The Overlander's Daughter

The Overlander's Daughter

a novel by

Amy Isaman

ISBN: 9781980941101

Editing by Genevieve Graham
Front Cover Image by Victoria Cooper of Victoria Cooper Art

Visit amyisamanbooks.com

To Gary, who is taking this journey through life with me.

And to my adventurous great-great-great-grandmother, Elizabeth Dixon Smith Greer, who recorded her journey on the Oregon Trail and inspired this story.

Chapter 1

I HAVE BEEN TO visit Agnes over a thousand times, but never to a place like this. I hug the ancient quilt she insisted I bring close to my chest, my steps slow and measured through the lobby. Despite the Manor's somewhat desperate advertising showing exuberant senior citizens, this is a place people come to die, not live, and I wonder what her room in this living morgue will look like. Eighty-nine or not, Agnes isn't ready to die, and I'm not ready for her to leave either. I've already lost one family. She's it, all I have left. And she should be next door, where I can run over for quick visit and check in on her. But, not surprisingly, her witch of a daughter didn't ask for my opinion when she moved Agnes.

The receptionist hands me the clipboard to sign-in, then points me to her room, 141. I feel like I should be tiptoeing down the elegant hallway. For Agnes' sake, I hope there's more life than death here, but it doesn't feel that way. Golden, gilt-framed pictures hang above tables claimed by giant sprays of silk flowers, like some sort of morbid funeral display. The color palette is soft: lavender, pale green, light blue. Nothing harsh or ugly that might in some way offend the senses, but also nothing to make it feel homey. Agnes' house is filled to the brim with knick-knacks displayed on crocheted doilies, not huge fake bouquets.

I knock on her door. No response, so I gently push it open. Agnes sits in a giant recliner. Even though she's tall, almost five foot eight and towers about six inches over me, the chair dwarfs her, and for the first time I can see her age. She looks frail, but I've never thought of her as old…until right now.

She's dozing, her chin resting softly on her chest. Her white hair has thinned and looks especially wispy today, but she's dressed, even if it is in one of her hideous color coordinated sweat suits she loves so

1

much. This one is bright turquoise with purple trim.

"Agnes?" I whisper. I set the quilt down on the coffee table, perch on the edge of the loveseat, and gently rest my hand on hers. Her skin feels paper thin, loose with wrinkles, and covered with dark blue veins, a sharp contrast to the taut, pink skin on my twenty-four year old hands. "Agnes, it's Harper. I brought your quilt, the old one from your cedar chest."

She sighs softly and opens her eyes, tensing as she tries to orient herself. Confusion clouds her eyes, and I wonder if they would notice if I kidnapped her and took her home, where she at least knows where she is when she wakes. I squeeze her hand softly. Without speaking, she surveys her room, a small studio, with a twin bed up against the wall, her chair and loveseat in the middle, a TV and a few shelves with some of her favorite mementos and photos. I wonder when she last slept in a twin bed, and shake my head. Couldn't her daughter even get her a real apartment? With a kitchen, a bedroom, and a normal size bed?

My heart breaks a little more with each passing second. She seems so small, so lost, trying to get her bearings. She lived in her old house for sixty years, and now…this. Finally, her eyes meet mine and she places her other hand over our entwined fingers, squeezing and creating a hand sandwich with mine in the middle. "I brought your quilt," I repeat and withdraw my hand.

I stand and pick it off the coffee table. The worn fibers are rough yet yielding against my fingertips as I unfold the material and prepare to shake it out.

She sits up straighter and eyes the quilt. "Gently, now. It's old!" She orders me, her voice sounding strong.

"Are you gonna let me do this?" I retort, lifting one eyebrow, but relieved that she at least sounds like herself.

She glares at me as I gently lay her quilt across her knees, but her eyes constantly flick toward the colors on her lap. I try to smooth out one of the fold creases as I spread it over her, but it seems permanent. Agnes runs her fingers across the flowery center design, and her entire body melts under the material.

The quilt is old. Ancient old. The cream colored fabric is yellowed in some spots, and some hues have faded, but patterns of squares and the triangles of color somehow seem to dance across the surface. A large middle square has some sort of flower design sewn onto its top.

A large star and a whole bunch of different brown, green, blue and pink blocks surround it. When I squint at it, I can barely see tiny, washed out signatures in the corners of some, but the writing has faded to almost nothing.

"Who made this, Agnes? It's amazing." I don't have an artistic cell in my body when it comes to creating anything visually appealing, but even I can tell this took a ton of work to create—and way more time than I'd ever have. I'd probably get one or two tiny triangles cut out before I got bored, gave up and moved onto something else.

"My great-grandmother made it when she was sixteen years old. She ... Her name was ..." A familiar crease forms across her brow, and I try not to show sympathy. Though she sometimes forgets words, she hasn't yet forgotten who she is. "Damn." She sits up straight, holding herself almost regally, then she lifts her chin and studies the ceiling as if the name is written there—except her eyes are closed as she thinks. "It's ..."

I wait for her to speak.

"Sarah." She relaxes a bit and grins.

Agnes rests her hands on the quilt. "Harper, I want to tell you this story."

"Okay, I'm listening." I lean back and relax. I've spent hours sitting with her on her porch swing or inside on her couch during Portland's rainy winters listening to her stories, and she listened to mine. All of them, the middle school drama, the high school angst. Maybe this will help her to feel more at home here.

She shakes her head. "Not just listen, Harper, you need to listen and write for me."

I have a brief moment of panic. Hopefully it's a short story. I haven't written anything in...forever, not since before my mom died. "Why don't I bring you a notebook and you can write it down? It might even be more interesting in your own handwriting."

She holds up her right hand. Arthritis has disfigured her knuckles. She can no longer knit or crochet, let alone write.

"Right. I forgot. Sorry." I feel like an asshole. I won't even mention her using a computer. I tried to teach her to play solitaire on my laptop and that was a technological disaster that ended in her telling me to "put the damn thing away and get the cards." She refused to even attempt email or Facebook.

"You," she lowers her eyebrows, glowering at me, "need to write this. I don't know how much time I have. I think you'll like Sarah, too."

"You have plenty of time." I don't want her talking about dying. Moving here has been bad enough.

"You're right. I could live another ten years, but you and I both know that by then, I probably won't remember a word of this story. It's the story I grew up hearing, and the story my mother grew up hearing, passed down for generations, Harper, and I don't want it to be lost."

Panic builds in my chest. I can't think about Agnes dying or even the dementia destroying her mind. When she's gone, who will I have? A father I haven't seen since I was eleven. Who knows where he is. My mom passed away two years ago. I'll be alone. She can't leave, but I don't think I can do this either. I started college with plans to go into publishing, either as a writer or editor, but those dreams fell apart. I quit when mom got sick, and now I wait tables. It's about all I can handle at this point. What if I can't do it? What if I don't finish? I'd be letting her down, failing her last request of me, kind of like I failed to finish college even though that's all she wanted for me.

I lean back and study the quilt. "Agnes, why don't you tell Rosemary? She's your daughter. Don't you think she'd be interested in it if it's a family story?" If she told it to Rosemary, maybe they'd have something to talk about, and Rosemary might understand that even though the quilt is ancient and faded, it's still pretty cool.

Agnes sighs. "This quilt *is* its story, Harper. It's not just the cotton and thread that make it up. Rosemary doesn't care about that. She's her father's daughter. She does...facts, numbers. You do stories."

"What do you mean? I 'do stories'?"

Her eyes narrow. "I'm not telling it to Rosemary because I want to tell it to you." She doesn't answer my question. Instead, Agnes points to the small desk shoved in the corner of the room, then folds her hands in her lap and waits. Apparently I'm supposed to get something to write with. Despite the fact that her hands won't allow her to write, she's got an old mug full of pens sitting on top as well as some pink stationary in a drawer. Not my usual note-taking supplies, but they'll do. I grab what I need and return to the love seat beside her recliner.

I wonder how long this will take. A few hours? Days? Can I get it all down before her memory goes completely? I've got about an hour before I need to leave for work, but I guess that's enough time to get

4

started. "So," I ask, "Who's Sarah?"

Most of her wrinkles are from smiling. At this, her entire face scrunches up in a big grin. She settles back in the chair and strokes the quilt, remembering.

I glance apprehensively at the clock on her bedside table. I won't tell her no, I could never do that, but what have I gotten myself into?

Agnes leans her head back and begins, "More than anything, Sarah didn't want to leave her granny behind in Indiana, but her Pa said the journey would kill her. She had to stay home."

"The…journey? What journey?"

"Hush, Harper. I'll get to it." She pauses and stares out the window. "They were heading to Oregon. Walking there. On the Oregon Trail. Sarah's Pa had heard of the bill Congress had passed. It gave free land to anyone who made it to the far west, and he decided to bring his family here. So, every night after Sarah and her Ma and Grannie had stitched and sewed in preparation for the journey, Grannie would get out her scrap bag and they'd work on this quilt. Granny'd pull the pieces out and tell Sarah the story behind each and every piece of fabric while Sarah cut them up. Granny could stitch but her hands were probably worse than mine. All the women worked with their hands back then." Agnes held up her bent fingers, so I could see them.

"When was this?" I ask, brushing my blond hair out of my face. I feel myself already pulled into the story as I grab a pony tail holder from my pocket and pull my hair back while Agnes thinks.

"Ah, it's right here." She points to a square on the quilt which I study. It says 1847 in faded script.

Holy crap. This thing is…really old. "So Agnes, how do you know all of this? I mean, it's not like your great grandma Sarah told you. Did she?"

"No, I never knew Sarah, but she told the story to her daughter and it got passed down. We all grew up on these stories, but I guess I never got around to passing it on myself. Rosemary wasn't interested anyway."

I wonder, then, what was real? Or what had been embellished over the years? I figured I'd never know but I take notes as Agnes continues, telling me of Sarah and her granny making the quilt and then having to say goodbye, forever. I can't blame Sarah for not wanting to come. Why would she want to say goodbye to everything she ever knew and walk two thousand miles across the country? I can barely handle Agnes moving three miles away, and I have a car to visit whenever I want.

"You know, the story really starts when they reached Independence, Missouri, when Sarah first saw Jed and he mistook her for a whore."

"Huh?" I lift my pencil and stare at Agnes, but she ignores me, fully ensconced in Sarah's world.

Chapter 2

April 1847 - Independence, Missouri

MORE PEOPLE WANDER the streets in Independence than I've ever seen in my life. And they're all moving in different directions. It took all of five minutes for us to mail our last letters home. How is it possible for Tommy to have vanished in that time? As soon as I think I've glimpsed my brother, the mass of people and animals shifts, then he disappears again, gone like everything else I've known for the past seventeen years.

People and wagons swarm the street, and the sharp odor of fresh manure, unwashed bodies, smoke, and animals assaults my senses. Every direction looks the same, so I choose the street across the square since it seems to vibrate with the most activity and wagons. Tommy would've gone that way, but I see no sign of his blond hair peeking from underneath his tattered brown hat. I lift my skirts, trying to avoid the sloppy muck that makes up the street.

Someone grabs my arm and yanks me back. "Watch out, Missy!"

A wagon driven by a green driver and team careens down the street, splashing through the mud and shooting brown fountains from the wheels. The team makes a sharp left turn—too sharp—and the driver leaps from the wagon as it slowly topples to its side. The crowd pauses and laughs, but I don't. Tommy could die here if I don't find him soon. A stranger strides past, accidentally bumping my shoulder, and I decide that maybe I don't need to cross the road if it means I might be crushed.

People throng toward me as I scan the crowd for my brother or Papa, and panic tightens my chest. An older woman runs into me then scowls as if it's my fault. "Hurry on now, girl," she orders. "We gotta get movin'."

Oregon Fever. Everyone's got it. Everyone. One of its major symptoms is that it causes people to lose all sense of manners.

Where is he? All the young boys wear the same dirty homespun trousers, flannel shirts, and hats. They look alike so I'd probably not notice him even if he was standing at my elbow. I take a deep breath and head down a somewhat quieter street off the main square, pausing halfway down. I lean against the building and shut my eyes for a moment so I can listen to the sounds of people and animals. Over here, far from the mass of bodies, it doesn't smell quite so bad.

A deep voice interrupts my thoughts. "Hey there, ma'am. You waitin' for someone?"

A young man in homespun long pants, a long sleeve shirt, and buttoned down suspenders stands in front of me. A farmer. Hopefully he's heading the same direction I am.

"Oh, no. I'm not waitin'. I . . ." He smiles and my voice trails off.

Oh my. My tummy does a little somersault. He's standing so close to me I can see he's trying to grow a beard but isn't having much success. His eyes are a deep blue, like the sky on a clear July evening. Actually, he's awful close. Too close. I try to back up, but my back's already against the wall. I wish I could rip this bonnet off my head so I could see all the way around me, but that wouldn't be proper, especially here in town. Mama would have my hide. But she'd also have my hide if she found me talkin' to this boy.

"Excuse me." I scoot to my left and step into the boardwalk, giving me a little space. I don't want to be sandwiched between him and the building.

He steps back and grins at me, the corners of his eyes crinkling up. He's much more pleasant to look at than Hiram.

"Find one?" another boy hollers as he lopes down the walk toward us.

"Nah, she's just a girl off the trail," says Blue Eyes.

"Ah, dang it. I just wanna look at a workin' one up close."

What is he talking about? Working? "No, I'm not workin'. What...?" As soon as the words leave my lips, I understand. How dare he even think such a thing? I step to the side, wanting to go around him.

Blue Eyes blocks me.

My heart speeds up a little bit. He's not letting me by.

They stand between me and the square, and his friend leans against the wall, eyeing me up and down. The town seems awful quiet and empty all of a sudden, except for the faint organ music on the other side of the wall.

I square my shoulders, despite the fact that this motion only accentuates my bosom—which is far too big for my liking. "Excuse me," I say, using my best big sister voice and stepping between them. "I was resting, but I'll be off now."

Blue Eyes takes a reluctant step back and lets me pass. *Thank you Lord.*

Despite the cool spring day, sweat drips down my bodice as I hurry back to the square. The only women working here are *those* women, I realize. The whores. That boy thought I was one. My hand goes to my bonnet which still sits primly on my head, and I glance down at my dress, checking. I don't understand. I look like an Indiana farm girl, not one of *them.* He must be daft. Or maybe he's just horrible. I walk toward the safety of people in the square, my heart racing.

If I only knew where to go.

The boys' footsteps and laughter follow me. I quicken my steps but the blue-eyed boy catches up to me anyway. My shorter legs are no match for his strides.

"Where you off to?" he asks, stopping at the corner next to me and hooking his thumbs on his suspender buttons. He is tall, gangly, and now I can see he has the beginnings of a narrow blonde moustache above a small mouth. He's not near as attractive as my first view of him.

I ignore him, look each way. I'm not going to walk in front of a saloon with him nearby. I'd rather get run over by one of the wagons in the street.

He laughs again. "Ain't no camps in that direction, but if you want to go for a walk, I'd be obliged to escort ya."

"How do you know there ain't no camps in that direction?" I scoff, still searching the crowds for Tommy. If he appears right now, I just might strangle him. Blue Eyes isn't going away. Maybe he'll tell me something useful. "I need to find my brother or my Pa. I think they're at the blacksmith shop. Can you tell me where that is?"

"Follow me."

"I don't need an escort."

"My name's Jed. I'll take you." He directs, like Pa does.

I clench my fists and take a breath. He's not gonna tell me.

Then he grabs my arm, as if he plans to escort me like a gentleman

9

would. He steers me in the opposite direction, and we pass a saloon. Music pours into the street. Shadows of men and women move in the dimly lit interior.

My face reddens, and I snatch my arm out of Jed's grasp. I give him my most scathing look, the one I usually save for Tommy when he's gone too far, but this insolent dolt grins. I wonder what I can say to make him go away without being rude. I can think of nothing.

Mama had warned me to be careful this morning, with all these people about. I hadn't paid any attention at the time. What was there to be careful of exactly? Now I knew.

We turn another corner and see the blacksmith shop. When I peer into the dark interior, I see strangers. My brother and my Pa aren't anywhere.

"See 'em?" Jed asks.

I shake my head.

"Well, I'll just take you back to camp."

I lift my chin, trying to look down my nose at him. "You don't know where we're camped."

"Sure I do. You're camped right near us."

Horror fills me. Had he followed me? "How do you know that?"

"Cuz I saw you come in last night. Maybe you oughtta take that bonnet off and try lookin' around sometime."

Truth is, I want more than anything to take this bonnet off, but it wouldn't be proper. With my fair skin, my cheeks would become permanently scarlet, and the few freckles that smatter across my nose would probably turn into one massive ugly spot. No thank you. And anyway, my bonnet has been the only proper thing about this afternoon, and I need to hold on to any shred of dignity I still have. Bonnet stays on.

He begins walking again, and I follow a step behind. I pray he's leading me back to camp, but he could be taking me anywhere. I can either follow him and trust that he's telling the truth, or keep on wandering the streets in Independence. I glare at his feet as we walk then decide I better pay attention and figure out where I am. I note the trees and buildings as we walk by. Nothing looks all that familiar during the ten minutes it takes to reach the edge of the camped wagons.

"Sarah? Sarah, that you?" Tommy's newly deepened voice cracks as he yells behind me. "Dang it, Sarah! Where you been?"

I don't realize how tense my body is until I see my brother. "Tommy!

Stop that cursin'. Mama'll have your hide if she hears you talk like that. I should have your hide."

"Well, where'd you get off to?"

"The general store where *you* were s'posed to be, too. What are you doin' anyway? You were s'posed to stay with me. Did you even look for me before you came back to camp?"

He barks out a laugh. "What do you think I'm doin'? I've been looking for ya, I found ya, and now I'm headed back. Just like you are. How'd you know how to go anyway? You didn't pay any attention when we left. Cripe, Sarah, you're hopeless. You couldn't get from the middle of the wagon to the front if it wasn't hitched up so's you could see the team's hind end."

Anger snakes through my body, and my hand itches to smack him. He'd just left me in Independence with this … this *scoundrel*.

"I'm guidin' her," Jed volunteers.

Tommy's smile widens as he reaches out a hand to introduce himself. "I'm Tommy. I was wonderin' how she got this far on her own. Now I know. She had help."

I glare at my brother. This afternoon could not possibly get anymore humiliating.

Jed shakes my brother's hand. "Jedediah Monroe."

It's a name I wish I could erase from my mind, but I have a feeling that won't be so easy. I keep walking with my eyes focused on the muddy path, Jed alongside me, until he speaks again. "Does yer Pa need help with the stock? He joined our train this mornin' and I'm hirin' out to help with the stock. They elected my uncle to be the train's captain."

We're on the same train? Six months? I'll have to spend six months with this cad? "That was *your* uncle they elected?" I squeak. I want to throw myself on the ground like a tot and thrash around.

"Sure was. We'll be headin' to Oregon together."

"Well, Tommy's watchin' our stock. We don't need no help," I snap. Tommy better not need any help. I pray he can convince Pa that Tommy and Jasper, my eleven year old brother, can handle the stock on their own.

He grins, and my stomach drops. "I'll be talkin' to yer Pa anyway."

Marching back into camp, I yank my bonnet off my head and wad it up in my fist.

Mama's at the wagon sorting through a bowl of dried beans, pulling out stones. "Where's your Pa?"

"I don't know. We lost him."

"And your brother?"

"Back there. He's coming. That company we signed on with today, do we stay with them for the whole trip?"

"If I could tell the future, I could answer that question, but I have no idea what'll happen once we start." Mama is always so reasonable. Of course she doesn't know. "Why don't you get some biscuit dough ready for supper?" Though she asks a question, I'm aware this isn't simply a request.

I don't want to make biscuits. I want to climb in the wagon, unpack the quilt I made with Granny, throw it over my head, and hide. But it's buried underneath the second floor. Half the wagon would have to be unpacked to get at it, and Mama wouldn't allow that ever. I reach for the flour and decide that's just what I'll do as soon as my chores are done. Sit in the wagon. Maybe I can ride the whole way, and I won't see Jedediah Monroe and remember this humiliating afternoon ever again.

AFTER SUPPER, I knead more flour into a ball, working it on my lap while my little sister Eliza packs up the last of the dishes, except for the Dutch oven. I'll set the dough in that and let it rise for morning. My hands work the dough, but my eyes watch a young man camped across from us. He sits in front of his family's wagon on a small stool. His left leg stretches out straight in front of him, his knee pointing normally toward the sky, but his left foot lies on the ground and points directly to his right. It sure looks odd. His right leg is perfectly normal. I wonder what happened to him.

"Sarah, you about got that dough done?" Mama asks as she climbs down from the wagon. "Let's get it set to rise."

"Yes ma'am." I lift the ball off my apron and inspect it. "This one ain't too bad." I eye the bug speckled dough. It's pointless to try to pick 'em out. I've tried. I set it in the pan and cover it with a lid.

"If you're done with your chores, you may go listen," Mama says.

"Listen? To what?" I've got a plan for the evening: get in the wagon to sketch while there's still light and hide from Jed.

"Well, it looks like that young man's getting' a fiddle out over there." Mama points across the meadow. The boy with the bent leg runs his hands along a black fiddle case.

I've heard fiddlers in other camps, but not in ours. They're a good break from the already monotonous trail routine. The sun has begun to set and a light breeze sends the campfire smoke every which way. There's no sign of Jed.

"Get your sisters before you go. Your Pa and I'll be over shortly."

I call for the girls. They have been playing with the other children in camp. People from the neighboring wagons begin to congregate, watching the boy get ready to play. I wonder who he is, hoping he's not related in any way to Jed, but as I get closer, I see a vague resemblance and kick at a rock, sending it skittering into the clearing. Of course he's related to Jed.

He gives the top of his case another quick rub before unlatching it and pulling out linens he had stuffed around the fiddle. Everything fragile in our wagon is either stuffed with linens or tucked deep in the flour or bean barrel to cushion the ride. I s'pose his fiddle is no different. Now that everyone else in camp is watching the boy along with me, I can study him without having to hide my glances. He's got light brown hair and a nose that turns up a bit at the end. His eyes are blue, the same as Jed's but he doesn't have the thin little moustache above his full lips.

When he finally gets his fiddle unburied, he sets the case aside and runs his fingers over the strings. His hands look strong with wide fingers, and I wonder how he can press one string at a time. Finally, he pulls the bow out of the case and runs his fingers along its length. His mother stands next to him, watching him unpack the instrument.

"It's traveling just fine, Ma," he says.

She smiles and sits on the ground beside him.

I pull two-year-old Katie onto my lap and accidentally catch the fiddler's eye. He smiles, and I panic. I look down, fiddling with Katie's dress. The only boys who ever smiled at me were Hiram and that Jed, but their smiles never made my heart start beating like this. Well, maybe Jed's did until I figured out what kind of boy he is. But not now. He could smile at me all day and the only thing I'd feel would be disgust.

Why can't I just smile back at this one? His blue eyes seem to look all the way into me. I peek again and realize I recognize his eyes. It's more than a vague resemblance. He's got Jed's eyes, and my stomach drops. Perfect. They've got to be related. Brothers? Twins, even?

He lifts the instrument and sets it in the crook just below his collar bone, pulling the bow across the strings. The fiddle sings, sounding eerily like a person, then he draws the bow back again on another note. After two long notes, during which his face is entirely concentrated on the sounds, he smiles at the crowd sitting on the ground and begins to play. He taps his good leg to set the beat as he pulls the notes from his instrument. The music begins softly at first then catches the breeze and travels through the wagons and trees.

As he fiddles, his eyes keep coming back to me. Each time his smile widens, and my tummy flips over. Is he a scoundrel like Jed? I've never met a crippled boy before, and I wonder if that'd make him meaner or nicer?

The crowd sits silently for the first song, listening, then they begin to shift and move, tapping their feet, clapping their hands, and finally rising to dance. He plays on and chooses a faster tune.

Katie crawls off my lap to grab Eliza, and my sisters jump and spin to the music. Mama and Papa clap their hands in time as the little girls twirl through the trampled grass. Finally, they spin so much they collapse into giggling piles on the ground. I laugh with them and reach out to tickle Katie's little belly.

The sun lowers in the sky until the light is dusky and the first of a million stars make their appearance.

"He plays well, doesn't he?" Jed says.

I pull my eyes away from the fiddler as Jed lowers himself down and sits between me and Papa.

"He does," answers my father.

I pull Katie back on my lap between Jed and me, like a shield. The fiddler focuses on Jed.

I don't want to speak to Jed, but I want to know this fiddler. "You related to him?"

"That's my cousin, Charlie."

Cousin. I take a deep breath and bite back a smile. That's good, much better than brother.

Charlie announces he'll be playing the last song of the evening. He pulls the bow across the strings and launches into a tune I don't recognize, the beat slower and steady. His mama's deep voice floats over the prairie and everyone quiets down, listening to the fiddle and the song. The tune is slow and haunting. I hope this journey is neither. I hope it is the happy adventure Papa keeps talking about. I'm not so sure though, given today's events.

The last notes fade into the night, and everyone sits quietly for a moment. The soft jingle of the cow bells and rustling of the wind through the grass sing to us now. Eventually people shake off the spell Charlie wove with his songs.

"Can I give you a hand?" Jed asks me.

Katie is on my lap, keeping my hands full. "No thanks."

I reach back with one hand to push myself up. He bends over, his fingers tightening around my arm, his knuckles slowly brushing across my breast as he pulls me to my feet. I step back and shift Katie onto my hip, forcing him to let go, shocked at what I felt.

Did Papa or Mama see?

Jed grins and winks at me. He did it on purpose.

I tighten my grip on my sister until she squirms to be let down. She's my shield, and I'm not letting her go. I loosen my arms but keep her on my hip between us.

"So you liked that last song?" he asks.

I nod, still too shocked to speak. I begin walking toward the tent.

"Hold up there."

I keep walking. "I gotta get my sisters to bed. You need somethin'?"

"I certainly hope not." Mama's voice stops us. "Mr. Monroe, if there's somethin' you need I'd be happy to help you. Otherwise, your tent is out there." She points her finger in the opposite direction and flicks her wrist.

"Yes'm," he mutters before sauntering off into the evening.

"Thank you, Mama," I whisper as soon as he's gone.

She's frowning. "Sarah, I realize that you have not been courted or spent much time with boys other than your brothers, but do *not* let young men follow you to your tent."

I stare at her in shock. If she knew what had happened this afternoon in Independence, she wouldn't let Jed anywhere near us. But I can't tell her. It would be too humiliating.

"I wasn't *letting* him, Mama. He just followed. I couldn't be rude."

"No, you couldn't be rude. He's help now. But even so, you should've stopped walking."

Panic tightens my chest. Katie squirms, and I realize I'm crushing her again. "What do you mean 'help'?"

"Papa hired Jed to help with the stock."

"Why?" My voice rises in panic, and I will myself to not yell at Mama. "What about Tommy? He's fourteen. Ain't he old enough? And Jasper could help him."

"He is, but Jed hired on with four families to help as a teamster and run stock for all of us. We'll take turns feeding him, and he'll help our boys. He can find cattle when they run off, help herd them, yoke the oxen, hunt. All that."

My heart races with anger. She needs to know what kind of scoundrel Jedediah Monroe really is. "But Mama, he's not a … nice boy."

Mama searches my face, giving me courage.

"He's a … a … snake. And he watches me." I glance at my chest, then back at Mama.

She nods in understanding, since she suffers from the same big-chested fate. Even though she's married with babies, sometimes I catch men still staring at her chest. Now they'd started to stare at mine. I despise my bosom.

"Why did he have to hire *him*?" I blink. *Don't cry. Not now.*

"Sarah, you've known him for all of an afternoon."

"That's long enough, Mama." I pause to calm myself then stomp toward the tent, trying to stop the tears. "G'night."

"I s'pose you ought to know your Pa feels it's high time you found yourself a husband," she says to my back.

I stop walking. "He does?" I try to keep my voice at a normal octave. A husband? Now? On the trail?

"Yes, he does. You best start lookin' at prospects."

"Why?" My dinner begins to churn around in my gut. I search the dimming light for Jed. *Please be gone. Please.*

"Sarah, you're seventeen years old. It's time you start thinkin' about those things. And as for Jed, well, he's twenty. It seems he's a hard worker, but time will tell."

I try to whisper, but it comes out loud, not a whisper at all. "He's a … a … no 'count—"

"Sarah!" she hisses. "You stop right there. I will not have you talkin' like that here in front of your sisters, or anywhere for that matter."

I hate it when Mama yells at me, but this time it doesn't even make

16

sense. I try again. "Mama, what about love?"

She shook her head. "Don't matter, Sarah. What does matter is that you're about old enough to get married, and a hardworking boy has taken an interest. I expect you'll be on your best behavior." She nods once. "You two get on to bed now. It's gonna be an early morning."

It don't matter? It mattered six months ago.

"What about Hiram?" I want to scream it at her, but I don't. I speak slowly, measuring my words.

Her brow scrunches in confusion. "Hiram? In Indiana?"

"Yes, Hiram in Indiana. When I asked if I could stay with Granny if I married Hiram, you told me that I gotta like somebody first if I ever expect to love him. Mama, I *do not* like Jedediah Monroe, and I *never* will. I'd take Hiram over him any day."

"You don't know him yet. Give it more than half a day." She kisses the top of Katie's head, pats my shoulder one more time, and sends us off to the tent.

I think I know enough of Jed already. I want to grind my teeth in frustration, and I wish for the hundredth time that Granny was here, but she's not. She's already hundreds of miles behind us. I'll never see her again.

Katie squirms again, and I finally set her down, letting her walk beside me toward the tent. A husband? Now? Does Papa want to get rid of me that much? He made me go on this trip to help out, but if I get married can I still help? I crawl into the tent behind Katie, my mind churning, and drop onto the blankets. I begin to unbraid my hair, pulling it over my shoulder and letting it fall across my chest as I run my fingers through the thick auburn waves, trying to untangle it a bit. When I lay down, Katie reaches over and twists her fingers into a strand and hangs on, anchoring herself to me.

I stare at canvas over my head, sleep eluding me. In the last four weeks, everything I've known has changed. I am sure of only three things: Granny is gone to me, I am stuck on this trail for the next six months, and I will not marry Jed Monroe.

17

Chapter 3

Late April 1847 - Independence, Missouri

THE LIGHT IN the tent turns from inky black to a soft grey. I lay on one side of the tent with Tommy, Jasper, and Eliza on the other side. Little Katie lies between us. Cool, moist air comes up from the river this early in the spring, so the little ones huddle together beneath their blankets and quilts to stay warm as our camp comes to life. It's no longer the soft, gentle sounds of a farm waking or the muted noises of the two or three wagons we'd traveled with across Missouri. Now we awaken surrounded by the frenzied sounds of people setting out on an adventure. Oxen bellow as they are yoked—cows too, their udders full—wagon tongues creak, and women holler at their children to get up and do their chores.

I lean over and nudge the girls next to me. "Time to wake up, sleepy heads. We've got someone to meet today."

Tommy looks at me. "Who?"

"Well, we're traveling with forty some wagons. I think there's lots of people to meet."

He raises his eyebrows at me for a quick second before pulling on his boots, ready to career headlong down this trail. His blankets are left in a jumbled pile.

The night before, when Tommy had come to the tent, I'd told him about Jed working our stock, and he'd left to immediately confront Papa. "Papa, I can do it. I can even crack the whip," he'd argued to no avail.

Tommy crashes through life without a worry for what others might think. I, on the other hand, spend my days wishing for the courage to stand up for myself instead of smiling and nodding in agreement so

18

as not to upset or offend anyone.

"Sarah will be stayin' with your Mama and helping with the little one. That's her work. You do yours and drive the stock. No arguments," Papa had replied, laying down the law. We each had a job to do, and he expected us to do it every day without question. Papa doesn't allow much for questions. Only sometimes from Mama, but she picks her battles, saves her arguments for what she really wants. Usually it works, but it hadn't with this trip.

Walking thousands of miles into an unknown land sounds as exciting to me as the two weeks we spent stitching and waterproofing the wagon cover, but it isn't my place to question.

Mama hadn't wanted to leave Granny neither, but Papa had decided. If she'd said no, he would have just packed her up like a sack of flour and tossed her in the wagon bed with the dry goods. We both know it. It took one whippin' in the shed with Papa when I was little to figure it out. Sometimes I want to fight back, but mostly it's easier to smile and go along for the ride than it is to fight.

But *now* they want me to get married. Married? I want to stay in the tent and hide. I should have hidden last night like I'd planned. Instead, I'd gone to watch Charlie, and Jed had found me and touched me.

"Jasper, get out there and see if you can help Papa," I tell my other brother.

Jasper yawns and opens one eye. He glares at me until he remembers that today we roll. He heads out, barefoot. He is only eleven, but like Tommy, he feels worthy of a man's work.

Little Katie lays on her side, her thumb shoved in her mouth. I rub her back. "Wake up wee ones, time to go."

The girls stretch and yawn as I begin folding the blankets and piling them by the door. We sleep in our clothes, and I try to stretch and smooth out my skirt. The pink calico print is a hopeless wrinkled mess. Instead I cover it with my apron, a plaid one that hides the dirt, and quickly braid my hair.

"Sarah, I gotta go," Eliza says, clutching herself and hopping.

"Mama, we need you," I yell, dragging Eliza out of the tent.

"I'll be right there." We are camped in a meadow with a hundred or more wagons, all waiting to head out. We scramble around the tent to the back side but since there are wagons behind us as well, it doesn't help much. Eliza crouches down while Mama and I spread our skirts to hide her. Even though the outhouse at home froze during the winter and I had to hold my breath in the summer, I miss it.

When it's my turn, I instruct Eliza to hold her small skirt all the way out. She glares at me. I crouch down as low as I can and hold my skirt up. "Hurry up," Mama whispers.

"I'm trying. Why?"

"Just hurry." I glance up and see her smile in greeting. "Good morning," she says.

I drop my skirt and stand to see Charlie standing just behind Eliza. Pee drips down the inside of my legs and blood rushes into my face. What I wouldn't give for our outhouse.

"Mornin'," he says, nodding to us as he walks by.

Mama bites her bottom lip, holding in a smile. "Best get the tent taken down," she says, before turning to walk away.

"Did he see you?" Eliza asks.

"I don't know! Did he?" Did he? How can I meet him now?

Eliza giggles and shrugs her shoulders. "I'm just glad it wasn't me."

I drop my face in my hands which sends her into full blown laughter. Heat from my cheeks seeps into my fingers. With my fair skin, it doesn't take much to turn my face the same auburn color as my hair.

We have just enough time to eat before Charlie's father, Captain Dixon calls, "Roll the Wagons."

After months of preparation, sewing, packing, planning, selling the farm, purchasing supplies, and more sewing, we embark on the Oregon Trail.

I WALK NEXT to the wagon, the ground damp and cool beneath my bare toes. My hemmed calico skirt hits above my ankles with each step, swaying like the prairie flowers in a breeze. *Swish, swish, swish.* The wagon rolls behind the yokes of the plodding oxen. Mama and Katie sit high on the trunks in the front, but I prefer walking to the wagon's incessant bouncing.

At noon, Mr. Dixon halts the train. Pa releases the oxen's yoke from the wagon's tongue and leads them to some grass to feed. Mama and I fix the noon meal. It's just breakfast leftovers, so we don't have to cook. That's the best part of the noon meal: no cooking. I serve Pa his plate of beans and cold biscuits. Jed stands next to Pa, waiting for me to serve him.

"Thank you, miss," he says as I hand him his plate. "Get yer food. You can sit here." He points to the ground next to him.

I return for my meal, trying to think how to get out of this invitation. I have no intention of eating with Jed, someone I don't even know who orders me around, but Mama will have my hide if I am rude to the help.

Eliza sits on the ground in the shade of the wagon, waiting for Mama to hand her some food. I nudge her. "Eliza, get up. You're coming with me."

Mama hands us each our plates.

"I'm just gonna eat here with Mama," Eliza says.

"No. Mama, will you come eat up here with us? You can sit on the wagon tongue with Pa and stretch your legs out in front." She nods, serves herself and Katie, then follows behind Eliza and me.

Jed has lowered himself to the ground and sits, leaning against the wagon's front wheel. I walk to the front of the wagon and sit, my plate in my lap, leaving room for Mama to sit between Jed and me. Eliza sits by my feet.

"How's it goin' back there? We got quite the herd," Pa says.

"It's loud and dusty. Had animals all over the place this morning. I think it'll take a day or two to figure it out. Where are you all from?" Jedediah asks. He doesn't look at my father, he looks at me.

"Indiana," Pa replies.

"You're not much of a talker, are ya?"

I can be, just not with him. I nod and let him think what he wants.

"How old are ya?"

"Seventeen."

"But you ain't married?" He raises his eyebrows, looking like there's something wrong with me.

I take a bite to hide my shock, and I look at Mama. She looks as startled as I feel, and I'm glad when she answers for me. "There's plenty of time for that. I need her here on this trip."

He grins.

I do not want to be talking about this with him. I shove the last bite of cold biscuit into my mouth and get up. "I gotta clean up." When I turn the corner of the wagon, I look back. Jed's watching me. It makes my skin crawl.

The tail gate is down on the wagon, holding the bean pot and biscuits. I want to ask Mama what she thinks of Jed, but I can't. I don't know how to start without her thinking the wrong thing.

We roll again after an hour and reach the Blue River late in the afternoon. Papa says we've made fifteen miles, and I wonder what trials the land ahead holds. The road leads straight toward the river's deep banks, steep and dangerous to the heavy wagons. The river flows clear and deep, and trees line the edges, leaning far over the water. We've already crossed dozens of creeks and rivers on this journey, but this one flows too deep and too fast to cross this early in the spring. Even I can tell that. For months Mama and Papa had debated leaving in April or May. If we left too early, the water runs too high in the rivers and the spring grasses might not have grown enough to feed the stock, but if we left later, we'd be stuck behind, with the best feed already eaten by the trains in front of us.

We left in April. Early. I think it's because men like my Pa like to be in front, be the first.

Supper finished and cleaned up, I lean over, somewhat precariously, and hold my left hand against one of the bows that holds up the wagon's canvas cover, trying to position and tack the red square to the side. This wagon needs something to mark it as ours among the whole village of them. We're camped in a large meadow, surrounded by oaks, sycamores and pecan trees which loom over the wagons.

I stand on Papa's tool box, smooth the square, and pin it in place. I can hear Granny's voice in my head, *if it ain't straight and true, just pull it out and do it again or if you're gonna do somethin', do it right.* The stitching doesn't have to be pretty, but the square has to be straight. I ready my threaded needle to run a wide basting stitch along the edge. That'll hold good enough. If not, I can stitch it stronger on the trail. I stab my needle through the red square then through the homespun double layer of linen and muslin that covers the wagon. Mama and I had wrestled that yardage for over two weeks, sewing it for the wagon. Then we'd had to paint the whole thing with linseed oil to waterproof it. Its thickness doesn't take kindly to my needle. I breathe in the oil's scent and remember Granny all bent over, painting it on.

I spent most every moment of the last eight months of my life with her, getting ready, wondering what this trip would be like. When Papa decided to head west, he and Mama read all the pamphlets and articles he could find. Just for making the journey, we can get land for free—more than we'd ever have in Indiana. After they had read it all, they put us to work. One book recommended a whole pile of bedding and clothes. I bet the man who wrote that never spun, wove, or sewed a single stitch in his life. He had no idea what that meant in practical terms, but Mama and I did. Callouses still thicken the ends of my fingers from all the stitching we'd done this winter.

The only stitching I enjoyed, looked forward to even, was piecing my quilt with Granny. She'd set her scrap bag on her lap and pull out a piece. Before we cut it and stitched it on as a leaf or flower, she'd tell me its story. Maybe it was a scrap from a dress granny made my auntie when auntie was young. Or maybe it was a scrap from her own wedding dress. When we left home, she'd held the quilt on her lap. "Here, take this. It's yers."

I'd knelt on the floor next to her chair, dropped my head in her lap and sobbed.

"This quilt," she'd said, "is who you are and where you come from, so it'll take you wherever yer goin' too." We'd christened it with our tears, then packed it up. When we said goodbye, it was to everything I'd ever known.

Now here I stand in a meadow far from home with a swatch of plain turkey-red, ready to stitch some more and try to guide my way. The wagon cover has become somewhat stiff with the oil and dirt, and my needle will not easily pierce it. I shove it in with the end of my thumb and wonder where a thimble might be packed, thinking this might take a while longer than I thought. By the time I get the top edge tacked on, my shoulders and arms ache. I drop my hands to my sides to let a little blood back into them and am stepping back off the box when I feel someone standing behind me. Startled, I jump back onto the safety of the box and turn around, ready to yell at my brother Tommy for sneaking up on me, but Tommy is not standing there. Instead, I look into two dark blue eyes and a grinning mouth. He has light brown hair that curls a bit above his ears. Charlie the fiddler.

"Oh," is all I manage to say as my face heats up. The last time he saw me I was squatted behind our tent.

"Sorry for surprisin' ya. Didn't mean to. I'm Charlie." He reaches out his hand to shake mine. I hold my hands up, filled with pins and needle.

"I'd rather not stab you."

He smiles, his eyebrows raised, and my tummy does a little flip. "What're ya doin'? I've been watchin' for a bit and I can't figure it out. You got whatever it is straight, if that's what you're checkin'."

I review my handiwork, trying to figure out what to call it. A marker? A flag? A block? "Well, I guess it's my ... uh, wagon flag? My little brother crawled into the wrong wagon today and about got whipped, so I thought I'd mark ours somehow so that wouldn't happen again. We both get turned around pretty easy, and all these wagons look the same to him, so I'm flaggin' ours. I'm puttin' one on each side."

"You really can't tell the wagons apart?" He points across our camp. "Look over at that one over there. It's about two feet taller than the one next to it, and the canvas on that one behind it a ways is all gray. Don't you see that?"

I survey the few wagons he pointed out, noting the differences in shading and shape of the canvas tops. Some are brand new, some already dirt grimed. My artist's eye discerns the subtle shadings of canvas. "Yep, I see it, but my brother don't. To him they're all wooden boxes with a big fabric sail on top. There's one that has a sign on the side. It's the only one he can tell. Did you see that one?"

"Yep, it looked funny."

"That's why this one's smaller. We saw one that had a big drape of calico over it. He'd recognize that anywhere, but Papa wouldn't ever allow it."

I stretch up to finish stitching down the sides. The sun will give maybe thirty more minutes of light, and I need to finish this. The wagon rocks as Charlie moves to my side and leans against it.

Most noticeable are his hands. The right hand, the one he'd held toward me to shake, is calloused and strong but somehow smooth. Not at all rough like Papa's or even Tommy's hands. His left hand grips a cane, which he holds tight to his left leg. I turn back to my stitching. I could probably stare at him all evening and stitch this square with

24

my eyes closed, now that I've got it straightened up, but Mama would definitely not approve.

As I stitch, I take sidelong glances at him. His left leg hangs from his body, a little shorter than his right, and his foot points sharply inward. How on earth is he going to walk thousands of miles to Oregon? I want to ask, but I bite back my question. It's not my business. I s'pose he'll have to ride. I finish the side of the patch and move my needle across the bottom edge. The hardest part of this project is getting the needle through the cover. It is like trying to pierce a hide with a twig, which makes my stitches zig zag all the way down the edge. Granny would be ashamed, but I decide this is a utilitarian project, nothing more.

Charlie watches my hands and the camp as I work, and I get used to the comfortable silence that he finally breaks. "Where's your family from?"

"Indiana."

"We're from Illinois. But we've moved a few times. My Pa's a bit of a wanderer, but I s'pose most everyone who's here is somethin' of a wanderer, lookin' for adventure. Or at least something' different. Who knows."

"Do you really think it'll be any better out there? Seems to me it can't be much different. A farm's a farm. It's hard work wherever you set your plow." I finish the bottom edge, tie off my thread, step down, and pick up the box. I head to the other side of the wagon to finish my project. Charlie follows, keeping right up with me as if the cane has become another leg for him.

"You know, they say it's an Eden. There's giant trees, and crops grow bigger and easier there. And we can claim six hundred forty acres of land. That's lots bigger than our farm in Illinois."

Whether they are full grown or half grown, it seems the male half of the species can spin dreams of Oregon without ever tiring of it. I have already had enough of it. There's only so much one can guess about it without seeing it for real.

"You think it's worth a couple thousand mile trek through the wilderness? With Indians?" I have had nightmares about the Indians ever since Papa proposed this whole journey. I stop pinning the second block and turn to look at him. "Are you planning on farming?" I doubt it. He can't even walk without a cane.

"As for your first question, yes, it's worth a long walk. For your second, don't you take me for a farmer?" He swings his cane in the air in a big circle and looks at me, eyebrows raised.

I blush and feel like a fool. I know better. I turn and begin stitching again so I won't have to look at him.

"Well, uh, no. I don't," I finally reply.

"Me neither. I'm planning on setting up a shop in Oregon City or Portland, whichever I like best or whichever needs me the most. I work with leather, saddles, harnesses, whips. I can sew too, so I might do some tailor work as well."

That gives me pause. I've never met a boy in my life who can sew worth a darn. Mama had tried to teach Tommy and Jasper, but it was more work than it was worth. She always just let them go. Eliza and I had to finish our stint before we were allowed to do a thing.

"A shop? You sew?"

"Sure. I can't very well work a field with my leg like this, and Mama had to figure something to keep me busy."

I smile a little. "I never heard of a boy who was any good at sewing, I guess."

"You never heard of a tailor before? They sew. That's all they do."

"Well sure, but that's not what you said. You said you work with leather and—"

"'T's just sayin' I know how to sew, but I prefer to work with leather."

He interrupts me which is good because I don't know what I was going to say anyway. I focus on my fingers pushing and pulling the needle in and out of the fabric, so I won't stare at Charlie, this beautiful boy who isn't a farmer. He doesn't seem to mind my silence and keeps talking about the journey ahead. He has a deep voice, gravelly almost, and I realize I could listen to him talk all evening. Though his eyes match Jed's, that's where the similarities seemingly end.

"What're you smilin' at?" he asks.

"Uh, I didn't realize I was." I can't tell him I was smiling because he's so different from his cousin.

"Yep, you were. Am I borin' you?"

"Not at all. I like it," I say before I can stop myself. I focus on the red square and feel my cheeks heating up as he laughs.

Two days we wait to cross the river, a thankful rest from the walking. My normally roundish body has already become harder and leaner, and I wonder how wiry I'll be by the time we get there. By this time, a whole slew of wagons are camping at the crossing, waiting for the water to go down. Sunday afternoon, Mama and I sit in the wagon's shade with the scrap-bag, our endless washing, mending, and baking done for the moment. Charlie sits on the ground across from me. His crippled leg turns out awkwardly when he sits on the ground. He is quiet this afternoon and soon lays back and closes his eyes. I steal glances at him when Mama's head bends to her handwork. He's tilted his hat over his forehead and his face relaxes in sleep, his mouth opens a little. A little bug flies around his head. He swats at it in his sleep and grunts.

I laugh as the bug makes a dive for his open mouth.

"What's funny?" Eliza asks. She sits at Mama's feet, finishing her stint. Mama looks up and catches my eyes before I can duck my head.

I nod in Charlie's direction. "I was just thinking if a bug were to fly into that trap over there."

Eliza squeals, a piercing little girl sound, as the fly circles his face.

Charlie stretches, closes his mouth, and lifts his hat off his eyes. "You keep laughin' at me, Eliza, you'll get your stitches all crooked and have to re-do it."

Eliza's eyes get big, and she ducks her head to her work. Now it's my turn to smile.

"Or you could just finish up for her and let her go," Jed interrupts, walking in on us.

"That I could," Charlie replies as he sits up. "But today I'll pass."

Jed stops next to me, and I keep my head bent toward my work. "I could get you a needle and thread, cousin. I'm sure one of the ladies would be happy to share."

Charlie grabs the side of the wagon and pulls himself to his feet before replying. "They would indeed be happy to share." He pulls his hat off his head and nods in my direction. "Especially with a man such as myself."

Eliza giggles again.

"You know, he really can sew," Jed says, smirking. "He can do all kinds of regular women's work."

"Yep, I know. He told me." Why he is so intent on embarrassing his cousin?

"What you got there?" Jed asks.

My diary sits on my lap, waiting for me to finish my piecing. I lay my block over it, hiding it from his view. "Nothing."

"Don't look like nothin'."

I refuse to look at him or answer, hoping he will get the hint to go away.

He doesn't. "What are you writin'?"

I push the needle in, my stitches small and even, wondering how to answer his ignorant question.

"My guess, Jed, would be that she's writing about what happens every day, what she sees, what she wants to remember. That's why people keep diaries like that, to remember," Charlie answers, saving me.

I don't bother correcting him. I haven't written a word, but I have started two sketches of Charlie fiddling along with quite a few of wildflowers, trees, and grasses. I tie off my last thread.

"You keepin' one too, cousin?" Jed asks Charlie. He says the words slowly, mocking both of us.

Charlie just shakes his head and stands up. He smiles at me, and his blue eyes crinkle up in the corners. "Goodbye, ladies. I've enjoyed chatting with you," he says before turning and walking away, leaving us with Jed.

"Can I join you?" Jed asks.

"You can sit by me," Eliza says.

"I'll sit here by yer sister." He lowers himself to the ground and reaches toward my diary.

"What are you doing?" I drop my full hands to my lap, protecting it.

"I just thought I'd take a look. See what you said about this whole trip so far."

"Show him your pictures," Eliza says. "They're real pretty."

"She's got pictures in there?"

"Yep. She draws in it."

I press my journal into my lap. "No," I say to Jed and Eliza. "They're not done, and I don't like showing them to anyone."

"Sarah, show him that one you were doin' yesterday. It's him anyway, isn't it?" she says.

I want to stab my sister with my needle, but I can't reach her.

Jed raises his eyebrows, a smile spreading across his face.

"N-no, Eliza," I stutter. "It's not … him, and it's not done." I hold up my completed stitches. "But this is done and I gotta get supper going." I fold my block, blinking back tears of humiliation and frustration. How could Eliza do that to me?

She grins, and I remember she doesn't know Jed like I do. My anger dissipates. I can't hate my eight-year-old sister no matter how much I dislike him. I shove the extra scraps that litter my lap back into the bag.

Finally, he rises and walks away. I wish he would leave me alone more often, but he doesn't. He flits around our wagon and camp like a mosquito searching for a meal. Buzzing and buzzing.

I search for Charlie, but he has vanished. Why couldn't Eliza tell Charlie that I'd been drawing him? I lean my head back on the wagon wheel and stare at the sky. If I have to pick a husband, would Papa accept a crippled one? A man who can't farm? Would it matter since he's got a trade?

Chapter 4

Present Day

THE SUN SHINES into Agnes' room, making it a little too warm. We've gotten quite a ways in the story, enough that I've started bringing my laptop to take notes since I can type so much faster than I can write. I tried to capture her words once on my phone, but that sent Agnes off. She thought I was texting or something and couldn't quite get that I was just taking notes as she talked.

But today I forgot my laptop, and my hand cramps from the notes. I'm either writing furiously to try to keep up with her, or I'm waiting for her to remember the story or a word that's escaped her memory. Her fingers trace the patterns on the quilt covering her skinny legs. Today her memory works like a mountain breeze, coming in strong gusts then calming for a moment before swirling in a circle.

The door whooshes open and Rosemary invades the room. "Mother?" She is tall like her mother, Agnes, but more elegant with silvery blonde hair framing her face. She wears a beige suit and heels, the ever intimidating professional woman.

Holy Crap. She came to visit. Agnes hasn't mentioned her coming even once.

I jump, the pen in my hand stopping mid-sentence over my spiral notebook, and Agnes falls silent. Her eyes and mouth widen in alarm. She shrinks back into her chair, closes her mouth, and drops her eyes. She looks…afraid. Nothing scares Agnes, or so I thought.

My protective instincts kick in, like she's my child and not sixty years my senior. I've only got twenty minutes to get to work, but I don't want to leave Agnes alone with her own daughter, and I want the rest of the story. It's so hard to figure out the timeline when she stops and starts. Already I've got a stack of notecards going to try to figure it all out. I'll have to go to the library later this week and get a book on the Oregon Trail. Who knew this would turn into such a research project, but I can't let Agnes down. She's never asked anything of me but this, well, besides finishing college. I hope I can at least give this to her but who knows. The story is damn confusing at times.

Rosemary surveys her mother's room, hands on her hips. "Harper, go get a nurse. I need to speak with them about … this." She waves her arm around the room.

This? I look around without any idea as to what she's talking about. Then I realize she wants me to fetch the nurse? Like I'm her dog or something?

"What is that smell?" she continues, scrunching her nose. "Do they not clean in here?" She focuses on me. "And please put that ancient rag away. How did that even get here? It's supposed to be in mother's trunk where it's always been." Rosemary raises her eyebrows at me.

I stand and step closer to Agnes. I want to protect her…or do I want her to protect me? I'm pathetic.

"Are you going to work now?" Agnes asks as she stands to say goodbye. Her voice is weak and timid, which is not how it's sounded through her hours of storytelling.

"Yeah, I'm sorry. I wish I could stay here." I don't want to leave her alone, but I can't be late again. I hug Agnes' bony body, thinking how every part of her seems to have shrunk: her mind, her memory, her body. Even her personality has somehow gotten smaller. I've heard Agnes use the same bitchy tone Rosemary uses every time I see her, but not now.

I turn back to Rosemary. "I've got to get to work. I don't really have time to get a nurse." I reach for the quilt and wink. Agnes clutches the fabric in her gnarled hands. "Uh, it looks like she still wants it," I say. "And when I first came to visit, they told me to try and keep her as calm as possible. I better let her hang on to it."

"Oh, Mother. Let the girl fold it up for you. Here, I'll help." She tries to pull the quilt from Agnes' grasp.

Girl? I want to point out that I'm twenty four years old, not at all a girl, but I stay quiet for Agnes' sake.

Then Agnes' voice creaks into the silence. "Rosemary, let go." She lifts her chin in defiance.

These two act like my mom and I did when I was fourteen. I can't decide if this is funny, pathetic, or sad.

I watch for another moment and realize there is no place for me here. I interrupt their silent showdown.

"Agnes? I've got to get to work, but I'll be back in a couple of days." Rosemary is still trying to wrench the quilt from Agnes' grasp, and neither of them pays attention to me. "I'm sorry but I've gotta go."

Rosemary glares at me. "Do you think—"

I interrupt her. "Yeah, if there's a nurse at the station, I'll send her down."

Rosemary nods, giving me the only goodbye I get from either of them. They are locked in the latest of a half century or more of battles.

I get halfway down the hall when I hear Rosemary calling my name. "Harper, wait. I'd like to speak with you."

I pause, not wanting to talk to her at all, but I stop and turn to face her anyway. "Yeah?"

The quilt is draped across her arms. Apparently she won the tug-of-war. "How did this get here?"

"I brought it." I hate how small my voice sounds and even how short I feel. I want to yell and tower over this woman, but I wore flats today, dammit.

"You broke into our home." She hisses her accusation.

"Of course not," I manage to snap back. "I have a key. I've had one since I was eleven. She wanted her quilt, so I brought it. And, uh, I've been watering her plants for you." I tack that on at the end, hoping to appease her. My voice gets stronger, but it's still shaky. Why can't I be confident and tell her where to go? I can't stand her, but right now I can't stand myself. If I had my heels on I think I could face up to her. What is it about great shoes?

"You had no right." She holds out her hand. "I'll take that key now."

"Are you going to water the plants?" I try to stall her.

"I don't care about the damn plants, and I certainly don't want you having access to all of my mother's heirlooms. This is a very stressful time for me right now, and I don't need you undermining all of my efforts with my mother."

I have no idea what she's talking about, but at this point, I don't care. "What? Your efforts? Oh, I get it, you mean like putting her in a home where she doesn't want to be? Those efforts?"

She ignores my questions and holds out her hand. "The key please."

"Agnes gave me that key, and it's her house. If she wants me to return it, I will." I mentally pat myself on the back and bite back a grin. That shut her up. I head toward the door.

"Don't walk away from me, young lady."

Who the hell does she think she is? My heart races, and I can feel heat in my cheeks, but I keep walking and wave my hand in the air in goodbye, feeling slightly stronger. She gives a loud exasperated sigh. Somehow I forget to tell the nurse who's manning the main desk that she's needed in room 141.

THREE DAYS LATER, I pull into the lot and survey it for Rosemary's blue car. The coast looks clear, thank God. An older woman with wildly tinted hair is sitting at the lobby's front desk. I wonder what color she was going for, or what pattern. It's got splotches of reddish and blonde, almost like a calico cat, but the reddish isn't red, more of a faded magenta. She's smiling, lipstick on her teeth. I guess she's still trying to look decent, even if she missed the mark a bit.

God, why am I such a bitch sometimes? At least she's trying, which is more than I can say for myself some days.

"Hi." I approach the desk. "Can I ask a question?"

"Of course, sweetheart. That's why I'm here. What do you need?"

"Well, my grandma is here, and my aunt comes to visit sometimes too." I lean in like I'm telling her a secret. "Well, um, we don't really get along cuz my grandma gave me something that my aunt wanted. It's been pretty bad. I saw her last week here, and she got mad at me in front of Grandma, who got really upset."

"Oh my, that's terrible."

"It was pretty awful. Do you by any chance know when she comes to visit? I don't want to call her and ask because she'll just yell at me."

"Well, I guess we could check the visiting logs. Of course people don't make appointments, you know, and they don't always check in, but I guess we can look. What's her name?"

I realize this probably won't work. I rarely check in at the front desk.

"Her name is Rosemary Smith. She's Agnes Blackwell's daughter."

She types something into the computer. "Oh, here it is. It looks like she comes every Sunday afternoon, and sometimes on Wednesday evenings. Isn't that nice?" She smiles up at me, forgetting that I don't want to see my "aunt." "You know, regular visits are so important." She leans in, like she's letting me in on a secret this time. "We have so many here who have no visitors at all. So sad."

"Thank you."

She beams a lipstick coated smile.

I back away and give a little wave before I can get sucked into a longer conversation. If I don't visit on Wednesdays and Sundays, I'm good. No problem. If nothing else, Rosemary is uber organized and predictable.

Today, Agnes wants to take a walk, something she hasn't wanted to do since she arrived. She grasps at my forearm and leans on both her cane and me as we shuffle down the walk outside the manor.

"Do you get to go outside much?"

She shakes her head. "I miss my flowers, my garden. Is my yard dead?" She stops walking when she asks this question, waiting for the worst.

"No, it's not. I've been taking care of your houseplants—well, at least the ones you left at home. The garden beds aren't as weed free as usual, but everyone is still alive and well." She stares at me, confusion crossing her face. "Your garden, Agnes," I remind her softly. "We were talking about your garden, your flowers."

She takes a few steps and lowers herself onto one of the numerous benches that line the pathways. "We need to get that story down," she says to herself. Then she looks at me. "I should have done this years ago, but I always thought there would be more time." We sit for a bit in companionable silence before she stands and begins to walk back to her room and her quilt. I keep pace with her.

As soon as we enter her room, she points to the closet. "Get it." She doesn't ask, just commands and points. Her directions won't get any more specific than that, and I don't think that's her dementia or Alzheimer's or whatever it is. It's pure bossy Agnes. I have never looked in the closet, but I helped packed her stuff at home. I can only imagine that she has crammed it full of every single keepsake acquired over eighty plus years. I find a few clothes hanging, but mostly her closet looks like a garage sale extravaganza. Nothing fancy, nothing expensive,

34

but only God and Agnes know why she chose each item. I stare at her collection and note the irony of it. People work their whole lives for the finer things in life, but when it comes down to choosing their crystal or silver or a child's picture framed in glue and popsicle sticks, people will pick the popsicle stick frame every time.

I look for a box but can't see anything resembling one. "Are you sure it's here?"

"Ah, I ..." She screws up her face in thought.

I kick myself for asking and drag a chair over so I can see on the top shelf. There it is, shoved in the top corner. How did she get it up there? It's a large gift box, the kind of box you open first on Christmas morning since bigger is better to every eight-year-old. But then you unwrap it, anticipation mounting, to find an exciting new ... coat.

I stretch my five foot two frame as tall as I can and pull the box from the top shelf. It's not heavy, and I set it on her lap.

"Sit down," she orders.

I perch on the couch, feeling a little bit like her pet. All I see is tissue.

"That's acid-free," Agnes points out. She leans forward and pulls the tissue back, uncovering the quilt.

I unfold the material for her and grin. Score for Agnes. "Rosemary didn't take it?"

"I wouldn't let her."

I wonder how that had gone, since Agnes was cowering when I left and Rosemary had the quilt over her arm when we spoke. Agnes must have recovered at some point.

She strokes the fabric as one would a sleeping baby. "My great grandma made it. She walked here all the way from Indiana with it, and it saved her, too, a time or two. I told Rosemary it just might save me." She falls silent; lost, it seems, in the quilt. She's also peaceful. The quilt calms her somehow, and maybe she's right. Maybe it will save her.

I wait for her to continue.

"Did I tell you about her biggest trial? The worst part of her journey?"

"I don't think so." I wonder what could be worse than walking two thousand miles and camping for six months with someone like Jed. I grab my laptop from my bag and begin to record her words.

She seems peaceful under that quilt, as if it removes some of her fear and agitation. She speaks of her great grandma and the quilt's story in bits and pieces. Sometimes it makes perfect sense, others not so much.

It's going to take quite some time and a hell of a lot of work to put it in order, and I'm not sure I have it in me. Agnes seems to think I do but I'm not sure that's enough.

These are stories that have been handed down, embellished. Who knows the actual truth? I type it all up anyway. She speaks slowly, pausing often enough to find her words that I can keep up with the story, and Sarah's story pulls me in.

Chapter 5

THE BELL CLAMORS through the dawn's murk, and Mr. Dixon's deep voice bellows, "We're crossin' today," breaking the morning silence yet again. My heart lurches. It's real. We'll be heading into Indian Territory today crushing any niggling hope I had left that somehow Papa would change his mind and turn around. Granny will be gone to me forever.

Light barely breaks through the murky darkness in the wagon. This early in the morning the men say Blue River is low enough to ford, for the oxen to pull the wagons across without needing a ferry, but it looks to me like we will be swept away. Mama clutches Katie tightly against her body as Papa drives the oxen closer to the water's edge. He sits on the wagon seat next to Mama, his jaw clenched tight and his back rigid. Eliza, Jasper, and I perch on the trunks in the middle of the wagon, gripping one another's hands until they are slick with nervous sweat. I pray we don't tip and drown and that the caulking will hold and keep our provisions dry. If we capsize or get wet, we'll lose everything for this journey.

My brother Tommy follows us along with Jed, holding tight to the rope Papa has tied off to the wagon's rear. I pray they are strong enough to brake the wagon and keep the current from pushing us. We haven't forded a river this deep before, and we need to cross before the water rises with the warming sun.

We roll down the bank in deep ruts cut by the wagons ahead of us, bumping toward the swirling water. The current pushes the wagon in front of us down river, and men's shouts fill the air as shrieks come from within the canvas cover. Three wagons have made it across, but it doesn't mean we will.

Jed holds the rope taut behind Tommy, hollering at him to hold tight. Their faces show the strain of holding us back, slowing our descent so we don't crash and capsize. We roll slowly down, the wagon's contents shifting with the slope. Eliza drops my hand and grabs tight to my skirt and the trunk.

The oxen bellow as the water rises up their legs, but the inside of our wagon is silent as we lurch into the now muddy current. Tommy skids down the bank behind us, his heels dug into the dirt, eyes on the water in front of him. His left foot catches on a tree root and stops his bottom half cold, but the rope keeps pulling his top half forward, and Tommy falls, taking the rope and Jed down the bank with him. The current shoves at the wagon like Mama's hands kneading dough, gentle but persistent. Papa hollers his command to turn the oxen right against the pull of the current and cracks the whip above their heads. Jed scrambles after Tommy, who struggles to get his footing. Tommy grabs at the rope, but it only drags him farther into the water, and when the current catches his legs, his head disappears under the murk.

"Jed!" I scream and point to where Tommy is struggling to get his head above the water.

Every muscle in Jed's neck is taut as he struggles to hold the wagon, keeping it from being dragged too far downstream with the current.

I kneel and begin crawling toward the back. "Grab Tommy!" If Jed doesn't grab him, I'm ready to jump in myself, though my skirts would probably drag me down. I can't just sit here while my brother drowns.

"Sarah! Hold still!" My father's voice rings through the wagon, and I freeze. Oh God. Either Jed gets Tommy or he dies—or we all tip over and more of us will die.

"Jed!" I yell again.

He finally drops the rope and reaches for my brother. Instantly the current drags at the wagon box, and I lose sight of the boys as they move further downstream. I can't move to see them or we might tip. I look out the front and see the oxens have almost reached the far bank, but I still can't see the boys. Mama's eyes are shut tight, and I hear her non-stop praying under her breath.

How can she not watch?

Finally, the boys reappear at the wagon's rear. Water drips from their faces, and Tommy coughs as he follows the wagon. The oxen strain to pull the wagon up the bank. We bump up the steep incline and finally reach level dry ground. The boys follow us out of the river.

I breathe. I didn't realize I had been holding my breath until cool air fills my lungs.

"Is it over?" Mama asks. She hasn't opened her eyes yet.

"Almost," I reply. "Just get Tommy out of the water and we're safe."

Tommy whoops, and Papa urges the oxen further, clearing the way for the wagons behind us. As soon as the wagon stops, Mama jumps down and helps my sister from her perch on the seat. I climb over bags full of flour, kegs of dried food, trunks, and bedding, clambering toward the back.

Jed is there, winding the rope neatly around his arm. Water puddles beneath him, streaming off his clothes. The wagon behind us is just entering the water when he notices me. He hangs the rope off the corner of the wagon box, and we both laugh, filled with a giddy sense of relief that we've made it across.

"Thank you," I say, "for grabbing my brother. That about scared me to death. I can't even imagine losing him."

"Why, you're welcome, ma'am," he says, grinning. "But we ain't done yet. Still gotta get the cows and horses across." We both watch the wagon behind us tilt its way down the precarious bank. Retrieving the stock will be Jed's third trip through the Blue. He'd had to help with the ropes on his uncle's wagon, our wagon, and now the stock.

"Mama and I'll have dinner ready when you're done." So relieved am I that we made it, I forget for the moment that I hate him.

Jed smiles at me. "That would be nice."

Tommy runs toward us, face lit up with the responsibilities he has been given this day. "I'm goin' to get the stock, Sar."

"I know. You be careful. Keep your feet underneath you. We'll be getting dinner and headin' onto the trail as soon as you get 'em across safe."

Jed tips his hat to me like a gentleman, and I wonder if I've been wrong about him. He saved my brother without even hesitating. Maybe he's not so bad after all.

"Would you like a hand before we go?"

"Yes, please."

I reach for his outstretched arm and swing my legs over the rear of the wagon, ready to jump. He grabs my left arm and reaches for my waist as I hop from the wagon, yanking me to him as soon as my feet hit the ground. I gasp as his wet body presses into mine. He leers at me, his blue eyes seem to darken, and my giddy happiness vanishes. I try to back up, but he crushes me to his wet body before letting me go. His grip is tight around my arm, so tight that it hurts.

"Jed, let go," I hiss. A man has never held me like that. Horror and shame fill me as I push away from him, terrified that my parents might see us.

He smiles. "Just givin' a pretty lady a hand."

Tommy laughs. "Come on, Jed. Let's go. We gotta get the stock."

Jed releases his grip and heads back toward the river with Tommy. I don't understand him. One minute he's kind and concerned and the next he's repulsive. I shake my head, trying to remove the disgust which fills me. How could I ever have thought he was a nice boy just because he saved Tommy?

AN ACHY THROB in my arm drags me from sleep. I roll over, attempting to take the pressure off it, and it helps a bit. The narrow confines of my blankets and siblings allow for few comfortable positions in which to sleep, so aches often accompany my waking from sleeping in the same spot for hours. But this one feels different. It doesn't ease when I roll over. I yank my sleeve up, and even in the grey morning light I can see the dark blue and purple fingers encircling my arm. Jed's touch lingers, stuck to my arm in a grotesque purple shadow. Anger twists my stomach. Maybe I'm bruising easy since I've only eaten cornbread and beans and bacon for two months.

Jed had saved Tommy, saved our wagon from capsizing in the river. All that morning, he'd been nothing but courteous, showing me a side I hadn't seen, and maybe even liked a little.

But then he grabbed at me.

Papa never sees the awful side. He sees Jed as a gentleman, perhaps someone who could even take me off his hands. And Jed knows how to act the part of a gentleman, but that's all it is: an act. Granny always told me, "When someone tells you who they really are, believe 'em the first time. You'll save yourself a lot of grief." I never knew what she meant back then, but I think I'm starting to figure it out. But do you ever know who someone really is? Is Jed the disrespectful scoundrel from Independence? Or is he the hardworking courteous teamster who sometimes steps over the line cuz he doesn't know any better? I wish Granny was here to help me sort it all out.

A bell clangs, piercing the morning stillness with its sharp, high pitched ting. I can spend hours each day as I walk imagining how I could sneak into the Dixons' wagon, find the hideous wake-up bell, and creatively dispose of it. If I never hear the sound again, it won't be too soon.

The bell rings again, and the day begins. Every day it's the same. Get up, help with the kids, cook the morning meal, milk the cow if she's still giving any, put the cream in the churn and hang it on the wagon so the bouncing will make butter by dinner, prepare the afternoon meal, break camp, walk. What had begun as an adventure has become tedium for everyone except the children. For them, this is a never ending picnic. I would be happy to never eat or sleep outside again my entire life, but we've still got thousands of miles to go.

All day, I walk along behind the wagon, carrying Katie on my hip or holding her hand as she skips along beside me. When I hold her, she grabs my bruised arm, reminding me of Jed. Our wagon slows and stops in a large meadow next to the Dixons' wagon. We've made twelve miles. I've just clambered into our wagon to grab the bean pot when Jed's voice breaks through the noisy bustle of setting camp.

"How's the sewing going, Charlie?"

I stop moving so I can hear.

"Ain't been doin' much, Jed. How're you doing?"

Jed laughs. "Too bumpy on the trail to keep yer stitches straight?"

"Sarah?" Mama hollers. "You got those beans yet?"

"Comin'." I hear no more from our neighbors. I haven't seen Jed all day, and I decide to keep it that way if I can. It seems the only time that boy's nice is when people are watching.

After supper, I rinse the last dirty plate in the creek and set it beside me on the grass. My feet tingle, and I wiggle my toes as I stand up from my crouched position, letting blood flow back into them. Grabbing the stack of dishes, I carry them back to their box in the wagon, the tin plates and cups tinging against each other with a hollow sound as I walk. The damp grass feels soft against my bare feet. It's a pleasure each evening to remove my shoes. Though my feet have gotten tougher and no longer blister as I walk, I still look forward to removing my shoes. I have one more pair in the wagon, but I don't know if I'll have any by the end of this journey. I have almost worn through the ones I've got, and we've only traveled several hundred miles.

The tent is set and supper cleaned up. Tomorrow is Sunday, a day to lay by, rest the stock, wash, and cook for the following week. Not much of a day of rest for me or any of the women for that matter. Maybe for the oxen, but no one else. Not with the laundry and cooking to catch up on. A few families are leaving our train, not wanting to wait. Papa wants the oxen to rest. Without them, we die.

By my judgment, I still have a good hour of decent light. "Mama?" She turns, raising her eyebrows at me.

"I think I've got an hour. May I go to the Alcove spring so I can sketch? I've heard its awful pretty."

"Yes, you may. Take one of your brothers with you, though."

I wave at Tommy as I climb into the wagon to grab my diary and pencil. They are stuffed in a pocket we'd sewn on the inside of the canvas cover, along with Mama's diary. While she tries to capture this journey in words, I try to remember in pictures as best I can. I slip the small book out, dig in the pocket for the pencil, and slide both into my apron pocket before backing out of the wagon. It creaks and rocks with my motion. As I crawl over the supplies, I hear Mama telling Tommy to walk to the spring with me and stay with me. She emphasizes the stay part, and I smile to myself though I am sure we can find our way back to camp by following the smoke of the campfires.

By the time we leave, my walk to the spring has turned into a regular expedition including me, Tommy, Jasper, and Eliza, who refuses to be left behind. Katie thrashes about in Mama's arms, crying.

"Hurry on up. Off with you now," Mama snaps as she struggles to hold tight to my baby sister.

We hurry off across the meadow where the stock graze and head toward the line of trees hiding the creek. Tommy leads the way, and I let him. We hear the creek before we see it. The water gurgles and pops, tumbling over rocks and making the plopping sound it does when it falls into a deep hole, almost as if two rocks are banging against one another. Tommy pushes low hanging branches aside, and he and Jasper hold them for Eliza and me to scramble through.

Someone has said there is a trail to the spring and waterfall, but we have missed it and are now blazing a new one. With each branch that Tommy pushes aside, he wakens a hungry swarm of mosquitoes. We swat at the bugs and duck our heads under the branches until Tommy stops short, his eyes wide. I peek over his shoulder and we both stare as Eliza and Jasper catch up with us.

We've found it. Water spills across a rock overhang and falls in a thin veil to a pool below. I'd guess the water falls eight feet or so, but I can't be sure. The rocks encircle the spring in a full half circle. The boys instantly realize that they can walk behind the falls, underneath the ledge of rocks.

"We'll be over there, Sarah," Tommy says as they scamper off with Eliza trailing behind.

"I'll stay right here. Stay where I can see you."

I walk down the bank to a rock that I can sit on, and Tommy laughs, pausing to look back at me. "Sarah, as soon as you start drawing the falls, it's all you'll see. We could be massacred by the savages right here and you'd never know it."

I pull my pad and pencil from my apron, ignoring him. I have few pages in this small book, so before I put a single line on my paper, I watch the water begin its descent into the pool below, the way the lip of the rock thrusts the water outward before it begins to fall, turning the water from a crystal clear to a sheet of pure white in an instant.

Despite the constant flow of water, the rocks aren't smooth and round like in a normal stream. These rocks are sharp and jagged, while the pool is placid, calm, peaceful. In other places, the water rushes, hurrying on its way to some unknown destination—just like me. I wonder where I will end up. In Oregon? Or in one of the graves that already mark the trail?

When I get a sense of the stream, I pick up my pencil and begin to draw, losing myself in the world of lines and shadows. I start with the waterfall itself, with the outline of jagged rocks at the top. I work my way down, outlining, enough that if I don't come back, I can fill it in from memory. It won't be perfect, but enough that I can remember the beauty of this place.

The sound of my siblings' laughter washes over me along with that of the other members of the party who had made the trek to the spring. It all combines with the sound of the creek and melds into one. I focus on each line I draw, glancing back up to see the rocks, then back down to sketch, absorbed in the process.

Suddenly a boot appears next to my foot. It's a man's boot, but not my brother's. I snap my book shut and lift my head.

Charlie. Relief floods through me.

He stands next to me, not looking at me but at the falls. He nods toward my pad. "Don't quit on my account. You've got a talent there."

My cheeks redden as I realize I hadn't shut it fast enough. My granny was the only one who'd ever seen all my sketches. "I, well, yes. Um, thank you. I don't like to show my scribblings to others."

"Why not? That one was pretty good."

"Well, I don't have anyone to show anymore," I explain. "My granny was my devoted audience. Eliza likes to look at it, but Mama don't have time to, and Papa thinks it's a waste of paper and time. I just do it for myself. I s'pose it's my picture diary."

"Never heard of one of those before."

I smile. "Me neither."

He sits on a rock a few feet downstream and a little bit in front of me, his cane propped against his hip. He pulls a blade of grass from the bank and twirls it between his fingers as he watches the waterfall, and he starts to talk. I open my pad to a fresh page and draw the line of his chin, his nose, the shape of his lips. His bottom lip is full, fuller than the top lip. I am not sure how to capture the look in his eye, so I sketch its shape without any shading.

"You still there?" he asks as he turns to look at me.

I freeze, my pencil in mid-line coming down his neck. "Don't move," I whisper. I enunciate each word, as if that will make him go back to the exact same position without any abrupt movements.

He lowers his eyes to my page without moving his head, realizes he can't see a thing on it from his angle, and turns back to face the creek. His mouth twitches a bit in a grin, but he tightens his jaw and holds it in.

"Sarah, look at me," Eliza screeches.

I ignore her. Charlie's jaw tightens again, holding in whatever words he wants to say. *Just five more minutes*, I think, absorbed in my work.

"Saaaarrrrraaaaahhhhh," she yells again.

"Can I move yet?" Charlie mutters without opening his mouth.

I laugh at his seriousness and shut my book. The light is fading anyway. "You can now. I'm done. Well, I'm done enough, at least."

Charlie's entire body relaxes as he turns to face me. His face falls when he sees the closed diary on my lap, and his eyebrows come together in a look of concern. "Don't I get to see it?"

"Nope. It ain't done."

"But it's me! I sat here, gettin' eaten alive by mosquitoes, and you ain't even gonna show me? That ain't fair." His lips lower into a pout.

"Maybe so." I don't mind if he don't think it's fair. I ain't showin' him.

"You better take a peek at your sister," he says.

Eliza waves from the top of the falls where she stands with Tommy. I wave back. "Come on down from there. We gotta head back," I holler at them.

"We're comin'," Tommy yells. "You go on ahead if you want. We'll catch up. Can you find it?"

Charlie laughs. "I forgot about your lack of directional sense. How's that wagon flag workin'? Does it help you? Cuz it sure helps me. I haven't lost your wagon since we left."

I scowl in reply. "It's very helpful, thank you. It works exactly like I thought it would. At least we've still got everyone with us."

"Well, I'd be happy to escort you back, Miss Sarah Crawford." He holds on to his cane with his left hand and holds his right elbow out toward me, as a real gentleman might. I grab it and take two steps with him before letting go and falling into step behind him as we navigate the creek bed, then the narrow trail back to camp. Despite the cane, he walks faster than most, as if to prove that he isn't slower than any other man. We walk in silence through the trees until we reach the meadow.

He pauses when we emerge from the trees and offers me his arm again. "How you get when you're drawing, I get like that when I'm playing. The whole world goes away. It's just me and my fiddle."

I accept his arm. "It makes my Mama crazy."

He laughs. "Mine, too."

I look sideways at him and catch his eye, see his face widen as he smiles, his blue eyes crinkle up. My chest tightens, and I look down. I'm too embarrassed to keep my eyes on his.

"Sarah's got a beau – o, Sarah's got a beau-o," Jasper and Eliza sing behind us, giggling.

I drop my arm from his elbow and whip around, horrified. "Hush, you two." My face feels hot as I hurry toward the wagon where Pa leans on the front wheel, speaking to Jed. They both watch us approach.

"G'night Sarah, Tommy," Charlie says as he nods to my Father. "G'night Mr. Crawford, Jed."

Papa acknowledges Charlie, then tells the the rest of us to get off to bed as it's getting late. I herd the kids around the back of the wagon toward the tent. Katie is in the wagon with Mama, so I have to get her before I can head to the tent and bed. They sit at the back of the wagon, rocking back and forth, Mama lulling little Katie to sleep. As I reach for her, Papa begins to speak.

"Excuse me, Charlie. I'd like a word," he says. I freeze and gape at Mama. She stops rocking and pulls Katie back toward her.

"Yes, sir?"

"I seen you walkin' with my daughter this evening. Do you suppose ye're going to ask to court her, or you just doin' it on yer own?"

"Well, I ..." Charlie struggles over his words, his discomfort obvious with his fumbling.

"Son, let me just ask this. How is someone like you gonna support a wife, a family?"

I imagine my father looking at Charlie's cane, humiliating him. My heart squeezes into a little wad in the center of my chest. I fight to stay quiet, bite into my lower lip as I listen. I hear nothing but the breeze through the trees and the creak of the wagon as Mama sways with the baby, but I don't hear Charlie's footsteps. Is he going to speak? Finally his voice breaks the tormenting silence.

"I plan to set up a leather shop in Oregon, sir. I've got a skill and a trade. I've been workin' in a saddle shop, well, seems like my whole life. I got a full trunk of tools in our wagon. In fact, I think I've even worked on one of your leads to repair it, didn't I?"

It is silent again. I can almost see my father thinkin' that one out. Charlie, it seems, has surprised him.

"And," Charlie continues, "I'd be much obliged if you'd allow me to court your daughter."

My hands tremble a bit as I release my fists. Mama nods at me almost imperceptibly. She heard it, too.

The next voice I hear isn't Papa's. It's Jed's. "What you gonna start a shop with, Charlie? Old man Smith did it all for ya in Illinois. What

46

were you then? An apprentice? No better than a crippled slave." He laughs then, a bitter laugh, and I have to wonder what could have caused such bitterness and hatred toward his cousin. How can they be related, raised together? It doesn't make even a bit of sense to me.

"I'll think on it, Charlie," Papa says.

"Thank you, sir," Charlie replies. "G'night Jed, Mr. Crawford."

He walks away. Mama lifts Katie off her shoulder and passes her to me. I grab my sleeping sister and run to the tent as fast as I can without alerting Papa to my presence. I have no intention of talking with either him or Jed. They would say something awful and ruin the words I'd just heard Charlie speak.

I creep into the tent, lay my sister down next to Eliza, and cover her before heading back out to take care of myself. I hear Papa and Mama talking as they settle in for the night.

"You heard that conversation out there, Rebecca, did you not?" Papa asks.

"I did."

Papa sighs wearily. "It's time that girl married." The wagon creaks as they crawl into bed.

I have never eavesdropped on my parents like this, and I feel like a criminal, but I cannot make myself leave.

"Both those boys seem taken with her," he says.

"They do," she replies, not offering an opinion. I can't believe Mama isn't telling Papa Charlie is the better man.

"Jed's a fine worker. A little rough with the stock, but he sees what needs to be done and he does it. That's a fine trait in a man. He wants to farm, to get a piece of land of his own. You know he never had nothin' and he's willing to work for somethin'. I gotta admire that in a man. Charlie wants to open a shop, but he ain't much use on this trail, that's fer sure."

"I think its best left to Sarah."

Thank you, Mama.

Papa scoffs. "That girl'd just as soon go off and draw a pretty picture than make a decision based on what's best for her."

"I think you might be surprised," Mama says. "She's a quiet one, but she knows what she wants."

Papa grunts. I can't tell if it's in agreement or not. The wagon rocks again as one of them moves.

47

I creep away. Does Papa not know me at all? Mama does. I do know what I want. I just have to find the courage to fight that battle because it's pretty clear that Papa wants something different for me. The night is still cool this early in the season, and I'm chilled by the time I crawl under the blankets next to little Katie. Though I am exhausted, sleep eludes me for hours this night as I imagine every possible scenario for my future. I try to build up my courage for a battle with my father, because this battle is one I can't afford to lose.

Chapter 6

Early May 1847 - Layin' by at Alcove Springs

I LAY THE LAST rag on the rock in the sun to dry and lean the wash-board against it. Done. Not done perfect, like Granny would have made me do it, but done. It seems almost pointless, washing in the freezing cold creek water. All it does is turn everything into a grimy not-white gray. At least our aprons, bonnets, and rags match.

I lift my skirt, sit on the grass next to Mama, and watch the water run over the rocks. After washing all day and standing in the creek barefoot, my feet are pink and clean for the first time in a week. My new calluses have soaked all day, puffed up, and softened like snails pulled from their protective shells. I wiggle my toes.

"Mama? I'm gonna head up the creek to get some wood for the supper and to maybe wash up a bit."

"Sarah, there's people all over this creek. You ain't gonna find a place to wash with no one in it."

"Can I try? Please?"

She sighs. "I'd best go with you. Go grab your sisters. We could all use a wash."

I stand up to get them. I also grab my diary in case I see something or have a quiet moment, though with everyone with me I doubt that will happen.

The stream meanders through the prairie with no rhyme or reason, and Mama leads the way as we walk up its middle. Katie squirms in her arms, trying to get down. It's easier walking this way than it is fighting the trees and branches that hover over this section of the creek bed. We come around a gentle bend and stop when we spy a small pool with a few feet of water nestled under the bank. A startled trout darts out and dashes by Eliza's feet. Thankfully, she has no idea, or she would have started screeching and squealing. We aren't too far from camp, but we can't hear any voices and I don't want them to hear ours. We've found our bathing spot.

Mama sets Katie on the bank and strips her down. Eliza is next. Their bellies and backs are the only clean parts on them. A fine covering of brown dirt coats every part of their bodies, and I know my body is the same. At home, I would have hated the grime covering me, but I have gotten used to the dirt here that coats me in an itchy layer. Mama unbraids Eliza's hair for the first time in over a month while I scrub at Katie with the chunk of soap. She squeals and giggles when I lift her arms, rubbing and tickling her with the soap. As soon as she's clean, I lay her down in the pool to scrub out her hair. My skirt drags in the water, but it has been wet all day with doing the washing. As soon as the little girls are clean, it is my turn and Mama's. Katie and Eliza sit on the bank, drying.

I pause to listen, to make sure I can't hear anyone coming before I pull my dress over my head and let my bosom loose. I duck down into the pool, sucking in air as the cold water hits my belly, my shoulders, and finally my head. My nipples tighten and harden with the cold water, and I hold my hand over my chest, self-conscious and uncomfortable. I haven't bathed with anyone for a long time, not since they have grown so big. Mama looks at me and laughs, her own large bosom spilling onto her belly.

She pulls my braids loose as I scrub my body clean. The cold water, while startling, feels invigorating and fresh. We are through with our baths in a matter of minutes, but the cool water feels like it has washed a month of grime from my body. We have one small towel between the four of us. The girls have air dried, so I dry off the most important parts and pull my dress from the bush on which it hangs. Once we're all dressed, we begin to walk back to the camp. The water has not only cleaned our bodies, it's refreshed our spirits. We have not bathed for over a month since leaving Indiana. Eliza skips off in front with Mama behind her.

A rock—a perfect spot for sitting—juts out of the bank on a bend in the stream. "Mama," I say. "I'm gonna sit here a minute where it's quiet."

She stops navigating the rocks in the stream and turns. "You'll be all right?"

"Of course. I'll be back in a bit, and I'll bring some firewood for supper."

"Don't be long."

I watch the water for a minute before spotting a game trail heading up the opposite bank. It looks like it might head to a little clearing in the brambles, a quiet spot to work on my sketch of the spring. I cross the stream and grab onto a willow branch to pull myself up the bank. The trail bends through the trees before opening up into a hollow of green prairie grasses and wild flowers. The light filters through the trees above, dappling the entire clearing with shadows. I breathe the beauty in and lay down to look up at the sky through the branches. I spread my hair in an arc around my head on the grass to let it dry before I braid it up again, and I watch the trees, searching for fairies. If any place on earth has fairies, this would be one of them.

Granny always told me the fairies might steal me away if they chose, and she said they'd leave an old man in my place that somehow looked like me. Ever since, I've always looked for the fairies, but I've never spied any. This afternoon I look at the sky and strain to hear a fairy song in the glad, but I hear nothing other than the breeze in the trees and some sort of bug clicking away.

Papa always thought it was all silly talk and told Granny to never speak of the old fairy stories she grew up hearing. She didn't listen to him but told me all kinds of tales as we stitched together. When I explore and find spots like this, I want to believe in her stories. I always search for the fairies.

Maybe they're here.

Perhaps I sleep; I don't know. When I open my eyes, Jed is standing in the clearing, watching me. With a start I sit up, glaring at him. He's invaded my privacy and I feel vulnerable. He leans against a small tree, looking down at me. He is close enough that if I reach out my hand I can touch his leg. Too close.

"Ya look awful pretty sleeping like that. You ought to leave your hair down," he says. "I like it."

I pull a ribbon tie from my apron pocket and began to divide my thick hair into three strands.

Jed steps toward me and leans over, reaching for my hair. "I said ya ought to leave it down."

I jerk my head back out of his reach and continue braiding.

"I'm just gonna touch your hair," he says. "It's purdy." He grabs my half-done braid and yanks my head back so I am forced to look up at him.

"Jed! Let go. That hurts," I try to loosen his hold, try to get to my feet.

He laughs and drags me down to the ground by my hair. "I got you now." He grins as if he is wrestling with a younger sister.

I grab at his wrist, but he wraps his free hand around my arm and pushes me back, lifting his knee onto my belly. My left arm is still free, and I swing hard, hitting him in the chest. He is solid. I feel as if I have hit the side of the wagon with my fist.

He stares at me with a look that terrifies me. His eyes are dark. Below them, his mouth curves into a smile. I twist and thrash, but I cannot even begin to move him.

"Jed, get off. Please. I won't tell Papa. Please. Just get off."

He slides his knee off my belly and straddles me, holding himself just above me with his legs. "I do got you now." His eyes blaze. "Oh, Sarah. I do love ya."

Horror fills me as he unbuttons his suspenders then his pants, using only one hand. I hit him again, so he lets go of my hair and grabs at both wrists with one hand, binding them together. I dig my heels in to try to get out from underneath him, but he tightens his knees on my chest. I am not going anywhere he doesn't want me to go. He finishes his last button and yanks on his pants. I squeeze my eyes shut and try to scream, but I can't utter a sound. It is as if my voice has failed me, left me, as if he has stuffed a rag right down my throat.

He starts to giggle, a childlike giggle that evolves to high pitched laughter as I fight. With his right hand, he grabs at my chest, kneading me as if I am a piece of dough. He digs his fingers into the soft flesh and moans.

"I'm makin' you mine. Charlie can go to hell, right where he belongs," he grunts, more to himself than to me.

I pray for Charlie to come find me, but somehow I know that won't happen. Jed will do what he came to do.

"I ain't yours, and I ain't never gonna be," I manage to sputter. I have yelled it in my mind, screamed it, but what comes out is a a weak, terrified whimper.

He reaches down between his legs and grabs at my skirt, yanking it up, exposing me. He reaches between his legs and grabs at me. I shut my eyes again and begin to cry as he lays on me, trapping me beneath his body. He lets my hands go so he can use both hands to knead my chest.

My hands dig into the dirt at my sides, grasping at weeds, anything to anchor my body. I clench a fistful, thinking those weeds were the only thing keeping me here. Without them, I would just float away, leaving my shell on the ground beneath this groaning man. I turn my head to the side and squeeze my eyes shut. Pain pierces me in two, never ending. A rock digs into my cheek. The weeds in my hands, the rock in my cheek. Those are real, the only thing that is real, not the sweating, mating male above me or the searing heat between my legs.

Then it stops. At least the physical pain lessens. I doubt the rest could ever stop. It is in me, on me. I will never be free of this. Finally, Jed rolls off, and I can breathe. His unwashed male scent roils my stomach.

"What you cryin' for, girl? You're mine now. Ain't no way round that," Jed says, smiling. He caresses my stomach, sickening me. He lifts my dress all the way up, around my neck and rubs his hands on my naked bosom.

I release the weeds from my grasp, lift my hand and slap his face as hard as I can. Then I lean to the side, and vomit. My stomach clenches again and again and again. My entire lunch of cold beans and cornbread comes up in a pile by his leg. I wipe my face on my skirt and try to stand, pulling my skirt down from its wad around my waist.

Jed is silent, watching. His horrible laugh has stopped. He stands and pulls his pants up, covering himself. Never once does he look at my face. Just like an animal, sniffing around.

"You're a beast," I choke, glaring at him.

He reaches a hand toward my face, caressing my cheek, but I recoil and turn away. I want to scream, yell at him to never touch me again, but nothing comes out. Silence and a glare is all I can muster. It isn't enough.

"I ain't no beast. Just a man like any other. And you are beautiful, my Sarah." He leaves his hand on my cheek, holding my face, and wipes at my wet cheeks.

I stare at him. He's had his way with me, like any beast in the field. Any farm girl knows the mechanics of mating, but did he actually think this could have been anything other than an attack? A ravishment? I rip his hand from my face and run, fleeing through the trees that such a short time earlier had exuded such a sense of peace. Branches tear at my arms and my face, but I won't stop. My right hand clutches my skirt, holding it up while I shove branches out of my way with my left. I reach the stream and race across it, needing to put something between Jed and me. My body hurts, every muscle is tense and sore.

I pause to listen. All I hear is the soft gurgling of the water over the stones. He hasn't followed. A wail begins low in my throat, building and rising. I climb from the stream bed and lean on a tree. The moan escapes, becoming a bellow which rises to match the wind in the tops of the trees. Tears and snot mix on my face. Sobs wrack my body until the hurt in my throat matches the pain in my body and in my soul.

If I see Jed again, I might disintegrate into a million little pieces. But on the trail, he's impossible to avoid.

How can I face Mama? Or Charlie? Or even Jed? Surely Mama will know. She'll look at me and she'll know. Can't women tell these things? That her daughter is no longer the virtuous young lady she was this morning? He stalked me like a wolf after his prey, mated me, claimed me, said he loved me. Can evil know love? I am on a two thousand mile journey with the devil himself, but only I know it.

I lean against a wide, proud oak and embrace it, burying my nose in its bark. Pulling the scent in, clearing out Jed's stench. The tree holds me up, keeps me on my feet because my legs are almost useless. I breathe deeper, calming myself before I head back to the wagons.

No one can ever know.

I think of all the precautions we take every night to protect ourselves from the savages in Indian Territory or from the threat of losing our oxen or cattle. I have listened to my parents, to Mr. Dixon, the train's captain. I have followed all the rules and been ravished by one of our own. And he will flaunt it. Point it out to me. I press my forehead against the bark and breathe again, taking long deep breaths before turning and making my way back to the stream. I need to clean up.

I come upon the stream just above the Alcove Spring. Near it, under a tree, is the crushed grass of a doe and fawn who had bedded there for the night. It looks like the spot where Jed bedded me. My innocence lies in a similar spot, upstream. It's no longer with me, but as palpable as the fawn itself, who had fled at first sight of my mud and tear streaked face. I kneel at the stream's edge and cup the turbid water in my hands, splashing and scrubbing hard, pulling handfuls of muddy grass from the bank and soaking them in the murky water before scrubbing my face, arms, and legs, wiping his scent, his touch, his manhood off as best I can.

No one can ever know.

Most of all I need Jed to know. I am *not* his and never will be.

I shiver and look up. The stream is in shadows. I have been scrubbing for far too long. I hear the high whine of mosquitoes and notice the infernal bugs lifting from the grass, hovering over me, sensing a feast.

I lift my chin and square my shoulders. I am a woman now, I suppose, but I am not *his* woman. I step slowly in the direction of the wagons, repeating my chant: *I am not his. I am not his.* My chin keeps dropping, my eyes filling. I pause every few steps, breathe deep, and lift my head. I can hear my granny. *You got grit, girl. Hold up and show it. You'll make this journey right fine.* She'd said that just before turning and wiping her tears. I'll never see her again, but I feel her there, holding me up.

"Sarah? Where you been? Mama's been callin' for ya," Tommy yells as he sees me coming toward the wagons. "Papa's puckered, too. You told Mama you wouldn't be long, but it's been awhile. Supper's about on." Tommy stops yelling and takes a step toward me, his face wrinkled up in concern. "What's wrong with you? You're all white."

"I...uh, fell asleep in a little meadow."

"We figured ya got lost. I thought you trotted off with Charlie, but I found him." He reaches his hand toward my face.

I recoil and back up, not wanting anyone to touch me, ever again.

"You okay, Sis? Ya fall? Ya gotta bunch a dirt in yer hair."

"Yeah. I tripped and fell." Can he tell? My fourteen-year-old brother? I look down to calm myself, my fists clenched with the effort to hold myself in one solid piece.

"Well, did ya get any firewood? Mama waited and then she sent Jasper and Eliza out. She's hoppin' mad you didn't come back quicker." Wood? And then I remember. My original errand. Wood for supper's fire. I shake my head and clasp my hands together to still them. They have begun to shake. My teeth, too.

"I don't feel so well, Tommy. Tell Mama I'm sick. I don't know with what." I manage to say between my gritted teeth.

"Did ya puke? You ... don't look right." He keeps staring at me.

I know I don't look right. I don't feel right, either. I'm not sure I'll ever feel right again. I step around him and head toward the tent. I feel him watch me go, but he'll never know why I'm not right if I have

55

anything to do with it. But Mama might know. She doesn't put any store in superstition or witchery, but somehow Mama always knows things. I feel as if a flag waves above my head, signaling my sin. I bend extra low as I reach for the tent's flap.

"There you are," Mama snaps at my back as I try to sneak into the tent. "Where you been? Supper's about on, but your brother and sister had to finish your chores. I'm surprised at you, Sarah."

I can't reply. What can I say? I can't tell her where I've been.

"Sarah Ann Crawford, you git out here when I'm speakin' to you."

"Mama?" Tommy says. "She ain't right. She's all white and shakin'. I think she's got somethin'."

Mama doesn't say a word. I can imagine the blood draining from her face as her worst fears for this journey come to pass. Her children, sick on the trail.

"Tommy, you go tell Eliza to serve up supper to your Papa and you boys. Then you go get my box, the medicine one, from the wagon. You stay outta this tent, ya here? Take the babe to Mrs. Baker. She can figure what to do there, and you stay out!"

I hear her moving toward the tent behind me. Eliza and I had set it on some nice grass, so at least my blankets provide a soft bed. No rocks digging into my cheek here. I curl up in the corner, shaking and chattering as if I am lying in the wagon, heading down the trail. Alarmed, Mama kneels by me and brushes my hair from my face. I never had managed to get it braided, and have no idea where my ribbon ended up. I freeze when I feel her soft touch on my cheek.

"My baby, Sarah. What you feelin'? You sick? Tommy's bringin' the medicine box. I'll try somethin' to calm you." She soothes me like she does to her babies as she rocks them to sleep in her arms.

"Mama?"

"I'm right by your side. You're shakin' like a leaf, girl. Let me cover you up."

I clench my teeth to try to hold them still, but this just makes my whole body convulse harder. The shakes have to get out somehow. It feels like the devil himself is holdin' on to me and rattling me from the inside out.

"Mama?" I manage to get out between clenched teeth. "I want my quilt. Granny's quilt."

Mama's hand stills on my forehead as she listens to my request.

"Sarah, my girl, I can't get that." She smoothes my forehead with her cool hand. "It's buried under the wagon's floor. You know that."

"Please, Mama?" I beg. Papa doesn't care much for the whims of a girl, but I pray Mama will light a candle and use precious wax to unpack to get to the quilt. She'd have to re-do it all before sleeping tonight or pulling out in the morning.

"No, Sarah. We ain't gettin' the quilt. These ones here will do just fine." A wedge of light falls across her face as Tommy cracks open the tent flap.

"I've got your box, Mama. Is she gonna die?"

"Sakes alive, Tommy. She's only shakin'. That won't kill her. She'll be just fine. Send your father when supper's over."

"Yes, ma'am." Tommy backs out of the tent and heads off. I can't hear his footsteps for long. I concentrate on clenching my jaw to hold off this infernal shaking.

"Sit up, Sarah. Take this." She holds a tin cup to my mouth.

I can smell whiskey fumes wafting up out of the cup. My eyes water as I grit my teeth, trying to get them to stop chattering.

"Just open up a bit. I'll pour it down."

I take a deep, slow breath, stilling my muscles through sheer will, and I open my mouth the tiniest crack, just enough for Mama to pour. The spirits burn as they run down my throat. I feel it hit my stomach and spread in a funny warm feeling. I haven't eaten since dinner, and I'd lost that entire meal ... after. I lie back on the blankets and close my eyes, feeling the whiskey reach all the way into my toes and my fingers.

Mama caresses my forehead, pushing the loose strands of hair back. Her cool hands feel nice against my sweaty brow. "You want some more?"

I nod and sit up again. With a second drink, I feel my body begin to calm. "You just relax. Stay right here, little one." She stops the bottle, returns it to its spot in the medicine box and leaves. "I'll be back for the night."

As if I'm going to head out somewhere. I don't think I could stand even if I tried.

I lie back. Alone. Though my body quiets with the whiskey, my brain won't take a breath. It shouts at me, yells at me. What have I done? How have I fallen so far?

"Sarah, you awake?"

My brain pauses for a moment in its incessant berating of me. Then

I hear a scratching on the outside of the tent.

"You in there? Can you hear me?"

It's Charlie, my wonderful blue-eyed, related to Jed-the-monster, Charlie. I wonder if I should answer, let him know that his cousin had his way with me just this afternoon. Virginal Sarah exists no more. What would he do, I wonder? If I told him? But I can't. Ever. He would get up and walk away as fast as he could. It doesn't matter anymore anyway. I have lost him. I start to shake again and wonder if it's the whiskey this time.

"Sarah?" he whispers. I bury my head in the blanket. "Sarah, Tommy said you're not doin' so well. I, well, I think you're asleep, but if you can hear me, well . . ." I hear a sigh, then, "I'll be thinking of you." He falls silent, and I hear him get up and walk away.

I imagine him fixing his hat, leaning on his crutch as he hobbles back toward his own tent. I can't speak with him. Not yet.

Not ever.

Chapter 7

Present Day

THREE DAYS LATER, as promised, I make it back. Agnes sits in her bed, propped up and watching TV at noon. Why isn't she up yet? Dressed? I hover in the doorway, studying her. Her color looks normal. She's awake. Maybe I'm panicking for nothing. I step all the way into the room.

"Agnes? You feeling okay?"

No welcoming smile softens Agnes' glare. "How would you feel, stuck in here with this god awful TV and all these goddamn old people?" Her voice cracks as if these are the first words she's spoken in days.

Crap. Guilt floods through me. She never had to "find time" for me. Every time I walked into her house as a teen, she never once told me to come back at a better time. Even though she's pissed and my cheeks feel hot with guilt, I have to look down to hide my smile. She's the feisty old lady I love.

"Yeah, I'd probably be as pissed off as you." I'm not going to argue with her, try to convince her that life here is great. I'd be lying. "Do you want the quilt today?"

Agnes nods and sits up a bit straighter, her anger seeming to relent a bit.

"Can I turn the TV off?"

Agnes clicks the remote, reaches for her walker, and sidles the few steps across the floor to her giant chair. As soon as she is seated, I drape the quilt across her legs and perch on the love seat. She seems to begin every one of our "quilt" sessions by tracing the pattern with her fingers while I get my laptop ready to transcribe her words. Some days she follows the outline of the flowers, other days she traces the quilting stitches that cross the surface.

Her crumpled fingers move across the quilt, and I think of my grandma. A heart attack dropped her to the kitchen floor. No chance to say goodbye. One day she was there, and the next she wasn't.

Agnes lingers. I am thankful, but at the same time—as her hands trace the patterns and I watch her try to get her bearings, to remember—I wonder which is best. After Grandma passed, I always thought I'd want time to tell everyone I loved them, but now I'm not so sure. Agnes has all the time in the world, but nobody visits. She's outlived her husband and most of her friends. Rosemary comes, but it seems she visits merely to manage her mother's care.

God help me if my life ever gets managed. It sucks. It's as bad, or maybe worse, then having a kid and being trapped in a hateful job, like my mom. At least as a waitress, I have some flexibility in my schedule, unlike somebody who has to clock in nine to five every single day which mom hated, but she was stuck. She couldn't be the chef she wanted to be, so instead every night she watched the Food channel and drank herself to death in her misery. The thought of getting trapped like her scares me as much as aging has trapped Agnes in her body.

Agnes' hands still gently caress the quilt, and I bring myself back to the present.

"What is that?" I ask softly as I point toward the quilt. I don't want to startle her. "That center part? Do you know what it's called?"

Maybe a question will get her started. Then I kick myself. The nurse told me not to ask super specific questions that she might not know or else she could get frustrated. I hold my breath and wait. She's already grumpy, and the last thing I want to do is remind her how quickly her memory is fading.

"This?" She points to the center block. "Why this is the center medallion. I can't recall what the design is." She pauses, but it doesn't seem to upset her, and I breathe a sigh of relief. Her eyes close in thought, head nodding slightly as if she's running through words or memories and checking them off when they're not what she's searching for.

Should I prompt her or wait? I don't know. She always had the perfect advice for me, despite our age differences, and I have no idea how to even talk to her, help her through this. The guilt I felt upon arriving begins a slow, hot metamorphosis into shame.

"I looked it up once, but I can't ... I don't know. You can look it up. All the blocks on the outside were Sarah's favorite blocks. Some of them are signed. See that?" She holds one up and I can see the faint outline of a name and a date. "All her friends made blocks and signed them. She put them in this quilt for her journey and then added more to make it bigger, of course."

It's hard to tell which blocks have signatures on them and which don't since the material's so old and faded.

She continues, explaining the blocks that she can remember. Most she can't. There's a star block, a flower block. I'm sure they have more specific names, but neither of us have any idea what those might be.

"Would Rosemary know the names?"

"No." Her reply is quick, curt. "We've been through that already." She pauses, reaching for the other side of the quilt. "Grab that corner. Are you going to help me fold this damn thing or are you going to sit there and watch an old lady struggle?"

I jump up from the couch and reach for the quilt.

"Don't do it *for* me. I asked for your help, not for you to take over."

I back up and hand her the corner of the quilt again so we can fold it together. "Sorry," I snap right back.

She smiles. "I think you have the gumption to tell this quilt's story. Take it. It's yours."

I look at the intricate and ancient cotton quilt that now sits folded on her lap. "I have the..."

"Oh, for God's sake, young lady. Have you not heard a word I said?" She sighs. "What have I been telling you these past weeks? This..." she waves her hand across the surface of the quilt, "this is my story, and now it's yours. It's more than just history. Please don't tell me I've been wasting my breath on you."

"No...you haven't." I know she wants me to tell the story, but I don't know if I can. I'd dreamed of being a writer as a kid, spent hours spinning tales and telling them to Agnes. I had files of half-finished pieces, nothing completed or at least nothing that I'd ever let anyone read. But I haven't written a word since my mom started to go, her liver shutting down. Panic seizes my chest. Then the meaning of her words hits me. "Wait...what did you say? You're giving me this quilt? Why? Don't you think it should stay in your family? I mean, I think it might be kind of valuable."

"Of course it's valuable," she exclaims. "That's why I want you to have it."

"You trust me with it? Are you sure?" I look closely at her eyes. They are clear, even piercing. She doesn't look confused at all. Can she mean it? Has she thought of what her daughter will do to her? To me? I don't want to upset Agnes, but the thought of Rosemary makes me cringe.

"Harper, sit," Agnes says, pointing at the couch in front of her. "Let me do this. Take the quilt. Please." Her watery blue eyes study me, waiting for my answer.

I can't tell her no and let her down. Taking the quilt is the easy part. It's the story part that's throwing me. "If you're sure."

"I'm sure. Of this, I'm sure."

I lean over and give her a kiss on her cheek. Her skin is so soft. It always surprises me when I touch her. It looks as if it would feel rough, but it doesn't, not at all. "Thank you, Agnes. Love you."

"Love you, too. Now where were we?"

I read her the last page of notes, reminding her of where she'd left off, and she begins. After an hour, she slows down then falls silent. Her head falls back, resting.

"I'm going to go, Agnes," I whisper as I pack my computer into my backpack. I have a few more pieces to the tale, but I think I know where these might fit in to the story.

She lifts her hand a bit in a wave. I turn and leave, the quilt tucked under my arm.

THIRTY MINUTES LATER, my best friend Claire meets me at my house. She is staring at the quilt which I've laid across the couch.

"Well," she says, then pauses. She brings her hand up to her chin and rests her head in it, her thinking pose.

I wait.

"If she wants you to have it, I think a couple of things. First, you should get it in writing, otherwise Rosemary will be her regular awful self and do something crazy like accuse you of theft."

My heart begins to gallop in my chest, like it's trying to escape.

Oh. My. God.

"Harper, close your mouth. Are you really that shocked?"

"Yes," I screech. "She would totally do something like that. And Agnes can barely hold a pen to write. Crap."

A grin crosses Claire's face. "You are easily the most panicky person I know." She crosses her arms and steps back, studying the quilt. "The second thing is that you need to figure out what this thing is worth and get it appraised like they do on that one show where people bring their old stuff in to experts and find out what they can get for it. Some of that old crap is worth tons of money. Harper, this is like a lottery ticket."

"A lottery ticket? What are you talking about?"

"If this thing is worth a lot, you could sell it and totally pay for your education. You could finally finish school."

"But it's a gift from Agnes. I can't sell it." I say this slowly, thinking about her words. "Agnes gave this to me so I'd take care of it for her, not post it on the internet for some random person to take home." But as I say this I realize she's right. The quilt could help with college. And really, what is it? An old blanket. It's not *Agnes*. She'd never know, anyway … would she? "I don't know. It seems, well, like I'd be betraying Agnes."

Claire slaps her first-grade-teacher face on. "I know, but you could think about it in a different way. Think of this as Agnes' gift to help you out. She never said you should keep it forever."

"Actually, she did. She asked me to keep both it and its story for her. And they go together. She said that 'I *do* stories,' but I haven't written anything, since..." I trail off. Claire knows exactly when I stopped writing. The same time everything in my life went to shit.

"Well then, I guess you have to figure out what you want to do, but I think regardless of what you decide, you should get it appraised."

I can't argue with that, so I nod, wondering how one gets a quilt appraised. Thank God for Google.

The next day, I'm crashed on the couch, enjoying a lazy day off from my job as a waitress when my phone chirps with a text from Claire: *Are you home? Can I bring someone over?*

Me: Sure. When?

Claire: Now. You have fifteen minutes. Get the quilt.

I reach my hand up to feel my hair. Blonde strands shoot off in at least three directions, and a matted mess covers the back of my head. Perfect. Serious bedhead. I look around the family room and grimace.

Not having the most active social life with friends stopping by, I don't always pay much attention to my house. I jump off the couch to begin a hurried clean up before racing up the stairs to at least change from my sweats to something a little nicer. I run a brush through my hair to try and make it look like a blond bob rather than a nest.

Seventeen minutes later, Claire pulls into the driveway. I grab the quilt and head downstairs. She doesn't bother waiting for me to answer the door but walks right in, followed by an older woman. The stranger is heavy, maybe sixty years old, with super short gray guy hair.

"Harper, this is Shari," Claire says in an officious voice. "She's the Art writer for the newspaper." Claire is an aspiring journalist, kind of like I used to be, but she actually got her degree, finishing her BA in four years while I'm barely done with my associates degree after six years of intermittent classes, but I don't know what to study. What if I finish my degree and find out I hate it? I'll be stuck. Like my mom and my biggest fear is drinking myself to death like she did, unable to change my life because I've chosen a path I hate. But at the rate I'm going, I'll be free but serving fajitas and tacos for the rest of my life.

I shift the quilt to my left arm and reach out to shake Shari's hand. Claire's taking full advantage of this opportunity to impress a local newsperson, even if this person looks like she might not be that influential.

Shari shakes my hand with a firm grip. "This must be the quilt."

"Yep." I lay it across the couch.

Shari stares at it, speechless. She walks around the entire thing, studying it. "Do you know when it was made?"

"1845-ish is when I was told."

She looks at me in disbelief. "1845?"

"That's what Agnes said. Is that really old?"

"Very. Textiles don't often last that long, especially in this condition. Do you know anything else?"

"I actually know kind of a lot. I've what I do have typed up, but I'm still piecing it all together. It came over on the Oregon Trail with her great grandma, Sarah."

Her eyes open even wider. "This came to Portland on the Oregon Trail?"

The repetition in this conversation is getting annoying. "Yes. It came with Agnes' great grandmother. You can see her name right here, along with the date." I point to the signature on the bottom right of the quilt.

"I had no idea this is what you were talking about, Claire. I'd love to do an article on it."

"What do you mean, an article?" I interrupt.

"In the paper. In the weekend Arts section. This is a fabulous story. And this truly is a piece of art."

I cross my arms over my chest. "Do you think Agnes would like an article about it? I don't know."

"Agnes would love it," Claire says without any hesitation. "She wants to tell the story, so why not publish a bit of it?" She frowns. "But what about Rosemary?"

I shrug. As far as I know she doesn't know I have the quilt. I step back and study it. "Would you take pictures of it? Or use actual full names?"

"Of course. In an article on an art piece, photographs of the piece are standard. Who's Rosemary?" Shari asks.

"Agnes' daughter. She's kind of, well, a loose cannon," I say.

"What do you mean?"

"Well, Agnes gave me the quilt, but I don't know if Rosemary knows that. I try to avoid her."

"Have you gotten it in writing that Agnes gave this to you?" Claire asks me.

"Not yet. I was going to see her tomorrow." I feel like a chastised five-year-old.

Shari's forehead crinkles in concern. "What are you talking about? Who legally owns this? I can't write about it unless you can verify ownership." She appraises me as if I'm a regular quilt thief, then she glances at Claire, eyebrows raised.

For Claire's sake, I give Shari a brief rundown of the situation.

Shari nods and scrunches up her eyes. It must be her thinking face. "You definitely need to get some sort of proof of ownership. A note or something."

"I can do that."

"Well, if you get proof of ownership, let me know and we can do this article. We'll need an official appraisal as well. I'd need the value for the piece." She pulls out her notebook to start taking notes. "That'll probably cost, oh, I don't know, maybe $150."

My mouth drops open. "What?"

She continues to take notes. "Well, if you want the article done, you'll need an official appraisal. Also, if you're considering selling the piece or getting it insured, you'll need one." She pulls a business card from her purse and hands it to me.

I start running my budget in my head. "If I figure something out, I'll let you know." There's no way I can afford to spend $150 on this quilt.

"I'd like to set up an appraisal as soon as possible. I'm not sure how long that will take. While I set that up, you can get the note from Agnes." She picks up a corner of the quilt, examining the threads. "This is an amazing piece."

Did she even hear me, or am I completely invisible here? I can't afford an appraisal. I glance at Claire who has joined Shari in admiring the quilt.

I break the silence. "Do you know what I am supposed to do with it?"

Shari looks at me like I've lost my mind. "Do with it?"

"Yeah. Do you know how to store these things?"

"What have you been doing with it?"

I'm embarrassed to tell her that it's been in a pile on my bedroom floor. I try to figure out something to say, but I'm not the best liar.

"It's been up in her room, folded in the closet. We figured keeping it out of the sun would be best," Claire says, covering for me.

Thank God for best friends. I smile and nod in agreement, going along with her lie.

"I don't know," Shari says, "but that sounds good. It seems like it's in pretty good shape for its age. Where has it been for the last a hundred and fifty years?"

"Well, I think it's spent most of its time in an old cedar chest."

She nods as if she thinks that's a good thing, but by this point I think she knows as much about this stuff as we do, which is not much.

"What kind of art stuff do you usually deal with and write about? This kind of stuff?"

"Generally, I deal with gallery openings, modern art, shows at the major museums down town." She shakes her head. "Antique quilts and folk art aren't my specialty. However, you do need to be able to prove ownership of it, or it could be a problem for you, especially if this woman's daughter would object."

Great. She has no idea what to do with this thing either, other than figure out what it's worth—and I can't afford to find that out. That's all anyone wants to know. Nobody has asked me about Sarah at all, and to me she's the most interesting part of this whole story.

After they leave, I head upstairs to work on it, wondering how she kept going. Here I am worried about getting an amazing antique quilt as a gift from Agnes and writing down her story. Sarah had to worry about a psychopath stalking her and walking two thousand miles. Last week, I had dragged the old card table out of the garage, wiped it all down, and set it up in my mom's room as a desk. I slump into my chair and stare at the research notes and fragments of Sarah's story Agnes has told me. In minutes, I'm engrossed, piecing together Sarah's tale, my worries receding with each word I write.

Chapter 8

WILDFLOWERS COAT THE prairie, looking as if a rainbow decided to lie down and take a rest. That's all I want to do: bury myself in their beauty and forget. Sleep. Rest. Stop walking.

Yellow, purple, and pink blossoms peek and wave from their tall, green stems, covering the hills. Their lovliness mocks me. We entered the wilderness, Indian Territory, when we crossed the Blue River, and we have all kept close watch to see the Indians. This country doesn't look savage, but it is there, underneath. I feel it hiding and traveling each step with me. I wonder how many its beauty has deceived as it has deceived me. I draw nothing.

We walk through Kansas then cross into Nebraska where the plains go on forever, dust swirling at our feet and the incessant wind tearing at our bonnets and skirts. I watch for Indians every day and though I have seen a few lines of them in the distance, I no longer feel terror at thought of them. What could they do that hasn't been done to me already? Nothing.

We make between fifteen and eighteen miles each day on this long, monotonous walk. The days are punctuated by moments of terror when I hear Jed's voice or see his face as he tries to speak with me. His attentions are agonizing and shameful at best, terrifying at worst.

I avoid him as best I can, but it's not always easy on this trail.

Our party has shrunk to twenty-five wagons which slither across the plains. Some families move ahead, not wanting to wait for others who decide to rest and lay by. The herd of cattle follows behind; the milk is a nice addition to our diet as long as the grass holds out.

We follow the Platte, a wide and sluggish river with almost no bank. Thousands of buffalo and antelope fill this country, and their meat is as good as any I've tasted. We can cook with their dung, too. At first this disgusted me, but it is a clean burning fuel and three bushels make a decent meal. Eliza can collect that it ten minutes, filling her apron with the dried chips. Me, it takes longer. Everything seems to. I feel like I'm moving through a swamp, sluggish and slow, every motion taking energy I don't have.

I am lost in my thoughts when Thomas careens into Eliza, next to me. "What are you doin'?" I snap.

"I need the gun."

"Why? Indians? What?"

Mama sticks her head from the wagon, her eyes wide. "Indians?"

"No. Ain't no Indians. Antelope. We're gonna get one for supper."

"Well, slow down. No reason to knock us all down. Can I go?" I ask, even though I know the answer. Anything at all to get away from Jed, even for a moment.

Tommy looks at me like I just sprouted an extra head. "Ain't no girls goin'."

"Why not? I can shoot that gun better'n you."

"You can't either."

I cross my arms and glare at him.

He ignores me, but he knows as well as I do that when Pa taught us to shoot, I beat him every time. "Got the gun, Mama?" he asks.

"With all yer shakin' you can't hit somethin' unless it's five feet in front of you and standin' sideways," I grumble.

"Sarah," Mama interrupts. "You let him have this hunt. You've got yer sisters to watch anyway."

"But why? You know if I go we'll have meat for supper."

"That's enough, Sarah. Not out here." She shakes her head at me. "I never did much like you with a gun. Now you hush and let yer brother go."

Tommy smirks at me as Mama passes the rifle down to him. I clench my fists under my crossed arms so I don't swat him upside the head.

"You better get one is all I got to say," I yell after him, and I do hope he gets one. Fresh meat and gravy sounds awful good.

The boys run up a small rise, and I wonder how far away the antelope herd is. I'd much rather be running with the boys, my hair and skirts flying, leaving all this behind me. Instead, I trudge behind the wagons, collecting buffalo dung in my apron.

An hour passes, then two. The wagons run five abreast to try to stay out of the dust, though those of us who walk next to them cannot escape the thick dirt. It coats our skin. We are becoming part of this trail. Eliza walks next to me, her bonnet flopping on her back, her cheeks red with heat and sunburn. At her side she drags a whimpering Katie.

"Sarah, stop. Katie's gotta go agin." Three-year-old Katie squats as Eliza and I hold our skirts out, shielding her from others' eyes. Hot water pours from her behind.

"My tummy," she whimpers, then she slumps to her side, curling into the fetal position on the hard dirt. I dump my apron full of chips and kneel to pick up my baby sister. Her body wilts as she lays her head on my shoulder, and blood covers the ground along with the diarrhea that had poured from her body. Eliza's eyes widen in alarm, and I seize my opportunity to run, to try and shake off the sluggishness that dogs me.

"Mama? Mama!" Eliza yells as we scamper after the wagon. The wagons are making good time today, rolling across the flat plains of the Platte River.

Mama sits on the wagon seat while Jed walks next to the oxen, driving them along. I don't want to go near him, but with my sick sister resting on my shoulder, I have no choice. He smiles at me and halts the team. I avoid his eyes and look toward Mama. Papa has yelled at me to be more mindful of my manners when I get up and move away from Jed at meals, but Papa could take his belt to me and whip me until I bleed before I ever acknowledge Jedediah Dixon's presence again.

Until right now. Pa, who always drives the team, is missing. "Where's Pa?" Panic tinges my words.

"In the wagon," Mama replies.

"In the day?"

"He's sick."

I stare wide-eyed from Jed to Mama. "Why's he drivin'? How come Tommy ain't drivin' the team? Tommy could do it." Anxiety spreads from the center of my chest throughout my body. In my panic over Jed driving, I momentarily forget that I'm here because of my sister. "Mama, we don't need him."

"Yer Pa wanted Jed to do it. He's better at it, anyway. And Tommy ain't back yet."

"Katie's sick too, Mama," Eliza says, interrupting us.

Mama wipes her arm across her face, swiping at the sweat that drips down her temples. She reaches for her baby, and I pass my sister up. It's as if I'm passing her a rag doll.

"What happened?" Mama brushes her hand across Katie's forehead, pushing her red curls back, and shushing her and rocking them both as if she's still an infant.

"I think she's got the bloody flux," I say. "I'll get some water from the barrel for her. She said her tummy hurts, and she's been kinda moanin' while I was runnin' here to get her to ya."

"Yer Pa's got it, too. You girls stay clear a here."

"Is she gonna be all right, Mama?"

"Let's pray that she is, Eliza."

"Do you want the water Mama?" I ask.

"Yes. And a wet rag." She lays Katie across her lap and holds her head in the crook of her arm. "Hurry, Sarah. This baby's burnin' up."

I run to get a cup of water from the barrel in the back of the wagon. When I pull myself up, I see Pa laid out on the supplies. His hat lies next to him, and he moans. One brown eye opens, watching me. He lifts his right hand toward the cup. I fill it and lean across, handing it to him. He drinks then lays back for just a moment before sitting up, lurching toward the back of the wagon, and jumping out.

Mama watches him move. She lays Katie down on his bed then jumps down from the wagon seat to meet him and hide him with her skirts. "Sarah, git over here."

Mortified, I walk toward them, turn my back and spread my skirts. He groans, and I can hear the splashing of his stool against the ground. I try not to vomit from the smell and the sounds. I clench my teeth and swallow, hard, but I can barely move my throat from the lump that has lodged itself there. What will we do? Without Pa, we'd have to rely on Jed. Charlie can't drive our team. I don't want to imagine what might happen if Mama also falls sick.

Finally, he's done, and Mama excuses me.

Eliza has put all the chips in the wagon bed.

"Let's go git more," I tell her.

She looks hard at me, eyes wide. "Do ya think we'll get it?"

"I got no idea." We pass graves daily. The first few we stopped to look at. Now we don't even stop, just keep rollin' along, as if passing a

71

baby's grave out in the wilderness is normal. And we count. We count how many graves we see each day, and Mama records it in her diary: how many we see, their names. It's her way to honor them, to note their passing, but it also constantly reminds us. Nobody makes this journey unscathed.

I head to the back of the train to where my brother Jasper drives the stock. Small rivulets of sweat run down his cheeks, coursing a path through the dirt and grime.

"Papa and baby Katie are sick. How're you feeling?" I study his face for any sign of weakness, but he looks like his normal, filthy, nine-year-old self.

"Sick? Pa? What's he doin'?"

"Lyin' in the wagon," Eliza tells him.

Alarm spreads across his face. Papa has never been one to lay in the wagon while it travels down the trail. Some days, he'll drive from the wagon seat, but never has he given completely over to Mama and Jed.

"We gotta stay away," I say. "Mama thinks it's the bloody flux."

"You feel all right?" he asks.

Eliza and I nod in response. My brother looks at the sun, judging the time. "I s'pose we'll be campin' here soon. I'll go help Jed out with the oxen."

"He's fine. You stay with the stock." I don't want anyone in my family near Jed.

Jasper doesn't like this but heads back anyway. Eliza and I return to walk beside the wagon, listening to my father's moans and the baby's cries. Other wagons maneuver around us as Jed stops again and again for my father. I do my best to hand Mama cups of the muddy Platte water and make cold, wet compresses for both Katie and Pa.

Jed walks slowly next to the oxen, matching their pace, the whip in his hand. He only uses it sparingly, never hitting them, but cracking it over their heads. He has learned, at least, that these beasts must survive. Without them, we are as good as dead, so he treats them with a begrudging kindness. In a way, Dee, Red, Titan, and Bean have more power than does he. They get water first. They get taken care of first, before he gets to even eat. That's as it should be. But he resents anything that doesn't put him first.

Each day, I look for signs of improvement, but Papa still rides in the wagon and Mama walks beside it carrying Katie, who grows limper with each passing hour and day. Their sickness is the only thing that has kept the shame at bay as my worry for them takes my mind off its relentless swirling around that afternoon in the glade. I jump up and down, in and out of the wagon, giving Papa water and taking Katie from Mama when her arms become too tired to carry the child. She seems to be fading into nothingness, her features pale and sunken in. Her eyes have that glazed, feverish shine, yet even with her fever her cheeks are pale.

If Papa dies, it will be Jed who saves us, gets us to Oregon. I will owe him everything I hold dear. I dip two rags into the muddy Platte and carry them, dripping, back to the wagon for Mama to press on Papa's head, praying that it doesn't come to that.

Yesterday Tommy saddled a pack mule with the side saddle, and I rode all day with Katie on my lap. Mama fetched them their water and kept them wrapped in wet rags. Today I must walk, as my bottom hurts too much to ride. Mama and I trade Katie back and forth. Eliza is in charge of collecting the buffalo chips to heat our supper. I pray we don't get sick.

It's been three days since Katie and Pa got sick. We've made good time with Jed driving, but I worry about the team since they must pull Papa's extra weight in the wagon. He's tried to get out and walk, but he's too weak. The sun is high in the sky when the wagons come to a stop for the noon dinner break.

Jed comes first to get his dinner of cold biscuits, coffee, and bacon. "Thank you," he says, the picture of politeness when I hand him his plate.

I refuse to answer.

"Sarah, why ain't you talkin' to me? Ya gotta talk to me."

"I gotta do no such thing," I hiss, keeping my eyes on the plate in my hands.

He can't hurt me here, with my family and all the other wagons around, but fear still grips me tight. My hands begin to shake, so I shove them in my apron pockets. I don't want him knowin' how much he gets to me, cuz he'll take it all wrong. He hurt me before, and I think he can probably figure out a way to do it again, especially since he doesn't seem to even realize what a monster he is. He stands in front of me long enough for me to count to a hundred until he walks away.

We finally finish the meal, pack up, and continue on, relentless in our westward movement. Jed walks beside the oxen, driving them. He cracks the whip, a nice clean crack, and I follow, carrying my sister. She lifts her head and looks at me, whimpering. This is her signal that she must stop and lift her skirts, so I bend down and hold her above the ground. Nothing happens, and she slumps forward, unable to hold her small body upright. Her eyes close, and I lift her back to my shoulder, walking again. Her body is warm against my chest.

"Sarah?"

I smile. It's Charlie. He's walking, not riding. This is unusual for him.

"How is she?"

"Not well. Papa seems to be getting better. He kept down his breakfast, and he's walked a bit today though he's back in the wagon now. How are the others?"

Our wagon is not the only one to take the hit with the bloody flux. At least seven of the wagons on the train have a family member or two suffering.

"About the same. Mrs. Baker just got it today, and she's pretty loud about it."

I smiled. I had heard her hollerin' earlier and thought perhaps one of the women who was expecting had come into her time, but I guess not.

"How're you feelin'?" he asks.

"I'm good." I don't tell him that yesterday I'd woken feeling nauseous, but that was all. I won't tell Mama that, neither. She's exhausted enough, takin' care of Pa and Katie. We walk for a bit in silence.

"I wish I could help you carry her," he says, patting Katie on the back.

"Me too." Her eyes flutter in a dream. "I'll pass her into the wagon. She might stay sleeping there."

"Jed, hold up," Charlie hollers at Jed's back.

Jed gives the command to the animals, and the wagon slowly rolls to a stop. He watches me, like he always does. Eliza jumps into the wagon and reaches down for Katie. I pass her up, leaving Charlie and me walking together, silent except for the creak of the wagons around us.

"I gotta talk to you," he says, breaking the quiet. His voice is soft, unlike his normal chatty self.

"What about?" We haven't seen much of one another these past days with the sickness, but I've avoided him too, almost as much as I've avoided Jed. What's the use of seeing him and speaking to him? He won't ever want me now.

"Yer Pa talked to me before he got sick."

I straighten my bonnet to hide my reddening cheeks.

"He said he don't support us courtin'. Don't think I can provide for ya."

I stop walking, anger ripping through my body. How dare Pa decide for me? But he can. He always has. I don't know why I would think this might be any different. I watch Charlie's hands as I grapple with a reply. His left hand grips his cane, which he holds tight to his body. In his right hand, he twirls a stalk of grass, unconsciously spinning it between his fingers. His hands are calloused and strong. Wide, man hands. I want to slip my hand into his, to feel the strength in them, but know that I can't. I think I could just watch them twirl the grass as we walk. Then, I think of Jed's hands, holding me, hurting me. It's always Jed who crowds my thoughts, reminding me of what I can no longer have.

Charlie stops walking and reaches for my arm. "That what you want?"

No, it's not at all what I want, but I can't say that. Charlie deserves better, not a whore like me. Maybe Pa has done me a favor after all.

"Yes, Charlie," I manage to croak, looking at the ground and not into his blue eyes. "I need to respect my Papa's wishes."

I memorize the way his hand grips his cane so I can draw it later. I can't have him, but I can remember him. I want to fall in a heap on the ground and cry, but I don't, instead I watch his back as he walks away.

I SET THE tent in the prairie grass about ten feet from the wagon. Eliza and I walk slowly through it looking for sticks or rocks that might poke us in our sleep. We find nothing and begin to lay out the poles and stakes we'll hammer into the ground so we can attach the ropes and spread the canvas tent over top of it all. It is tedious work to put up every day, but Eliza and I put it up quickly as soon as we find a suitable spot for it.

I look up from laying out the stakes, startled to see Papa out of bed and watching us. He places each foot with care, as if he's walking across an icy pond and not a dusty plain. His face is gaunt, older than it looked four short months ago when we left Indiana.

"Thomas!" Mama screams from the rear of the wagon.

Eliza and I look at each other and run toward her. Mama cradles my sister's limp, lifeless body against her chest. She's rocking back and forth as if Katie's merely sleeping.

I cover my mouth with my hand. We have seen too many graves along this trail. Death surrounds us, ever present but always an unwelcome visitor.

My father wraps his arms around Mama, embracing with Katie between them. I can't breathe. This journey has brought nothing but loss. Finally he releases Mama. "Go git yer brothers," he tells Eliza, then points to me. "You get a quilt to bury her in."

I climb into the wagon, my heart torn. I get to see the quilts, but one will be left here in the wild, wrapped around my baby sister. Mama sits on the ground, clutching my sister's body as Papa takes a shovel and begins to dig. We will bury her inside the circle of wagons, protecting her small body from wolves for at least one night.

The good quilts are buried in a trunk deep in the wagon, but that is what Mama will want. To get to them, I must unpack almost the entire wagon. I begin to hand supplies to Eliza who stacks them in a pile on the ground. Finally, I reach the box that holds the quilts, our good clothes, and some of Mama's special service, all wrapped up in the soft material. I open the lid and pull out the quilt she will want for Katie. It's a smaller baby quilt, the one Mama wrapped us all in as infants. It had been destined for future babies in Oregon but won't ever get there now. I pass it down to Jasper.

Then I pull out my quilt, the one I'd made with Granny. Papa's shovel scrapes at the hard earth, and I get the sense that we're not only burying Katie here, but Granny too.

My fingers trace the large center piece on which I'd appliquéd a pattern of leaves and flowers. It's surrounded by a whole bunch of different blocks. I made at least one of all the blocks Granny'd taught me, needing to remember her. My school friends had made some too. Those are all cutwork. There's a small, solid border then a big, lovely, chintz border. Granny saved her egg money to buy that border for our quilt. I rub my right hand on the block that Granny had signed. Her hands had touched this quilt. My chest hurts, holding in the giant, painful memory of saying goodbye, of her leaving me. I look up, lean

76

my head all the way back, and blink, holding in the tears that threaten to spill down my cheeks.

If I start to cry now, I'll never stop.

"What you doin' in there, Sarah?" Jed's leaning on the back of the wagon, peering in at me.

I catch my breath, and shove the memory of Granny back into a safe corner of my mind where I can take it out when I am alone and needing her. I glare at Jed, the devil himself, and my sorrow is instantly transformed into a white-hot fury.

"How dare you speak to me."

His eyes widen in surprise. "Why wouldn't I speak to you?"

I can only stare at him, dumbfounded. He waits for an answer, his thumbs hooked in his suspenders.

"Jedediah, you … hurt me," I finally manage. "I despise you." My hands shake as I speak these words, so I grip the quilt tighter to still them.

"Hurt? I didn't hurt you. Sarah, I, well, I wanna marry you. I thought ya knew that."

Marry me? Does he really think he loves me? I don't know what to say to him, how to even think. How can he think that?

"That'll happen all the time once we're married," he continues. He looks at me from his clear blue eyes and smiles almost shyly, not at all scary like that day in the trees.

My hands shake harder. He can't possibly think that what happened was love, can he? "You need to leave, Jed. I just lost my sister and now you want to talk? Leave. Now. I will *never* marry you. You get that clear in your mind. The only reason I even look at you now is because I can't get away from you on this trip. When we get to Oregon, if I never see you again, I'd be just fine."

His eyes go wide, and then fill with an anger that I've seen before. "You gotta marry me," he whispers. His lips curl into a mocking grin. "Ya gotta marry me cuz ye're mine now, Sarah." He pauses. "I made ya mine. I s'pose I could tell yer Pa."

My entire body stiffens as the impact of his words hit me. "You wouldn't."

But he would. He knows it, and I know it. If he tells, I will lose everything. If I admit what happened to Mama and Pa, they would make me marry him, force me to spend the rest of my life with Jedediah. If

I tell Mama and Papa what really happened, would they even believe me? If they did and could convince the rest of the party of the truth, Jed would hang from the next tree we came to. Then everyone would know what happened, including Charlie. He would never look my way again, knowing I was not only responsible for his cousin's death but also a sinner, a whore. I would lose Charlie forever. My family could be banished from this train and would probably end up making the rest of this journey alone, in which case my entire family would die, end up in a grave just like Katie.

If I just denied it, said it was all a lie, people would still wonder if I was Jed's whore, and Charlie would think I belonged to his cousin. He'd move on.

All the possibilities run through my head, each one ending in a ruined reputation, death for my family, a life with Jedediah, or all of them. I want to beg him not to say anything, to just let it lie, but I can't. He'll do what he will do to get what he wants, and I refuse to beg. I turn my back and begin to fold the quilt.

"I'll be talkin' to yer Pa soon."

He is evil. I hate him, and I'm not gonna even ask God to forgive me for these thoughts. I begin to repack the quilt into the trunk but then stop. I will need it tonight. Mama will not notice as long as I keep it wrapped up in my blankets. She won't notice anything at all. I can hear her muffled sobs and the continued scrape of the shovels digging the ground.

MR. DIXON READS some words from his bible over my sister's grave, and Charlie stands near him, his violin in hand. He pulls the bow slowly across the strings, his eyes closed as he listens to the sounds. It is a mournful sound, a song I am not familiar with, but I'm too numb to listen to the words or care.

Charlie opens his eyes. They find mine, and for the first time, I don't look away, I don't fidget. I look back, right into his deep blue gaze until he nods, just barely and looks back toward the grave. He plays for a few minutes more but never again looks my way. I keep my eyes on him. He's the only thing that's keeping me from flying apart into a million little pieces.

Tears spill down Mama's face. Papa's face is rigid, his hands clenched tightly at his side.

It is June 8, 1847. We have been gone from our farm just over eleven weeks, but our world has completely changed. We stand in a desolate land near one of the many creeks that run into the muddy Platte, still on dusty plains though we have glimpsed mountains in the distance. Laramie Peak lies to the south, and I can just make out its shape in the distance, across grass covered plains.

My sister's grave sits at the base of a small tree. I stand with my brothers, holding Eliza's hand in mine. We are now a family of six. We will leave Katie alone here in the wild wilderness and pray that wolves won't dig up her body.

The trail wears on me, but we cannot stop to rest. We must keep going, leaving bodies, innocence, our hearts farther behind us with each step.

The land we are in is less than plenty. It is starvation and death.

That night, after I crawl into bed and listen to my siblings falling to sleep, I cry. Pulling my quilt from underneath the blankets where I have hidden it, I hold it close to my face and sob. I cry for my sister, for my granny, for myself. My tears soak the corner of the quilt that I am clenching between my hands. I cry until I sleep.

WE HAVE TRAVELED the last few weeks through a barren and desolate land, what they call the Black Hills. It's a rocky, spiky place, and we can't go barefoot or our feet get all filled up with stickers. I wake to the morning bell, feeling sick and forever exhausted. Katie is gone, Charlie is lost to me, and Jed haunts me.

Tommy groans and rolls over. We all lay wrapped in our blankets for one last minute before rising and resuming the drudgery of this journey.

My mouth waters, and I swallow the saliva, trying to keep down the vomit while I think back to what I ate the day before. We have all suffered from diarrhea and stomach ailments, and I dread a jolting day of riding in the wagon, but I think today I will ride.

I sit up and instantly lay back down, roll to my side and heave. "Mama, Sarah's pukin'," Eliza shouts to my mother.

"Eliza, hush," I snap as I try to sit up for the second time. It's a little bit better.

"Then you get out here Eliza and start breakfast. Leave her alone. I'll be there in a bit."

I can hear the strain in Mama's voice. After losing Katie and six other people on this train to the bloody flux, Mama hovers over the rest of us, just waiting, it seems, for another one of us to up and die on her.

As Eliza heads out of the tent, I ask her for some water to rinse out my mouth. She brings it quickly, and I feel a bit better. Well enough, at least, to stand up and leave the tent. Mama sees me and instantly heads my way, grabs my hands and leads me to the wagon. She hasn't yet put up her bed.

"Lay down. You just stay right there fer now."

"Mama, I can help," I protest.

"Not today. Just rest. Please." I relent and climb into the wagon as Eliza protests that she will have to take down the tent on her own. I heave again over the front of the wagon just as Jed brings the yoke of oxen around the side to Pa, who's back driving the team. Jed still sticks around to help, much to my dismay. He speaks softly to the animals. They are weary and now must pull an extra load: me.

He hollers as I spit yellow bile toward the ground. "Sorry," I mumble, aware of my Mama standing close. I crawl toward the bed, my stomach roiling.

"You sick?" he asks. "Do ya want some water?"

I ignore him and roll over.

As soon as he has the first yoke of oxen hooked up, he heads toward the back of the wagon. "Sarah?" He hands me a cup from the water keg. I take it wordlessly, not wanting to talk to him.

He goes to get the second yoke of animals, hooks them up, then Mama calls for breakfast. From the bell to heading out is less than an hour.

I close my eyes as my mouth begins to water again. I swallow, willing the nausea to subside until Jed says my name. He has set his tin plate of bacon and pancakes on the seat at the front of the wagon. He looks down at his plate.

"I, uh, well, I haven't had a chance to talk to ya much lately."

I stare up at the canvas wagon cover, trying to ignore him, but he's got me cornered.

"I talked with yer Pa."

I refuse to acknowledge him.

"He seems to like the idea of us makin' it official." His voice sounds shaky, nervous, as if he's given me the choice of refusing.

"And if I say no?" I ask, just to see what he'll say.

"Ya won't."

I sit up to look at him. I need to know. "Do you really want this, Jed? You wanna marry me?"

"Yep. I do. I, well, I love ya." He looks down as he says this, and I wonder, for the hundredth time, what exactly he thinks love is.

I have no choice here, and he knows it. "I'll tell you straight up. I don't love you. I never will. You understand that?" I ask in one last effort to get him to see reason, to let me go.

He grins as if I have just said the opposite

Nausea rolls over me again, and I lurch to the rear of the wagon to heave. He grimaces before walking away. I don't care. He's the one who proposed while I am puking. Idiot.

The nausea subsides mid-morning, and I'm able to suck on some hard tack. I want to walk, but Mama insists that I ride for the entire day. She's so worried about losing another one of us that she has become extra protective. I lay across the trunks and boxes of supplies, bouncing and jolting, while the same words ceaselessly run through my head . I won't marry Jed. I won't be Mrs. Monroe.

I stare at the canvas walls and see my sketch book in the pocket. I pull it from the pocket and flip it open. Charlie stares at me from the pages. I slam it shut and shove it back in the pocket, my throat tight.

Chapter 9

July 1847 - Independence Rock, Wyoming

DISTANCES DECEIVE IN this wide open land. Mountains and the odd rock formations we have begun to see are always farther away than they seem. This entire journey is like that, unimaginable and misleading. I had no idea what two thousand miles actually meant when we started out. It is a distance I still cannot fathom, though I travel it each day.

Independence Rock juts out of the desert, breaking up the flatness of this land and making it a major milestone. We must reach the rock by July 4th, or we might not make it over the mountains in the west—at least that's what all the guidebooks say. Half of what the guidebooks say has turned out to be false. I've learned there is much more to fear than these wide open spaces that offer no place to hide.

We are south siders. Mama and I walk near the Platte River which flows to our right. Others travel on the north bank of the Platte. At some point, we will all come together on a single trail meandering west.

"Sarah," Mama says to me. "Did Jed speak to you?"

I stare across the placid river, not wanting to have this conversation but knowing it's unavoidable. "He has," I finally reply. "He seems to think he loves me."

"What do you think of him?"

"I don't feel that way about him, Mama."

"Sarah, he'd be a good provider. Yer Papa approves and gave Jed his word. Are ya hopin' for a proposal from Charlie?"

My throat is so tight, I don't try to speak.

"Papa and I talked about Charlie, too. He's a nice young man, but he can't walk right, Sarah. He can't do what he needs to do to provide."

"How do you know that, Mama? Have you seen the work he can do with his hands?" My voice barely works as I utter these words. She can't seem to hear me; it's like I'm speaking from the bottom of the muddy Platte. But even as I say them, I know they mean nothing. He'd never have me anyway.

"Where's he gonna get the hides and the leather? Are you gonna tan it all? Do you have any idea what that takes? You can't do that, girl, and neither can he. He's dreamin'."

I shake my head. She doesn't see that everybody on this entire trip is dreamin'. Papa actually believes some of the tales we've heard about how big the trees are in Oregon, but she doesn't call him a dreamer.

"Did you love Papa when you married him?" I look her straight in the eye and try not to dip my head in cowardice. "Or did your Mama make you marry him cuz he could farm?"

She can't hold my eyes. "I loved him." She pauses. "We're just trying to think about what's best for you, for the future. Jed's a hard worker."

"So's Charlie." I can't do this, listen to them ignore me. I expect it from Papa but not her. "I think I'll ride."

I head toward the rear of the wagon where I can jump in safely. If I trip and fall, I won't get run over and have my head crushed like a melon. Or maybe that would be a good thing.

"Sarah, your gonna need to do what's best. Think on it," Mama says to my back.

But what's best? It's not Jed. I know that much. It's the one thing I'm sure of on this journey. Jed wants it, my parents want it. I'd rather die than marry Jedediah Monroe. That's all I can think of. I can't propose to Charlie myself. I've caught him watching me from a distance, trying to respect my father's request. I try to blink away the never ending well of tears in my eyes as a horse comes up behind me.

"Sarah? That you?"

Oh God. It's Charlie. Why now? I stop walking, and the wagon creaks away in front of me, Mama walking by its side. She glances back and shakes her head.

I take a deep breath to try to compose myself, and I wave in his direction.

"You all right?"

"Fine," I say. We walk in silence for a bit. Finally, I just decide to tell him, see what he'll do. "Charlie, Jed talked to my Pa." I pray that he knows what I mean, that he won't make me explain, but God is apparently not with me on this journey.

"What do you mean? Doesn't he talk to your Pa every day?" He looks genuinely confused as he says this.

"I mean, well, I mean that Jed talked to him about me. About him and me," my voice cracks as I say this. There is no 'him and me' and there never will be, but now Charlie will think different. His face has lost all expression.

He knows exactly what I mean. He is silent.

A giant void of emptiness gapes between us. I make a feeble attempt to fill it. "Mama thinks I ought to accept him. I s'pose my Papa does too, but I . . ." What can I say?

"You should," he replies, staring straight ahead.

I pull my bonnet off and look up at him. "I ... should? Is that what you just said?"

"Yep. You should. Jed's a good man. He'll do well for you."

A good man? What? Charlie knows the same Jed I know: the vicious one. "Charlie, look at me."

He doesn't. He heels the horse and rides ahead, leaving me alone. He won't overstep his cousin. His cousin beat him, and he'll honor that. I know that now. There is no one to save me but me. Independence Rock looms in the distance, a place to stop and celebrate our freedom. I shake my head at the irony.

Dry Sandy River, Wyoming – July 1847

For eight days I avoid Jed as much as possible, I watch Charlie, and I think about all the horrible ways people have died on this trip. Why can't I escape that way? Maybe this nausea is the bloody flux. That might be the easiest, but then Mama would have to watch me die. Or maybe it's just that I've been eating the exact same food for the past three months and my body is tired of it. If I never eat bacon or beans again, I'll be just fine.

I could trip when I jump out of the wagon and hope the wheels crush my head, but they might also miss my head and crush my legs, leaving me perfectly alive but crippled. At least Charlie and I would be a matched set. Jed would probably reject me then, but living that way would also mean months of pain. Quick is better. I could accidentally shoot myself, but Papa never lets me handle the guns even though he knows I can handle 'em just fine. He taught me. That would be bloody, though, and maybe too much for Mama. Each day I consider my options, but they are either too painful or too traumatic. At heart, I'm a coward. But I do have one idea.

What if I leave? Disappear? Simply vanish into this never ending landscape? I don't want to think about what might happen to me out there between the Indians, the wolves, the snakes, all sorts of things. But whatever happens, it happens only to me. I wouldn't have to worry about Mama trying to save me or me having to see her pain.

"Haw!" Pa yells as he snaps the whip.

"We're at the top?" Mama yells from inside the wagon.

"Yep, South Pass."

We've been climbing slowly for the past month, and we've finally reached it: the place where the water runs west instead of east. We camp three miles below the pass on the west side, and I decide that tonight I will leave. It's the only solution I can think of. It's Thursday, July 8, and I'll take nothing but my quilt, my own burial shroud.

I lie in my bed and listen to Tommy's, then Eliza's, and finally Jasper's breathing fall into the quiet softness of sleep. A new moon shines tonight, dark enough that the watch won't see me if I can sneak good enough. I'll head northwest, into the desert.

Mama still hasn't noticed that I've had my quilt wrapped in my bedding. I pull it from underneath the blanket, rolling it up and clutching it to my chest as I begin to crawl to the tent door, avoiding Tommy and Jasper's feet. I pull open the tent flap and slip out. No one sighs or rolls over. I can't make out any details of their faces, only the shapes of their bodies beneath the quilts. They sleep the sleep of exhaustion. If anyone can keep me here it would be them, but losing me is preferable to the shame the entire family would endure if I stayed because the only way to avoid a marriage with Jed would be to admit what he did, and I refuse to shame my family.

I can get from the tent to the wagon with no problem. If the watch saw me, they would assume I was relieving myself. The challenge is to go farther, beyond the stock, beyond the world of the train, without them being able to track me. I need miles between me and the camp before they rise to that infernal bell.

I say a quick prayer over my brothers and sister, shut the tent flap, and creep to the wagon. I huddle there, peering into the darkness, listening to my father's soft snores and letting the rhythm of his breath calm me. The men sitting watch are three wagons up from ours. Several weeks ago, Indians stole blankets from a man sleeping underneath his wagon, so I know I can get away if I can walk as silently and stealthily as the Indians can. I'm just not sure I can do that. I peer around the wagon toward the north, the direction I intend to run, then look west but see nothing.

I take a deep breath and steal forward, hunched over and low to the ground. I creep along for what seems like hours, looking down to avoid rocks and bushes. My back begins to ache but not enough that I stand up tall. Not quite yet. I freeze with fear at every sound. Will Indians find me? Will the guards shoot me in the back as I flee?

The sky is inky black, but the stars shine bright and clear. Millions of them. They watch over me as I trek to the northwest, inching through the vast wasteland until something, anything takes me away from this journey. A light breeze begins to blow as I pick my way through the sage and rocks. Time and again I find myself frozen in position as a bush bends in the breeze, its shadow mimicking the terrifying shape of a hungry wolf on the prowl. I have never seen a wolf, but I have heard them howling in the night. Other overlanders have seen them, told us stories, and whenever Eliza annoys Tommy, he tells her tales of wolves sneaking into camp to eat little girls. That led to Eliza sharing my blankets more often than not. If the truth be told, I enjoyed the comfort of my sister's warm safe body lying next to mine on the hard ground.

I'm not sure of my direction, but I try to continue to move away from the wagons. I pray I haven't gone in a giant circle. If I have, I'll hear the bell when Mrs. Dixon rings it in the early morning light. I want no part of that, no part of hearing my mother's cries when she finds me gone, or of them finding me and asking, "Why?"

I have no answers.

The endless night continues as I alternately run, creep, and stumble over bushes, or stand frozen in terror. It's a miracle I make any progress at all without alerting everyone to my escape. My steps slow as the night wears on. I have never stayed up all night, and fatigue grabs at me. Still, I cannot stop. Not until I have gone at least eight miles or more. But I have no idea how far I've gone. I have no sense of time or distance in this black night. I fumble over a bush, and my legs fail me. I cry out as I fall, and my knee hits a sharp rock. I land in a heap and lie there, deciding I've gone far enough. I unfold the quilt and throw it over my body, hoping to fall into a sleep from which I will not awaken.

My tongue sticks to the roof of my mouth in thirst, but I hear no creeks or flowing water. It's as if God turned this land upside down and shook all of the water out of it before setting it back down, a withered and bleak place covered with rocks and sage. My lips are dried and cracked, and the metallic taste of blood fills my mouth. I shut my eyes and give into the sleep which pulls at my body, ignoring my thirst and aches.

THOUGH THE SUMMER days can reach one hundred degrees or more, during the night the desert temperatures plummet. I had wrapped the quilt over my head and buried myself in it, but now I feel stifled. The heat of the sun has warmed my cocoon. Thirst racks my body, and I wonder vaguely why I am even awake. My plan had not included waking up sore and thirsty; I had wanted just to flee into the wilderness and die a peaceful death. I pull the quilt from my head to see if I can judge the time.

It seems I have slept far longer than normal, my body craving a rest from this interminable journey. I squint against the bright sun and look in the direction I think the mountains should be, and I freeze. Sitting in front of me, not five feet off, is a young man. A brown man. An Indian. He watches me, expressionless.

"Ay, up," a raspy female voice says.

The words are thickly accented but clear. I turn my head and see an Indian squaw. Her face is lined, her hair pulled back in a long braid. She wears a filthy white deer skin dress that covers her knees. It has wide sleeves with fringe. Moccasins cover her feet. She sits on the ground, watching me shrink back into my quilt and pull it over my head. I curl into a ball and decide they can just kill me now. I won't go with them to their Indian camp where I will surely be skinned, or scalped, or abused again. The woman begins speaking to me, the slow melodic sounds undecipherable to my ear, and I squeeze my eyes shut, willing myself to sink into the ground and disappear. My heartbeat increases its tempo as the possibilities of this situation become clearer.

For the past three months, I've heard stories of emigrants who have been terrorized and murdered at the hands of the Indians. But I had allowed myself to forget those stories. All I wanted to do was die, to save myself and my family the humiliation of my life. It should have been a simple task. Now, rather than peacefully dying, I'll be sold or enslaved. I suck my breath in and feel my eyes begin to water, but I don't want to cry. So far they haven't done anything to me.

Come to think of it, I have absolutely no idea how long they have been sitting here, watching me. I take a deep breath to calm myself. As I do, the woman sighs right along with me, making a noise not unlike the exasperated sighs Mama is prone to. Thinking of Mama doesn't help. By now she has discovered me missing, and she has panicked. For one small second, I regret running. Then I think of Jed.

"Girl!" She tugs on the quilt, which I grip tighter, but I'm no match for her. "Get up."

She rips the quilt out of my grasp, reaches for my arm, and pulls on it, forcing me into a sitting position.

I crack open my eyes. Is this worse than a life with Jed? I'm not sure. She offers me some sort of skin that drips with cool, clear water, and I try not to grab it out of her hands too greedily. The water drips down my chin as I guzzle it. When I return the skin to her outstretched hand, she takes a long drink as well.

"Come. Get up," the woman repeats. "You will come with us. We watch you."

She doesn't sound crazy, and she speaks English. Can I trust her? No. The young man approaches us. He wears buckskin pants and a shirt and looks terrifying.

"No." My voice shakes when I finally answer. "I'll stay here."

The woman frowns at me, puzzled.

"Here?" the boy asks in good English. He looks around in confusion at the sage covered plain. Mountains rise from the ground to the north east, but behind them and to the west lays a seemingly endless desert of sage. "There's nothin' here."

"You speak English?" I ask, alarmed.

"Yes."

"How?"

He ignores my question. "You hungry?"

"Uh, well." I don't want to beg, to tell them I'm starving. I'm not keen to admit that my plan to lie down and die is in the process of failing miserably.

"Get up," the woman says again and reaches for my arm. I instinctively pull back, and she sighs again and looks toward the young man, seeming exasperated.

I could run but that seems silly. Where could I go to escape these Indians and their horses? I could go with them. That seems worse because Lord knows what could happen to me as a lone white woman in an Indian tribe.

I stare at my quilt, wishing it would give me an answer. The woman kneels in front of me. Her wide face is round with full cheeks. Lines etch her forehead and around her dark eyes. She isn't a young woman, but she isn't old either. Maybe Mama's age. We study each other.

"Girl," she says again. "Get up."

I shake my head, panic and indecision freezing me—until she lifts her hand and slaps me hard across the face. My head whips back, the sting of the slap reverberating through my head and knocking me sideways toward the ground. Out of the corner of my eye I note a rock … just before it slams into my temple.

Chapter 10

July 1847 – Northwest of the Oregon Trail, Wyoming

MY HEAD BOUNCES rhythmically against something, and pain shoots through my skull with each bounce. I concentrate on my eyes, but only one will open to let in small crack of light. The brightness bites into my skull. I squeeze my eye shut and try to hold my head still, an impossible task.

When the memory of my last few hours comes back, it does so in a rush. Running away, sleeping, waking to find Indians staring at me, the slap, then … nothing. I groan and try to assess the situation. I'm a captive, and my body is draped across a horse. My head knocks against the animal's side with each step. My arms aren't tied, but a tingling in my limbs tells me both are asleep. The horse finally stops, and strong arms lift me from it. Every muscle in my body both protests and welcomes the changing position. I open my one good eye and reach out for the horse, needing balance. An arm is wrapped around my waist. As soon as I am steady, it vanishes and I lay my cheek against the horse's warm side.

I have no idea how long we have been riding or where we are headed. All I know is that I sorely regret my decision to leave the wagon train.

Out of my one open eye I see the Indian boy standing next to the horse's head. Finally he speaks, alarming me again with his almost perfect English. Of all the Indians we have seen, few spoke any more English than was necessary to trade with or beg from the emigrants.

"We'll feed you." He nods toward the woman who has stopped her horse and watches us. "Just do what she says."

He reaches toward my eye and I jerk back my head, causing sharp pains to shoot through it. I gasp at the renewed agony.

"How long have we been riding?" I'm sure that I am now days away from my family.

He shrugs. "We need to go. Now." He speaks sternly, using a tone he hasn't used before, and I follow his gaze. Far across the desert, dust rises in the afternoon heat. More Indians? A rescue party? Maybe it's just an antelope herd. My head throbs. I wonder vaguely if I can get this boy to shoot me.

"What is that?"

"I don't know, but I'm hungry and I want to eat."

"Who is that?" I try again, pointing toward the dust. "Do you know?"

He looks closer and shakes his head. "Can you walk?"

I take a mental check of my body. My head pulses with pain, and my muscles are stiff and sore from the horse ride, but I think I can move. "I'd rather do that than ride across the horse like I was." I want to yell it at him but my head hurts too bad to do anything but whisper.

"Can you ride?"

"If you help me up."

He cups his hands for me to step into. I mount the horse and sit sideways on its bare back, holding on to the horse's mane as it trudges along behind the boy's horse. I watch the ground beneath my horse's feet out of my one good eye. My swollen eye will not open. I reach up and feel sticky blood crusting around my eye, but I can't feel the pain of a cut. I wonder how deep it is and how long I was knocked out, how long we're riding. My stomach growls and gurgles, but they have not offered food or more water, and I don't ask.

"Ya got 'er yet?"

All three of us look up when we hear a man yelling, and my head throbs with the movement. I stare in alarm as a filthy white man appears over a small rise in front of us. He walks down the hill toward us. Who is he? What's he going to do with me?

"Christ almighty, girl. What the hell you doin' all the way out here anyway? You gave Nettie here a scare, ya did."

Nettie?

"She thought you was dead and just about took yer quilt from ya, but when you coughed?" He roars with laughter and the woman smiles. "About scared ol' Nettie to death. Good to see ye're alive and well. Let's git. I'm hungry. Help Joseph git them horses put up," he directs me.

The squaw follows him on her horse, and I gently lower myself to the ground.

"Your name is Joseph?" I ask, surprised the boy has an English name.

"Yes." Joseph dismounts as well and stands next to me as I take my first tentative step. We've ridden for several hours though, and we are far from the wagon trains. I have no idea how I could possibly get back. The land behind me looks much like the land in front of me. I could wander for days then die out there, but it hadn't worked for me the first time.

I steady myself and lean on the horse. Then it occurs to me that my hands are empty. "Where's my quilt? What did you do with it? Did she take it?" My voice gets shriller with each question, and I try to still the panic I feel coursing through me. I fail. The blood dripping down my face didn't cause the same sense of alarm I feel now without my quilt.

Joseph points toward the old woman, and I breathe again. There it is, draped over the shoulders of the savage squaw who had slapped me. I watch it disappear as she descends the hill, determined that I won't lose Granny's quilt like I've lost everything else.

I follow Joseph who leads his horse after his mother. Within a few minutes, I hear the sounds of water bubbling over rocks, and I smell smoke. We come across a creek flowing through a little meadow, and next to it, tucked up against the trees, stands an Indian lodge made of buffalo skins hanging over tall poles. Joseph hobbles his horse, lets it loose, then watches me. This is my brother's job. I have no idea how to do it.

"You gonna hobble him?"

"I, well, I don't know how."

He shakes his head as he strides toward me. Grabbing the rawhide hobble from the horse's neck, he reaches down and expertly winds it between the animal's front feet. "You know now."

Apparently that was my lesson in hobbling. My stomach rumbles with hunger as I follow Joseph toward the lodge. I have seen other lodges as we crossed the plains and camped around Fort Laramie, but I never got near one. None of the immigrants did. Dirty animal hides cover long poles, and smoke wisps out the top. Several skins hang on a rack next to the lodge, drying.

"Hurry it up," a gruff voice yells, and I realize the old trapper is hollerin' from inside the lodge. His grizzled head pokes out, reminding me of a bear peering from its den, and he reaches toward me with filthy hands. Grime covers his beard, which hangs down to his chest. "Come on in. We got some food fer ya."

I cringe away from him, but the smell of food pulls me into the lodge. I duck through the door first with Joseph just behind. As we enter, the smoke makes my eyes water, but I only care about the bowl of stew the woman hands me. I sniff at it and the old man starts to laugh.

"You afraid you eatin' a puppy there?" He chortles to himself, and we all watch him.

A puppy? Is that what they eat? Horror fills me as I realize that what we've heard about these people is true. I hold the bowl out in front of me, no longer hungry.

He laughs as he watches my face. "Yep, we've eaten our share of 'em when there ain't nothin' else, but that ain't one. That's just some plain old antelope. Ye're safe."

I stare at my bowl. How am I supposed to eat it? My fingers? Nobody offers a spoon, so I dip my fingers into the bowl and pull out a chunk of meat that's so tender it breaks apart in my hands. It smells delicious, but I'm still not sure about it. My mouth has a different idea. It waters in anticipation of an actual meal. I poke around in the bowl and find some sort of root looking vegetable. I pull it out and look at the old man to see if he will identify it, but he is absorbed in eating his own bowl of food.

I have eaten nothing but bacon, beans, pancakes, and the occasional piece of meat when we had managed to down a buffalo or antelope. I decide that if I'm going to have a miserable end to my life, I might as well not suffer hunger as well, and I dig my fingers into the bowl, not caring that I don't have a spoon. The stew tastes like manna, and my headache finally begins to lessen with the meal.

The family eats in silence, and I decide that the old man has domesticated these Indians at least a little bit, even though he is nothing if not rough. As soon as he is done, the squaw refills his bowl from the pot that hangs over the fire. Smoke and stuffy heat fills the lodge. My eyes still water, but I find that as long as my belly continues to fill, I don't mind the smoke.

The old man breaks the silence after downing his second bowl of stew. "What happened to yer face?"

I point at the woman. "She hit me and knocked me into a rock."

At this, he really starts laughing. "She did, did she? Well, that's

Nettie fer you. She's just tryin' to wake you up, or get you to listen, I'm thinkin'. She thought you was dead at first."

"I *was* awake. I was already sitting up."

"Well, I'm guessin' you weren't doin' somethin' she asked. What was it, Joe?"

The old man looks at the boy who sits on the other side of the lodge. I can now see the resemblance between them. This is a trapper, his squaw wife, and their half breed son. I cannot begin to imagine what Pa and Mama would think of me sitting here with them. If they knew where I was, would they leave me here? Well, Pa would. I think Mama might take me back, but as I dip my hand back into my bowl and lick the food from my fingers, I'm not so sure.

"She just wadn't gettin' up like Ma asked her to. We didn't know if she was hearin' us, so Ma's just tryin' to wake her up."

The trapper looks at me again and raises his eyebrows. "I guess you got a bit of a scare, wakin' up and seein' Nettie?"

I nod in response, and he howls, laughing so hard he has to wipe the tears from his face. "Aw, God. I wish I coulda saw that. A little white girl wakin' up to Nettie. Damn antelope. I tracked the antelope, and Nettie here tracked you." He pauses, studying me.

It makes me feel uncomfortable, and I cannot hold his gaze. I finish my stew and stare at the bowl in my lap.

"What ya doin' out here anyway? Ye're about fifteen miles off the trail. You get lost?"

I weigh my options, not sure how to answer. I can tell him the truth, or I can lie and finally decide on a variation of the truth. "I couldn't stay with my train anymore."

"Why not? It's a lot safer with a train of emigrants—no matter how ignorant they might be—than it is out here with wolves, bears, or Indians."

I ignore his question. "Why are you out here?"

"Belong out here. Ain't nothin' for me or them where ye're headed or where you came from."

He's right. Anyone on my train would run him and his squaw wife off. "You gonna live out here forever?"

"Safer for me and my family out here than it is back with yer folks, and I ain't gonna give this up." He waves his hand around the lodge and smiles.

I look around and wonder what he sees. It seems a rough life to me. "This ain't safer for you, though. Much less danger for you back with your train."

I shake my head. "I haven't felt safe since we left Indiana." I think about Jed. Was I safer with the train? Looking around at this family, I don't think so. I reach up and feel the stiffness of my check and realize I still have blood covering the side of my head. My hair is flying around in every direction, and my eye is still swollen and painful. "I'd like to clean up."

Nettie reaches her hand toward my face, and I instinctively shrink back. She lets her arm drop and rises to her feet.

"Come," she says, then she bends over and walks out the flap of the door.

I look toward the old trapper.

"Git, girl. She'll get ya cleaned up."

I set the bowl on the ground, not sure what to do with it, and stand up.

"What's yer name?" he asks as I walk toward the door.

"It's Sarah. I'm Sarah Ann Crawford." It feels good to say my name, to announce to him that I have a name other than "girl."

"Nice to meet ya, Sarah. Name's Jim Pierce. Been trappin' this country fer close to thirty years, but that's done. No more trappin' out here, so's we's just livin'. Gettin' by. But that's about done, too. Not sure where to go from here." He shakes his head. "I got lotsa stories I could tell you, but not now. You gotta git on out there with Nettie. She's waitin' on you."

I stiffen at the sound of her name, and he grins. "She's harmless." He tilts his head slightly. "You know, she watched you sleepin' fer close ta four hours to make sure no wolves got you."

My one good eye opens wide at that news. "She did?"

"Yep, my Nettie would'na let nothin' happen to you. Now git on out there."

I consider this new information as I head outside. If the woman had watched over me, then why had she hit me so hard? It doesn't make any sense at all.

Nettie kneels by the creek, so I head toward her. She's holding some sort of cloth which she dips into the water. She wrings it out, her brown hands strong and calloused. Her knuckles are like Mama's, wider and bonier than her fingers. Her hands are working hands, hardened and marked by her life. When I sit on a rock near her, Nettie reaches up with the soft leather cloth and gently wipes at the dried blood. I close my eyes as she dabs repeatedly at my face. When she's done there, she rinses out the cloth and holds it above my head, dripping water into my hair. I cringe as the icy droplets hit my head.

"Does it hurt?"

Her question surprises me. "No, it's just cold."

She smiles, and I watch her closely. I hadn't expected a smile to crack across her lined, dark face.

"Ah, it is that." She pauses and keeps wiping. "Ye're awake now."

A stinging pain covers my entire face as she wipes at the cut just above the edge of my eyebrow, and I clinch my eyes shut. I wonder if I'll have a black eye. Nettie pauses to rinse her cloth, and I reach up to feel the cut. The skin is puffy and tender. As I press at my face, Nettie begins to untie the ribbon holding my braids in. I wonder if she'll steal it and then decide I don't care. She can have it. But as soon as she gets it unknotted, she drapes it over my shoulder like Mama does and runs her fingers through my hair.

She gets to her feet. "Stay here," she says, then walks away toward the lodge.

I wonder where she thinks I can possibly go then remember she'd found me wandering by myself in the middle of nowhere. Who knows where she thinks I might flee? The water burbles over the rocks in the creek, and I listen to Nettie's soft footsteps as she returns. She sets one hand on my head and runs some sort of porcupine quill contraption for a brush through the tangles. I shut my eyes and pretend Mama's brushing it out and braiding it for me, just like she has my whole life.

One braid completed, Nettie's hands still. I've almost fallen asleep in the warmth of the sun, but her stillness alerts me. One dark hand is twined through the strands of my hair, but her other hand hovers in mid-motion, paused. Her head is cocked to the side, and she stares off. She looks as if she's listening. Then I hear it, too. Horses running. Fast. Nettie grabs my arm and pushes me toward the lodge as Pierce emerges with a rifle in his hands.

"Git in there," he shouts at us. "Let's see who this is."

Nettie drops my braids, grabs my arm, and hurries me to the lodge. Is it more Indians? Mountain men? Emigrants? I want to stay and watch but apparently that would be too dangerous. I slide through the slit in the hides they call a door, expecting Nettie to follow me, but the hides remain closed, shutting out the light. The sound of the pounding hooves slows, but I don't hear any voices.

I try to lift a piece of hide up from the ground to peek at the visitors, but I have apparently chosen a part that is staked down. I crawl a few feet to my left and try again, yanking enough up that I can make out the bottom of a boot of one rider and nothing of the other.

"You seen a white woman out here, old man?"

It's Jed. His voice is rough and lacking any pleasantries. Bile crawls up my throat, and I clench my jaw.

"No white women. Just me and my squaw here."

Nettie's moccasined feet head toward the lodge.

I try to see who's with Jed, but I can't. Nettie's brown hand reaches in the door flap and her squat body follows. She stares at me, seeming to accuse me, but I'm not sure of what crime.

"Is he your man?" she asks in a low voice.

I shake my head. My heart races. She keeps her face blank as we listen to the men.

"You lyin' to me?" Jed says in a low voice, challenging Pierce. "Cuz if you got 'er, she's mine, and I'd just as soon kill you as anythin' else."

Nettie grabs at my arm, pulling me up behind her. I'm again surprised at this small woman's strength.

"Git," the older woman hisses. She shoves me toward the door, clearly wanting to get rid of the crazy white man outside.

I grab at her hand and hold it, but she pulls me toward the door anyway. The only way to stop her progress is to fall. I do, landing hard on my knees, the fall jarring the pain in my head and causing it to pierce through my skull. "I can't. Please," I whisper desperately.

She pulls harder and tries to drag me toward the door.

"Please," I beg. "He'll hurt me."

"That ain't my problem."

Tears run down my face, and my whole body shakes. "He might kill me. Listen to him. Please. He's crazy."

"You're the crazy one," she hisses, but she stops dragging me. "What we s'posed to do with you?"

"Just don't give me away. Don't give me to him. Please."

She drops my hand and puts her hand on her hip then whispers, "If he hurts Pierce or Joseph, you die."

I sit back on my heels and drop my head in my hands, massaging my temple that isn't cut. I know, without any question, that she is telling the truth. If Jed's anger gets the best of him out there, she'll kill me. I'll die in this desert at the hands of an old Indian squaw. I also know that if I go with Jed, I'm a dead woman. I wonder if he would take me back to my parents if he found me. Or would he torture me and let me die out here? Maybe he would torture me then take me back half dead, talking like he had rescued me, make it look like he was a hero. I don't know, but I'd bet on the last option.

Jed is still here, and Pierce invites him for a bite to eat. What? Why isn't Pierce getting rid of him? I glance at Nettie, panicked. Jed is going to come into the lodge, and there is nowhere to hide. Nettie shakes her head at me then gets a bowl of stew, which she promptly takes outside. The voices quieten. Either they are not talking or they have walked away, farther from the lodge.

I sit in the lodge's dim light and finish braiding my hair, listening to the sounds of horses leaving. The muscles in my back and neck hurt from holding them so tight. I had braced myself to run again after hearing Jed's voice. Had Papa found this camp instead of Jed, I think I would have rushed out and told him that I couldn't marry Jed, but I wouldn't have told him the truth. I couldn't ever tell him the truth. Charlie, too. I would have run to Charlie. But they hadn't come for me. Jed had, and that twist of fate makes my decision for me.

When I'd first concocted my plan to run, it had seemed so simple. Just disappear, take all my humiliation, and vanish. I never considered Indian abduction or the discomfort of actually dying. I say a small prayer that this family found me and wonder if I can find my way back to the wagon. If I manage to do it without Jed's help, would they have me back?

Chapter 11

THREE DAYS LATER, I lie beneath a heavy buffalo robe. Gray light filters in, the sun barely risen, but my body, used to rising at the same early hour each day, awakens. For the first time in two months, I welcome morning without a start of fear or dread for the day ahead. I don't worry if Jed will watch me or try to talk to me, or if Charlie will visit. I am in another world here, one in which I don't belong. At least here I feel safe, though that doesn't make sense. I burrow deeper into the buffalo robe. Birds flit and sing outside, and Pierce's soft snoring reverberates through the lodge. Pierce and Nettie lie on the other side of the lodge, and it's not much different from sleeping in the tent with Eliza, Jasper, and Tommy—though with the fire always burning the lodge stays much warmer, too warm. And there is the choking smoke. I definitely prefer having the fire outside, not in.

I relish the soft morning sounds and the absence of the bell. The tedium of the daily routine with the wagon train does not await me this morning. I wonder when they began the journey again. How long did they search for me? Did they lay by? They were probably well on their way this morning, taking advantage of the cool air.

For right now, just this single moment, I lie in bed enjoying the quiet and stillness. No pancakes to make. No cows to gather or milk. No wagons to load or unload as we come to yet another river. No little sisters to dress—but I can't think of them. One sister lies in a grave miles back, and the other is miles away, lost to me. When I ran, I had not thought of Eliza, only of myself. Now, in the silence, I wonder what they think of me. Do they think I have died? Are they mourning me?

The others sleep soundly as I stretch my legs and roll onto my back, only to feel my stomach clench. Bile rises in my throat as a wave of nausea rolls upward from my gut. I jump to my feet and hurry for the door, making it to the creek just as my stomach clenches again. My mouth fills with bile and the remains of last night's stew. I heave again, squatting on the ground next to a boulder. Nothing comes up the last time, but my stomach continues to clench as I gag and spit.

I jump as a hand smooths back my hair.

"Water?" Nettie asks.

I reach for the tin cup, filling my mouth with water from the creek before spitting it out. I cannot make myself swallow because my stomach is knotted in cramps. Despite the coolness of the morning, I feel sweat dripping between my breasts, beading on my forehead.

Nettie reaches out her hand and helps me rise from my squat in the dirt.

"I'm sorry," I mumble, embarrassed that this woman has seen this.

Nettie doesn't respond, just guides me back to the lodge. I lie back down, and she stokes the fire. Pierce and Joseph are no longer in the lodge. Apparently my hasty exit woke everyone, so I lie back down and shut my eyes, praying that this sickness is from the rich stew the night before, not the beginnings of dysentery or something worse.

I must have drifted back to sleep because Pierce's booming voice wakes me. "Can she move today?" he asks as he enters.

Nettie shrugs in response.

Pierce's blue eyes bore into me. "Can ya?

"Move? What do you mean?"

"I mean move, leave. Pack up. Head out. I need a new book, and I've got some tradin' to do to get set fer the winter. Time to move on."

I sit up, my stomach gurgling at the movement. "A book? You need a new book?"

"Yep. I've done read this one three times." He lifts a brown leather covered volume from the buffalo robe on which he had slept. I can't make out the title.

"Where do you get books out here?"

"The library," he responds matter of factly.

"There's a library?"

"Yep. At Fort Hall. They've got a decent selection."

I stare at him, trying to understand what he's saying.

"What d'ya think we do out here? Especially in the winter."

Even if I had never thought about that before, a library would never have been a part of my thoughts. "I, well, I have no idea. I guess I never really thought about how people out here spend the winter."

"Well, one thing we do is read, so I need a few more books. Then, we got to be headin' out for the winter."

"Out to where?"

"Ah, one of the forts, most likely. We've just been out, huntin' and trappin' a bit, but there ain't none of that left. No place to sell the fur. But I ain't fit for the city life like some of them old guys. Nah, not me. I'll be out here til I die. Kinda like you was tryin to do, right?" He looks pointedly at me, but I can't hold his gaze. "Damn foolish of you, if you ask me. But then, I guess you didn't ask now, did you?" He laughs at his own little joke. His white hair hangs in long straggles down the sides of his face, mixing with his beard. He no longer scares me, and I find his appearance fascinating. I want to draw him.

"What are you planning for me?"

"Ah, plans for you." He sits down and leans back against one of the lodge poles. "As I see it, you was on a suicide mission, so I don't much think you care one wit what happens to you. You didn't seem much inclined to come out and welcome that no 'count varmint when he rode in three days ago, neither. So," he says, pulling at his beard and watching me, "the way I see it, I ought to be askin' you that question. What's your plans?"

"My plans?" My plan had already failed miserably.

"Well, sure. You do have a plan for yourself, don't you?"

I have no plan and no idea what to say. Nobody's ever asked me. Nobody's even cared.

"Somethin' got yer tongue, girl? Did'ja puke it up this morning along with the rest of ya?" His eyes crinkle with his smile. My face reddens, not in shame but in anger. I look Pierce in the eye.

"I guess I don't have any plans right now." Though it scares me— being in charge of myself—I think I kinda like it.

"So you ain't headin' to Oregon to grow pigs as big as wagons? You heard the stories about the place, ain't you?"

"I've heard the stories, but I ain't lookin' for paradise. That's my Pa." What exactly am I looking for? "For now I guess I'll stay with you."

I hope he'll consent. I speak as decisively as I can, with him chortling at me from across the lodge. I can't imagine rejoining my family and Charlie after spending time with a squaw and this family.

"Nope. You can't do that." He falls silent for once.

My stomach drops. "But I can't go back," I say. "I can't. He . . ." I stop talking and glance toward Nettie who stirs the stew.

Joseph watches me too, a small grin on his face.

"Well," Pierce says, "it sounds to me like you got yourself a bit of a dilemma."

I sit silently since I have nothing to say. I think about running again, but the thought of actually dying scares me this time. I'd managed to get the courage to do it once, but that well has run dry, and I know it.

Pierce speaks up again. "Why can't you just tell this fella no? It seems like that'd be the easiest thing to do."

"I can't go against my parents."

Pierce shakes his head at me. "Ain't their life. Look at my wife, would you? You think I care one wit what my Pa or anyone thinks? I got me one life, and I'm livin' it on my terms." He waves his hands in front of himself, circling them widely, encompassing the entire world. "I tried to live it out there and it didn't work so well. I live each day my way now, like I want to. Don't get better than that."

"Well, that's great for you," I whisper, "but I can't do that.

His eyebrows furrow as he studies my face. "Why can't you?"

I let out an angry, breathy sigh, and I realize I sound exactly like my Mama. "I don't know," I finally snap. I can't even begin to explain all the reasons why I can't just live like he does.

"Yeah, well, you're probably right. You probably can't," he says after studying me further. I'm not sure what he sees to help him finally reach that conclusion. "So what are you gonna do?"

I have no idea. I want to scream at him, but I don't. I hold it in, like I have everything else, and I watch Nettie stir.

Chapter 12

Present Day

SHARI WORKS FAST, well, faster than me. I still don't have any ownership evidence from Agnes, but I haven't figured out how to ask Agnes. What if she can't write? I'll be pointing out another way her body has failed her, and I don't want to do that to her.

I find myself trailing Claire and Shari into some woman's house—a quilt appraiser extraordinaire, apparently. Shari decided we could get the appraisal done without the note, and Claire has come to my rescue yet again by covering the cost of the appraisal. She's in charge now, and for the first time in our friendship, I resent it. I asked for her advice, I didn't ask for her to take over, to use the quilt as a stepping stone for her own journalistic dreams. I'm not sure how to rein in the two women standing in front of me, but for now it doesn't matter. I'll find out how much this thing is worth and take it from there.

The house looms above us, a giant brick two-story home with a long circular driveway. I'm glad Shari drove us in her car, so I'm not polluting her neighborhood with the classy chariot I drive. I scan the street and don't see even a single car older than ten years or with chipped paint. Yep, way out of my element here.

Shari takes charge. She knocks on the huge double wooden door with its leaded glass panels, and a middle aged woman opens it.

"Hello. Come on in. My name is Sandra," she says, reaching her hand out to shake each of ours.

She leads us through the front entry, which is almost as big as my entire downstairs, and to her "office." Two long tables are shoved together in the middle of the room and covered with white sheets. Quilts decorate the walls, and a bookshelf lined with fabric books stands in the corner. Another corner is obviously her quilting space. A sewing machine sits on a table and giant cabinets run along the entire back wall. One of them is open, revealing drawers and drawers full of fabric. I can't even begin to imagine how much it all cost.

I stand in the back, not really knowing what to do with myself. I know I'm small, but as this woman begins filling us in on her credentials, I feel invisible. She says she's been appraising quilts for ten years now and has earned her certification. Apparently that's important—or at least she seems to think so—because she goes on about it to Claire and Shari for quite a while. She even points to her certificate she has framed on the wall. She's clearly pretty proud of it. She pretty much ignores me other than to shake my hand during introductions.

She reminds me a bit of Rosemary, though without the scary, wicked stepmother vibe. She's got that elegance that some older women have. Her pure white hair looks striking with her blue eyes, and she's even dressed in a white pant suit. I wonder if she dresses like this every day or if these are her "work" clothes. It's a little nicer than the jeans and apron I don every shift.

Finally she acknowledges me, but it's only to tell me what to do. "You can lay the quilt out there on the table."

I pull it out, and she eyes my hands as she pulls on white gloves. Shari and Claire both look at my gloveless hands now too. I feel like I did something wrong, but I'm not quite sure what.

The appraiser helps me spread out the quilt, then she stands back and looks at it. "It's lovely," she finally says, but that's all.

I want to tell her it's a masterpiece, but she's reaching for a clipboard and a camera and looking quite official all of a sudden.

"While I'm looking at it, I'll need you to answer a few questions." She hands me a clipboard and a pen. Clipped to the top is a form asking all kinds of questions about the quilt. Four straight wooden chairs sit along one wall, and we sit as if in a doctor's waiting room, filling out insurance forms. Thankfully, I know most of the answers.

She gets out a little magnifying glass and goes all the way around the quilt, checking out the blocks and whatever else she needs. I'm not really sure. She takes a million photos of the front, the back, the edges, the blocks. Then she zeroes in on one of the flowers in the corner.

"What can you tell me about this piece?"

"That block right there? Or the entire thing?"

"The entire thing, but if you know about specific blocks, tell me that, too. The more information I have the better."

I fill her in on what I know: the date, the maker, the quilt's journey to Oregon from Indiana. As I talk, she puts down her spyglass and listens. I get to the part about Sarah running and meeting Pierce when I pause and realize I've been talking for quite a while. I'm also done with what I know, other than the fact that the quilt obviously made it. I still don't know if Sarah does. I look at the flowers and smile at myself. The quilt's story pulls at me just like it does to Agnes. I forget myself a bit when I'm around it, and I wonder briefly if there's something more to it than cotton fabric and thread. The appraiser interrupts my musings.

"Wow! This is a fabulous story. So this has been passed down in your family?"

"Well, yes, but not my family. The maker's great-granddaughter, Agnes Blackwell, gave it to me. She's eighty-five and recently moved into an assisted living facility. She's kind of a grandma to me." I hand her the clipboard which has a lot of the information on it that I just gave her.

"Did she not have any children to pass it on to?"

"She has a daughter, but Agnes told me she wanted me to have it. I don't know if her daughter even knows she gave it to me."

"Hmm. Interesting. Do you have it in writing that she gave it to you?"

I hesitate, wondering what the appraiser would think of the situation. "Not yet."

"You should. With a valuable family heirloom like this, there's a good chance her kids might want it. It wouldn't hurt to get something to back up that it was a gift."

Crap. Now I definitely need to ask Agnes to write something.

"You do seem to know a lot about the provenance of the quilt, though. That would certainly help your case in any ownership disputes."

"The what?" Claire asks. "What does Harper know a lot about?"

"The provenance. The story. She knows where the quilt came from, the maker, all that. It actually adds to the value of a quilt."

"It does?" I ask. Well, that's one bit of good news.

"Sure. It makes it a lot easier to date a quilt with that information."

"But you don't have to date it. I told you the date, and it's on there. Did you see that?"

"Yes, I noted that. I do have one question. What can you tell me about the tear in the corner? How did that get there? It looks like it's been there a while—well, actually a long while. The repair work is quite good. The bat is also a bit different there."

"Uh, I don't know. Agnes hasn't told me that part of the story yet. I don't know if she knows, but I can ask her this week when I go see her. What do you mean, 'bat'?"

"The batting, the filling. Have you felt it? The quilt is slightly stiffer there."

I nod as if I know what she's talking about. I hadn't noticed it at all. Oops.

"Anyway, let me know what you find out. Overall, it's in pretty good condition except for that one part. How it got there, when it got repaired, that sort of thing will help with its valuation."

"Will that impact the value a lot?" Shari asks.

"Certainly. A quilt's condition is a huge factor in the valuation of it. You want me to give you the replacement value, correct?"

"Um." I look at Claire. "Are there other values?"

The appraiser seizes the moment and launches into lecture mode. Here we go. She explains what each of the different valuations for a quilt are, why you would need each one, the benefits of each of them. "With that said, I can give you the market value, if you are interested in selling it, or I could give you the replacement value for insurance purposes. Or I can give you both."

"We'd like both, please," Shari replies.

I wonder why, because I'm not selling the quilt. Nobody seems to understand that.

"We're not yet sure what we're going to do with the piece," Shari explains.

We? I raise my eyebrows at Claire, but she avoids my eye. She heard it, too.

"I see. Have you considered how you'd sell it? There are a couple of different options." As she begins to outline them, I want to ask her where her PowerPoint is to go with all of this, but I don't. Claire would kill me as she's obviously trying to impress Shari. I keep my mouth shut as the appraiser goes on and on about how to get an antique quilt to some sort of market.

Finally, it's too much, and I interrupt. "You know, we haven't really gotten that far yet. I doubt I'll sell it, anyway."

"I see." She taps her bottom lip with her finger. "Well, if you should decide to change your mind, let me know. It's worth quite a lot, and I have some contacts in the antique textiles industry that might be helpful." She reaches for her clipboard and starts jotting down some more notes.

I know I don't want to sell it, but how much is "quite a lot"? I watch her for a moment before getting the courage to ask. "So, what do you mean by 'quite a lot'? Do you mean like a couple of hundred dollars, or do you mean way more than that?"

She lifts her head and takes off her reading glasses. "Oh, sweetheart, much more than that. This," she looks down and runs her hand across the edge of the quilt, "is a one of a kind heirloom piece. And just from my first survey of it, it looks like a museum quality piece. I'll let you know the numbers in a few weeks, but this is worth quite a bit, especially for the right buyer."

Museum quality? My stomach begins to curl around on itself. I need to get out of here and think about all of this. "Are we done?"

"Almost." She looks up from her writing. "I'll get this to you as soon as I can. Let me know about that tear."

"Sounds good." I reach for the quilt to fold it.

"Oh, I've got it," she says, holding up her gloved fingers. "You know, you really ought to store this flat if possible, like on an extra bed if you've got one."

The only other bed in my house is my mom's bed which is currently blanketed with Oregon Trail books and note cards as I've tried to piece together the timeline in Sarah's story, but I'm not ready to share my attempts to write this whole thing down yet.

"I don't have one. Do you have another suggestion?"

"Well then, let's roll it up. That'll avoid folds which can weaken these old fibers."

We get the quilt packed up in a more appropriate manner than it arrived, and she ushers us out the door.

THE NEXT DAY I decide I need to meet with Agnes about the note, and I need to go early, before work. She tends to be somewhat happier in the morning than she is in the evenings. I climb into the Chariot, the sun heating the inside to just below 1500 degrees, and my legs immediately glue themselves to the seat with sweat. This is the first really hot day of summer, and I would swear that Portland is being hit by a heat wave. Agnes has a quality air conditioning system in her new place, so it'll be nicer to stay there for the two hours I have before work than it would be at home. I can sit with her and enjoy the AC. I wonder if that's completely selfish of me, but then I feel sweat dripping down my chest and turn my peeling car toward her place.

When I arrive, I enter through the large lobby as usual and sign in to make sure Rosemary isn't here already. This morning it's not empty, which is unusual. An ancient woman sits on the couch across the spacious room. She seems sort of slumped in on herself, her head swiveling as she watches the comings and goings of the other residents. I wonder if this wing is where she belongs. Many of the residents who live near Agnes don't seem sick at all, but this lady seems confused, much more so than I've ever seen Agnes. She is wearing a pink robe over her clothes and slippers, white hair shoots out in every direction, and her mouth moves incessantly. Is she talking to herself? Or can she not control her mouth, like some sort of ancient meth addict? I can't tell, and I don't want to get any closer to figure it out.

She terrifies me, sort of like the Ghost of Christmas Future haunts Ebenezer Scrooge. I try not to cringe as I stare at her, but I almost can't help myself. Will Agnes get like this? For the first time, I begin to see what my friend may become, the vision that must haunt her every single day. My throat tightens as I swallow back tears. I've seen the signs, moments that have signaled that her memory is going, but nothing like this.

The woman stares at me. I lift my hand in a lame wave and flee toward Agnes' room, trying to concentrate on how good the air-conditioning feels. When I arrive, Agnes is headed to lunch. I join her for an edible—if somewhat mushy—meal of meatloaf, mashed potatoes, and peas. When we return, her door is ajar. I know I'd shut it all the way when we'd left. I push on the door expecting to see a nurse. Instead, I spot Rosemary sitting on the floral loveseat, her hands in her lap, her ankles crossed. Her purse sits at her feet. I paste my best customer service smile on my face, say hello, and continue to escort Agnes to her chair. I give her a hug and get ready to leave. Damn. No stories or note today.

"Oh, don't leave, Harper. You can stay here and visit," Rosemary purrs, lifting my antennae.

I grab my bag. "I've been here a while. We ate together. I'll let you have some time with your mother."

"Well, before you leave, let me ask a question. I looked for mother's antique quilt." She waves her arm to encompass the small room. "I can't find it. I know you brought it here. Do you know where it is?"

Agnes' face goes completely blank.

Damn, she's good.

"Quilt?" Agnes says, in a small shaky voice, giving me a minute to try and figure out an answer.

Rosemary tries again. She speaks slowly and a little louder. "Yes, Mother, the ka – wilt," she says it phonetically, in two syllables, as if Agnes is learning to speak herself. "You know, the one from your grand-mo-ther?"

"Ah, my quilt."

"Where is it, Mother? What did you do with it? I can't find it." Rosemary studies Agnes' blank face. Then she turns on me. "How was she at lunch?"

"Uh, well ..." I have no idea what to say. Agnes bitched all the way through it. She lost a word here and there, but that's all.

"Well then, have you seen the quilt?"

"You mean the one I brought her?" I try to buy myself another minute.

"Yes, that one," she snaps in frustration. She glances at her mother, but Agnes is deserving of an Oscar. I want to roll out a red carpet right now. Her face is slack, her mouth slightly open. She is staring up to where the wall meets the ceiling as if something fascinating is occurring there.

Rosemary raises her eyebrows at me, puts her hand on her hip, and waits for an answer.

While Agnes has turned into an A-list actor, I start fidgeting and focus on keeping a poker face. I grew up listening to lies, lies like, "I'll be there Friday to pick you up" from my dad who never made it, or my mom telling me "I have to work tonight, so you can stay at Agnes' house" when I knew she wasn't working—especially when I found her passed out on the kitchen floor the next morning. I grew up in a soup of lies, and I hate them. Agnes was the only person in my life who

109

never lied to me, and here I am, about to tell a lie.

"I have no idea where that quilt is." I look directly into Rosemary's eyes as I speak. Just because I despise lies and liars doesn't mean I never learned how to do it. "The last time I saw it was when I brought it to her."

"When was this?"

"I don't know. I don't keep a visiting schedule."

Slack-faced-Agnes finally decides to join our little party. "Rosemary?"

I watch, fascinated, as Rosemary morphs from a witch into a loving daughter. She instantly turns toward Agnes, kneels, and sets her hand gently on her mother's knee. "Hi there," she says sweetly. "I was talking to Harper about your quilt, your favorite one. Where is it?"

Agnes smiles. "Safe. I'm keeping it safe."

"Where is that?" Rosemary tries again.

Agnes smiles and resumes staring at the corner, and Rosemary rises to her feet with a sigh. I try to hide my relief. Agnes won't sacrifice me to her daughter's craziness. Not unless her brain accidentally betrays both of us.

"Well, I'm going now," I say.

She turns on me. "Harper, do you honestly not know where her 'safe place' for the quilt is? I've searched this room, and it's not here. I'm going to have to talk to the administration. That is a valuable heirloom. It's one of the reasons I didn't want it here. All kinds of people have access to this room. Somebody could just come and take it. If it's gone, I might even have to file a police report."

My stomach lurches. The quilt is in my closet at home, and I have no doubt Rosemary would happily accuse me of theft. She likes me that much. But in this moment it seems to me that she's more worried about the quilt than she is about her mother. It doesn't bother her that all these people also have round-the-clock access to her mom? This is one crazy lady, and she hates me. Super.

"You know, I can talk to Agnes about it next time I come," I offer. "Sometimes she's pretty lucid. Other times, well," I glance in Agnes' direction, "she's not." My voice feels shaky. I hate myself for the lie I've told and for the predicament I'm now in. I shrug. "I'm sure it'll turn up. She says it's safe."

I turn back to my friend. "Goodbye, Agnes." I give her a soft hug and flee.

The woman in the robe still sits in the lobby. She's sound asleep, drool dribbling from the corner of her mouth and down her chin.

I DON'T MAKE it back for four days even though I need to ask Agnes about writing a note and the tear in the quilt. When I do come, I drive the entire parking lot scouting for Rosemary's car before I go in.

It's clear.

"Did you bring the quilt?" Agnes asks as soon as I'm seated in my spot on the couch.

"Nope. Remember? It's in a 'safe place'." I glare at her. "You need to tell Rosemary you gave it to me."

Agnes glares back but doesn't respond.

"Did I tell you I took the quilt to an appraiser?" I say, trying to get her attention. When she doesn't respond, I repeat myself.

"Why?" she finally asks.

I decide honesty is the best policy. Thinking about the lies I've already told makes my stomach twist. "I did it for Claire. She wants to do an article on it for the newspaper."

"Are you selling it?" Agnes heads right toward the key issue, like a dog on point. She can still be relentless, even if she can't remember what she ate for lunch.

"No. She wanted to know its value for the article. But she also thinks I ought to sell it, figures I can use that money for my education." I watch Agnes' face for a response, but it remains placid.

"I see," she finally says. "Well, it was a gift." She leans her head back and closes her eyes.

"I don't want to sell it," I admit. "I won't." I try to read her reaction. Is she angry or just sleepy? Her eyes crack open.

I decide to change the subject. "Before you start telling me more of the story, do you think you could come to your desk for a minute? I need you to write something for me. It's something the appraiser said."

"I suppose," she mutters.

I grasp her scrawny elbow and help her up. Moving seems to be getting more and more difficult, though I'm not sure why. She never had problems with getting around until she got here. I swear this place is aging her faster than being at home alone. She'd never needed to lean on me like this before, and she'd never used a walker regularly. As we step across the floor, doing an awkward, lurching dance, I stare out the window at the gray Portland sky. The rain and clouds hover low across the treetops, but at least it's cooler today. Drizzle drips down the one window in her apartment, mixing with our slide and shuffle. Agnes lowers herself into her chair in front of the desk.

I set a piece of her pink stationary on the desk in front of her. Her fingers quiver as they wrap around the pen. "What do you want me to say?"

I'm not really sure what she should say. "Well, I guess I want you to say that you gave me the quilt as a gift."

"Why?"

It's a simple question with a complicated answer. Do I tell her that I need it because her daughter is a scary bitch, or do I say that if I get in a more desperate financial situation I might sell it? I look at her watery blue eyes, her shaking hands, and I tell Agnes a lie—my second lie about this quilt. Until recently I'd somehow felt like the quilt had been turning me into a better person, that writing the story was something I could do for Agnes. Lately I'm not so sure. It makes me lie, and I'm beginning to hate the quilt for that.

"I, uh, want something in your handwriting to go with the story. I think it'll make it better when I put it all together."

The old Agnes would know I was lying after the third word, but not this Agnes. She continues to stare at me. Then she looks down at her hand that holds the pen and her expression says she's forgotten why she's got it. Slowly, she releases the pen and sets her hand on the table next to the paper.

I pick up the pen and kneel in front of her. "Agnes? Can you write exactly what I tell you to?"

Her eyebrows scrunch together as she looks at me. She nods.

I put the pen back in her hand and begin to dictate. This feels wrong, and my stomach clenches with guilt. I'm not sure why. She did give me the quilt.

I dictate, "Dear Harper." Her letters are shaky, as if the table is vibrating beneath her. She grips the pen, seeming terrified it will fail her as so much has failed her lately. "I am giving you the Oregon Trail quilt . . ." I pause, and repeat the line several times. This is going to take forever, but she's not giving up, which is good. "That my great grandmother, Sarah Ann Crawford, made in 1847."

At the end of this sentence, Agnes sighs. She probably hasn't written anything since she got here. I take the pen from her hand and gently rub her fingers and palm. Her knuckles are twice the size of mine, swollen by arthritis. Her left hand curls in on itself like a lettuce leaf.

She closes her eyes, enjoying the touch of my hands on hers. She's not sleeping, just feeling. I wonder when she had last been touched by anyone, and I decide to add that to my visits with her.

"Can you write one more sentence?" I whisper.

Her eyes crack open, and she clutches at the pen again.

"This quilt," I say, "is a gift for you."

She adds, "My friend" to the last line, and my eyes tear up. Oddly enough, she's my best friend even though she was already the ripe old age of sixty-five when I was born.

"I guess that's it. Sign it, then write the date on it."

She sets the pen down.

"Agnes, can you sign it?"

She pushes herself from the chair and reaches for my arm. I look at the unfinished note. Is this good enough?

She shuffles away as I pick it up. This note, even without a signature, means as much to me as the quilt does, but I still need her to sign it. I guide her back to her giant lounger-chair and try to hand her the note one last time, but she waves me away. She is done with writing today. Great. Now what? Rosemary will probably try to have my sorry ass thrown in jail for grand theft quilt.

She's done with the note, so I hand her the quilt and see if I can get the question the appraiser wanted answered.

"Do you know what happened here?" I lift the lower left corner of the quilt and point to the tear. It's not an insignificant rip; it's big, as if somebody wanted to rip the entire corner off, but it's peculiar in that it was painstakingly repaired, the little flower pieces removed and the rip sewn back together, then the leaves and stems stitched back on again over the top. Whoever repaired it did a good job. The blemish doesn't jump out at you when you look at it, but it's there.

Agnes relaxes her hands in her lap, studies the tear, and begins to tell me perhaps the most intriguing part of the story yet.

Chapter 13

July 1847 - Southwest Idaho

"CAN YOU TAKE me to Fort Hall with you?" I finally ask, realizing that Pierce isn't going to tell me what to do. He isn't going to get me out of this dilemma I've created for myself.

"I was wonderin' when you'd figure that one out."

If I wasn't so scared, I'd laugh. I don't hate Pierce like I hate Jed, but he infuriates me in the same way. I finally have a choice, a chance to make my own decisions, and I am handling it like a hot coal that I can't get rid of fast enough.

"So you'll take me then? You won't leave me out here?"

"Wasn't plannin' on havin' a murder on my hands, young lady," he says. "We'll drop you at the Fort. Get you hooked up with some train that'll take you on. I'm guessin' you can work as hired help or somethin'. Somebody'll take you on."

"You're just gonna leave me with strangers?" Somehow the fact that he was a stranger didn't seem to matter anymore.

"Well, who else do you got in mind? Seems to me you don't want much to do with the people you know. The way I see it, we ain't leavin' you, we're returnin' you. And if you see yer Pa ever again, you tell him that varmint—that one that came by yesterday—he ain't no good." The lodge falls silent except for the hissing of the stew over the fire. I consider Pierce's words. After all this, could I?

"What you gonna do about the babe?" Nettie asks.

All three of us look at her, confused.

"The babe? What babe?" I ask. "Do you have a baby?"

"The one your carryin'." Nettie calmly stirs, her spoon never leaving

114

the bottom of the pot.

I feel as if a spear, a real life Indian weapon, has lodged in my chest. "I'm not carryin' a baby," I say, appalled that this woman would even speak such words to me. "I'm *not* carryin' a baby," I repeat, but I can hear the panic in my voice as it gets higher and shriller.

Nettie smiles gently at me as she serves her husband and son bowls of the leftover stew. Pierce and Joseph leave the lodge, leaving me alone with Nettie. She sits next to me on a pile of skins.

"Sure you are. When was your last . . ." She pauses, searching for the word.

I do not offer it to her.

"Your last ... with the moon?" she finally manages. The word she searched for was not one she needed to know in English, not a word she would have used with her husband.

My face flames. "I ... I don't remember."

Fact is, I haven't had a monthly since since Independence, Missouri. I had thought the endless walking, the jouncing in the wagon, the same food every day, maybe all that had made it go away. I hadn't asked Mama, and she hadn't asked me. I sure didn't miss washing the rags or dealing with it, especially considering the total lack of privacy on the trail. I'd been thankful it hadn't come to visit ... but now ... now, thinking about it drove the spear deeper into my heart.

"Why do you think I have a baby?" My voice sounds small. I can barely get it out.

Nettie looks at me, surprise covering her face. "The sickness. When you wake."

I lay a hand on my stomach and feel for a lump between the bones of my pelvis. I feel nothing, but it's there. I know it like I know the sky is blue. I'm carryin' Jed's baby.

CLOUDS OF GNATS swarm the air above my head. I swat at them, but it's as effective as trying to dam up an entire stream with a single rock. They follow us as we travel west with the sun. It seems to me we keep up a much more westward path than we had on the trail, which had wound around and zig-zagged across rivers, always searching for the easiest path for the loaded wagons.

On the train, a fearful weariness had pervaded each long day: would the Indians attack, steal the women or the stock, and kill us all? Could the stock hold up? Would the train hold together? Would we make it? Or would we die out here, buried in a shallow, unmarked graves, our bodies dug up by wolves? These fears were punctuated with the endless speculation as to what Oregon would actually be like. With Pierce's family, I ride in silence, a new set of fears now rattling around in my brain. How will I care for a baby? Who will take me on? Will my family ever take me back now? Considering all the shame I feel, do I even want to see them again?

Pierce leads two pack horses which carry all the supplies. We have no heavy wagons, no stock, no children, and—perhaps the only blessing—no noise but the sounds of the horses breathing and the bugs buzzing.

I have no idea how many miles we travel each day, though it feels like we go much farther than the wagon train did. The irony of it all is that I have walked and ridden for hundreds of miles but have not yet managed to get anywhere that I planned on going. But have I ever really had a plan? No. I've spent my life following orders, doing what I'm told.

One evening I sit on a rock, letting my aching hips and legs rest. I rub my still flat belly and don't move when steps approach from behind. During the first few days, Joseph had startled me every time he appeared, but now I can identify his soft tread. He squats in the dirt next to my rock. I wait for him to speak. If he has come to find me, he has something to say.

"Supper's just about ready, if you can eat anythin'."

"Thanks," I mutter. I've been sick on and off for the past few days. The thought of food does not help my nausea.

He's still studying my face. "You don't look so good."

I have not seen myself in a mirror, since Nettie does not own one. I can only imagine the dark circles under my eyes, the dark freckles on my sunburnt drawn skin, the scar over my eye from the rock. I left at night and didn't think to bring a bonnet. I'm probably as brown as Joseph by now. I don't feel well at all, and I wonder yet again if the child is causing this, or if something worse has taken ahold.

Joseph is holding my quilt, and he hands it to me. I haven't seen it since we left our original camp, and I grab at it, holding it tight in

116

my grasp. I bury my face in its folds, hoping to get scent of home, but I only smell horse. I have looked for the quilt but Nettie has kept it well hidden.

"Why do you have this?" My voice sounds sharp, but I can't help it. He stands and shakes his head at me.

"Don't touch it. Keep your filthy hands off of it," I yell at him. My quilt is all I have left, but he's kept it from me. I don't care that he brought it back. How dare he take it from me in the first place.

Joseph merely watches me, shrugs, then heads back toward the lodge. My anger hasn't even touched him. I watch his back as he walks away, his head held high. He is not one to chat, and I don't want to talk to him anyway. We've ridden in silence for days, and I don't think that needs to change. He is a half-breed: half-white, half-Indian, wearing his hair in a long braid down his back. I feel my father's derision flow through me as I watch him leave.

He lives in his world, I live in mine.

The sun dips lower, due west. I have spent the last months of my life following the sun on its trek across the sky, listening to Papa, to Jed, to Mama, and now to Pierce while every cell in my body urges me to run the opposite direction—right back to Indiana, a land where green plants and trees thrive, unlike this barren, rock and sage strewn plain. But I can't. I would die, and this time I would not only be killing myself.

I watch the desert colors—like nothing from home—shift and soften in the graying light. Soft grays, yellow, browns, and oranges merge into a completely foreign landscape. Most people find it horribly ugly, and at first glance it is, but to see the sun set over the desert takes my breath away most evenings. My fingers itch to sketch these scenes, to capture the subtle colors of this desolate land. Maybe with a pencil in my hand, I could figure out a plan, one to save myself, this child, and my sanity, but no pencils or paper exist out here with this family. I had asked Nettie earlier, but she'd only stared at me, not understanding my request. Pierce had "harrumphed" in response.

I stand as the sun sinks just below the horizon, my butt sore and numb from my rocky perch, and I unfold the quilt. I trace the center medallion with my fingers, following the leaves as they swirl about it in a joyful dance. Just five short months ago, I had put the final stitches in the quilt. I had dreaded the walk but hoped Pa would be right, that taking this trip was the best decision. It wasn't. He'd hoped for a new life for his family, never imagining a new life growing in my belly with no husband and no home.

The sun has left an orange and pink sky in its wake. The air cools with each passing minute, so I wrap the quilt over my shoulders and head down the slope to the camp. I smell venison cooking and my stomach clenches, not in hunger but in revulsion. Bile rises and I lean into a large sage, but when my stomach heaves nothing comes up. My gut spasms in waves as I support myself with my arms on my knees. Wretched, sour bile fills my mouth, which I spit until the waves of nausea cease. I lean back onto my heels, eyes closed.

Finally I straighten, and though the light has become duskier, I can still see my way back to the lodge. I grip the edges of the quilt tightly in front of me, drawing strength from the fabric as I will my stomach to calm itself. I zigzag, searching for the easiest path through the brush, but a bush grabs at my quilt. Without thinking, I tug to loosen it and am awarded with the sound of a rip as the spiky branches release their hold. I stop tugging as soon as I hear the tear, but apparently it isn't soon enough. I lift the corner to survey the damage. A tear, about eight inches long, runs straight across a block in the lower left corner of the quilt. A bit of cotton still clings to the lower branches of the bush. I bite my lip, holding back my sobs, and bend to unhook the shredded fabric from the branch. The tear is jagged and hasn't followed neatly along a seam. It is a gash that bleeds cotton batting from the inside. Ruined, like me.

Sliding the quilt from my shoulders, I pull each corner together without making the tear worse and fold it up, hugging it tightly to my chest. Tears try to spill over, but I blink furiously, refusing to let them.

"Girl!" Pierce's voice rings out from the camp below. "You comin'?"

I take a deep breath to pull myself together and make my way back down the hill to my temporary home. Pierce perches on a buffalo robe and leans against the filthy hides that make up the lodge. Nettie sits in a wooden chair, and Joseph is perched on a log. I stand, undecided as to where I want to sit.

Pierce breaks the awkward silence. "You eatin'?"

A dark red venison steak lies across Nettie's plate in a pool of bloody juice. I shake my head. A month ago, I would have given anything for food other than bacon, beans, or biscuits. Now I wish for any of that with every ounce of my being.

"You just gonna stand there?" Pierce asks, knocking me from my reverie.

I seem to be doing that a lot lately. Perhaps it is the baby. More likely, I am losing my mind. I look toward Pierce. "I tore my quilt."

"You tore it? How?" Nettie asks.

I don't always understand Nettie, but I do know that she loves the quilt, covets it even.

"It got caught on a bush. Up there." I wave my hand in the general direction from which I have come. "Do you have any thread? Maybe a needle?"

Pierce laughs and Nettie shakes her head.

"Aw, we can get that at Fort Hall," he says when he gets done chuckling. "Nettie'll git it all fixed up.

"I'll do it. She ain't touchin' it."

Pierce shrugs in response and begins eating again. He doesn't use utensils, just holds the steak in his fingers and rips bites off. Meat juice drips into his beard. I turn away, disgusted.

"How much longer til' Fort Hall?" I ask, braving a glance in Joseph's direction. Maybe he'll answer.

He looks right past me, as if I am no more than the bush that had torn my quilt. Nettie also ignores me. Joseph must have told his parents what I'd said to him, how rude I'd been. But what did they expect? He's an Indian. In my world, he doesn't deserve any better.

I head toward the lodge to escape this moment, but as I pull back the hide door and lean over to enter, I realize I'm not in my world anymore. I'm in theirs. Here, a whole different set of rules applies, and I have no idea what they are.

Fort Hall, Idaho – early August 1847

After several days at the quilt tearing camp, we leave. Pierce intersperses several days of riding with two or three days of rest. While the routine with Pierce's family couldn't be more different than my family's on the trail, it is still a routine. Two weeks later, the white walls of Fort Hall come into view. I am not sure what I feel upon seeing the billowing covers of the forty or fifty emigrants' wagons standing in the meadows around the fort. I have no idea whether it's relief or sheer terror.

People mill about the wagons, cooking, checking stock, relaxing. I survey the wagons, searching for the telltale red patch that I sewed on a lifetime ago, back in Independence. I smile to myself, remembering Charlie talking with me as I stitched, his endless teasing, his music, his voice. I miss watching his wide, calloused hands as they run over the strings on his fiddle or play incessantly with the small pieces of leather he carries and tools. I had sketched his hands once. It was a small sketch, but I hadn't shown him the picture. I had never gotten it quite right.

Shock covers a young mother's face when she spots us. Her hands fly to her mouth, covering a squeal, then she hollers at her kids and begins loading the brood into the back of the wagon. A small group of four boys stares at me, their eyes wide in alarm. The tallest of them turns and runs toward the line of camped wagons, and the others scramble after him, trying to keep up. The smallest falls and cries out for the larger boys to wait, but they don't. The child turns his head and stares at me, past me. I pull on the reins, slowing my pony before sliding down its side. I want to check on the child, but my movement seems to send him into a greater panic. He yelps and scrambles to his feet.

A woman in a filthy calico dress runs toward the child. "You stay away from my boy, ya hear?" she yells at me. "You stay back where you are."

"Me?" I ask, partly to myself. I stop walking and smooth my hand across my dress. It's in no worse shape than anything the women here are wearing. I'd rinsed my face this morning. I've not got a bonnet, and I'm sure my face is browned and freckled. What is she afraid of?

The woman doesn't answer, just grabs the boy's arm and yanks him to his feet before half pulling, half carrying him back to the wagon. The other boys have already made it to the safety of the camp, and they watch the proceedings from behind the relative safety of a wagon's rear wheel.

Alarmed, I turn and scan the mountains and hills behind me, trying to figure what's scaring them. Pierce chuckles, and his pony plods up beside mine.

"What just happened?" I ask him.

"They's afraid of Indians."

"What Indians?" He laughs again, and I narrow my eyes at him. "Look again," he says. "Tell me what you see."

Nettie rides her pony and leads the pack animals, which hold the travois and lodge. Joseph rides in front of her. I realize how accustomed

120

I have become to their presence, and now, looking at them, I can understand the boys' alarm. Joseph wears the fierce scowl that seems always to cover his face, and his mother looks just as unfriendly. Frown lines crease her forehead. I recall the same fear I'd felt when I'd first encountered the family.

"Yep," he says, "the Indians ain't in the mountains behind us, girl. They's with us."

My memory of waking to Nettie and Joseph rushes back. I see the two of them standing above me, and I remember how my heart raced, sure that murder, a scalping, or being sold into slavery was in my near future. Every scary story I had heard as a child had flitted through my mind, but none of that had happened. Instead, I realize, it will happen now that I'm back with my own people. Probably not the murder part, but the sold into slavery part most likely. A new family? Strangers? Would they welcome a pregnant young woman? Another mouth to feed? Pa would never take on someone like me. Maybe they won't either.

It is odd, this turn in thought. I consider my situation. I both welcome and abhor the idea of returning to the crushing work and exhaustion that life on the trail brings.

"You ready?" Pierce hollers, interrupting my musings. He surveys the line of emigrant wagons with interest. Nettie and Joseph have caught up.

"I suppose."

The pony I ride follows Pierce. I have no need to steer him. As we get closer to the wagons and the fort, I can see the outline of several lodges on the other side of the fort. Apparently that's where we're headed. My pony plods along until it almost bumps into Pierce's horse, and we all stop. A man stands with his rifle across his chest, staring at Nettie and Joseph. He seems to be guarding the wagons.

"She's just my squaw," Pierce says to the man. "No need to panic."

He jerks his chin toward the other side of the fort. "She ain't allowed over here. Take them yonder. That's where the Indians is at."

"That's where we're headed. Came in from the North side. Why'n't you put yer gun up," Pierce says, his voice soft as he stares down the emigrant.

"You get these Indians away from my family, and I'll be happy to put it down."

Pierce lifts an eyebrow and turns to us. "Nettie, you get along. I ain't puttin' my back to this man. Take Joseph and Sarah over yonder."

Nettie nods and clicks to her horse. We plod away, and I note with alarm the rifles that disappear into the wagons as we leave. The thought of dying as we entered Fort Hall had never occurred to me. I'm not sure whether to laugh or cry.

Nettie leads us to a clear spot on the far side of the fort, and I turn when I hear a horse trot up behind us.

"Let's just set the lodge here, and then we'll go find yer people," Pierce says.

The faint edges of panic begin to tickle my heart. Pierce is looking for my family? "No," I say. "No, not them." Panic weaves itself throughout my gut.

"You don't wanna find 'em?"

"No. I can't go back there. Not like this." I lay my hand on my stomach, emphasizing my point.

"Aw hell, girl. It's yer Ma and Pa."

"I won't go." I stare at Pierce. He must understand. "Please." I fall silent, hating my dependence on him.

He shrugs. "All righty, then. Help Nettie with the lodge and I'll see what I can do."

I grimace. It is difficult and heavy work, setting up the lodge. It was Nettie's job, and I had become her helper. I hate every minute of the work. I wonder if I shouldn't just run to one of the emigrant families and claim I have been kidnapped, but then they might hang Pierce—or even worse.

"Wait. What are you going to do? Don't you think I should go with you?"

"Fer what?"

"To . . ." I don't know what. "To help?"

"You can help set up the lodge."

He heads to the wagons, leaving all the work to me and his wife. Nettie waves at me to follow her. We begin to set camp while Pierce and Joseph head toward the fort. I obey, hating myself for my weakness and glaring at their backs as they walk away.

I remember my quilt. "Pierce," I holler at his back.

He stops and turns.

"Can you get some thread and a needle?"

"You got anything to buy it with?" He knows I don't. Why is he taunting me? "Git to helping Nettie, girl."

122

I clench my fist, wanting to run after him and beat on him, but I can't, no more than I can run into a wagon screaming. I'd end up being the crazy one, not him.

My arm muscles scream as I lift the last lodge pole in place. It's draped with heavy buffalo hides. Sweat drips into my eyes as I look again toward the fort, hoping to see Pierce returning with some news. He had gone in then come out again with a group of men, and they had headed toward the wagons, but none of them had made an appearance since. I pull the bottom edge of the lodge taut as Nettie pounds in a stake. We move around the entire base together, pounding in stakes to hold it down.

"Go on," she says as she hammers the last one in.

"Are you sure?"

I have wanted to leave ever since Pierce walked away, but now that I have been given the opportunity, I am not sure if I want to stumble across a random party of men discussing my fate. Would he trade me like a slave? Or was he just finding a wagon that would take me on? I cringe as I think about him speaking of me. What was he telling them? We have not discussed any possible stories, which I now realize was a mistake. My entire life is in his hands.

"Go," Nettie repeats.

I survey the wagons on the other side of the fort, take a breath, then screw up my courage and head over. The wagons look so familiar—the blowing, filthy canvas, the campfires and tents—but I don't recognize any of them. None have any of the markings that had become so familiar on our train. Nor do I recognize any of the exhausted looking women who huddle over their meager sage fires, trying to get some sort of flame by which they can cook their family's supper. I continue walking, surveying the families, wondering which one will take me in, if any will. Maybe nobody will accept me, and I'll have to wait here indefinitely for some family to take pity on me. What if my family arrives? They would have Jed with them, and I can't begin to imagine the shame they would suffer if they found me here, pregnant and living with a trapper and his squaw wife. That thought sends a sharp spike of panic straight to my gut, so I banish it.

My meanderings through the wagons slows when I hear men's voices. Pierce's laughter stands out most clearly, and I listen hard. He's telling the story of how Nettie found me. When he tells of the slap Nettie'd given me, the entire group of men erupts in laughter. How dare he? He is supposed to be finding safe passage for me and instead he is entertaining them at my expense. I reach my hand out to steady myself on a wagon.

"Are you the source of all that merriment?" a soft voice asks.

I start, so focused am I on listening to Pierce disparage me. A small, kindly looking woman stands next to me. "Yes, ma'am."

"I'm sorry," she says. "I didn't mean to disturb you."

"Disturb me? I don't think I could get any more disturbed after listening to this … this … I don't even know what to call it."

She smiles at me, a gentle smile, and pats my arm. "It'll get better. It always does. We've laid by these two days, and I'm feeling oh so much better about this trip." She takes a deep breath and looks toward the meadow. "It's been a long journey."

"That it has," I reply, though I am not sure if she is asking for a reply or not. "I'm Sarah Crawford."

"Pleased to meet you." The woman reaches out her hand and introduces herself as Rachel Smith. She appears to be in her mid-twenties, with dark brown hair tied back in a bun, wide-set eyes, and round cheeks. "Will you be joining us?"

"I … well, I don't know." I try to smile, to convey some sense of confidence, but I fail miserably. I blink back tears.

"I think you best join them," Rachel says, pulling me around the corner of the wagon to the men.

"Why?" I yelp, digging my feet in.

"Don't let them decide for you. That's the last thing my John said to me before he passed. I'd think that's good advice for you, too."

I let her pull me forward.

"Ah, there's the girl," Pierce's voice booms as he sees us approach. "Git on over here. I gotta introduce you to the captain of this train. He says he might have a spot for you."

"He's a good man, Captain Sawyer is. You'll be fine," Rachel says, leaving her hand on my forearm.

"Git goin', girl. We ain't got all night," Pierce yells as I head toward him. His shouts are accompanied by the men's laughter, and I cringe in embarrassment. The man has no grace whatsoever. The group eyes me as I approach, and I drop my gaze to the ground to lessen the humiliation, if that's possible.

"This here's Sarah. She's a hard worker, and she can cook. Any wagon would do fine to take her on."

I wish I could become a bird and fly away. Never have I felt such mortification. I lift my chin and glare at Pierce. "It sounds as if you're tryin' to sell me," I hiss. "I am not chattel."

He raises his eyebrows at me. "I's just tryin' to find a wagon for you." He grins, obviously entertained with the proceedings. "I s'pose it does sound a bit like the auction block, don't it." A couple of the men in the group laugh at this as well, but they have the decency to look down as they do so.

"You say you can cook?" a man asks.

I keep my eyes on the ground. "I can."

"So's your husband didn't die of starvation I'm guessing?"

"No sir, he didn't," I look toward Pierce, my rage lessening. He's brilliant. I can pass off as a widow. "No, he died of, uh …" I pause, realizing I might contradict Pierce's story. Thankfully he picks up on my cue.

"I told you that part. The man got sick, and the train wasn't up to waiting. They figured the wagons a day or two behind would take her on, but we found her before they did. Figured the safest bet was to bring her in with us."

"They just left you out there?" the captain asks me.

"Well, I thought my family was a day or two behind, but they, uh, never showed up," I say, hoping my lie isn't completely obvious. "My husband hadn't wanted to lay by when they did earlier in the season, so we were a bit ahead and had joined up with another party." All the men nod at this, understanding the fluidity of parties on the trail.

The captain looks around at the group before speaking again. "John, do you think she could help your Gracie out?" He stares intently at the man who asked if I can cook.

"That might work," John says, looking me up and down. "We all know Gracie's been having a time on this trip."

A few of the men chuckle, and he shakes his head. Whether it's in defeat, anger, or frustration I cannot tell. I'm not sure if I want to meet or live with this Gracie woman.

"That settled then?" Pierce asks. "When you pullin' out?"

The Captain looks at Gracie's husband. "Sound good to you? If it does, we'll take her." He glances toward Pierce. "We're pullin' out at dawn tomorrow. Get her ready."

My rage returns. "I can get myself ready, thank you, sir," I say to the captain. The deal for my life has just been made, and not one of them thought to ask me about it. It doesn't matter. Apparently, I am no different than the stock they trade back and forth.

The man who'd agreed to take me on stands and approaches. He stops and reaches a hand toward me. "Name's John. I'd be obliged if you could help out my wife with the kids and the cooking. She's having a time of it. Follow me, if you would."

Is that a question or a command? I'm not sure, but I follow him regardless. The deal has been made. I've been sold. We wind through several wagons before stopping behind the open tailgate of a wagon with a light blue box. A woman stands at the rear preparing biscuit dough. She seems fine, though a little worn. But we all are dirty and exhausted from the journey.

"Gracie?" John says, sounding a bit tentative. He approaches her from the side, reaching his hand toward her as if he is approaching an animal that might bite.

"What? You need somethin'? Supper ain't ready yet," she snaps. "Can't you see I'm workin'?" She has taken off her bonnet, and loosened hair from the knot on the back of her head flies around her face in the light breeze. The sun sits behind her, low in the sky, creating a halo of wild, windblown hair. A blond head pokes out of the wagon, above his mother's.

"Who's that, Pa?"

Gracie looks up at her son's words and notices me standing near her husband. She surveys me then turns her gaze on her husband, waiting for the answer to her child's question.

"Gracie, this is Sarah Crawford. That trapper just brought her in. She got separated from her train when her husband died, and the trapper and his squaw picked her up. She needs to get to Oregon." He pauses and studies her reaction, waiting for something. I am not quite sure what.

She does nothing but stare at him. Her hands rest on the dough which she has already patted down. The blonde head slowly disappears back into the wagon, like a turtle retreating.

John continues. "She'll give you a hand. She can cook and help with the little 'uns." She still stares, silent. "She'll sleep in the tent with the kids, and you can move the baby to the tent, so you can sleep a little better. That'll help you out a bit." Not one word out of Gracie. "She'll be joining us at dawn when we leave."

That means I have one more night in the smoky lodge. Despite my anger at Pierce for treating me like chattel, I quickly decide that I'd rather sleep in the tent with the children tonight, just as I had done with my own brothers and sisters. "I'd be happy to start helping this evening," I offer. I try to smile at Gracie, let her know that I'm more than willing to help, just to please get me out of the lodge. "In fact, I'd prefer it, if you'd have me. I can help. I've, well, I've had enough of the trapper and his family."

She slams her hand into the middle of the biscuit dough. I hear the kids in the wagon scurrying over the supplies to the front, getting away from their mother.

John sighs, hooks his thumbs into his overalls, and hitches up his pants, readying himself for … what?

"Why not?" she exclaims. "Just bring her right on in. This wagon is worthy of a show. Why not add a widow to the lot of us?" Her voice has risen to a yell. "Sure, I can feed another mouth. Did you think of that, John? Did you think of feeding her when you decided I need the help? Am I not doing good enough for you? You need to bring in another woman? Or is it that you wanted to head south from here to Zion or whatever them Mormons call it? Because if you do, I ain't goin'. I got no intention of bein' part a you havin' two wives."

I gasp, shocked, as Gracie continues on her rant. "I won't have no part of *that*," she hisses. "You hear me, John? You won't be takin' no other wife. This train won't take that."

I take a step back as John moves toward his wife. "I ain't takin' no new wife, Gracie. Ye're my wife. I just thought she could help you out is all."

The boy whose head I'd seen lowers himself from the front of the wagon and creeps toward me, his eyes on his mother. "Mama," the child stammers. "She can help. She can help you with the wagon and the cookin'."

Gracie whips her head in his direction. "You think I need help with the cookin' too? You think you can run this wagon? You think, Ian

Stone, at twelve years old you can make those decisions?" She's goin' good now. Her voice pitches higher and higher with each question. Ian ducks behind his father to try to escape the tirade. "How much flour we got? How much meal? How many beans? Can we feed her?"

"That's enough, Gracie." John's voice is firm and loud.

She pauses, her eyes wide. Spittle covers her chin.

He speaks before she can begin again. "She's comin' with us. It's the Christian thing to do. Her name's Sarah. She'll be building the fire for you." He points to a small pit where they'd had a fire earlier. Though the biscuit dough is ready for coals, the fire pit lies cold and empty. "You need the help." He turns and walks away, leaving me alone with Gracie.

I hurry to follow after him. "Mr. Stone?"

He keeps walking.

"Mr. Stone? John?"

Finally he stops.

"Are you sure this will work? She's, uh, she seems angry," I manage to get out, not quite sure what to say.

He nods. "This journey's taken its toll on her. I just got to get her there, and she'll be all right. If you could help me do that, I'd be mighty obliged."

"Would you be all right if I stayed with your kids tonight? I think that'd make it easier on everyone."

"Whatever you think, Sarah." With that he turns and walks toward the group of men who are still gathered where Pierce had auctioned me off.

I return to the wagon to find Gracie Stone standing in the same spot, glaring at me.

Ian kneels warily near the fire pit, watching his mother's malevolent look. "Pa said your name's Sarah?"

"It is, and you're Ian?" I reach out my hand to shake his. He grins sheepishly and holds his hand toward mine.

I feel like I might have a potential ally in Ian. "Would you mind helping me find some firewood?"

Together we leave Gracie with her dough. More than anything I want to ask Ian about his mother, but I know that until I have his trust, that topic is probably better left alone. We head through the wagons toward the edge of the meadow where we can gather some sage for the fire.

Ian keeps glancing at me. "Wasn't that you who came in with the

Indians today?" he asks as we begin gathering the meager fuel.

I smile. Of course he would want to know about the Indians, and I feel a pang of guilt as thoughts of Tommy and Jasper flit through my mind. They would love to hear this story. I hadn't thought about the last several weeks in those terms until now, but I suppose my adventure will make a good story if I live long enough to tell it. There's no telling on this trail.

"Yep," I say.

"What were they like? Are they as savage as they say? Did you see them scalp anyone? Did they try to scalp you?"

Questions fly from his mouth, one on top of the other, without any pauses in between. At his last one, I flip my thick braid over my shoulder, showing him my long brown hair.

"Nope, they didn't try to scalp me. When they first found me, I was pretty scared. I thought they were going to kill me, and I panicked. Nettie slapped me to bring me to my senses, but that only scared me more. I actually fainted."

Ian's eyes widen as I talk. I tell him about returning to their lodge and finding a white man there. I don't get much further in the story before we have our arms loaded and we must return to get the fire going, but just in the pieces I have shared, I think I might have made a friend for life.

Chapter 14

I'M SITTING ON the back porch in the shade, holding my hair off my neck with my left hand and waving my magazine in front of me with my right, trying to create some sort of cool breeze. The grass has begun to turn yellow and crunchy from thirst, and even the trees seem to droop in the still, pervasive heat. The door slams, and Claire walks toward me, a cool glass of iced tea in her outstretched hand.

"Oh, hi." I reach for the tea and take a gulp. "When did you get here?"

"Just now, and you're welcome." She sits, and we both look at Agnes' sad, empty house next door. "How's she doing?"

"Not great."

"Made any decision on what to do with the quilt?"

"What do you mean? I'm keeping it. I already told you that."

She shrugs. "I know. I just thought maybe you might have changed your mind."

"Claire." I try not to give a big exasperated sigh like my mother used to when she was annoyed. "She *gave* it to me. She wants me to keep it, to remember. If I forget it or lose it, then I've forgotten Agnes."

She sips her tea, and I can tell she's not done with this discussion. She squints, which means she's brooding, trying to come up with a new approach to convince me she's right. "Harper, you're saying that Agnes and the quilt are one, but they're not."

I don't respond.

"Okay. Let me ask you this. Why did Agnes give you the quilt?"

"Why do you care so much about this anyway?"

"Cuz I see you struggle to pay for ... well, everything. The appraiser said its worth a lot, like thousands of dollars. And it seems to me like selling this quilt could make your life a lot easier. But you're too damn stubborn." She smiles at me. "And that's why I love you. So back to my question. Why did Agnes give you the quilt?"

I glare at her. "I told you already. She gave it to me to honor it, to honor its story, to remember. She wants me to do it for her since she can't keep it anymore."

"Do you need the quilt, the actual physical object, in order to do that?"

"Yes, I do." I lean back in the chair and rub my face with my hands. I feel like I'm always on defense when it comes to this damn quilt, and I wish for the umpteenth time I had the courage to take the offense.

"Harper, what was Agnes always encouraging you to do?"

"Oh my God!" I cry, exasperated. "What is this? Am I on the stand?"

"Just answer the question."

"I *am* on the stand." I set the tea down and run my hands through my hair, pushing it off my face. "She wanted me to finish college, get a degree, take care of myself," I recite. It is a lesson she pounded into me from the day I met her. She was always about being independent. It seems to me the definition of irony, considering her situation.

"Exactly. She wanted you to be able to stand on your own two feet, and she wanted you to get your degree so you could do that." She pauses and watches me. "But she also wanted you to write," she adds softly.

I close my eyes, praying for strength. "You are not allowed to watch any more courtroom dramas. This is ridiculous. Could you make your point, please, without all this questioning?"

"My point is this, Harper. Agnes has given you a gift, a gift that will help you to achieve everything that she wanted for you to achieve. If you sell the quilt, you can pay for your education or at least a big chunk of it. You could also write her story, maybe even sell it. Remember that dream? Honor Agnes that way. There's more than one way to honor her."

I lean forward, resting my elbows on my knees. I do remember that dream, and I've started writing it. It feels good, but I'm not ready to share my words yet because that's what Claire would want, to read it.

"I don't know what to do," I groan. "What you're saying makes sense. I could pay to finish school, but in my heart of hearts, I *know* Agnes didn't give me the quilt and share its story with me so I'd turn around and sell it. She didn't. And what if she finds out I sold it? What if her last coherent thought is that I betrayed her? I know what that feels like, and it's not good."

"Yeah," Claire says. "I guess you do. I just hate seeing you struggle sometimes."

"Me too." I lean my head back and close my eyes, letting the sun heat my face. It's my first day off in a while. I should be typing up the latest Sarah tale. Actually, I should be doing my laundry so I have something clean to wear to work, but right now, sipping tea and sitting in the sun with Claire is about all I feel like doing.

A car stops in front of the house, and a car door slams shut.

"I'm gonna go see who that is," I say when the doorbell rings.

Claire, her eyes on her phone, nods.

When I peek out the side window, I freeze. It's Rosemary, in full intimidation attire. She's sporting a suit, high heels, and a Coach bag. Her blonde hair reaches her shoulders in soft curls. She has money, and it shows. I don't, and it shows too.

I look down at my jeans, t-shirt, and flip-flop clad feet. I quickly kick my flip-flops off and slide into my three-inch platforms that are lying by door. Sometimes being a slob and kicking off my shoes the second I walk into the house is a good thing. I can now face her eye to eye.

When I open the door, I try my best to look and sound surprised. "Rosemary! Hi. What can I do for you?"

"May I come in?"

"No, I think we can chat here." I block her way as she begins to step forward.

She hadn't expected my answer. She stops and takes a step back.

I stand a little taller and look her in the eye, even though I think my heart is going to beat out of my chest. Never in my life have I been this rude. Or maybe I'm not being rude. Maybe I'm actually standing up for myself. I look down to keep her from seeing my smile before I can wipe if off my face.

"I visited with mother this morning."

"Oh, you did? That's nice. How is she?"

"Not well. She started in on the old quilt again." She watches me, and I try to nod casually though I can feel my face beginning to redden. The quilt is upstairs in my closet. "That reminded me that I still hadn't gotten the key from you, so I thought I'd grab it while I was over here."

"Okay. It's on my key ring." I don't want to give her my key, but I don't know how to get out of it.

"Can you go get it, please? I don't have much time."

"I'll be right back." I shut the door in her face. I'll be damned if she's coming in here.

I grab my keys off the scarred kitchen table and head back to the front door. I have no fingernails whatsoever, and it takes a minute to get the key in the little slot so I can unwind it off the ring.

Rosemary watches me the entire time in awkward silence. Finally, she speaks up. "I'm selling the house."

I look up at her, forgetting the key along with my determination to be rude. "You are? Why?"

"Because my mother isn't ever going to go home." Her voice is soft. Sad, almost.

I understand what she's saying, but I don't want to admit it.

"Have you been to visit her lately?" she asks.

"Yeah, I went a few days ago."

"She told me that she gave the quilt away. Apparently that's her "safe place" for it. There are some days she doesn't speak to me at all." Her voice begins to shake, and I watch her, somewhat awestruck. The ice queen has cracked, and a little bit of emotion is spilling out. "It's like my mother is there, but she's not really."

I don't want to tell her that her mother tends to be worse, much worse, with her around. I focus on my key, giving Rosemary a moment to pull herself together and put her icy façade back in place. It doesn't take long.

"If you could try to get out of her who she gave the quilt to, I'd appreciate it."

I nod in response, not trusting my voice.

"When do you plan to visit again?" she asks.

"Tomorrow, before work. It seems to be a good time to visit with her, before she goes to lunch."

My cell rings and Claire answers it. Really? Is there no privacy?

"Let me know what she says about the quilt," Rosemary says.

I hand her the key. "Is that all you needed?"

"I suppose so."

As I step back in the house and shut the door, I hear Claire finishing "my" phone call.

"Harper!" she yells from the back porch. "That was the quilt appraiser. She had some sort of family emergency so the appraisal will take longer than she thought, but she says so far the numbers look really good. She just wanted to let you know."

I want to scream "shut up" to Claire's bellowing, but I don't. Instead, I drop to the ground and peek out the corner of the wide open window. Every window in the house is open. Rosemary has stopped on the front steps and is staring at the door. Shit. She heard.

Claire saunters into the front room and finds me still crouched on the floor by the window. "What are you doing?"

I shake my head and stand. What can I even say?

She gives me a hug and heads to the door. "Think about what I said, okay?"

I nod, but right now, it's the last thing I want to think about. Instead I head toward the stairs and my mom's room. A map of the Oregon Trail covers one wall. Library books on the Oregon trail sit stacked on the floor and the dresser, and notes cover the bed in a rough timeline. This room has become my escape because every time I think my life can't get any more depressing, or confusing, or unbearable, I think of Sarah. Her summer was worse...way worse.

Chapter 15

FOLLOWING SUPPER, THE Stone family joins the rest of the party, just as the families in my train had, especially following a day of rest. Someone pulls out a fiddle which reminds me of Charlie whom I have—until now—managed to avoid thinking about. It hurts too much to remember, and I have no desire to listen to this fiddler play. I search the faces around me for Mr. Stone. I need to return to the lodge and retrieve my quilt, but I am not sure about the expectations of my new "family." Can I just leave? Do I need to ask? I am now a widow, a woman of experience, not a child—though I feel more like a lost girl than anything else. I decide I'd better at least let him know where I'm headed. So far, I like him. He seems a calm, even-tempered man, though perhaps this is only in comparison to his wife.

Gracie Stone seems to have lost an important part of herself somewhere along the trail. Earlier, as I had built the fire and begun cooking the bacon for supper, she had muttered to herself non-stop. Though I hadn't been able to decipher her words, I did empathize with her despair and anger. Now, with the whole party collected to listen to the music, Gracie sits near her husband, her face relaxed and peaceful for the first time since we met. She stares toward the west, where the sun has begun its slow descent.

I approach the couple tentatively. John notices me first and nods his head, acknowledging me. His wife's gaze never leaves the setting sun.

"I just wanted to let you know that I am going to head back to Mr. Pierce's to get my belongings."

He frowns. "I didn't think you had anything. We can't handle any more weight in the wagon. The oxen are tired enough as it is, and we've had to drop some belongings on the trail."

"I don't have much. Just a quilt, and if necessary I can carry it. I'll need it for sleep too, so I won't use your blankets. It was all I could bring with me, but it's important."

"You don't need to be wandering around over there alone. Take Ian with you."

Ian stands up immediately, ready to head into Indian territory. "Ye're gonna let me go, Pa?"

John gives his son a sharp look. "That's what I said. Hurry back and don't let nothin' happen."

Ian's body hums with excitement as we leave the group and head toward the fort and the Indian lodges. This excursion will make him perhaps the most envied boy on this train, if not on the entire Oregon Trail. He walks next to me, matching my pace, his chin held high, and I think again of my brothers.

Nettie and Pierce sit outside the lodge. I cannot see Joseph. The door flap is open, and Ian tries to see as much as he can inside the lodge without acting like it. My quilt lays across Nettie's shoulders, the bottom edges dragging in the dirt.

"What you doin' back here? Thought we got you all set to go," Pierce says, taking a bite of stew from the bowl on his lap.

"I came back for my quilt. I'd like it back. It's all I've got."

"You got more than that," Pierce replies.

"What do you mean? That quilt is all that I have from my family."

Nettie tightens her grip on the quilt and pulls it tighter across her shoulders.

Pierce challenges me with his words and his eyes. "You got your life, ain't you? Without us, you'd have died. And Nettie likes the quilt. It's awful nice of you to give it to her."

"I didn't give it to her. You're stealing it." My voice rises, and I check myself. I don't want to sound like Gracie Stone on one of her rants. Those seem to fill the air at least hourly.

Pierce begins to chuckle, filling me with rage. "It's my quilt," I repeat. "My granny and I made it."

"I heard you the first time, and I ain't givin' it to you. I already gave it to Nettie here. She likes it. We fed you, we brought you back. I think it's a fair trade. That's what I do, trade. Anyone here would agree with me that it's a fair trade. Yer life for a quilt."

"Please. It's all I've got."

He ignores me, continues eating his meal. I realize the one thing that has held me together, reminded me of Granny, filled me with some sense of peace might all be gone.

Nettie stands, lifting the quilt from the dirt, and nods toward me, as if in thanks.

"Let's go, Ian. It ain't no use." I clench my fists and stare at my quilt, draped over her shoulders. One last time, I study its colors, the blocks, and the shapes, then I leave with Ian beside me. I wonder at the amount of hate I can hold inside before I up and burst with it all.

Chapter 16

Present Day

THREE DAYS LATER, I sit at the kitchen table, laptop on, trying to decipher my handwritten notes, but it's like trying to read an ancient Hebrew text or something, with all its random lines and dots. I need to remember to not only take my laptop on my visits with Agnes but also to charge the damn thing.

As I finally begin to make some sense of my scribbles, my phone chirps. I don't recognize the number. Hopefully it's a wrong number, but then it chirps again, notifying me of a voice mail. Who leaves messages?

Out of curiosity, I listen. "Good afternoon, Harper. This is Rosemary, Agnes' daughter." What the hell? How did she get my cell? And then I remember it's stuck to Agnes' refrigerator like a piece of child's art. "I wanted to set up a time to meet with you, to get this whole quilt situation worked out. Would it be possible to meet me for coffee this week? I'm available on Monday afternoon or Tuesday morning. Please let me know which works for you. I look forward to hearing from you."

I so do not want to meet with this woman, but maybe I can get her to see reason and back off. I'm not giving her the quilt. If Agnes didn't want her to have it, then I don't either. I finally decide to text her and tell her I can meet her Friday at ten. My schedule. She responds immediately and gives me the address for the coffee shop where she wants to meet.

I think it's all set when my phone chirps again with a text. "Bring the quilt with you, please."

I sigh. Do I take it? The only reason to bring it would be to return it, which I'm not going to do. Or I could bring it and not return it which would probably piss her off more. My brain is telling me to return it, but my heart is telling me to tell Rosemary to fuck off already. She needs to figure out why her mom picked me instead of her.

AGNES PAUSES IN her story and stares up at the ceiling, her face tight and her lips pursed. She breathes out heavily in frustration. "What is it? What is that damn place?"

I think she's looking for "Fort Hall." I've filled in for her twice before. The first time she got pissed. The second time she almost cried. I've pretty much got the entire route memorized from studying the map, trying to figure out Sarah's journey. I keep my mouth shut for as long as I can before I blurt out, "Fort Hall? Is that it?"

Confusion creases her forehead.

"You were talking about the trapper, remember?" I continue telling the story I know so far, hating myself for prompting her, for all my worthless chatter, but I hate the silent void of her memory loss even more. Even to myself, I sound like a mosquito buzzing throughout the room, annoying and loud. She waves her hand, brushing me away and silencing me.

She has been telling me about Sarah meeting the trapper's wife and son. I can't even imagine how scary that would have been. She built the suspense up well in her telling of it, pausing often at exciting moments, but I'm not sure if that was intentional. Her pauses are getting longer as she looks for the words she needs for the narrative.

"Harper?"

I raise my head, and she looks at me with a sort of desperation in her eyes.

"Do you mean Fort Hall?" I repeat, softer this time.

"Yes." She pauses again, waiting for the words to come. "I want to finish this soon."

"You have lots of time," I assure her. Or am I reassuring myself? I know what she is saying, but I don't want to admit it. In the few short months that she has been here, she's gotten older somehow. Her language is slowly fading; her short term memory is shot. I often have to remind her where she'd left off only minutes later. She has repeated some pieces of the story and included different details. I have no idea what is real and what is not. It's all her interpretation of it at this point. And then as I write it, it becomes my interpretation, my story. Doesn't it?

"I don't know how much more time I have to tell you, to remember the whole thing. I found a book in the medicine cabinet yesterday morning. I don't remember putting it there."

"Agnes, don't talk like that."

"Harper, let's not sugarcoat it. If I've taught you anything, it should be that. Dust yourself off, pick yourself up. I'm almost ninety. It's been a good go."

I drop my head and whisper, "No."

She's silent.

She can't go. I lift my eyes to hers, wanting to drop on the ground and plead with her. "How can you say that? You can't just give up." I shake my head, panic beginning to slowly wind it's tentacles around my heart where they begin squeezing. My breath hitches. "What am I supposed to do if you leave?" I shout the last words then wish I could grab them out of the air as soon as they escape my mouth. What have I said?

Silence fills the room. She rises and shuffles toward me. Her ancient wrinkled hand takes a hold of mine. It is cool and soft. "It makes me angry, too."

I lean my head back on the couch as tears fill my eyes and drip down my cheeks.

I HAVE DREADED this meeting all week, creating scenario after scenario in my head as to how it will play out, but the reality is, I have no idea. As I approach the coffee shop door, I hold the quilt bag by its straps like it's a lifeline and I'm drowning. I still don't know if bringing it was the right choice. I've been staring at it all week as I've worked on the story, wondering what to do. Life would be so much easier if I just handed it over to Rosemary, but then I couldn't take it with me to visit Agnes, and she's the one who really needs it, not Rosemary. Maybe I need it too. Maybe, like Agnes, it's saving me.

The strong coffee smell assaults me as I survey the room. Newspapers litter the tabletops and empty chairs. People type frantically on their laptops or chat on their phones in an annoying public display, trying to convince others of their importance.

Rosemary sits in the back of the shop, watching me, eyeing the bag in my hand. Even though for some weird reason I feel like it gives me strength, I instantly regret bringing it as soon as I see her eyeing the bag. I wish I had left it sitting in my closet, right where it belongs.

She smiles and lifts her perfectly manicured hand in a wave. I nod in her direction and stand in line to get a coffee. I think I'll need the sustenance to get through this interview, but then I change my mind. If I get a coffee, I'll have to stay here with her until it's done, or else I've wasted three bucks. I'd rather be able to leave quickly without wasting any cash, so I step out of line and head back toward Rosemary.

"No coffee?"

"Not today." I really don't want to tell her that three dollars is quite an expense for me for a cup of coffee.

I sit down and wait for her to start. This is her deal, not mine. She grips her cup, her unease obvious in the whiteness of her knuckles. I bite my cheek to hold in a grin.

"Harper, I'll get started here. You have a valuable family heirloom that belongs to my family. I want it back. I expect you to return it to us. I see that you brought it with you, so I'm hoping that you will be doing that now." She looks at me expectantly.

I have set the bag on my lap. It is in a large gift bag, a bright fuchsia one with royal blue, purple, and lime green polka dots on it.

On the way here, I thought I might return it to her, have this whole thing be over with, but she's such a condescending bitch. I ask for the thousandth time how on earth this woman could be related to Agnes.

She reaches for the bag. "Let me have it now."

I fold the top of the bag down. "No. It's not yours anymore."

Her eyes harden and her hand freezes in mid-air over the table. "It *is* mine. It will always be mine. I have more than enough documentation to prove it. Don't make this ugly, Harper. You don't want to do that." She pauses and looks me up and down, taking in my worn T-shirt and jeans. "You can't afford to take me on, young lady."

She's right. I can't. But if I give in to her, right here, right now, I won't be able to take anything on for my entire life. I promised Agnes. I need to keep that promise.

"Actually, I can't afford not to. I've got my own documentation and a promise I made to your mother. I'm actually curious as to what your documentation is."

She laughs mockingly. "Documentation? You have something from a woman with dementia? A woman who some days can't remember where she lives? That's not documentation honey. That's pathetic."

I bristle and stand. "Uh, I don't think it's pathetic at all. Want me to tell you what's pathetic?"

"No, not really," she says into her coffee cup as she sips, "but I'm guessing you will anyway."

Yep, I hate her. "What's pathetic is that your mother gave me the quilt in the first place. Did you ever ask yourself why she did that? Do you wonder why she's telling *me* the story about it?"

At this, she drops her eyes. It's not a lot, just enough that I know I got to her at least a little bit. I turn and walk out of the shop, proud of myself for once. But what am I proud of? Pointing out to an old lady that her even older mother doesn't like her?

Thankfully it's not raining today, so I can walk to my beat up old car with my head up and not sprint, all hunched over. I don't want to look like I'm running away. I shove the key into the door as I hear my name. Rosemary walks toward me.

Great.

My moment of comeback greatness and fantastic exit slips away with each one of her steps.

"I want to be clear here," she says coolly. "Regardless of what you may think, I love my mother, and as far as I'm concerned, you stole a family heirloom. You broke into my mother's home and took it. I'll get it back."

Would she really lie like that? Of course she would.

She reaches out her hand. "If you hand it to me right now, all of this will go away."

It would be so easy to give it to her, to hand it over, to let this damn obligation go, but I can't. I can't give Agnes up. Rosemary looks just enough like her mother that I see Agnes' eyes staring at me, challenging me to do what I need to.

"Rosemary, let me ask you a question. How did that tear get into

142

the quilt?"

Surprise makes her eyebrows lurch upward. "You tore the quilt? You've already ruined it?"

"No. The one that was repaired years and years ago. I'm talking about the tear in the lower left corner. How did that get there?"

"I have no idea what you're talking about. Now just give it to me."

Exactly. She has no idea. "You don't have a clue about this quilt. I think I have all the documentation I need." I open my car door and climb in.

She doesn't walk away, just watches me as I put my car into reverse, back out, and leave the lot. When I turn onto the street, I check my mirror. She is still standing there. My heart races, and a giant lump sits in my throat. What have I done?

AT 8:30 THE next morning, my cell rings, jarring me from my sleep. My schedule is specifically designed so I can avoid waking up early. I always work either lunch or dinner, never morning. I roll over. Whoever is calling doesn't know me very well. It rings again, then thankfully stops. It chirps to alert me of a voicemail.

Now I'm curious and won't go back to sleep until I check it.

"Hi, this is Sandra with Worthy Quilts Appraisals." Her voice is high pitched and chipper. If I only heard her voice, I would imagine that a much younger woman had left the message on the machine. "I wanted to let you know that I've worked up some figures for you, and I'd like to get the appraisal to you. Give me a call at your earliest convenience and we'll set up a meeting. Thank you."

I roll over and try to go back to sleep, dreading the meeting. All this will mean is more grief about the quilt. I truly hope it's valued at nothing, because its already worth way too much.

On Monday after I work the afternoon shift, I pick Claire up so we can go to Sandra's house. She meets us as the door and ushers us into her quilt room as she had before, only this time we sit at a table upon which she has spread several sheets of paper. It feels very much like a business meeting. She goes through each of her valuations of the quilt and explains how she reached those amounts.

I am stunned. She has put the quilt's market value at $8400 but feels that if it went to auction, there is a chance it could be worth more. Claire instantly begins to ask questions about how to go about doing that. I let her. That's a lot of money. Tuition. Almost enough to finish school. Now what?

Chapter 17

Shoshone Falls, Idaho

THE NEXT MORNING begins with a bell. It has a slightly different ring to it than the bell on the Dixon train, but it is a bell nonetheless, a clanging hateful sound. As soon as I hear it, I realize how much I have not missed it, and I vow for the hundredth time to never allow any bells in my life once I arrive wherever I'm going.

I lie in the tent between Ian and his two little sisters. They are all blonde and have the sharp, thin features of their mother. The night before they had crawled into bed as soon as the last fiddle note died, before their mother even rose from her seat. An older quilt I hadn't noticed earlier lies across the kids' blankets. I sit up and study it in the dim light, but I cannot see much of it. I want to check the stitches. Granny always said how a quilt was made said a lot about the maker. That's why she spent so much time making me rip out my stitches and re-do them. I can't see this quilt's stitches well enough to tell, but I figure if Gracie made it, it'll show in the stitching and won't impress me much.

The children stir and sit up, beginning the morning routine. I slept soundly though I've lost my quilt, my family, all my pride. I am now masquerading as a widow and a child bubbles in my belly. N ausea rolls over me as I climb from the bed, and the little girls follow me behind the tent, where I heave. They watch with big eyes as I get sick three times, then we all hold our skirts up for one another to hide their morning duties from prying eyes. Ian leaves the tent to help round up all the train's stock.

We haven't yet heard Gracie's piercing voice. For that, at least, I am grateful. The girls scramble back into the tent to clean up the bedding and get ready for the day's journey. They know the daily routine. It seems that regardless of the train or the family, the routine of this journey doesn't alter. I fall into it gratefully. Without thinking, I do the chores I have done hundreds of times before.

I have dwelled so long and so often on the problems of what I should do that I give it up this morning. I don't worry about my family finding me or the shame they would surely feel. I don't mourn the loss of Charlie. I don't dwell on my hatred for Jed and my almost as much hatred of Pierce. I don't think about the quilt I gave up without a fight. I don't think about how I will care for a child on my own in a strange land. I don't think. I just pack up the blankets and quilts, help Gracie serve the beans I soaked and cooked the night before, squeeze the tiny bit of milk we can get from the cow, set it in the churn hanging on the side of the wagon for butter, and then, as I have every day for the last four months, I walk.

We make good time today. At each stop Gracie yells at me, taunts me, tries to get some sort of reaction, but I don't have the energy to respond to the words of a crazy woman. Exhaustion bites at my heels.

The country gets rockier and drier, which I find almost impossible to believe. How can it? Strange rocks litter the land, cutting the animals' feet as they trudge along the trail. Each day runs into the next, with one day much like any other. Rise, fix the morning meal, pack up, walk, break for dinner, walk, set camp, fix supper, and fall into bed with an exhaustion I have never before felt. My body fights the constant walking, but neither can I sit in the wagon and withstand the constant jolting. It sickens me, even worse than I already am.

The repetition and boredom of each day deadens me just as it maddens the woman with whom I travel. I have learned to avoid her as much as possible. Most often I walk next to Rachel, the kind, widowed Quaker woman whom I'd met when I first approached this wagon company.

The extent of Gracie's madness becomes clearer with each day. The trail gets to everyone, but it seems especially hard on Gracie for reasons I do not fully understand.

When we rise early one morning and the kids pack up the tent, we finish another breakfast of bacon and beans. "Can I have your plate, Gracie?" I ask, as gently as I can.

"No. I ain't done." Her plate is empty.

"We need to get going now, Gracie." I kneel in front of her. "Hand me your plate."

"I ain't goin'. I'm stayin' right here. I can't do this no more."

"You got to, Gracie. You can't stay here." Desolate brown land surrounds us. "Nobody can survive here."

"You get away from me. You ain't part of this family." She waves her hand, shooing me away. "Git, girl." Her voice rises as it does whenever she becomes upset.

I look around for John. He seems to be the only one able to calm her.

"You leave now," she says. "I don't want you eating my food no more." Her voice drops, becoming almost sinister as she hisses her final words. "Find another wagon to help you, you beggin' whore."

I stare at her, too shocked to respond. Finally I stand, unsure of what to do.

"Did you not hear me?" Gracie screams. She hurls her dirty plate at me. She misses my head but it hits my shoulder, bounces off and lands in the dirt. The last time anyone hit me it was Nettie's slap.

"Gracie! That's enough!" John yells as he walks briskly toward his wife. "I'm sorry, Sarah."

"I ain't sorry! How dare you say that to her, to that little whore you brought on to this wagon?"

My throat is tight with anger and fear. "I'm gonna go now."

"That'd be fer the best," John says. "And Sarah, you best find another wagon to take you on. We ain't doin' it no more."

"Where? I ain't got nowhere to go."

"That ain't our problem," Gracie tells me. "*You* are."

I walk toward the line of people who are gathering to watch another of Gracie Stone's rants. What now? Gracie screams at her husband, and I turn to see. John grabs her arm and pulls her to her feet. She fights him, refusing to stand. She even grabs a rock off the ground and hurls it at his head.

He backs off. "We're leaving here in ten minutes. You best be on the wagon," he says before walking away, leaving his livid wife sitting in the dirt.

She drops her head, and a sob starts deep in her body, rising upward before forcing itself out in a wail. She crouches on the ground like a beetle frozen before the vibration of a wagon's oncoming wheel, unsure which direction to turn to save itself though its death is imminent.

Tears drip down her cheeks, and for the first time, I realize how much I have in common with this woman. I wonder if she started this journey looking forward to the possibilities that lay ahead, or if—like me—her family dragged her along, offering her no other option.

The crowd begins to disperse. I consider approaching Gracie then think better of it. I have to find a new host. I follow the others and search the wagons for Captain Sawyer.

Five minutes later, I am still searching for him when a small voice hollers.

"Sarah!" I turn just in time to grab Ian as he throws himself into me. "You gotta come. Mama's trying to burn down the wagon. You gotta help me!"

I grab his hand and run. Gracie grasps a flaming branch just behind the rear wheel, holding it right where all the axle grease collects. Thankfully, the morning breeze is extinguishing her kindling or else the Stone's wagon would already be ensconced in flame. I run to the woman and try to grab at the flaming branch she wields.

"Ian, get the other branches from the fire!" I shout.

"I told you to stay away," Gracie yells. She swings the flame toward my head, and I scream and jump out of her reach. She is no longer trying to ignite the wagon, she is trying to ignite me. I back away as she lunges toward me again, and the heat from the flames brushes my hair. If my hair catches on fire, I will die. For the second time this summer I am faced with my imminent death, and I decide I'm not yet ready to meet my Maker. I wrap my hand protectively across my belly and realize with a shock that I want this baby to live, too. I back up more quickly.

Gracie pauses in her attack, eyeing me. I take one more step back and my foot snags on one of the millions of rocks strewn across the land. My upward momentum keeps me going. I reach back to catch myself and manage to stop my fall with my left wrist. It crumples beneath the rest of my body as I crash to the ground. Pain shoots up my arm.

"What in the hell are you doing, woman?" John hollers as he crosses the space between the wagon and his wife.

Gracie whirls around and threatens him with the flaming branch. "I told you I was done with this trip. I ain't goin' nowhere," she screeches, waving the torch toward her husband. "You just try to take me."

"Papa, she's tryin' to catch the wagon on fire!" Ian huddles with his siblings underneath the wagon. Their eyes are huge as they watch their mother try to set me and now their father on fire.

John looks toward his terrified children, and anger transforms his face. He marches toward his wife, ignoring her threats with the torch. He grabs it from her hand and throws it to the ground. He reaches his hand back and slaps the side of her head. She reels from the blow but still manages to lunge at him, her hands reaching for his throat. John reaches his right arm back and swings a second time. This time he catches her on the temple, and she crumples to the ground not far from me, where I sit clutching my arm to my chest.

John surveys the scene, shakes his head in disgust, and walks back toward the stock. He does not help his wife or even check on his children. I push myself up from the ground with my right hand, as my left wrist has already begun to swell.

"Is she dead?" Ian calls from his spot under the wagon. He blinks rapidly, desperately trying to hold back the tears that threaten to spill.

I walk with more than a little trepidation toward Gracie. She hasn't moved. A bruise is forming on the side of her face where John hit her, but she is breathing. Her chest moves up and down with each breath.

"She ain't dead," I tell Ian, reassuring him. "You can come out."

The kids crawl out and tentatively approach their mother. My attempt at a smile for the kids' sake has turned into a grimace of pain. Ian picks up a stick and pokes at his mother from a safe distance before he actually tries to touch her and help her up. She doesn't move.

Neither do I. Where can I go?

Gracie Stone. She now ranks right up there with Jedediah Monroe and Jim Pierce. If Gran knew how much hate has grown in my heart on this trip, she'd worry it'd soon be turning a nice shade of black. I hold my wrist and glare at the woman who lies curled in the dirt.

"Ian," I say, "you best head off to get Mrs. Black. I think we need her."

Ian drops the stick he was using to poke his mother and runs to fetch the older woman.

"Sarah!" Rachel's skirt almost trips her as she careens around the rear of the Stones' wagon. "Are you all right? What happened?"

Janie, her eight-year-old daughter, runs along behind her usually composed mother, and they both stop when they see Gracie lying on the ground.

"Oh my." Rachel grabs Janie's head and crushes her daughter's face into her side to prevent her daughter from seeing the woman crumpled on the ground. "Is she dead?"

"No, she's not. She's quite alive but knocked out. John had to hit her to get her from killing either one of us. Ian's off to get Elizabeth."

Rachel finally notes the awkward way in which I hold my left arm across my chest. "Oh. Are you hurt too?" she asks, reaching for my good arm.

I nod. "She tried to hit me with a flaming stick, and I fell back. I caught myself with my left hand, but I think it's broken." I gingerly remove my arm from my chest, but the movement causes me to take sharp intake of breath. Tears well in my eyes, and I look up at the sky, blinking them back.

"Hurry up, Mrs. Black. I think she's dyin'!" Ian yells as he runs around the wagon and kneels by his mother's side. "Mama? You alive?"

She moans in response.

"She's alive, Mrs. Black, but she don't look so good."

Mrs. Black is a large woman, though her girth has shrunk considerably over the last three and a half months as evidenced by her dress which hangs loosely on her frame. Even so, she cannot keep up with Ian. Mrs. Black—or Elizabeth as most call her—serves as this train's resident medical practitioner, dispensing rum, delivering babies, setting bones, and consoling bereaved parents. She squats next to the prone woman and feels Gracie's face.

"She's comin' 'round. What happened to her?" Elizabeth peers up at Rachel and me, where we stand a safe distance away. What do we say? That she's a crazy old coot who has completely lost her mind and tried to kill her family?

Thankfully, Ian saves us both. "She got real mad. Started swingin' round a torch. Then she tried to light the wagon on fire. Said she wasn't goin' to Oregon no more." His voice drops as he tells the story to Elizabeth. "Sarah got here, and Mama almost kil't her, but then Sarah fell down. I thought Mama was gonna get her, but then Pa got here, and he knocked her right out. Took two swings, but he got her good. Took her torch away, too."

Gracie moans again.

"She's wakin' up. Go get a cup of water, Ian," Elizabeth says.

He races off.

"Is what he said true? I'd imagine it is from the ways she's been worsening the last few weeks, but is it really?" Elizabeth asks me.

"Yes'm."

"Well, you two help me git her up and loaded in. She's in for a bumpy ride today and a bit of a headache. Maybe he knocked some sense into her, though." Elizabeth chuckles to herself and shakes her head as she reaches an arm out to grab Gracie. "Help me out now."

Rachel steps forward and bends over. Together the two women manage to right Gracie, who has opened her eyes and now stares at them in confusion.

Elizabeth croons softly to her, "Now you just stand up now. Right easy. We'll git you to the wagon."

Gracie groans and tries to lay down again.

"Ah no, you don't. You git up I'll give you a nip of that laudanum I got. It'll help yer head now."

Gracie stands slowly, leaning all her weight on Rachel and Elizabeth. The threesome move awkwardly toward the wagon. Gracie pulls herself in just as John arrives with the oxen. He shakes his head in disgust.

"I'll go get her something to settle her down." Elizabeth assures him. "You won't need to worry about her for today at least."

"I thank you for that, Elizabeth." The lead wagons are about ready to head out, but the Stones need a little more time. "Ian," John commands his son, "git on up there and tell Captain Sawyer that we need a half hour or so. I figure he's heard about yer mother's fit, but if not, tell him she's not well. Tell him we'll be comin' along in the back today."

"Yes, sir." Ian runs toward the day's lead wagons.

"Elizabeth?" I say before she can leave. "I'd like you to look at my arm. I fell when Gracie was havin' her fit. It don't feel right."

"Another one? Lordie, is it gonna be one of those days? I'm thinkin' it is," she says in response to her own question. She reaches for my arm. "Lay it out here, girl. I gotta see it if ye're needin' me to fix it."

I gently lower my arm, releasing it from my chest. It no longer makes a straight line from my elbow to my hand. A large, painful bump has grown between my hand and my forearm, and I feel sick to my stomach. Again.

Elizabeth lets out an exasperated sigh. "Come with me," she says before turning to Rachel. "Get me a plank, about this big." She points to my arm and holds her hands about a foot apart.

"A plank?" Rachel asks.

"And some rags or cloth to wrap it in."

"Where might I find a plank without chopping one out of the wagon box?"

"I don't know, but one ain't gonna jump out at you, girl. You gotta go find it. Now git goin'."

Chagrined, Rachel heads toward her wagon, her daughter following close behind.

"You come with me," Elizabeth says. She waves her hand at me and heads toward her wagon.

Most of the others have moved out, so I can clearly see Elizabeth's wagons from where we are. Elizabeth and her husband James have two wagons on this journey. One is filled with their provisions, and the second one is filled with provisions and supplies for the store they plan to open in Oregon. They've even got a few fruit trees packed in barrels of dirt back there. James has big plans to build a store with an orchard and start a thriving business, where he has heard his trees will grow fruit bigger than anyone has ever seen.

He stands next to the oxen, watching his wife. "Is it gonna be a while?" he asks.

"Yep. Up to you whether you want to unhitch the team or not. Don't know how long this'll take." She rummages around in the wagon, and the box bounces with each of her movements. "I gotta take Gracie Stone some laudanum then set this one's arm." Her hand reaches out of the canvas cover and hands her husband a bottle. "Give Sarah a shot of this, would ya?"

James grabs it and heads toward me as he twists off the top. "This'll take the edge off," he says. "Ever have any spirits?"

I think back to the night at Alcove Springs when Mama had fed me some, when I couldn't stop shaking. I nod and eye the bottle warily.

"Well then, you know what's comin'. You got somewhere to ride today?"

"No. I can't go back with the Stones'. I ain't got nowhere right now. I gotta walk till I figure somethin' out."

"Not after my Lizzy's done with you. No way you'll be walkin'. Just take a swig of that, let it settle, then take another one. She'll figure somethin' out for you. You'll be ready for her when she gets back."

"What is it exactly?"

"The finest rum a man can buy. Lizzy swears by it. Take a swig and you'll see what she's talkin' about."

I hold the bottle in my good hand, keeping my left snug to my chest. The lump seems to be getting bigger and more painful with each passing minute.

"Hurry up. The sooner you take that the better you'll feel," he says.

Fumes roil out of the bottle as I lift it toward my mouth, causing me to bend and cough. Pain shoots up my entire arm as the movement jars my broken wrist.

"I don't think I can," I gasp.

Laughter fills the air as James watches me. "Sure you can. Don't smell the stuff. Its vapors don't work. You gotta drink it."

I close my eyes, press the bottle against my lips, and tilt back my head. The warm liquid runs down my throat, burning the back. I feel the liquid travel all the way down into my stomach, like it really is a live snake.

"Let that one settle a minute then take another swig," James advises. "You'll need it, Sarah. You ain't gonna like what's comin'."

I look up into the kind lines of his face and try to trust him. A man who babies and nurses the saplings in his wagon like he does cannot be a cruel man.

"Go on now. You'll be fine."

I lift the bottle and take another swig. This one doesn't burn as badly, and I can already feel a subtle warmth spreading into my limbs. I hand the bottle to James who stoppers it and sets it on the wagon bench.

"We might need that again, young lady." He guides me to the ground so I'm leaning against the wagon's rear wheel.

I wait another few minutes, feeling the rum dull the pain. Soon enough, Elizabeth returns with Rachel close at her heels. Rachel holds up a pile of rags and a small plank for Elizabeth's inspection. With dismay I realize she has wrenched off a plank from her treasured side table, the one piece of furniture she has not thrown out of the wagon to lighten the load. Guilt mingles with the rum in my veins.

"I'm sorry, Rachel."

"Aye. Ye're more important than a table."

"That'll work just fine," Elizabeth tells her before asking me, "Did you get some spirits?"

I give her a weak smile and she turns back to Rachel. "I'm gonna need you fer this. Wrap that plank in some rags so it won't chafe Sarah's arm, then set it here." She points to my lap.

Rachel does as she's told, her face paling as she sees the swelling and bruising on my arm. Sweat beads on her brow, and she begins to take deep breaths to calm herself.

"Do you need a swig too?" Elizabeth asks, chuckling.

"No ma'am, I'll be fine. Just tell me what I need to do."

"You need to set behind Sarah and hold her up and still. If you can't do that, I'll get James to."

I scoot away from the wagon and Rachel moves behind me, squatting in the dirt. She tries to wrap her arms around me but cannot while she's kneeling, so she sits on the ground, her legs stretched out in front of her. She turns her body so I can lean on her, then she wraps her arms around my waist to help hold me up. I realize what she is doing just as I hear a soft gasp come from her. The dress I wear every day has easily hid the small lump growing in my belly, but my dress cannot hide it from Rachel's hands.

She removes her hands from my belly, raises them up closer to my chest and grabs my right hand with her right hand. "Hold on tight here," she whispers. "You'll be fine."

I lean back on her sturdy body and grit my teeth, preparing for the pain. Elizabeth lifts my arm and feels the bones. I grit my teeth to hold in a moan that wants to break free.

"I'm gonna have to pull a bit," Elizabeth tells me. "Take a deep breath."

I do, but it doesn't help. I scream in agony as Elizabeth pulls the crushed bones apart and fits them back together as best she can. Sweat pours from my face, dripping onto my dress as Elizabeth works for a good five minutes. The crunching of my bones washes the rum from my veins.

Finally she finishes and sets my arm on the rag-wrapped plank. She takes the rest of the rags and tightly winds my arm and the plank together.

"Now, if yer fingers turn blue, you gotta loosen it up some," Elizabeth says to me.

"Blue?" I cannot understand what she is saying.

Rachel nods in response. "I'll watch it, Elizabeth."

I sit with my eyes closed, my head thrown back on Rachel's shoulder. "Is it over?"

"It is. We can git goin' now. You just rest today. Don't try walkin'."

"I gotta walk. Ain't got nowhere to ride."

Rachel gently disentangles herself from my grasp and stands, pulling me up behind her with my good arm. "You can ride with me," she says. "We'll figure somethin' out."

I lean heavily on her and head toward her wagon, my arm and plank cradled gently against my chest.

WITHIN A WEEK, Rachel and I have settled into a routine. For the first time since I joined this train, I find moments of relaxation with this kind, soft-spoken woman. I rest for a few moments on a trunk in the wagon bed with Angelina, Rachel's two-year-old, and our bodies sway with the endless jolting and rocking. Even a slight breeze can set the box to moving. These wagons are prairie schooners, ships never settling as they cross the land, jarring every bone and muscle. I pray for stillness, just a single moment of quiet, free from motion, but I know that prayer will not be answered for at least another month, maybe two or even three. And that will only happen if I survive.

Rachel hollers at the oxen and the wagon slows. Her voice, usually so soothing and gentle, becomes a bellow and the wagon halts. Hugging my injured arm close to my chest, I creep over the trunks and toward the front of the wagon.

"Sarah?" Janie squeals, her head framed in the canvas hole in the rear of the wagon. "The cap'n said there's someone here for ya."

She heaves herself over the edge of the rear wagon box and scrambles all the way in. Her cheeks glow red with the excitement of running back to the wagon with news, anything that breaks up the drudgery of a day on the trail deserves attention.

"And ... he's a boy." Her cheeks redden with this news. "I seen him myself."

"A boy? Here? Who is it? What does he look like?" Questions fly out of my mouth without a break as scenarios of Jed finding me run through my brain. Who would come for me? I back up and return to the middle of the wagon, where I'm not so visible. Who is it? Whoever it is, it can't be good. I watch Janie crawl over the goods toward me, and we listen to the jingle of horses coming alongside the wagon. The last time anyone came for me, I had huddled in an Indian lodge, terrified that Nettie would give me up to Jed. I grab Janie's hand and pray it is not Jed sitting that horse just a few feet away.

Finally I whisper to Janie, "Ask your mama who it is."

She looks at me, confusion crossing her face. "Why don't you just come on out?"

"Janie, please."

She crawls to the front of the wagon and peers out. "Mama, who's there?"

"Don't know yet," Rachel replies softly from where she stands beside the team. "Git back on in there now."

"You saw him?" I whisper to Janie. She nods. "What did he look like?"

"He's a man on a horse. He's got a hat."

I want to scream. She gave a perfect description of every man on the trail. I try to hide my frustration. "Anything else? Did you notice anything else about him?"

A horse stops and stamps its feet. Janie shakes her head, then we fall silent as the visitors begin to speak.

"How ya doin', Mrs. Smith?" Captain Sawyer hollers.

"Fine cap'n. You?"

"We're makin' good time today, but even so, this fellow managed to catch us." He pauses to chuckle at his own little joke. The train is no match for a man on horseback. "He says he's lookin' for a woman who might be the young gal we picked up back at Fort Hall. She here with you, or she back with the cattle?"

I wish I could see right through the wagon cover. I close my eyes, take a deep breath and wait to hear who sits on that second horse. Is this a rescue, or will it be an inquisition? Charlie? Jed? Papa? It could even be Joseph or Pierce. Well, maybe not. The captain wouldn't have brought either of them over.

The wagon rocks as Rachel steps on the tongue and lifts herself in. She's smiling as she waves her hand to beckon me outside. "Come on out here." Then she lowers her voice, speaking just to me. "You'll be all right. You're not goin' nowhere you don't want to go. You're welcome to stay with me." Her head disappears as she jumps down from her perch. "She's coming."

As I move toward the wagon's front, Janie grabs my hand and repeats her mother's words. "You'll be all right."

I smile toward her, wondering how my fear is so obvious to the child. "You sure you can't tell me what he looks like?"

"He's just a man on a horse is all."

I see Rachel's back and her bonnet, and when she turns her head, I wave her over. "Can you tell me anything else?"

Her bonnet hides her profile from the men. "Well, he sits a horse well, but it looks like one of his legs ain't quite right. You know him?"

For the first time in weeks, a real smile spreads across my face as relief floods my body. "Blue eyes?"

She shrugs.

My reaction does not escape her gaze. I look down and chew the inside of my lip, trying to hide my feelings, compose myself before I see his face: a face I've dreamed about for weeks, months even.

"She comin'?" asks the captain again. "I gotta get back to my team." His voice is harsh now. He's annoyed at the interruption this visitor has made to the tedium of his day.

I crawl to the front of the wagon as best I can. "I'm right here."

Charlie sits on his old horse. My stomach drops. Why is he here? How did he find me? I have no idea what to do. Should I approach him?

"Sarah?" The smile that had lit his face when I'd first emerged from the wagon has tempered into a look of concern. His blue eyes study me for wounds or scars, but he can only see a sunbaked, dust covered young woman with her arm tied to a plank with filthy rags. This seems to settle him. I'm broken but alive. "You all right?"

I cannot reply.

After pulling his cane from its holder behind his saddle, he dismounts, props his cane against his body, and reaches for the pack behind his saddle. He pulls a bundle from its depths, balancing on his one good leg as it takes two hands to untie the bundle.

"I got somethin' fer you," he says. He grabs his cane and waits as I clamber awkwardly down from my perch to stand next to Rachel.

"Is this the one?" the captain asks him.

"Yes, sir. This is the one." I don't know where to look, so I finally settle on Charlie's boots. They are barely holding together, the leather soles are worn thin. The toe on his good foot looks like it about has a hole worn right through it. I wonder that he hasn't patched it somehow with his tools.

Finally the captain breaks the silence and his gaze moves between Charlie and me. "Well, I gotta ask, young man. Who're you? That ol' trapper that had her said she's a widow, and it sounds to me like she is. Ya'll come back from the dead?" He laughs at his joke, though he is the only one who does. It does nothing to break the palpable tension in our small group.

Rachel gasps at his audacity and reaches out to grab my shaking hand. I hold on tight to her fingers, thankful for her strength.

Charlie reaches up and tilts his hat back, looking into my eyes for the first time. "A widow?"

He's asking for help, wanting to protect me, to not reveal any secrets I'm hiding. I give him an almost imperceptible nod, but it is enough. "So he died, did he?"

Rachel squeezes my arm, and I feel breath begin to flow into my lungs. I hadn't realized I had even been holding it. "He did. He, uh..." I wonder how thick I should weave this lie. "He got sick, and the trapper found us just after he died. I couldn't even bury him without Mr. Pierce's help. I didn't know if another train would take me on. I didn't know what to do, so I went with them."

The captain watches our exchange. I wish he would leave, but he won't. Not until he gets the whole story here.

He looks at Charlie and asks again, "So who are you? Why didn't you go find her before this? Ain't it been a while?"

Charlie stares at the man for a moment before answering. "I'm her brother-in-law." He watches me as he says this then turns back toward the captain. He raises his eyebrows. "And to answer your last question, captain, let me ask you one. Does every man get along on this train? Have you had any families split off cuz they just can't figure out how to get along?"

The captain nods sagely, knowing the difficulties of this trip and the conflicts families have had with one another. We all know it.

"Well, her husband, my brother, refused to stay with the train, and we figured they'd joined up with another. We had no idea anything was wrong till we got word of her at Fort Hall."

I watch Charlie during this entire exchange, and the captain turns and catches sight of me staring. I manage to drop my eyes just as Charlie turns toward me, but I don't think I have done it fast enough. His wife will wheedle every single bit of information out of the captain.

"You made yer point, son. Let's get this wagon goin', Rachel."

He heads back to his wagon at the lead of the train which has continued to move past us, providing each and every wagon with all kinds of gossip. I dread setting camp tonight and wonder which woman will come visiting first.

"We best get moving, Sarah," says Rachel softly. "Janie can stay with Angelina if you'd like."

"I'd like that, thank you. I'll walk with Charlie."

She stares at his leg, twisted and small. "He can't walk, can he?"

But Charlie only smiles as Rachel's cheeks redden in realization of her comment's rudeness. "I can walk just fine, ma'am. I can go faster on a horse, though, so I'll ride. Sarah can walk with me if that's all right with you."

Though my arm throbs, I'm ready to get out of the wagon. "I'll be fine," I assure Rachel.

As soon as I am clear of the wagon, Rachel picks up her whip and gives it a fine crack above the teams' heads as she hollers. They slowly resume their amble westward.

The wagon creaks along, leaving Charlie and me behind and alone for the first time in months. I had thought I would never see him again, and he'd thought I was dead. Despite the dirt covering every inch of his clothing and face, my breath hitches. He has tilted his hat back a bit, so I can see his eyes and his entire face. A scraggly beard has started to grow, but it is his eyes which take the breath from my chest. They are clear and blue and looking right into me. I have to look down.

"Whaddya got in that bundle?" I finally manage to whisper.

He smiles and hands me package he had removed from his horse. "Yer Mama wanted you to have this. If it really was you I was chasin', that is."

The bundle is soft, covered in a muslin wrap and tied with twine. I untie the knots and peel back the wrapping. I gasp as the colors of my quilt peek from beneath the filthy muslin covering. The green leaves, the blocks signed by dear friends, the hours spent with Granny. A smile crosses his face as I pull the quilt close to my chest and swipe a hand across my face.

"How did you get this?"

Mama never had my quilt. Nettie had it, which means Mama somehow found Nettie.

Charlie doesn't answer.

I can't think of any scenario where Mama finding my quilt over the shoulders of an old Indian squaw could end up good. "How did you get it? What happened?"

"Walk with me. I'll tell you, but you ain't gonna like it." He says, confirming my dread. "But first, why'd you run off?"

I ignore his question. "What happened? How did you get my quilt? You tell me, Charlie Dixon. Tell me now." I sound whiny and petulant, even to myself. I clench the quilt to my chest and glare at him.

He surveys me like he is surveying stock at an auction. I feel the same humiliation I did when Pierce had traded me off to this train. My dress is filthy as I have felt no desire to wash it and saw no need. My face has darkened with the sun, a bonnet Rachel loaned me shoved in some corner of the her wagon. Loose strands of hair fly wildly about my head, and the tears I'd shed over the quilt probably ran dust tracks down my face. I withstand his scrutiny for a full minute, bearing it, until he finally speaks.

"Looks like we both got stories to tell," he says. At that, he mounts up then clicks to his horse and ambles away. "You comin'?"

He'd said he wanted to walk with me and now he's just riding away, but no matter how happy I am that he's here, I refuse to chase him. I want to pelt his back with rocks, make the horse throw Charlie's mean, insensitive self right onto his backside so he'd have to answer all of my questions, but I know I won't throw a rock at him. Just as I know he isn't going to say a word unless I tell him why I ran.

Clouds of dust spew up from the wagons' wheels and animals' hooves. How had he gotten the quilt? Nettie would not have given it up. That meant she and Pierce had to have been at Fort Hall when the Dixon train arrived. How long had they stayed? How far behind this train were my parents? Did Papa kill Nettie or Pierce for it? Did Mama? Did Papa buy it back? No, he wouldn't have bought what he would have viewed as rightfully his, and he probably didn't care much about the quilt anyway. But Mama would have. I watch Charlie's back and decide it doesn't much matter anyway. I have my quilt back, and Charlie is here.

No matter how infuriating I find him, I cannot deny my pleasure at seeing him. Despite that, deny it I must. I'm pregnant, and he knows I'm no widow. He needs to leave before he figures that out.

160

Charlie heads to the far edge of the wagons where he can ride outside of the dust. He doesn't once look back to see if I have followed. I head in the opposite direction and search for Rachel's wagon. She is not far ahead. If I walk with her, Charlie can't see me from where he's riding, and I won't be tempted to watch him.

I could feel his anger at me. He's like a parent who is worried when their child runs off then gets furious instead of relieved and ecstatic when the child is found. If he doesn't tell me, he can find his supper elsewhere, and if he thinks I will be filling him in on the real reason I left, he is dead wrong. He needs to leave, and hopefully he already has.

Chapter 18

Present Day

"CHARLIE RETURNED THE quilt to Sarah when he caught up with her," Agnes says while I type. "Her mama had fixed it. That's why the stitches look a little different." She studies the tear and presses it between her fingers. "It's stiffer here. I always wondered if she stitched something else in there, but none of that is in the letter."

I look up at her from my note taking. Letter?

She caresses the seam with her hands. I reach over and feel it too. I want to ask about the letter, but I don't want to confuse Agnes. This is frustrating. One thought at a time.

"What kinds of things do you think she might have sewn into it? She wouldn't have had the same kind of filling as she had in Indiana, would she?"

Agnes rubs the repaired seam between her fingers. "Maybe part of the canvas from her wagon, something she could have written on. Maybe it's a thin piece of leather that Charlie worked for her. He was a leather smith, you know." She closes her eyes, remembering.

I take advantage of her pause to change the subject, hoping I won't confuse her. "Agnes, what letter are you talking about?"

She looks at me blankly. Crap.

"Letter?"

I nod gently. "You mentioned a letter. Did Sarah write a letter?"

"No." Her hands tense around the quilt.

I wait while she searches her mind. "It's okay, Agnes. You can tell me later."

Her silence drags on. Finally, she looks at me, questioning me.

"The letter? You mentioned a letter that talks about the tear somehow. Who wrote the letter? Do you know where it is?"

I've made the mistake of stringing together too many questions, and I want to kick myself. It's too hard for me to remember all the best ways to communicate with her. I hate it, and it's hard not to take out my frustration on Agnes.

She finally begins to speak. "It's … it's Charlie's letter. Charlie's letter to Sarah." Her face relaxes into a smile as she accesses the memory of the letter.

"Do you still have it?"

She nods.

"Is it here?"

She slowly shakes her head.

I feel like I'm playing I-Spy or Twenty Questions like we used to when I was younger. "Is it in your trunk where the quilt was?"

"Yes, with the quilt."

I stare out the window at the rain matting down the fallen leaves. The letter will fill in some of the gaps. Except now that I don't have my key, I have no excuses for being in Agnes' house. Rosemary hasn't contacted me again about the quilt, but if she catches me breaking in, she will. But I'm not sure which scares me more? Rosemary having me arrested or me coming one day to visit and Agnes not knowing Sarah or Charlie? Or me?

I STAND AT the kitchen sink and stare out the window at Agnes' empty house. It is no longer a safe haven. I miss walking through the gate and visiting. I miss listening to Agnes sing to herself as she puttered around her backyard garden. I miss my friend. The quilt sits on the kitchen table. I pull it out of its bag and feel the stitches. My hands come across the tear, and I wonder what happened. Who fixed the tear? What's in there? The answer is in Agnes' trunk, and I want that answer.

The quilt situation cannot possibly get any worse. I've become a liar and been accused of being a thief. So why not become one for real and go find Charlie's letter? I decide to go for it before I overthink the very idea. I scurry out the back door, through the gate, and up Agnes' back steps. Hopefully, the hide-a-key is still under the third planted pot from the left, and Rosemary has no idea about it. I smile when I spot it under the planter and unlock the back door.

The house is musty but still smells like Agnes' house – a mix of lavender from her garden, old books, and coffee. I head upstairs. The plants are still in the bathtub with a little bit of water. That's good. At least Rosemary is taking care of them. I wonder when she is planning on putting the house up for sale. I'd like to ask her, but I think I've probably lost any hope of a civil conversation with her ever again. To her I am nothing but a criminal, and as I look around me, I realize that right now, I am exactly that. I have officially broken and entered into a home with the intent of taking something. I say a quick prayer that Rosemary has no idea this letter exists.

I open the trunk. It's still full of all sorts of linens, so I pull out a few stacks of them and set them on the floor next to me. Kneeling, I dig through the fabric until I see the yellowed corner of a large envelope peeking out from beneath the last stack of little embroidered doilies.

Agnes has written "Sarah" on the front in her spidery script. The envelope is thick. I reach in and pull out a stack. First I see the leather covering of a small, ancient notebook. I gently lift the cover and see "Rebecca Laney Crawford." My breath hitches. Rebecca's diary? Agnes never told me. The writing is faded and will take time to decipher. I set it on the floor. Next in the pile is a smaller envelope. Agnes has written "From Charlie to Sarah." I feel like I found a winning lottery ticket, even though it is merely an ancient letter from one lover to another.

I set the letter on the bed and put the diary back into the larger envelope, trying to calm myself. I return the linens to the trunk, hoping they're in the same order they came out, though I seriously doubt Rosemary would notice any difference. I wonder if she's ever even looked in here, to figure out what family heirlooms she even actually owns or if she's only focused on the one she doesn't have. Does she know about this envelope of her family history? I can't imagine that she does. She'd have taken it, or maybe she's really not interested.

I perch on the edge of Agnes' bed and take a deep breath as I reach for the letter. The rest can wait. I want to read this now. I gently open the envelope, and pull the pages out with the tips of my fingers. They are yellowed and incredibly faded, almost illegible. I can barely read some of it, but I begin deciphering it anyway.

My dearest Sarah,
I am writing to tell you why I am here. I thought you'd be pleased
to see me. It seems, however, I was wrong.
When we woke and found you gone, your ma collapsed. She could
not take finding you missing so close to losing Katie. She refused to
speak or leave the wagon. Your Pa organized a search party. The watch
hadn't heard Indians the night before, so we didn't know what to make
of you being gone. We all thought you'd been stolen and prayed that
we'd find you before they could hurt you or kill you, but I'll be honest
and tell you that I didn't think that would happen. We broke into
groups and headed out with no signs at all as to where you'd gone. It
was as if you'd vanished into thin air. As for me, I have never felt so
guilty. I'd told you to accept Jed's hand even though that's not what I
wanted. I thought that was for the best. Maybe he could provide for
you better than me. As I rode that morning, I prayed that the lies I
told you were not why you left.
When we returned to the wagons that evening, I learned that
nobody had found any sign of you anywhere except for some horse and
moccasin tracks some five miles to the northeast, but we didn't know
if those had anything to do with your vanishing. That evening, your
Pa began to organize the party to continue searching the next day,
but some of the men on the train refused to allow it. They argued, and
the camp divided. Your Ma wouldn't leave. She begged and pleaded
with my Pa as the train's captain to allow the party one more day
to search. I've never heard such cries of agony from a woman and
don't wanna ever hear them again. Jed wanted to move on, to reach
Oregon before winter. I stood with your father to stay and look for
you. It was at this point that I truly began to realize my feelings and
Jed's. I let him know I was disgusted with him wanting to leave you
behind. We argued around the campfire that night. I cannot tell you
the exact words that we threw at one another, but they led to punches.
We fought. Jed's a bigger man, and since he's got full use of his legs,
well, he can just stand up better. My ma cried and begged us to stop
as we rolled around. The other men tried to break us up, but Jed got
the better of me when he grabbed a rock and swung it at my head.
If not for your Pa, I'd probably be dead. He grabbed Jed's arm so the
rock still made contact with my skull, but not with the full force of his
strength. I remember nothing else after this until the next day when
the bell rang to break camp. I lay in the wagon, the worst headache
of my life. I'd just about rather die than live with that pain and
knowing you were gone fer good.
Tommy told me that the men stayed up late into the night trying

165

to decide on a punishment for Jed. Some saw his actions as attempted murder and felt he should hang, others saw our fight as nothing more than a fight between two young hot-headed cousins. It was far more than that. I'd a killed him and he me, had your Pa not separated us. My father finally won out, convincing the train that we needed Jed to survive, we needed all the healthy young men we could use, but your Pa refused to have him work for him any longer. I worried that with your Ma in such a state and you gone that your family would not make it.

Your Ma begged to stay behind and join with the next train coming, but he refused. If you'd been taken by hostile Indians, he wouldn't risk losing any more of his children to the same fate as a lone wagon in this wilderness. Following his declaration, we heard no more from her.

In the following days, your sister and your brother grew up, doing all the chores you, your Ma, and Jed used ta do. I couldn't do nothing but lay in the wagon and nurse my head and bruises, feeling like the weakest man alive.

We began to move that morning, and I asked my Ma how your family was doing. She said that your Ma had not spoken a word since we left. The losses on this journey continue, more every day it seems, and I wonder if in the end it will have been worth it, or if we are merely chasing a dream. Maybe we'll know someday. Your Ma refused to get outta the wagon fer three days. My Ma and Pa prayed for her sanity, but in all honesty, I thought of those prayers as somewhat futile.

I rub my eyes which ache from squinting at the small text. Agnes' telling of Sarah's story hadn't fully conveyed the agonies of the journey, or perhaps I had only romanticized it in my head. I think back to old re-runs of *Little House on the Prairie*. In the later ones, they even have a restaurant in their little town, and I realize how truly ridiculous that was. Agnes always wanted me to read the books, and maybe I should have instead of just watching the show. Frontier life pretty much sucked. I flip through the pages. Three more. I squint again at the teeny script.

After three days, the trail made a turn toward the southwest and Fort Bridger, and we saw your Ma fer the first time, though she wasn't talking at all. When we reached the Green River, we laid by for two days, and it was then, while she washed, that she discovered your favorite quilt was missing. She'd dug it out to be closer to ya. I heard her hollering for your sister, yelling about a quilt. Eliza couldn't answer her questions bout it. Finally your brother admitted that you had it after Katie died. He figured you got it when you got out the quilt for your sister's grave. He'd forgotten it.

Your Ma then called me to her side and began to question me. For the first time since little Katie died and you vanished, she sounded a bit more like herself. She asked if you ever mentioned the quilt, and I told her of our talks of it. She became convinced that you had not been kidnapped but that you had run away and taken the quilt with you. We both understood, without saying, what you were running from and hoped that you had joined with a train in front of us or trailing behind us. If that hadn't happened, you were surely dead, your quilt as a shroud, somewhere out in this lonesome, never-ending land. We didn't want to think on this and felt heartened that maybe we'd see you again someday at the end of this God forsaken trail.

The letter draws me in, and I have no idea how long I read, trying to decipher the faded scrawl on the page, pausing frequently to try to imagine the scenes as Charlie describes them. So absorbed am I in the writing, that I hear it too late: the sound of a key in the front door, the squeak of it opening, the ancient screen door banging, then Rosemary's voice gently telling Agnes to be careful and not trip.

Oh. My. God.

Every single floor board in this house squeaks. If I walk anywhere, they'll hear me. I grab the envelope and slink off the side of the bed where I huddle, weighing my options.

In our last encounter, she said she would have no problem accusing me of stealing a family heirloom—which I didn't steal—but how the hell will I prove that if I'm found here, actually stealing a family heirloom. My heart races. If Rosemary finds me, she'll have me arrested, without question. Her feet hit the bottom stairs. Thankfully, I'm on the side of the bed away from the door. I lie all the way down and try my damndest to scoot underneath Agnes' bed, feeling like a ridiculous fool playing hide and seek, but for real this time. Hopefully, nobody comes to this side of the room because Agnes has so much crap underneath her bed that I can't fit all the way. I try to fluff the bed skirt over me, but I'm hiding about as well as I did when I was four and could never figure out how my babysitters always knew where I was.

I think back to what I have done in the past hour. I'm fairly sure I re-locked the back door. I know I put everything back in the trunk. Did I shut the lid? I think I did, but I can't remember exactly.

167

Agnes and Rosemary slowly progress up the stairs, and I realize how much Agnes has deteriorated, but I'm thankful she's slowed down as much as she has. It means Rosemary is slow too. As I listen to their laborious progress, I finally admit that Agnes probably couldn't be living on her own, though I don't think the facility she's at is the best choice either.

They enter Agnes' room, and I hold my breath. "Sit down in your rocker here mother," Rosemary says. The old chair creaks with Agnes' weight. "I'm going to give your plants a drink."

Agnes makes all these loud sighing noises as she rocks, but I can't tell her mood from them. She's either happy to be at home but angry that she's not still living here, confused about where she is at all, or annoyed that Rosemary is yelling at her like she's deaf.

I look at the underside of Agnes' box spring and try to calm my heart. One time when I was about ten, I found a small bird that had fallen out of its nest. I carried it in my cupped hands all the way home. I couldn't see the nest in the tree, and even if I had I couldn't have climbed the tree to put the baby bird back in it. The bird's heart raced like a little jackhammer the entire time despite my trying to talk to it and calm it down. Laying underneath the bed, listening to Agnes' agitation, I feel like the little bird must have felt, lost, heart racing, being carried away by something much larger than itself with no power whatsoever to stop it from happening.

I hear the water run in the bathtub for a few minutes, then Rosemary speaks. "Mother, I'm going downstairs. Do you want to come or stay?"

Agnes doesn't reply, and Rosemary's heavier footsteps head back down the hall and the stairs to the first floor.

I'm trying not to hold my breath, to breathe steady and listen. They can't be here for much longer. Agnes' rocker creaks, once, twice, and then I hear her shuffling footsteps. I turn my head to the side and try to see where she went. I can't see her feet, so maybe she left. Then I hear a little gasp and her feet appear, heading in my direction. Oh God.

She kicks me hard in the side. I suck in a yell and squeeze my eyes shut. At any other time, I might be able to see the humor in this situation, but right now? Not even a little bit. I stay where I am and pray that Agnes thinks I'm a box or something. Her feet are still there and then her face appears as she lifts up the bed skirt.

Her old face lights up with a smile when she sees me hiding under there, like an insect under a rock. "Harper," she croaks.

I stare at her and try to communicate with my eyes, but she completely fails to read the panic in my face. I put my finger to my lips. "Shh. Don't say anything to Rosemary."

She nods, and I pray that she understands.

"Go sit back down."

At this she looks a little hurt. Her eyebrows knit together and her eyes squint a bit. She waves me out from under the bed. "Come out."

"Agnes, quiet," I hiss. "Go sit down in your rocker."

"Out." She waves her hand at me. She is not going to go sit down, and it seems she has forgotten how to whisper.

"I can't. I don't want to see Rosemary." A lucid, younger Agnes would completely understand my dilemma. This Agnes? Not at all. For a moment, a brief flash, I hate this old woman who is bent over, staring at me, not understanding anything. I need her to figure this out, and she can't. If it wasn't for her, I wouldn't be laying under a bed like a common criminal, clutching an ancient letter, the evidence of my crime. My throat tightens as I stare at a face I love so much. If she could only come back for a few minutes right now and understand.

"Here," I whisper and shove the letter toward Agnes. "Take this, and go sit back down."

She reaches for it, her face relaxing, but she doesn't leave. She shuffles her feet around and sits on the bed on top of me, almost crushing my face as the mattress lowers an inch or two with her weight.

I poke my head out from under the bed. "Agnes, stand up." I try to be as firm as possible but it's really hard to convey my panic when I'm whispering.

She ignores me and looks at the letter in her hands.

I'm going to have to take her back to her chair. Rosemary is puttering in the kitchen, turning the water on and off at intervals. Still watering. I scoot out from underneath the bed skirt, roll over, and kneel in front of Agnes.

I reach toward her. "Let's get back to your chair."

She smiles and takes my hand. We stand together and traverse the room. I think my heart is going to leap from my chest. As Agnes sits, Rosemary's footsteps cross the front room toward the stairs.

Shit. Shit. Shit. I smile at Agnes, put my finger to my lips and run back to my hiding place which now has pages of antique, yellowed paper scattered across it. I grab the sheets and pile them up. Agnes must have dropped them when I hurried her back to her chair.

"Mother? Is that you?" Rosemary calls and her feet speed up.

Agnes is silent, as I lie down and scrunch myself into the space under the bedskirt.

"Harper?" Agnes says.

I cringe and shut my eyes, as if that will help me stay hidden. It worked when I was little, so what the hell. My heart hammers in my chest. Agnes' voice cracks a little as she says my name again. I cower down further, not completely hidden, but willing my body to shrink.

"No, Mother. Harper isn't here." Rosemary enters the room. "What's this?" It's quiet for a long moment, and Rosemary takes a few more steps. I'm guessing she's moving toward Agnes to get whatever pages of the letter Agnes managed to hang on to. "Mother? What is this?"

I hear the old paper crinkling, and I guess that Rosemary has taken the pages from her mother's grasp.

"Charlie's letter," Agnes says, her voice raspy from disuse. I wonder if she's getting sick or if it's the aging that's making her sound like a pale version of herself.

"Whose letter?"

"Charlie's. To Sarah."

"Where did you get this?"

I'm doomed. I'm sure of it. Agnes, bless her shriveled little brain, remains silent, but only for a moment. "Harper?" Her small voice reaches toward some sort of validation I can't give.

"No, Mother. Harper isn't here."

For the first time in my life, I don't hate Rosemary. I hate myself.

"Let's get you home. I think maybe this wasn't a very good idea."

"Rose, Harper gave it to me."

Agnes sounds sure of herself this time, and I hope Rosemary thinks this is one of her mother's more confused moments. An immense wave of guilt washes over me for wanting Agnes' disease to get worse to save my sorry, thieving ass.

Rosemary lets out a big sigh. "Come on, let's get you up." The rocking chair moves against the floor, and I hear their footsteps head toward the door.

I try not to breathe too loudly in relief.

"Mother, don't cry," Rosemary says as they leave the room.

Now I feel like a real asshole. Agnes sniffs as she navigates the stairway. Is she crying? She's completely lucid, but nobody believes her. Their steps head out the door which slams behind them. I pick up the remaining pages and sort of run, all hunched over, to the front bedroom. Thankfully, lacy curtains cover the window, and I can peek out without completely revealing myself. Rosemary has parts of the letter, and I had only read through half of it. I truly hope she has what I already read, but who knows. Rosemary helps Agnes into the car and I see the rest of the letter poking neatly out of her purse.

This sucks.

As soon as Rosemary's blue sedan disappears down the street, I run to the back door, let myself out, lock it, and flee for home, trying not to grip the pages of Charlie's letter and the envelope with Rebecca's diary too tightly. I pray my sweaty hands won't smear the writing, making the words even more difficult to read. When I finally reach the safety of my kitchen, I set the stolen letter on the table and turn on the water to make tea, needing desperately to relax. My heart still races, and I wonder how people can become criminals. I hate this panicky feeling, but then I guess some people thrive on the adrenaline rush. I want to drink tea and take a nice long nap on the couch.

While the water heats, I put the pages into some semblance of a pile. I have five pages of the letter, but I can't remember how long it actually was. Eight pages? Ten? I grab an empty file folder from my mom's old filing cabinet, place the letter in it, then carry it to the kitchen table where I gently spread out the sheets. I have no idea what I have and what Rosemary has. Charlie wrote on both sides of each sheet, but they are not numbered. The sheets are small, maybe four inches by five inches. I find the first page and begin sorting through the rest. I am missing two of the pages that I've already read, but I have three that I haven't. From what I could see sticking out of Rosemary's purse, Agnes has at least two pages, but she might have four or five. I think I read five pages. I re-read the last page and begin the slow process of deciphering Charlie's faded scrawl, putting them in order as I read.

As our train wound on through the desolation, I wondered if I should go after you, but I knew my father wouldn't ever allow it, and I couldn't tell Jed. Every time I saw him, I thought of all the times I ignored his meanness. I knew this last time led to you leaving. I wanted to kill him.

The train headed south toward Fort Bridger. We laid by there for three days to rest the stock, wash, and trade. Nobody there had seen you. We all expected much more than the lone building there. It was a desolate place. We headed out on July 23. The trail turned north toward Fort Hall, our next stop.

I have a difficult time deciphering the rest of this page. My sweaty hands had smeared the already faded pencil writing, smudging the words beyond recognition. The best I can tell it is a brief narrative about the weather and their progress toward Fort Hall. The next page is relatively free from smears, but I can't tell if I've missed a page.

We reached Fort Hall in the mid-morning. I looked forward to arriving, but was sorely disappointed with the actual fort. Pa wanted to check it out but not lay by since we had gotten rested and re-stocked at Fort Bridger. Prices were high. It's plain thievery what they charge for supplies out here. The Fort itself was hardly worthy of the name fort, but it seems you must know this already.

We stopped the wagons a ways off and a group approached the building on foot. An Indian squaw stood near the door to the trading post. There was a young Indian man near her. Nobody paid much attention to them until your Pa ran back to the wagons. I had stayed back at the wagon, and we all watched as your Pa, his anger clear with the set of his jaw, pointed toward the fort and grabbed his rifle. I still did not understand what was bothering him, but we all could see the anger on his face. Your Ma asked him why he needed his gun, but he refused to answer, just turned and headed back. We followed behind. Your Ma's hands were all twisted up in her apron which she hadn't taken off. She ordered Eliza and Tommy to stay with the wagon but they weren't bout to listen with the guns out.

We'd avoided the Indians as much as we could as they'd steal us blind if we'd let them, so my father didn't like what he saw. He hollered at me to grab his rifle as he headed up to the Fort behind your parents. By the time we all had got there, a white trapper came out of the store and sat next to the squaw. He was a filthy looking man with a tangled beard halfway down his chest. I didn't know what your pa meant by approaching him. He didn't say a word, just pointed at the squaw. When your ma got close enough to see the Indian woman, she stopped cold in her tracks. We could finally see what the squaw held. Wrapped tightly in her arms was your missing quilt. She had it rolled up in a tight bundle. Dirt covered it, but I could see the colors and the blocks. Your ma walked right up to that squaw, grabbed at it, but she held tight. The trapper grabbed your Ma's arm and pulled his rifle right out. Everyone got real still. The squaw never made a sound but she kept her eyes on your Ma. She didn't lower her head none either. Your pa was standing behind your ma, his rifle in his hand but when he saw trapper's gun he started talking all soft. He had your ma's arm in his hand, and I could see him trying to pull her back. Eliza hid behind me but Tommy would have none of that. He ran right up to the trapper and your pa.

At this point, my Pa approached with his rifle and a soldier came out of the fort as well to try to sort the mess out. It didn't help none. Your Pa shouldered his gun, right close to the trapper and demanded the trapper tell him where he got the quilt from. The trapper just laughed, and your mama crumpled to the ground letting out an awful cry. We all thought the worst. The trapper got all serious then and pointed at the guns, told your pa to put his gun up.

I want to scream. That's all I have.

What happened next? I can't get the rest of the pages from Rosemary, which means I need to get the rest of the story from Agnes. I lean my head in my hands and groan. Maybe I can call in sick, so I can spend some more time with Agnes.

I check the time on my phone. It's 6:30, and I wonder if that's too late to go. I know Agnes has a tougher time at night, but maybe not tonight.

By the time I finally pull up it's after eight, and I'm surprised to find the Manor's front door unlocked. I'd thought they'd lock up in the evening so random people like myself couldn't walk in off the street. The lobby is deserted: no nurses, no residents, no noise. It's not that late, but this place feels like it's about midnight. Now I do feel like some sort of intruder or thief—again. Should I tiptoe down the hallway to Agnes' room? Maybe I should have called her first. What if she's asleep? What if I scare her?

Well, it's too late now. I knock softly, but she doesn't respond. I try the handle. I wonder if these rooms are ever locked as I push the door open. Agnes sits up in bed watching TV.

Her face lights up when she sees me. "Rosemary?"

I walk all the way to her bed. "Hi Agnes. It's me, Harper."

She frowns and pats the bed next to her. "You're my Rosemary."

I fight a moment of panic. Do I argue with her, try to get her to see who I am, or do I go with it? I decide to go with it. I've done it all my life, so why stop now?

"Hi."

Her face relaxes, and she smiles at me. "Cocoa?"

"I, uh, don't know how to make it here."

"Oh." She pats my hand. "How was school today?"

I'm not sure if she's talking to me or to Rosemary, and I don't want to upset her. "It was good. I like my teacher."

Coming this late was obviously a bad idea. She falls silent, and I pick up the remote to turn off the TV. She doesn't seem to notice at all. The room is dark except for the light coming in the window from the street lamps outside, a cozy glow.

"Can you tell me a story?" I ask.

"Mm-hmm."

I lean back on the bed next to her. "Tell me about Sarah, your great grandma."

She purses her lips and looks toward the ceiling, searching for the stories, for the words in the tangled neurons of her mind. I grasp her hand in mine. She leans her head back against her pillows and begins to talk, slowly and haltingly telling me about Sarah and Charlie and their deep love for one another, a love to which neither can admit. I put my legs on the bed next to her and lie down. I want to ask about the letter, but I don't want to upset her. She's pretty confused right now.

She pats my head, even makes shushing noises, as if I am her long grown baby girl that she gets to tuck in one last time. For once she looks peaceful, even though the words don't come easily. She speaks hesitantly, and I fill in words when I can figure out the one she wants. The stories don't flow. She seems to bounce between stories with long pauses in between. I don't mind. I feel safe here. She isn't alone. And neither am I.

I awake in the middle of the night, my right arm sound asleep. I get up from the bed, cover Agnes, then move to the couch where I drape an afghan over me and crash. I awaken to the nurse shaking me.

"Who are you? What are you doing here?"

I sit up, alarmed. "What time is it?"

An older woman in the room in her nurse's scrubs heads in my direction. "6:00 am. Who are you? You shouldn't be here!" she hisses in my face.

I glance at Agnes, who sleeps soundly. "I'm a friend. I was visiting

174

last night, and I guess we both fell asleep. Sorry. I'll leave."

"Get out now, or I am going to be forced to call the police." She backs away from me, eyes narrowed.

Really? I reach for my head and try to smooth down my hair. Do I look that bad? "You don't need to do that. I'm leaving."

"You aren't immediate family. We can't have people coming in off the streets."

I stare at her, stunned by her arrogance. "Then maybe you should lock the doors."

Her eyebrows lift, and she heads toward the telephone.

Agnes mumbles in her sleep. I do not want her to see this. I grab my backpack and head toward the door. "No, no, no. Really, I'm sorry. I didn't mean that. You don't need to call. I'm leaving. I didn't mean to spend the night, but she was up late and we both must have fallen asleep."

She glares at me. "Don't let it happen again."

I pause at the door and watch her check on Agnes. I can only guess that she's making sure she's still breathing. That's comforting. Wouldn't want any family members to stumble in on corpses. I guess that would be bad PR.

I head home where I spend the day reading and sorting through the memorabilia in the envelope. I was hoping for Sarah's sketchbook but that isn't there though there are some ancient unlabeled photographs of stern looking people and a yellowed newspaper article with names I don't recognize.

Though the quilt situation with Rosemary is still a disaster, Sarah's story is finally beginning to take shape and for the first time in a long time, I begin to see the end of it and hope I can actually finish writing the story and putting together the disjointed snippets of Sarah's story Agnes has told me.

Chapter 19

THE SCOUTS FIND a spot to camp with plentiful feed and water for the stock this evening. There is no sign of Charlie. Has he gone to the captain's wagon for his supper, or did he turn back toward his family's train? I wonder for a moment then dismiss the thought as I cannot allow myself to hope for anything. I break some tough sage from the rugged bushes. It's the only fuel we have to build a fire, and it's a bugger to try to collect enough to cook with—especially since I can really only use one hand. We finally manage to collect a small pile, and Rachel gets it lit despite the strong breeze blowing from the west. The meager flames flicker against Rachel's intent face while Angelina plays near her skirts, stacking small rocks.

"Can I help you with anything?" Charlie's voice comes from behind the wagon. We both turn, but only Rachel smiles at the sound of his voice.

"No sir, but I thank thee for asking. Sarah might need help. She's heading off to see to the stock, if you'd like to help her." I stare at Rachel, surprised at how easily and seemingly innocently she manages to put Charlie in my path.

"Would you like some help?" he asks.

"You didn't leave," I answer.

He draws his eyebrows down and looks at me in confusion. "Where would I go? I just got here."

"I figured you delivered the quilt, so you might have headed back."

He chuckles to himself and gazes across the barren, rock strewn plain. Finally he takes a deep breath and looks straight at me, right into my eyes.

"I came all this way to find you Sarah, not just make a delivery. I thought I lost you once already and …" He pauses and studies me. He breaks his gaze by looking toward Rachel who is stirring the beans but listening intently. "Can we go get the stock?"

"Why don't you two go get some water?" Rachel suggests softly. "We could use some more.

I head toward the back of the wagon to retrieve a bucket. At least the Snake River is accessible from this camp, not hundreds of feet below us in a deep ravine. As we start to walk he continues talking, as if he hadn't ever stopped.

"I ain't losin' you again," he says.

My heart lurches. Those are words I have dreamed of hearing, but I can't take them from him, not now. I keep my eyes on the ground, knowing they will betray my lie if I look at his face while I speak the next words.

"You might as well leave. There ain't nothin' for you here."

As I utter those words, a small bubble pops in my belly, a butterfly spreading its wings and flying. I had thought earlier it might be too many beans, but it is more than that. It is the child, quickening. I want more than anything to reach my good hand toward my belly and touch the baby back, but I clench my fist, willing it to stay at my side.

Charlie grabs my closed fist and stops walking, forcing me to stop too. He stands close, close enough that I can smell his Charlie smell of salty sweat, the dust from the trail, his horse, and the leather he's always playing with.

"I don't believe you."

My breath hitches, and I take a step back. He is too close. I feel my face reddening, and I yank my arm from his grasp. I can't talk to him now.

"Rachel needs help. Why don't you get the water? And then you can tell us both how you found me and all about the quilt. She really wants to hear the story."

He harrumphs as I walk away, then I hear the crunch of his footsteps behind me. "Runnin' again, huh Sarah?" he says to my back.

I stop walking and take a deep breath as he continues. "Seems to be the easiest thing for you to do. Don't know why I'd think you'd do any different now."

My nervousness and fear instantly changes to anger. I turn to face him. "How dare you. You have no idea what ye're talkin' about."

"You're right. Cuz you run instead of telling anyone what's goin' on." He walks right on past, not looking at me, just leaving me standing there as he approaches Rachel.

I do not want him speaking to Rachel, *my* Rachel, asking any questions he wants, so I lift the edge of my skirt and hurry to catch up.

"Rachel!" I holler just as he reaches the fire and her side. Startled, they both turn and look at me.

"Have you got the water already?" she asks, somewhat confused.

"Uh, no. Charlie decided he couldn't navigate the bank, so he wanted to come back, and I realized that I didn't ever get the chance to introduce you. Forgive me."

"I can git to the water just fine," he snaps, glaring at me.

Rachel watches both of us, silently waiting.

"This is Charlie." I finally manage to say. "He's, uh, my husband's brother."

He tips his hat toward Rachel. "Pleased to meet you, ma'am. I thank you for your generosity in helping my sister here."

"Sarah has been generous with her help and friendship. She has made these past few weeks more bearable than the preceding four since my own husband passed." She looks around. "I wish I could offer you a seat, but they're in short supply here."

"I'll be all right."

"Sarah and I've been talking, wondering how you found her," Rachel says.

I want to throw my arms around her in a hug for creating this opening. Charlie removes his hat and rolls it between his fingers. I wait for him to start.

"I'd be happy to share. But I'd like to hear about my dear brother's demise as well." He looks down and swallows. I glare at him until he continues. "We got to Fort Hall in the evening. We thought we'd reach it in the morning hours but the Aldrich's wagon threw an axle and we got delayed."

Rachel nods in understanding.

"We arrived in the late afternoon and set camp. There were the typical Indians camped around the fort, trying to trade or just begging. After we ate, Tommy came running into camp. He hollered to your Pa that some squaw had your quilt and you were bein' held hostage."

"When did you get to Fort Hall?" I interrupt.

"Uh," he looks up as he thinks, counting back on his hand. "I believe it was about August 11 or so. When did you get there?"

"I don't rightly know the exact date. I didn't have my journal or mama's calendar to take note of the date, and it didn't occur to me to ask."

"It was August 4. A Wednesday," Rachel replies.

Both Charlie and I turn toward the soft spoken woman. "That's when we got there, and I saw you that night. I think you recall that," she says with a small grin.

"Not likely to forget it." I return Rachel's smile. "Go on Charlie." I try not to sound too commanding.

"Well, when we heard that, everyone panicked. Your mama jumped up and asked where, started dragging your brother along to show her. Your Pa made her sit back down. He took Jed to go investigate it. I think quite a few of us followed along. We all thought you were dead. Taken by Indians, eaten by wolves. Somethin'. Nobody figured you'd turn up further down the trail."

He paused as Angelina toddled over and set her handful of rocks on the ground next to him.

"And the quilt?" I prompt.

"I'll get there."

He stacks up the pebbles, much to the child's delight. The breeze blows the sage smoke over them as they play. I want to rip the story from him, but he makes me wait, and I don't really have a choice.

Finally, he speaks again, but he keeps his eyes on the pebbles he and Angelina are stacking. "Tommy had come along too, to make sure yer Pa knew where to go. It wasn't hard to find. Right there at the entrance to the fort stood a squaw with your quilt draped over her shoulders. I heard your Mama gasp when she saw it. I couldn't believe it. Nobody could. I don't even think your Ma knew it wasn't in your wagon anymore, but it was unmistakable with all the signatures and what not on it.

"Yer Pa walked right up to that old trapper and asked where he got it. The trapper just said he traded for it. Yer Pa grabbed the squaw and shoved her up against the wall. He was yellin' and askin' about you. Jed jumped in when the trapper went after yer Pa to get him off his squaw. I was watching it all happen. I didn't even notice Tommy. Nobody did."

Charlie stops and looks down at the pebbles he still holds in his hand. He takes a deep breath.

"What happened? What did Tommy do?" I interrupt. "Did something happen to my brother?" My voice is almost a whisper, and though I want to know the answer, a feeling of dread has settled over my body.

"I heard your Mama first. We were all so focused on your Pa and the trapper and Jed fighting. Your Mama screamed at him to put it down. I turned and looked. We all did. She hollered that loud. Tommy had a gun. He must have run back to the wagon and grabbed it. He had it loaded and aimed, right at the whole group of them."

"Did he shoot it? Did he kill one of them? Did he kill Pa?" Questions fly from my mouth. I couldn't imagine my brother pointing a gun at a group of people, much less shooting it, but this journey had brought more surprises with it than anything else.

"No, no. He didn't kill anyone. Everybody froze though when they saw the gun. Your mama said real quiet to put the gun down. He turned to look at her, and as he turned it went off. I don't think he did it on purpose. He wasn't aimin' or nothin'. It almost hit the squaw, but it was high."

"Who'd it hit?"

"It didn't hit no one, but the squaw dropped like it had hit her. Scared us all. Everyone dropped, especially the group around the quilt. Then out of nowhere comes this Indian boy."

"Joseph?"

"Yeah. I think his name was Joseph."

Charlie stops talking again and looks out over the camp. He still holds two small rocks in his hand which he plays with, rolling them over each other, back and forth. The clink of the rocks and the gentle bubbling of the beans in the pot sound soft and gentle, calming somehow though every muscle in my body is rigid, waiting for the end of Charlie's story, for the part he didn't want to tell me.

"Charlie, go on. What did Joseph do? What do you mean he came out of nowhere?"

"I guess he figured his mother had got hit. He, well, he came out of nowhere with a gun … and shot him."

"Who shot who?" I feel like I am screaming, but my voice comes out in a whisper.

"The Indian boy, Joseph you say? He did it. Joseph shot Tommy."

"Is he? Did he … die?"

Charlie looks at me and nods, so much sadness in his blue eyes.

"Tommy died?" I stare at him, looking for any signs of his usual teasing. There are none. He's told the truth.

"Yes."

I can't breathe. "What about Joseph?"

"They hung him. And at the hanging, your Mama took that quilt straight off the squaw's shoulders while her boy swayed from the tree."

180

My legs fold beneath me as I sink to the ground. I had been standing near the fire, listening to Charlie, but my legs can no longer hold up the weight of my body. *Tommy is dead. Joseph is dead. Tommy is dead.* It goes through my head like a chant, followed by the whisper that all the blame is my own. *I killed Tommy. I killed Joseph. They're gone.*

I LIE UNDER the blankets next to Rachel. The canvas cover glows in the moonlight, and I watch the shadows play in the gentle breeze. Though the moon isn't yet full, it is bright enough that it wakens me, though I doubt I could sleep anyway, even if the night had been moonless and black. Angelina lies between us, a small source of heat though one is unnecessary, and Janie sleeps on a pallet toward the rear of the wagon. I throw the coverlet off with my good arm and let the night breeze blow across my body, cooling me.

The tragedy that I have left in my wake has consumed my every thought since Charlie shared his story. It is a story I wish I had not heard. I would give up my quilt, my life, everything to have my brother back. But I'm the one who gave him up in the first place.

I turn my head and stare at the quilt, folded in the front of the wagon bed, on top of a trunk. I have not replaced the muslin wrapping as the process would have been awkward with one hand, so I had set it just inside on the seat. I have not been able to touch it since I heard its legacy.

But is it the quilt's fault? Or is it me who's caused all this tragedy? Or perhaps it's just fate. I don't know. I sit up and crawl as gently as I can toward the front of the wagon, so I can sit next to the quilt. I pull it onto my lap and run my fingers over it. It looks the same and feels the same. I awkwardly unfold the blanket with one hand. I know every stitch, every block, every thread. I want to feel it with both hands, but my left hand and arm is still wrapped tightly to a board.

As I unfold the material, something falls out and onto my lap. I pick it up, feeling the flat pages between my fingers and realize it is a letter. It is too dark to make out the writing, so I don't know who it's from. I set it aside, frustrated that I have to wait for the light of dawn, and let myself feel the quilt and its details. I stitched the blocks and quilted it, my hands had felt every inch of the fabric over and over again. My fingers track each corner, seeking the rip. I remember that walk I'd taken down the hill after speaking with Joseph. My relationship with sagebrush has not changed. I despise walking through it, cooking with it, even the smell of it.

I cannot find the tear, so I start feeling each corner again, frustrated with the use of only one hand. I go over each corner until I finally discover the mend. It has been stitched up neatly, far better than Nettie would have been able to stitch. This is Mama's work. It feels slightly stiffer where it was torn and mended, as if she has added some sort of batting when she repaired it. What could she have used? There would not have been any wool. Perhaps it's layers of cotton. I rotate it and run my fingers along the mending from every direction, but I cannot figure what it is. The material is just slightly thicker, slightly stiffer than normal. One who did not know the quilt as I do might not even feel it.

Maybe it is a little piece of Mama's heart. She had repaired the tear after losing her oldest son. She'd lost two children on this journey. And I suppose she had also lost me.

The wagon's cover is cinched down tight, but a hole maybe two feet in diameter lets in the breeze. I loosen the ties so I can see out and get some more air, but despite the breeze, I find that I can't breathe. My throat tightens, and I swallow back a wail of grief, burying my face in the quilt and letting the tears come.

I don't know how long I cry, but it's long enough for my eyes to burn and swell, my throat to ache with the effort to keep my sobs inside. I do not want to awaken Rachel, but I fail at that too. The wagon box rocks gently as she crawls toward me. She says nothing, just sits next to me at the front of the wagon and gently spreads the quilt out across her lap and mine. Sucking back sobs, I look into the face of one of the kindest women I have ever met.

"Would you like to talk about it?" she whispers as she puts her arm around my shoulders, pulling me into her body. She does what my Mama would have done, and a new well of tears springs to my eyes.

"I killed my brother, Rachel. That's all that I can think."

"You didn't kill him. You weren't there."

"But everything I did somehow caused it. If I ... if we ... hadn't left the train, if we'd stayed with them, none of this would have happened."

"You had to follow your husband's word. He desired to stop with thee at that place," she says, laying a hand on my head and stroking my hair. "You did right by him and by the Lord."

The guilt I already feel about Tommy is compounded by Rachel's gentle reminder of the lies I have told her. She believes I have behaved in a righteous and godly manner. She believes I truly am a widow, that I was a good wife, not a ruined girl, a liar running from her sins. If she knew the truth, what would she do? I don't want to imagine losing Rachel on top of everything else I have lost or given up, so I stay silent.

"Charlie's a kind man," she continues.

"He is," I consent. "I treated him horribly today. I was so shocked to see him, and he wouldn't tell me what I wanted to know. And then when he did tell me, I didn't know what to do. I couldn't speak to him. I almost couldn't bear to look at him."

A deep sigh escapes from Rachel. "I have learned that this journey can do that to a person. I have never known such heartache, nor had I ever imagined how I might deal with such pain. Sometimes I regret how I acted when I lost my husband and my son, but this is not something you shall be judged for. You shall be forgiven."

"I doubt it."

"What will you do?"

"What do you mean?" I lift my eyes and study her expression. She doesn't answer, so I say, "I guess I'll just go on to Oregon. What choice do I have?"

"Why not return to your mother? I would love for my mother to be here with me now."

"I just … can't." I cannot begin to unravel the web of lies I have told my friend who welcomed me into her home.

"Is it the babe?" Rachel asks.

I start then peer at Rachel in the dark. "The babe?"

"You're with child, are you not?"

I take a deep breath and decide to tell the truth. "I am. How did you know?"

"Ah, it was mostly a guess, but you've got the rounded face a bit, and you keep rubbin' yer belly. And I felt it when Elizabeth set your arm. Has it quickened?"

"Yes. A bit."

"T'is good." I can see her smile in the dim light. "Babes are always good, though they can cause us much heartache too."

I know she has buried at least one child on this trip, and I wonder if there are more.

"You've got to think of the child."

I smile weakly. "I feel like I never stop thinking of it."

"I mean there's a man who traveled quite a ways—alone—to bring you a quilt. He looks awful kindly at you. It's no shame to take another husband, Sarah."

"You think I should marry Charlie?"

I had thought of this when we'd begun this journey a lifetime ago. I'd spent time entertaining myself, thinking of nothing but that. But not since the entire incident with Jed. Charlie would never want me if he knew I was not an innocent girl, if he knew I was expecting Jed's child. I can't begin to explain. He knows the truth. I had never married his brother, a man who did not and never had existed.

"I think you should think on taking him as a husband, Sarah."

"He would never marry me." I can barely eke out the words, my throat is so tight.

"You never know what men will do. Sometimes they surprise us. For the sake of your baby, you best be wed. Especially in this country. It's no place for a woman alone."

I shake my head as Rachel removes her arm from my shoulders. "What will you do?" I ask.

"Oh, I suppose I'll find someone, though he won't ever replace my husband."

Rachel is right. She'll find somebody to love, somebody who will love her. She understands, first hand, the difficulties this country presents a woman with two small children and no husband. I can't marry Charlie. I can't tell him another lie. I can't imagine being with a man in that way anyway.

Rachel begins to crawl back toward her daughter and the warmth of her bed. "You best be comin' back to bed and sleep. We've still got a long way to go."

When she's gone I wrap my arms around my middle in an attempt to hold myself together. I'd left in the first place because I couldn't hurt Charlie or disappoint my family. I couldn't live a life with Jed or tell Charlie the truth about what Jed had done. I'd rather do anything than hurt Charlie, but that's all I seem able to do.

I return to bed but don't sleep. As soon as the light begins to spread across the sky, I sit up and reach for the letter that sits on my quilt, next to the pallet. The writing is small and cramped, not my Mama's handwriting at all. I turn to the last page and see Charlie's name scrawled at the bottom. He had already given me everything I demanded from him yesterday: the quilt and the story. Had I only been a bit more patient or just opened up the quilt, I would have known that. He also told me he doesn't want to lose me again.

What have I given him? Nothing but lies, frustration, and grief.

EXHAUSTION PERVADES MY body after the sleepless night. We've been on this trail for hours, and I need water, cool fresh water from the river. I stand above the bank of the Snake River, watching it wind through the dry, rocky landscape. Some days the river rushes into gorges hundreds of feet below the trail, other days it runs placidly near us, offering easy access to the water. Today, the bank is steep but navigable. The water runs maybe twenty feet below the edge on which I perch.

By the end of each day, the wagons, children, drivers, supplies, and food have a thick dirt coating. I am so tired of the dust. People back home do not know the true meaning of the word dust, but I know it means dirt clogging the air until neither the cattle nor the immigrants can see far enough in front of them to navigate without following the vague, ghostlike shadows of the wagons, hoping the lead wagon will find its way and not send us all off a cliff and into the churning waters of the river below. If the first wagon falls, we would all follow like stupid and fearful animals running in a stampede.

Dirt even coats the inside of my mouth. We had not been able to fill the barrels this morning due to the steep, rocky bank, so the water in them is hot, stagnant. I listen to the river rush in the canyon below and crave a cool drink. I holler to Rachel, letting her know that I am heading down toward the water, but she doesn't respond. Her focus is on the animals and on her children, who ride in the wagon behind her as she works to keep her team moving forward, always moving forward. She holds the whip high over the yokes of oxen; she can crack it well now. The first time she managed to crack it we had jumped and screamed for joy.

I use my right hand to steady myself as I step down the steep embankment, and I say a prayer of thanks to Rachel for fashioning a sling for me out of an old dress. She had cut a skirt into strips then knotted them together to make a loop which I draped over my neck. I put the splint through the loop to help hold it up. While it isn't ideal, it at least allows me the use of my right hand, which I had been using to hold my broken left arm. It also helps ease the pain in my wrist.

I follow a faint trail, either a game trail or a path prior emigrants had made, and step carefully, placing each foot solidly and checking my footing before taking another step. Despite my caution, I slide on the loose sand and rocks. I reach my good arm out, flailing, but I cannot catch my balance. I gain speed and fall back on my butt, hitting hard, not catching myself at all as I grab my broken wrist with my good hand. I see the river below me, and my feet struggle to catch a hold and stop my slide. It doesn't work, and I scream as my body slides off the trail and over the edge of the cliff. I drop five feet and land with a thud, crashing into a stand of willows at the river's edge. They bend under my weight but hold, keeping me from sliding all the way into the swiftly flowing water.

I lie there, panting and shaking, mentally reviewing each part of my body before I try to move. My rear end hurts from the fall, my wrist throbs, pain shoots up my arm, and rocks and branches have dug into my back. I open my eyes and see the sky and willows, but that image is swiftly replaced by images of Jed looming above me. My breath hitches and starts to come faster as panic sets in. My legs can't move, twisted and tangled as they are in my dress. The branches of the willows, the blue sky filtering through the trees above my head, and the mottled shadows on the ground take me back to the glade in the woods. I can't scream, I can't move. I'd let it happen the first time, and it's happening again. I feel the weight of his body, the pain ripping through me. I feel my muscles clenching, protesting, and I start to scream.

The first scream comes out in a low wail, and it builds. I hear it, but it is not a sound that I associate with myself. It seems to come from somewhere so deep within me that I don't recognize it. I kick my legs, freeing them from my dress as my screams fill the air around me. I scratch at the air with my good arm and back myself up until I am sitting, wedged between the dirt embankment and a willow, reliving every moment of that afternoon, though it had all happened on another river a thousand miles back.

My body shakes, but I force my eyes open and stare at the river, quieting myself, taking deep breaths to ward off the panic which sits just there, ready to pounce if I let down my guard. I close my eyes and focus on my breathing. It takes a few minutes before I am finally breathing normally. My wrist throbs and scratches cover my legs, but I don't think my body is any more broken than when I'd started my trek to the river.

Except my mind is somehow broken, scarred.

I feel my stomach and want to hit it, take vengeance on Jed through the child I carry, but I cannot. I press my fingers into the hard bump where the baby has begun to grow bigger. It feels fine since I'd landed on my back and side. I wish it would just go away, that I would lose it. I want Charlie, not this child.

I lean my head back and rest it on the dirt behind me. I can see the deep blue of the sky in stark contrast to the swaying green branches above me. The sky is never this blue in Indiana, and I don't understand why it is so blue here. I think how I could draw it but decide that pencil won't capture the colors. I don't have my sketchbook anyway. I close my eyes and breathe again, feeling my body relax as I listen to the water below me. If I could just stay here and sleep, it would be easy. I hear the wagons passing above me on the bluff. They would never know.

But I have already tried that, tried to stay behind, go on my own, make the pain go away, and it didn't work. I sit up and decide not to test my luck again. As I stand, I survey my landing spot and realize I have fallen off a bit of a cliff, and I am not sure I can get back up, especially with one arm. I can't go the way I came down, as it is far too steep. The only way to get back to the path is to get in the river and go upstream about ten feet, but the current is deep and swift here, swirling around the bank. I can swim a bit, but I'm definitely not a strong enough swimmer with one arm to go through that. I turn to survey any escape routes in the other direction. Just below me, the river's bank becomes a sharp cliff, almost vertical up to the bank fifteen feet above my head. I sit back down and begin to weigh out my options.

Now that I want to stay alive and stay with the train, I have managed to leave without a trace. Nobody heard my screams when I fell. I look at the river and realize that at least I can get a drink now. I splash the cold, clear water on my face, cup my hand and drink deeply. It takes several handfuls to slake my thirst, but as soon as I do, I begin to yell. I don't know what else to do. I call for Rachel, for Charlie, for Janie, Rachel's eldest daughter—even though I know she is in the wagon far up the trail by now. Nobody responds, though I can hear the creak and groans of the wagons at the rear of the train as they pass by me. I yell again and again, until the sound of the wagons and stock begins to dissipate as they move away from me, up the trail.

My throat stings from the hollering, and I can feel my voice fading. I am stuck down here on the Snake River, and nobody knows it. I let out a few more good yells, hoping one of the boys who stayed with the animals behind the train might hear. Nobody responds.

Chapter 20

Present Day

I KNOCK LIGHTLY THEN push open the door, only to be greeted by a sour smell. Agnes sits on her bed, her scrawny legs hanging over the side, her shoulders hunched over like she's trying to shrink even more than she already has. Judging from the pictures covering the nightstand of her and her husband—a man who had died well before he could age like Agnes has—she's already done quite a bit of shrinking. God, I don't want to get old like this.

Her blue eyes, already watery, spill over. She clutches both hands in her lap. She hasn't yet gotten dressed. Her robe hangs open, revealing an ancient cotton nightgown. Her breasts lay flat against her chest, almost resting in her lap. It looks like that would hurt, but it obviously doesn't—or at least Agnes doesn't seem to notice.

I approach her bed and kneel in front of her. It only takes moving within three feet of her to figure out the problem. The awful stench hangs in the air around her. "How long have you been sitting here, Agnes?" I reach for her hand, and Agnes clutches my fingers. "How long?"

She ignores me.

"Agnes? How can I help you?"

She grunts and finally pokes her head out of the turtle shell she's created with her shoulders. Her steely blue eyes lock onto mine. They are clear, lucid, and I take my cue to step lightly today.

"Harper." Her voice cracks in humiliation. "If I could get to the bathroom, I wouldn't be sitting here like a cat in a goddamn litter box."

Oh boy. Her walker is far out of reach. I drop her hand and grab it for her.

Agnes grimaces and knots her hands. She shuts her eyes to keep in the tears.

I reach for her elbows to pull her up and get her situated with her walker. She grunts as she stands, an anguished sound of utter humiliation. I avert my eyes to give her as much privacy as I can and head to the bathroom. As I sit on the tub, letting the water run over my hand to feel for the temperature, I watch her grip her walker and prepare herself to get to the bathroom.

She flinches and rests for a moment, taking a breath before she takes her first step.

"I'll be right there, Agnes."

She ignores me and begins to walk slowly, leaning heavily on the walker's handles. I start the shower and head toward her.

She grunts again as I get nearer, so I take a step back. Pissed off about her infirmities and fighting aging with every cell in her body, she is like a small child, wanting to do everything all by herself but sometimes not quite able to make it happen.

Reaching the bathroom, I pull the robe from Agnes' shoulders, and her nightgown slips to the floor. She is quiet as I help her undress. She is not wearing old people diapers, but regular old lady underpants. They are full, and wet, and disgusting. Agnes drops them to the floor, and I help her into the shower.

While she bathes, I get the cleaning supplies and wipe everything down, change her sheets. She lingers in the shower, and I can't blame her for that. I leave a clean outfit from her dresser on the bathroom counter and crack the door so I can hear if she needs me. By the time I'm done cleaning, I'm fuming. Where the hell is the regular nurse on this floor? She was here to kick me out a few weeks ago, but now, when Agnes needs her, she is nowhere to be found.

I look out in the hallway. Empty. There would be hell to pay if Rosemary had found her like that. Good God.

The water shuts off, and the air is silent, silent for far too long. Finally, I knock on the door. "Agnes? Are you okay?"

She stands in the tub, her towel held up. She clutches the hand rail, afraid to let go, but at least she's clean. I reach out my arm, and she grips it as she steps from the tub. As soon as Agnes has her footing on the bathroom floor, I begin the process of dressing a full grown woman who can move and speak but who can no longer easily do the buttons on her blouse.

Finally, I lead Agnes to her chair. She sits and lifts her chin to reclaim some sense of dignity. We sit in silence for some time. I don't know what to say, and I'm not sure she can say what she wants to. "Harper." Agnes breaks the silence. She points to her closet. I know she wants the quilt, but it's in the bag at my feet. I pull it out and set it on her lap. She pets it, smiling, and we fall back into silence. I really want her to tell me more of the story, but today is not the day to push her. Our silence is broken by the swishing of her door swinging open.

"Oh, Agnes. Look, you've got a visitor," a nurse says as she traipses into the room. She says this loudly, with an extra cheerful lilt on the end, as if Agnes has no idea that I'm here. As if she is deaf and possibly blind, too. Do they teach that annoying tone in nursing school, some sort of horrible 'bedside manners' class? I hope not.

"Yes, she does have a visitor," I snap. The woman stops flouncing through the room. "Are you her regular nurse on the morning shift?"

"No. Why?" She's no longer talking to Agnes, but to me. Her entire tone of voice changes.

I stand and give Agnes a hug. As I walk to the door, I touch the nurse's arm and ask her to follow me to the hall. I will not complain in front of Agnes. I will not make her relive the morning's humiliation. But as soon as we step out the door, I let the woman have it.

She shakes her head in disgust. "Yeah, the girl in the morning is pretty much worthless. She's on Facebook on her phone more than she is with the patients. I'll let the supervisor know. But next time you ought to come get someone to help her. If something would've happened, you would have had hell to pay. Might even have been liable if she'd fallen or something. That's what we're here for."

"Somebody should have found her way before I did," I reply, anger rising. "I'd think you guys would be happy I didn't go get someone or complain. *You'd* have hell to pay, not me. Don't let it happen again."

I'm proud of myself for not caving. It must be my new spike-heeled boots. The nurse has the decency to stay quiet. She heads back into Agnes' room, and I follow. We're so close to the end of the story, and for the first time in a long time, I know I can finish this, even if it kills me or lands me in jail as a quilt thief. I owe it to Agnes, but I'm beginning to realize that I also owe it to me, to see this through. Today I

191

have time to wait for the words to come to Agnes if she wants to talk. She does, so I settle in.

A FEW DAYS later, I fire up my laptop and start googling antique quilts. Despite all of her threats, Rosemary hasn't had me arrested for stealing the quilt, and thankfully, I haven't seen her in months. But even though I've been working every possible moment, my bank account balance is infinitesimal. Between my stupid car breaking down, the gas and insurance, and an occasional movie, I've barely saved enough for the next two semesters … at a community college. At this rate, I'll graduate with my associate's degree when I'm thirty, and there's no way I'll be able to afford transferring to a university. Unless I figure out a way to finance my education, I'll be serving burritos and margaritas, or coffee, or whatever random job I manage to get until I die. Not a happy thought.

My mom always warned me against getting trapped. She'd wanted to be a chef but ended up pregnant and becoming an office receptionist. She'd spent her evenings making me mac and cheese from a box while she guzzled wine and watched cooking shows until her liver couldn't take it anymore and shut down. I always swore I wouldn't get trapped like her in a life I hate but really, it's only made me a commitment phobe…stuck in a life I hate.

Agnes is never coming home. Who knows if she'll even be able to finish the quilt's story, and I don't even know if I want her to tell me anymore. Every time I look at the quilt, I think of everything she isn't, and that's not the Agnes I want to remember. I want to remember the tall, proud Agnes who welcomed me into her home, who set up a bedroom for me, who "babysat" me all those times my mom didn't or couldn't. I want to remember the one who remembers who I am.

As I surf around different sites, I realize that people will spend a shit load of money for old pieces of fabric. If I get the whole story typed up to go with it, I might be able to get more money for it. I could sell the quilt with the story, get rid of them both, and remember Agnes as I want to, not as the shell of a person she's become. Maybe that's the

best way to honor her.
  But I'm still not sure.

Chapter 21

I WAKE TO A throbbing pain in my wrist. I have become accustomed to the pain, but the fall has jarred the jagged bones. I wonder briefly how long I have slept then decide it doesn't matter. Nobody has returned to rescue me. Or maybe another train will rescue me, and Charlie will think I have run off again, unable to face a single problem in my life.

But I can. I've made it this far. I realize I may not make it any farther, but if I do, I will face it. I'm done running.

The water flows below me. It's quiet here, so I hear the footsteps when they crunch through the rocks above me. They stop, and a head appears. It's Charlie. Relief, then anger dances across his features. I am overwhelmed with happiness at sight of him, but he is determined to dampen that.

"What are you doing?" he demands. "Why would you try to navigate a cliff with a broken arm? Why didn't you tell anyone where ye're going?"

"I did tell. I told Rachel," I reply with indignation, knowing that I hadn't really told her anything.

"Well, Rachel didn't hear you. Nobody would've known what happened to you if the little kid running the cattle hadn't heard you bellowing. I'm about done chasing you down." He glares at me. "You hear me?"

"Well then, why did you come get me? If it's that much trouble, leave me well enough alone." I turn and glare at the water as a rope snakes down by my side. I feel foolish. He is right, but I don't want to admit it. I don't really want to admit anything when it comes to Charlie.

"Can you grab that?" he asks. "I've got the other end rigged to the saddle. Just hold on to it and I'll try to pull you up."

I lift my splinted arm to remind him. "Did you forget this? I can't pull myself up at all."

He sighs. "I'm gonna have to get some more help then. Can you wait here?"

I smile and then start to laugh. My life can't get into any more of a tangled mess, so I might as well laugh about it. "Do I have a choice?"

"I guess not. But I think that's maybe a good thing. At least I'll know where you are." He smiles, and I realize we have just had our first civil, happy exchange since he found me. "I'll be back."

His head disappears and the rope he'd thrown disappears up the cliff as he walks back up the game trail. I sit down and wait, then decide I ought to be doing something to help. I grab a flat rock and begin to scrape out a foothold in the dirt face in front of me with my good hand. I manage to get two dug in by the time Charlie returns with several men to help with my rescue.

Charlie's head reappears at the top of the cliff, along with two other heads. "Watch your head," he yells. "We're throwing a rope down."

"How in the hell did you git down there, girl?" Mr. Sawyer, the train's captain asks. "We're sending John Stone down. You'll have to grab the rope as best you can. We'll pull and he'll give you a boost from below."

I nod, my cheeks reddening. Mr. Stone, whose wife despises me, would be grabbing my backside and shoving me up a rope. This could be awkward. I stand next to the willows and watch him come down the rope to join me on my little willow-covered beach.

He takes a drink from the river then looks at me. "Are you ready? I'll just lift you up nice and easy, and they'll pull, but you're gonna have to hang onto the rope. Can you do that?"

I nod, adjusting my sling so it holds my arm tight to my body, then I grab the rope with my good hand. I set my right foot into the lower foot hold and lean back on Mr. Stone. He hollers for them to start pulling as he squats down behind me and places his hands flat on my back side.

I am mortified. The rope tightens and pulls right out of my hand, along with a fair amount of skin. I feel myself falling backward for the second time today, but this time I land right on top of Mr. Stone. I let out a small screech as I struggle to untangle myself and stand up.

"I'm so sorry, sir," I falter, as I finally gain my footing and stand.

195

He laughs loudly. "Quite all right. We gotta go slower," he finally manages to say between chortles. He hollers up instructions to go a little slower this time, and we all get in position again.

This time the rope becomes taut slowly and stays in my grasp. I manage to hang onto it with help from Mr. Stone. Halfway up, my hand begins to burn as the rope slides through it, but I hold onto it with every muscle fiber in my hand and arm. I do not want to stay down on the bank with Mr. Stone any longer than necessary. I don't want to think about what his crazy wife would do to me if she saw him helping me like this at all. She'd probably break my other hand. Even worse, if this doesn't work, I'd have to swim with Mr. Stone, and I don't want to drown.

Finally, when I'm within a foot of the top of the cliff, Captain Sawyer reaches down and grabs my right forearm. "Keep comin'. Don't let go."

I hold on but find it difficult with him gripping my upper arm. My feet scramble, searching for footholds, but I don't want to accidentally kick Mr. Stone in the face. I move another six inches upward, high enough that Captain Sawyer can grab underneath my armpit and yank. At the same time, Mr. Stone gives me an extra shove from below. I fly over the lip of the embankment and land with a thud on the rocky ground, jarring my arm. I say a quick prayer that Mrs. Baker won't need to reset it after today's adventures.

The captain lets out a whoop and a laugh. "Got 'er John. You ready?"

I lie on the ground, panting and holding my throbbing arm close to my chest. Charlie's got the rope tied off on his horse's saddle, and he's working his horse, coaxing him to slowly back up and pull Mr. Stone up the embankment. I sit up when I see the top of Mr. Stone's hat appear. As soon as he is up, they begin to wind up the rope.

"This one seems to find trouble," Captain Sawyer says as he nods in my direction. "Can you get her back to the train, son? We need to get back to find a camp."

Charlie nods and thanks them for their time. I approach the men to give them my thanks.

"Don't let it happen again. We're about done rescuing you," the captain says, then he laughs, but I'm not sure he's joking.

I drop my eyes, my face heating up in further humiliation. "Yes sir," I answer as the men walk toward the train, which has continued its westward march. Then I turn to look at Charlie. I am indebted to him … again.

"Why don't you come up here, away from that bank," he suggests.

I want to be angry. I need to make him go away, but he makes me smile. He's the only one who can make me smile, and I want him to stay.

"Thank you for the rescue. I just thought I'd get a drink from the river. That blasted dust had covered every inch of me."

"Yeah, it does that."

I can see billows of dust beyond us, but I cannot judge the distance. "How far to the train?"

"A mile or so, not too far. Look at that."

I follow the direction where his hand points. The sun has begun its descent beyond the western horizon, stretching pink and orange fingers across the sky toward us.

"We best get going. I don't want to worry Rachel," I say.

"Hang on a second before we go. I got somethin' for you."

"You have something else? I think you've given me enough." I think of the quilt, the letter, the news of my family. "I guess I owe you."

He's smiling as he returns to his horse and pulls something from the pack on the side of his saddle. It's a small bundle, and I can't tell what it is. He turns and holds it out in my direction.

I grab it and my fingers touch his. It is the first time I have touched him since his arrival, and I quickly pull my hand away. I cannot think about him like that. He deserves better. He has been traveling with our train for several days, but I have not initiated conversation with him. I don't know what to say. *I love you, but I'm carrying Jed's child.* If I can't forgive myself or see past it, how can I expect him to?

"You gonna open it?"

I fold back the piece of cloth and see the paper cover of my sketchbook. My mouth drops open, and when I look at him I see the beginnings of a smile lifting across his face.

"You've had this the whole time you've been here?"

His smile falters. I'm not angry, though I do wonder why he hasn't given it to me before now.

His voice is calm, almost steely when he answers. "I was going to give it to you when I gave you the quilt, but, well, I sort of forgot about it and since then …" He stops talking and looks at me.

I fill in the blank. "Since then, I haven't really spoken to you."

"With your wrist, I figured you couldn't have used it anyway."

197

"Thank you." I open the pages and skim the images.

"You're really talented."

"You looked in here?" I ask, surprised. I feel like he read my diary. He turns to look back at the sunset. "I did. I didn't actually think I'd ever see you again, remember? We thought you were gone. Your Mama showed it to me after you disappeared, before we ever got to Fort Hall. I didn't think it would do no harm."

I pause to consider his words. "I had forgotten that part. I suppose I can forgive you for that." I turn the pages. Sketches of flowers, prairie grasses, buffalo, my sisters, and then him. I had sketched page after page of Charlie, his face, his hands. Even several of his eyes. I had studied him in the evenings as he fiddled, thought of him as I walked each day, then drawn him. He had seen the sketches. All of them.

I look up, my cheeks hot, and find him studying me like I had studied him all those long weeks and months ago.

"Why didn't you tell me, Sarah?" I do not need to ask what he is talking about. We both know. My sketches tell a story, one he had read. He reaches out toward my good arm, grabs it, and turns me so I face him. "Why didn't you tell me? Why did you run?" His voice shakes, just slightly, but I can't tell if it's with anger or fear or what.

His eyes show pain and confusion, and I give up. I decide to tell him the truth, not able or wanting to lie any longer. My hands begin to shake as I think back to my fall from grace. "It was Jed."

"Jed? What about Jed?"

"Jed's ... he's evil." I choose my words carefully, slowly, and watch his response.

He does nothing as I say this about his cousin, just continues to watch me closely, pain in his eyes.

"He scared me." I pause again, not sure how to tell him. I have decided to do it, but now I have no words.

He's leaning in, trying to understand me. "What do you mean? How did he scare you?"

"He showed me that I had no choice but to leave. He *made* me pick him and not you." I look at Charlie who watches me with an intensity that makes me want to either jump back over the cliff or fall into his arms. I'm not sure which.

"What do you mean he made you? What did he do?"

"He ... he wanted me," I say then gauge his reaction. My patient

Charlie just listens, so I continue, but I can't tell him about the attack. It's still too raw. "He asked my Papa for my hand in marriage. My Papa said 'yes,' but you knew that. I couldn't do it. I couldn't marry Jed, but I couldn't tell my Papa 'no'." I look back up into Charlie's face. "And I couldn't hurt you."

He stares at me, and I can see him weighing his words. I wait, giving him whatever time he needs. He deserves that at least.

"So somehow, you decided that dying would hurt everyone less? Sarah, that doesn't make any sense. How could running away and dying make anything better?"

I ponder an answer, one that might make him understand. "You're right. Running didn't make anything better or even any easier. It made it all worse."

"I found you now. How could it be worse? I don't understand. I won't make you go back." He takes the sketchbook from my hand and opens it up to a page which had become slightly dirty and wrinkled. He had obviously looked at it a lot since my "death." This page had a flower, a part of Charlie's left hand resting on his crutch, and a small sketch of his profile. It's one of the better sketches.

I knew which page he would turn to as soon as he took the book. I also now know, without a doubt, what had made him come after me. Why hadn't I taken my book? In all my haste, I hadn't even thought of it. Or maybe I had, and I'd left it behind on purpose so he would know.

"Sarah, I know you see what I see on this page." He pauses and watches me.

Tears fill my eyes, and I let them fall. "I do see it. I drew it."

"So why don't you talk to me now? I'm here now. I came for you because of this." His voice cracks, and I see what leaving his family and finding me cold and angry has cost him.

"Charlie, I can't."

"Why not?"

"Because … because Jed and running made everything worse. It won't work."

"Can't we fix it?"

I shake my head.

"Sarah, I don't—"

I grab the sketchbook, set it on the ground, and rise up. With my good hand, I reach for his and take a step closer to him. I am close enough now to smell him, his sweat, the dirt, his scent. I take a deep breath and lay his open palm on the hard curve of my belly. It is the only way to get him to understand. He starts and tries to pull his hand away, but I hold it firmly. His hand's warmth penetrates the cotton of my dress and spreads to my skin. I watch his face intently, as discomfort, then confusion, and finally understanding dawns and he feels the hard swelling of my stomach.

He doesn't respond as I release his hand, but neither does he move it. He holds it there, spreading his palm over the curve of my belly for a moment before he lets it drop. "I was wondering why they called you a widow," he finally says.

Then he turns and walks toward his horse, leaving me alone to watch the sun say its final goodbyes. I bend down, pick up my sketchbook, and head back toward the safety of my lies and Rachel's wagon, my throat tight with the effort of holding in more tears.

It takes me more than an hour to reach the camp. By the time I arrive, Rachel has supper prepared. Charlie has apparently assured her of my well-being. He must have left after that, because I don't see him anywhere. As soon as Rachel sees me she rushes over to check on me. Even after walking for an hour, I am not sure what I feel. Anger? Humiliation? Relief? Or maybe just grief. He's gone.

Rachel reaches around me and gives me a gentle hug. "Are you all right? Charlie said you'd be in late but he didn't say why."

"I fell. He came and got me and then left."

"What happened? Why did you need rescuing?"

I reply, chagrin in my voice. "The dust was choking me back there, so I headed down to the river to get a drink. I slipped and went over the edge of the little trail I was on and landed on some willows just above the water."

Rachel gasps, her eyes widening in alarm. "How far did you fall?"

"It wasn't too far. Maybe eight feet, but it was far enough, and too steep for me to get back up, especially with my wrist. I thought I was going to get left there, but one of the boys who was in the back with the cattle heard me yelling."

"We shall praise the Lord for that." She looks me over. "You look a mess."

I survey myself and note my filthy dress and hands. I can only imagine the mud on my cheeks from all the tears. "Can I use some of the water in the jug to rinse my face? I'm not sure I'm up for another trip to the river."

"Of course you can. The water's not far. We can fill it tomorrow before we leave." Rachel looks at my hand. "What did you find?"

I look down and see the forgotten sketch book crushed in my grip. "Charlie brought this to me when he rescued me. I guess he got it from my mama."

"What is it?"

"It's my sketchbook. Sort of my diary of this trip, but in pictures. I had forgotten it."

"May I?" Rachel holds her hand out toward the book. Nobody would ask to read someone's diary, so why does everyone think they can look at my sketches? Though I hesitate, I hand her the book. I cannot and will not tell her no, though I remind myself to never ask to see anyone's private writings or drawings.

She takes it and gently opens the pages. As she gazes at the flowers and grasses, her face softens into a smile. "Angelina, Janie, come on over here." She kneels down next to her daughters and together they look at the pictures. I turn to wash my face when Rachel reaches the pages covered with images of Charlie. She will know exactly who they are, and exactly what they mean.

I pour some cool water into a small tin cup and splash it on my face, then I dry myself with a rag which instantly turns a dirty brown color. Repeating the process, I scrub my face and neck, trying to rid it of the dirt, and to rid myself of the memories of Jed that had come rushing back this afternoon.

I try but fail to wash myself clean of my conversation with Charlie this afternoon. He has left me, just as I had left him, but now he knows. He won't be back. Tears well, but I squeeze my eyes shut tight. I am done crying for today. I hadn't wanted him or anyone from my family to find me and share in my humiliation and shame, but now that he has I realize I don't want to lose him again.

Rachel's soft footsteps approach as I finish my attempt at washing myself. Judging from the rag, I don't think I have been all that successful. I feel like I've merely smeared mud around my face.

"Charlie has seen these, yes?"

I nod into the rag, my face still covered.

"Sarah, may I ask ye something?" She waits until I uncover my face to ask me her question. "Why did ye draw Charlie and not your husband?" Her words are soft, spoken with kindness, not accusation, though she must know I have kept something from her.

I lift my eyes and look into my friend's trusting face. "Can we get in the wagon, Rachel? I'll explain it then."

"You need to eat first, and then we will."

She returns to the bean pot to serve me. I don't realize how hungry I am until she lifts the lid and the smell of bacon and beans permeates the air. My mouth waters as I reach for the bowl she offers. As soon as I am fed, we begin the process of settling in for the night. We made almost twenty miles today, so we'll crawl into our beds as soon as the evening meal and morning preparations are complete. No fiddles will play this evening, and I wonder, briefly, where one particular fiddler might be.

I climb into the wagon, brush my hand across Janie's forehead to wish her good night, then lay down on the pallet next to Angelina. The small girl is already sleeping soundly, having walked for some of the day with her sister.

As soon as Janie's breathing becomes soft and regular, I begin to tell Rachel the story, to break down the web of lies I have woven in an attempt to save whatever self-respect I have left. The lies have diminished me, made me into something I am not. This evening, as I'd walked back to camp, I'd decided I needed to tell Rachel the truth as I told Charlie. I need to be honest with at least one person. Perhaps she will kick me out of her wagon and leave like he did, but I have to trust that she won't. I have no other choice because I can't keep living in a world of lies. It doesn't work.

I start at the beginning, with my first sighting of Jed those months ago in Independence, then my relationship with Charlie. I share my parents' views on the two boys and how they didn't believe Charlie was good enough for me with his leg. At this Rachel grabs my hand and holds on to it. She married for love. I think she understands.

When I get to Jed's attack, I stop talking and begin to cry. I had relived the attack this afternoon, and I don't know if I can tell her, if she will believe me when I say I had tried to fight. What if she thinks I had asked for it? What if she thinks I was a woman like that?

I have never spoken of this to anyone, and now I find myself telling a deeply Christian woman, a Quaker, about my deepest, most fearful shame. She lies next to me, listening, quiet. I cannot judge from her silence what she thinks, so I continue to speak. I tell her of the ravishment, of my father sanctioning my marriage to Jed, and of my decision to run, my deep belief that the only way to escape the pain and a life with Jed was for me to die. I speak of Nettie and Joseph finding me and taking me with them to Pierce, of my initial terror for my life when I saw them, and my weeks traveling with them to Fort Hall. I tell her of my discovery that I carry Jed's child.

Finally my story comes to an end. I lie back, my good hand clutched in Rachel's, my broken wrist by my side. Tears drip down my cheeks as I have no way to wipe them away. They fill my ears, soak my hair, and puddle on the pallet beneath me.

Rachel has not spoken during my entire tale, and finally she breaks her silence. But when she speaks, she does not chastise me or question me. In fact, she asks me a question.

"Have I told you about my babies?" she whispers.

"No."

"Angelina is my youngest, my baby, and Janie is my second eldest, but I had three others. My oldest, Carrie lived to be four. The other two died as toddlers." She is silent for a few moments, and I keep silent as well. "They passed before we left on this journey. And now I've lost my John, too. It is just Angelina, Janie, and me left. I can't say that I understand why or what the Lord's purpose is in all of this, but I have these two children that I must keep going for, though He has taken all else away. I am burdened with completing this journey alone." She rolls over and looks at me. "You don't have to do this alone. Charlie came for you, Sarah, and you love him back." She doesn't mention Jed, or my shame, or the weeks I spent living with an Indian woman.

I take a deep breath and point out the obvious problem with her solution. "Rachel, I told him about the baby, and he left me. He did not say another word to me after he realized what I was telling him. He just got on his horse and left. No man will have me now. You are a widow. Someone will have you again. I ... I am a whore." I whisper this last word and Rachel falls silent.

I listen to the breeze rustling the wagon cover. "May I stay on with you? I understand if you can't have me. Perhaps Gracie will take me back."

Rachel scoffs. "Of course you can stay with me. We shall pray. You are carrying a child. I could no more kick you out of this wagon than

I would one of my girls. I saw your sketches, and I know your heart. And if nothing else, I enjoy your company and appreciate your help."

"But what about the baby? I'm not married, Rachel. I never have been."

I want her to understand. To hate me as much as I hate myself for not fighting, not screaming, for letting it happen.

She says nothing, only squeezes my hand and falls silent for the night. I lie awake though the emotion of the day has left me empty. Telling my story has relieved me of my sense of isolation, but it has rekindled my fury and hatred of Jed. It enrages me that his evil reach continues to touch me, months and miles away. Will I never be rid of him? I feel the baby move, just a slight flutter, and I realize that I will not. Jed will be with me, in some way, for the rest of my life.

Rachel's right. She keeps going for her girls, and I must do the same for this baby.

Chapter 22

T WO DAYS LATER, when the bell clangs, I feel a chill in the air, one I haven't felt yet on this trip. It smells different, too. Today we leave the winding Snake River behind. I won't miss it, but the mountains ahead will be difficult.

I climb from the wagon and lift Angelina down behind me. Rachel kneels by the fire, trying to get it going, while Charlie works on lining up the oxen and preparing them to be yoked. I stop helping Angelina and watch him. He and I have not spoken since our discussion after my rescue, but he has surprised me by staying here. He can yoke the animals by himself, but it is a bit of a struggle for him to do it without falling down. Rachel gazes intently at the fire, avoiding any eye contact with either me or Charlie. Apparently she wants me to help him. Even two-year-old Angelina abandons me, leaving me alone with him in front of the wagon.

"You're still here," I say. "I thought you'd left yesterday and headed back to your family. Or are you just resting your horse?"

"I'm still here. I thought about leaving." His eyes drop back to the task at hand. "Can you give me a hand here?"

I wonder where he has stayed, but it doesn't really matter. He's here, and that's all I care about. I hurry to his side and lift the yoke in place over the animal's neck as he fits the neckpiece to it. We repeat the process for the other team without speaking to one another. We have hills in front of us today, so everyone yokes all their available teams into position; no rest for any of the animals today. Rachel only has two teams, and I pray they will be enough to get us through the mountains that lie ahead. If not, like others before us, we will shed more of Rachel's belongings along the trail. I look toward the hills, dreading them. We are entering what the guide books say is possibly the most difficult part of the journey.

When all the animals are yoked, I break the silence. "What made you decide to stay?"

He glances silently at me, shakes his head, and continues to harness them to the wagon's tongue.

I think I know the answer, but I want to hear him say it, so I repeat my question.

"Sarah? What do you think?" he finally asks.

"I just want to hear you say it, Charlie. You're the one who left the other night."

He doesn't look away. "I'm staying because of you," he says. "I've thought about it. The child, it doesn't matter."

I stare at him, shocked. "It doesn't matter? How can it possibly not matter?"

He looks at me, hurt etched in his eyes. "I don't want to hear about it. I don't want to know. I'd kill him myself if I could. Understand?"

I do. I head to the fire to help Rachel with the girls and breakfast, wondering what this means. I don't think we can be a "we" if he thinks this baby doesn't matter.

The three of us, Charlie, Rachel and I spend the next few days getting into a routine on the trail. While Charlie can't walk with the teams, he can drive from the seat of the wagon, giving me and Rachel much needed rest from our duties. In the evening, he plays a borrowed fiddle for the camp. We have not had music since the train's fiddle owner drowned in a river crossing a month or so back. Couples dance and clap, enjoying the respite.

Each evening that he plays, I sit near him, watching his face, his hands on the strings. I have missed this. I remember why I fell in love with him. And now I'm sure. That's what this is: love. But I won't ruin him in order to have him.

He watches me too, nodding his head and tapping his foot in time with the music.

On the fourth night that he plays, I sit next to Rachel. He ends with a song I have heard him play, but this is the first time I have heard the words because Mrs. Sawyer, the captain's wife, softly sings them. It's as if they were written for us. Charlie never takes his gaze from me as he plays, and it takes me halfway through the song before I realize he is playing for me.

Tell me the tales that to me were so dear,
Long, long ago,
Long, long ago,
Sing me the songs I delighted to hear,
Long, long ago, long ago,
Now you are come all my grief is removed,
Let me forget that so long you have roved.
Let me believe that you love as you loved,
Long, long ago, long ago.

Do you remember the paths where we met?
Long, long ago,
Long, long ago.
Ah, yes, you told me you'd never forget,
Long, long ago, long ago.
Then to all others, my smile you preferred,
Love, when you spoke, gave a charm to each
word.
Still my heart treasures the phrases I heard,
Long, long ago, long ago.

Tho' by your kindness my fond hopes were raised,
Long, long ago,
Long, long ago.
You by more eloquent lips have been praised,
Long, long ago, long ago,
But by long absence your truth has been tried,
Still to your accents I listen with pride,
Blessed as I was when I sat by your side.
Long, long ago, long ago.

When the music dies down, everyone quietly enjoys their brief moment of fun on the arduous journey. Charlie lays the fiddle in its case and shuts the lid as they disperse to their wagons and tents.

"Sarah, can we go for a walk?"

"I'd like that."

I have been sitting on the ground, my legs crossed in front of me, my splint resting on my lap. He reaches for my good hand and pulls me to my feet. We walk toward the edge of the camp, and our shoulders bump as we walk in silence. For the first time in a long time, the silence is comfortable, and neither of us speak until we are safely out of earshot of the wagons.

Charlie finally breaks our silence. "I'm going to ask you something. I ain't askin' your Pa or Rachel or Captain Sawyer. I'm askin' you."

He stops and reaches for my right hand with his. We can only hold those hands as my left hand is all wrapped up and his left hand clutches his cane. I look at us and start laughing.

"Sarah, I'm bein' serious here."

I try to compose myself. He waits for me to do so, again. It seems he has spent a lot of time these past few months doing just that, waiting for me to compose myself. I take a deep breath and look down at the ground to calm myself, then I lift my eyes and face him.

"Are you ready?" he asks.

I nod.

"Will you marry me?" He speaks softly, but he holds my gaze as he asks.

This is not the question I had been expecting. My heart lurches in my chest. "You want to marry me? Why?"

"I love you. It's as simple as that. If I didn't want to marry you, I wouldn't have asked you. You can't help what happened to you, Sarah. You shouldn't have ever run. Stayin' put would've avoided this whole mess."

I feel the warmth of his hand in mine. I want to tell him about Jed, to be totally honest, but he doesn't want to hear it. He said as much himself. If he'll take me despite this baby, I'll take him, no matter how selfish that may seem.

"I'd like that, Charlie. If you'll have me."

He smiles and pulls me into his arms. My splint separates us awkwardly, but I finally know what it feels like to have his arms around me. I feel safe for the first time in months. He knows what happened, and he still loves me, still wants me.

I wake in the night, shaking, remembering Charlie's arms around me, the heat in my belly when he kissed me, but the joy evaporates as I realize what I've done. A wedding to Charlie means a wedding night with Charlie. I see Jed's face above mine in the grove, and my heart speeds up. Suddenly I'm back on the Snake River's bank, reliving that horrible afternoon. I rub my belly and take a deep breath to calm myself. I'm not sure I can give Charlie what I know he wants. I'm not even sure I want to.

DESPITE MY FEARS, the wedding takes place the next evening. Babies, weddings, death. They just happen as we creep our way westward, without months of planning. Nothing, it seems, stops the train. My wedding isn't what I had imagined it would be as a young girl, but the wagons are circled, the camp is set. Charlie has supped with the Sawyers; he had spoken with the captain shortly after we had decided to marry.

I sit on a barrel in Rachel's wagon and watch her dig down into her trunk. She pulls out a rather plain calico print, blue with small yellow flowers. Dust flies from the cloth, and she shakes her head.

"I don't know why I thought it might have been spared the dust."

She looks at me through the cloud of dirt floating in the air between us, and we both begin to laugh. The dust spares nothing, and now we both wear a fresh layer from Rachel shaking out the dress.

I washed this evening in a cold creek, but it doesn't seem to have helped. I still feel gritty. She tosses me the dress.

"You're going to have to help me with this," I say.

She shuts the trunk, crawls over to me, and loosens the rags which tie the splint to my arm. I set the wooden plank on my lap and lift my arm. My wrist throbs with the movement, and I note the odd lump where it had broken. I hold it as still as possible as Rachel undoes the fastening on my dress and pulls the sleeve down my arm.

As she pulls on the sleeves, my bosom, already large and cumbersome but now even larger with the baby, erupts from my dress and cascades down my chest. Rachel begins to giggle again.

"Oh my," she says as I grab at the blue calico in an attempt at modesty. She turns away to try to hide her smile, but it is too late.

"What? Why are you laughing?"

She ignores my question. "Charlie's waiting. Let's get you dressed."

I glare at her but can't help grinning, and I reach my arms through the new dress which she helps to pull over my head. My old dress is still wadded around my waist, but I can't remove that until I stand up. I sit and wait for her to fasten this one up. She gets it done, so I stand and pull my old dress down and step out of it. Finally, she replaces the splint on my arm, and I am ready—at least physically. All day I've thought of the wedding but avoided thinking what will happen after. My stomach clenches, but I take a deep breath and ignore it. I can do this, I tell myself yet again. I have a pretty dress, and I have a man who loves me and wants me. That's enough.

It is.

It has to be.

I repeat these words, hoping to convince myself they're true. I crawl toward the front of the wagon.

"One last thing and then you're ready," she says, and I pause.

"What is it?" I can't imagine what else this sweet woman has done for me. I'm already indebted to her far beyond anything I'll ever be able to repay.

"Janie? You got it ready?"

Janie clambers into the wagon. "It's not too pretty, Mama. There ain't no flowers here." She hands me a bouquet of grasses and sage that have been tied with a ribbon.

"It's lovely."

Janie grins sheepishly at the complement.

"They're all waitin' on you. Can you do this?" Rachel asks.

"The wedding? Yeah. I can do this."

Rachel gives my arm a squeeze, and we climb from the wagon to find the majority of the emigrants, probably a hundred or more people, waiting for me and for the ceremony to begin.

Captain Sawyer and Charlie stand near the Sawyer's wagon. He watches me approach, a small smile on his face. It's my favorite smile of his.

"Ya'll ready?" Mr. Sawyer's voice booms out over the crowd.

My left arm still rests in the sling, which I hold tight across my body. In my right hand, I clutch my bouquet. Charlie slides his hand into the crook of my elbow, and we face Mr. Sawyer for the ceremony.

My wedding takes a grand total of three minutes, at which point we are herded off to "our" wagon which sits fifty yards from the rest of the camp. Elizabeth and her husband have donated their second wagon for our wedding night. Trunks and barrels loaded with goods and trees fill the wagon box, and every bow is hung with supplies. It must weigh far more than a regular load.

Every boy from the train follows us, whooping and hollering. The girls and women smile and giggle. Rachel waves, a wide smile spread across her face.

"Ya'll right?" Charlie asks. His face is red with embarrassment or excitement, I can't tell which.

Suddenly the full force of what is about to happen hits me. I feel my knees buckle and almost drop, but Charlie still has his arm in mine and holds me up.

"There ain't nothin' to be afraid of, Sarah. Just get in the wagon. We'll talk."

Talk? He just wants to talk? I doubt his intentions but quicken my steps. We climb in as quickly as possible, pulling on the string ties to tighten the canvas and keep the boys' prying eyes out. A narrow tick covers the trunks in the middle, and my quilt lies on top. I crawl over the goods and perch myself on the side of it.

Charlie follows and sits next to me. He is close enough that our arms and legs touch. "Are you scared?"

I sit down hard on the blankets that have been piled in here to make a bed, and I listen to the hoops and hollers, the jeers and taunts that follow us. It sounds like they've circled the wagon now. We have held chivarees on our old train and on this train, but I never thought one would happen to me and Charlie, though I'd imagined it a time or two to entertain myself as I walked.

I can only nod in reply to his question. My heart sped up when I saw the bed in the middle of the wagon. It is there for one purpose and one purpose only; it is our wedding bed. I have a weird, floaty feeling in my gut, one I get when I'm nervous and can't escape, like a swimming lesson when I was young and Papa would toss me in the creek to sink or swim, a river crossing now, or a steep downhill descent in the wagon.

Charlie takes my hand in both of his. Now the yelling boys outside rock the wagon, and my body crashes into Charlie. He wraps his arm around me to steady us. We sit and wait for the laughter and baudy comments surrounding the wagon to calm. I take this moment to breathe, to try to relax myself. Charlie deserves better than a panic attack on his wedding night.

"I don't want to hurt you, Sarah. And more than that, I don't want you to think of ... of before while you're with me. You're my wife now. I want you to be *my* wife."

My throat tightens as he says these words, and I close my eyes to ward off the tears I feel coming. As soon as my eyes close, memories fill my mind. I open them and look at Charlie. I'm terrified of what comes next, but I don't want to tell him that.

"I want that too, Charlie," I manage to croak, and I do. I want to feel normal and excited about my wedding night, but I don't know if I can. I feel like I might disintegrate into a million little pieces if he does anything other than sit next to me and hold my hand.

"Do you want to do this? Can you?"

I keep my eyes on his. "I think so."

I need to, for him. I owe him that, and I love him. This terror makes me hate Jed even more, if that's possible.

He lets go of my hands and cradles my face in his rough, warm palms. He leans in close, until our noses almost touch. "Are you sure? Be honest with me, Sarah."

I nod, my throat too tight to talk. Do I really have a choice?

He drops his hands to my shoulders, leans in and kisses me.

I keep my eyes open, so I can see him, my Charlie. I want to only see him, not the horrible image of his cousin which fills my mind each time I shut my eyes. His kiss warms me, and I kiss him back.

His hands drop to my bosom. His touch is gentle and slow as he begins to undo the buttons on the front of my dress. I am surprised to find that I don't feel embarrassment or shame as he slips the dress from my shoulders and my breasts escape.

He catches one in his hand and smiles at me. He lifts my broken arm and pulls the sleeve over the splint. He holds my hand, sits back, and observes me. "Your turn, Sar."

I hold my splint up.

"You're going to have to undo your own buttons. I can't." My voice is a little shaky, but I focus on Charlie, on right now, not on anything else but the man with me. He laughs and pulls his shirt over his head. I gasp, and his eyes widen in alarm. I have never seen Charlie without his shirt.

"Are you all right? Do you want me to put that back on?"

Despite the fact that I am sitting there half-naked, my dress pulled down around my waist, my throat has relaxed a bit. I can speak, but not loudly.

"Not at all," I whisper. "You're beautiful." I reach out my hand to touch him. His breathing quickens and becomes a bit shaky. "Charlie?"

"HmmmmH?"

"I just need you to do one thing for me," I say as I rest my hand on his chest. We sit close to one another, our bodies almost touching, but not quite.

"What is it?"

"I need you to keep your eyes open and look at me, to see me. I don't know if that makes sense, but I need you to see *me*. Will you do that? Can you?"

"Is that all?"

"I think so."

As he slips my dress from my hips and slides his pants down, he never takes his eyes from mine. When he lays down beside me and caresses me, he looks at me, and I know that he is here for me, Sarah Ann Crawford Dixon. I am his wife, and I know that he loves me.

Afterward, we lay side by side. I reach down and feel my legs, my arms, my belly. I am in one piece. I have not flown apart, and for the first time in months I consider reaching Oregon and having a family with this man beside me. I begin to think maybe I can make it, and I fall asleep with him holding me tight.

The Dalles, Oregon – September 1847

It takes three long weeks to cross the Oregon mountains, but we finally make it into the Columbia River gorge. The way is narrow next to the mighty river, but at least the water is plentiful. I walk next to the wagon as Rachel drives. Charlie is in the back of the train, driving the stock from his horse. We are pulling into the Dalles, a mission, but the place does not look much like God has blessed it. As my Mama would say, the place looks like starvation.

"Charlie wants me to leave a letter here for my Mama," I tell Rachel, "but I can't. What if Jed is still with them? What if he catches up to us?"

"I'm surprised Charlie isn't concerned about his cousin. Did you mention that to him?"

"I did, but he didn't seem concerned. He thinks I owe it to my Mama. He saw how afraid she was when I ran. If you include me, she's lost three kids on the trail. I don't want to hurt her, but I'm afraid."

"You ought to speak to your husband about this." She is always reasonable, thoughtful, and right.

"Rachel, if your Mama was within fifty miles of you, would you go to her?"

She looks at me, surprised. "Of course I would."

"That's what Charlie thinks, too. He doesn't understand why I'm hesitant, and I don't know why he doesn't. I *told* him Rachel. He knows about the baby."

She frowns. "I think you ought to consider carefully what you do. There is a man who has done you harm, and he lives near your mother. You have a child coming. You best think about that."

I wonder if Jed would really come after me. If he knows I'm married to Charlie, would he still? I don't know how he'd figure out the baby I'm carrying belongs to him. I know Charlie wouldn't tell him. I wonder again why Charlie feels so strongly that I should write, but he has spoken of it enough that I know it's important to him.

"I suppose. I'll let Charlie decide what to do with it, though I hope he'll hold off on sending it."

"What are you going to write it on?"

"I'll just take a page from my sketchbook. That way Mama will know it's from me."

I spend the rest of the evening composing the letter in my head, and as soon as I complete my chores, I climb into the wagon and begin writing. My fingers tire from writing so small, but if I'm going to write her, I want to fit as much as I can on the two sheets of paper I have allowed myself. I tell her of Charlie finding me and giving me the quilt. I tell her of our marriage and the baby we are expecting this spring. Mostly I try to tell her that I am alive and well. I have survived this journey, and though I didn't think I would or even that I wanted to, I have made it this far alive.

When I am done, I sign my married name, fold the letter in half, and go in search of my husband. He is sitting with Mr. Black, discussing their plans for the store they plan on constructing this spring. Charlie will have to find his parents, because they have all his leather working tools and money. We have nothing and continue to live off the charity of others.

Charlie looks up and a grin crosses his face when he sees me, sending my heart on a little dance.

"I wrote the letter, but I'd like to take a walk," I say.

Thankfully, the rain has subsided for the time being, and though the ground is muddy, no more water is falling from the sky. Charlie excuses himself from Mr. Black, and we walk toward the river.

"I wrote this, but I think you ought to wait, and we'll send it on in the spring."

"Why? I would think you would want your mama to know that you're alive, that we're married." He doesn't mention the baby, and I wonder about that. He hasn't said much about the baby.

"She can know this spring. I don't want Jed around. I'm afraid he'll come up here if he knows I'm here."

"I don't think he will if he knows we're married. That means I won something that he wanted. He won't come around knowing that."

"You think you *won* me? That's what I am? A prize?"

Charlie stops walking and grabs my arm to stop me. "Sarah, you know that's not what I think, but I've told you how Jed competed with me while we was growin' up. He always has, and I don't think he's probably changed much, but you never know with him. We grew up together, so he might come up. Why do you look so scared? I can protect you. And you know how to shoot, too."

I stare hard at him. *Why wouldn't I look scared?* I want to scream at him, but I swallow my fear. "I just really think you ought to wait until after the baby is born to get in touch with anyone."

"They gotta know where we are, Sarah. I need my tools."

"So why don't you write a letter to your Pa and leave it here?" This seems like the most obvious solution.

"I already have. I left one at the Indian Agency on the Umatilla River." He shakes his head. "You need to write because you owe it to your mama. You're the one who ran. You owe her a letter at least."

Alarm courses through me. "You left a letter back over a hundred miles ago, and you didn't think fit to tell me?"

"I just thought of it as we pulled in and didn't think much of it. I told them that we married and that I need my tools."

I bite my tongue and follow him through the drizzling rain as he escorts me back to camp, my letter in his hand. He will leave it here for Mama, but I realize that my concerns with my letter are nothing. Jed already knows where we are. I wonder how long it will take for him to catch us. He's coming.

Chapter 23

Present Day

AGNES ROLLS OVER *in her bed, the urine pressing uncomfortably on her bladder, and readies herself mentally to get up, an event which has, through the years, become more of a process than she ever thought it could. She sits up slowly, turns, and gingerly lowers her feet to the floor. Her toes, out of pure habit, inch across the floor almost with a will of their own, until they sink into the plushy softness of her slippers. Satisfied that they have sniffed out their rightful home, they inch their way in.*

She sighs, a deep sigh, one that speaks of the intensity of focus necessary to raise an eighty-nine-year-old body from a sitting to a standing position. In her one foray into the world of yoga, twenty-nine years ago at the spry old age of sixty, she had learned this deep kind of breath was called a cleansing breath. She needs cleansing, all right. Though she isn't sure a breath will give her all she needs, she gives it a shot anyway. What the hell. She breathes again, placing each hand on the edge of the bed then slides off, pushing herself upright as she does so, praying her legs will hold. They do.

Light peeks through the vertical blinds. Blinds should make one just that—blind—but these fail miserably. And they're ugly, except for the light that peeks through this morning. It is a bright light, the kind of light that speaks of an early spring morning, not the gray light of a rain or snowstorm. She slowly peels one of the slats back and peeks out, squinting to avoid the glare.

She doesn't see any tulip and daffodil leaves poking up from the soil, but she decides they are coming soon. Leafless trees reach toward the blue sky; no clouds today. The grass is dry, and she knows it would

217

crunch under her feet if she were to venture onto it.

Agnes turns from the window, pleased. It is time for coffee and the porch swing. Those have always been her favorite mornings.

The house, quiet with sleeping child; the air, cool and fresh. She can sit and swing, get her head on straight for the day. She cherishes those mornings. Oh, she doesn't have a child anymore, but her porch swing time is her time, a sacred gift to herself. During the winter months when it was too cold to sit out there, she'd sit at the kitchen table and stare out the back window at the yard, a poor substitute for the swing.

She shuffles toward the bathroom and her morning rituals. Ah, today she would dispense with those, except for taking care of her bladder. Her first porch day. Tugging her robe off the hook on the back of the bathroom door, slipping it on, and tying it tightly around her waist, Agnes totters to her door, nodding in anticipation.

She pulls it open and pauses, momentarily confused. Then she recalls moving her bedroom downstairs so to avoid a fall.

"I walk out of a room for fifty years, I guess I get used to the view," she mutters to herself.

Her daughter worries far too much, though she has to admit she doesn't miss the daily hikes up and down those steps. And there had been nights when she had slept on the couch in the front room rather than navigate those damn stairs. So yes, moving downstairs had been good, though she still can't get used to it. Agnes moves down the hall to the door which she slowly pulls open, stepping out into the morning air. She breathes in.

"Seasons smell. They should bottle that. I'd wear it every day." She had always been able to smell the first day of spring, summer, and fall. Winter not so much.

The door clicks shut behind her, startling her out of her reverie. She turns and looks at the handle, realizing she has forgotten her coffee.

"Never mind that. I'll take a stroll then get a cup. I've got all morning. Shoot, I've got all day."

Today would be a good day, a day with a plan: a walk, a swing, a coffee. That is all, but that is good. Some days stretch endlessly and empty in front of her.

She steps gingerly down the path in front of her. Rosemary would yell if she fell. Oh, how she'd holler! She'd always been a loud one when *she got mad, even as an infant. So Agnes moves slowly, admiring the flowers, the beds that are so well kept. The yard is lovely.*

She walks on, holding herself as tall as she can. She knows she isn't as tall as she used to be, but she can try to reach 5' 8" again. Maybe if she holds her chin up a bit. Reaching the corner, she decides to cross the street.

"The street has gotten busy," she says quietly. "People moving, moving, moving."

"You okay?" a man asks from just behind her.

Agnes pauses then glances around and faces a young man, well, he's maybe fifty-ish or so.

"Oh," she says softly. She's not sure where this man came from.

"Can I give you a hand across the street?"

She grasps at his outstretched arm. Slowly, they navigate the street.

"Thank you. Can you stay for a cup of coffee?"

He stares at her, looking slightly alarmed. "No coffee today, thanks. Are you okay?"

She nods. "I'm going for a coffee and a swing. I wish you would slow down a bit and stay with me."

He shakes his head. "Uh, I've gotta run."

Agnes walks on, unsure. She feels an all too familiar knot of fear begin to curdle the inside of her stomach. She clenches her gnarled hands. Time to head home to her swing, though the walk has been lovely.

This way.

She lifts her chin and takes one small, dignified step at a time.

Breathing a sigh of relief, Agnes sees her swing. The clenching in her stomach relaxes, and she steps off the sidewalk and onto the drive. Her swing is right there, welcoming. She has made it. She is ready for a rest, too. But dammit, she still doesn't have that coffee. Oh bother. She'll sit a bit and get the coffee later. One has to learn to be flexible at some point. She reaches the swing and slowly lowers her ancient body into it. A barrel, empty of its spring flowers, sits next to it. Agnes rests, laying her head back, letting the fall sunshine warm her skin. Her breath evens out after the exertion of her walk. So many cars. And so noisy nowadays.

"Ma'am? … Uh, Ma'am?"

Agnes peels her head up from the cushion and gasps. Her bony hand flutters to her chest. "Why, Rosemary! You're here." *She stops speaking, and her forehead wrinkles up as she struggles to think.* Where is the coffee? "I'd ... offer you some coffee, but I ... I don't seem to have any." *She pauses then pats the seat next to her.* "Sit with me, Rosemary?"

The young woman kneels. "Are you okay, ma'am?"

"Why are you calling me 'ma'am'? I'm your mother."

The girl shakes her head, so Agnes repeats herself.

"What are you saying? I, um, I can't understand you," *the girl says as she rises.* "James!" *she hollers. Then she speaks into a microphone.* "I need some assistance in the Garden Center."

Agnes wonders who James is then decides perhaps he's the gardener Rosemary has hired to keep the flowers nice. A young man approaches wearing a horrible orange vest.

"James, can you go call the nursing home please? I think they have an escapee."

"Rosemary," *Agnes says.*

The girl pats her leg. "It's okay. We'll get you home."

Agnes looks around her. She is already home, she wants to tell this girl. She's on her porch. But the words don't come.

Chapter 24

Late September 1847- Columbia River Gorge

OUR WAGON IS last in line, waiting to board a raft to float the Columbia. The icy water laps over the boards of the rafts as the heavy wagons load up, one wagon per raft. We remove the wheels and set the wagon boxes on the raft logs. Rachel and I watch the proceedings, wondering if rafting the river is the right decision. It is either two days by river to Portland, or two more weeks on the trail if we take the Barlow road. After much discussion, we've decided to float the wagons down the river. The oxen can't take much more. Charlie will drive the oxen along the Barlow road. If all goes well, we'll meet up again in two weeks in Portland.

We haven't seen a river like this since we crossed the Missouri. The heavier wagons weigh the rafts down, water coursing over the tops of the logs. I can't imagine surviving rapids on these rafts.

I'm watching the river when I feel a hand on my shoulder. "By God, it *is* you."

Jed.

The corner of his mouth crooks up. That same smile. Six months ago, when I'd first seen him, it was his smile I noticed. It's the first thing I see today too, and it still unnerves me.

"Get your hand off me." I swipe at it and step back.

He laughs and lets his hand fall, but his eyes bore into me. "Where's your ... what is it? Husband?"

"I'm right here, Jed," Charlie says, and I thank the good Lord right then and there that Charlie's not off with the stock. I step back to stand next to him.

221

Jed hitches his thumbs in his suspenders and leans back on the wagon, then he looks me up and down. I can't hold his gaze. I look away toward the wagon, then decide I don't need to be here.

"I'll leave you two alone."

Charlie looks at me, his eyebrows raised, but I ignore him and climb into the wagon. I don't want to see Jed. I don't want to hear his voice either, but the wagon is the only place where I can hide from his eyes.

I lie down and close my eyes, trying to shut out the image of Jed's face, when he begins to speak again. "She's havin' a baby?" he asks Charlie. I want to scream at him. I can't lay here and listen to this without doing something. If nothing else, I've learned that lesson. I reach up to the hooks which hold Rachel's rifle and take it down. I make sure it's loaded, take the safety off, and point it toward Jed's voice.

"When she ran off, Indians got her," Charlie says. Indians? What is he talking about?

Jed laughs, his loud booming laugh. "That what she told ya? That she's carryin' a half-breed?" He doesn't wait for an answer, just keeps talking, and I want to shove the gun right in his mouth. "That ain't no half-breed she's carryin'."

"Like hell it ain't. It's that damn Indian we hung at Fort Hall. Glad we got him for it though."

Joseph? Charlie thinks this is Joseph's baby? I thought I'd explained everything to him, but … The gun drops to my lap as I realize I never did.

"That what she told ya?"

"She ain't told me nothin' and I ain't gonna ask about it. I'm just gonna get rid of it when it gets here."

Get rid of it? *What?*

"What if I told ya that she's carryin' yer cousin?" Jed says, his voice low.

"What the hell you talkin' about?"

I am frozen, the gun useless on my lap.

"Just what I said. That baby's mine." He chuckles, as if he's played a big joke on everyone. "Yer wife's mine. Always has been."

Charlie doesn't make a sound. Why doesn't he argue? Why doesn't he fight for me?

"Why you think I was gonna marry her?" Jed asks. "She was all over me."

Finally, Charlie speaks in a low voice. "You're a lyin' son of a bitch."

"I ain't lyin'. Ask yer wife yerself."

I stop breathing. Every lie I've ever told clogs right in my throat. The wagon cover sinks in on me, suffocating me, and I need to get out. I grab the gun with my good hand and crawl toward the front of the wagon. I feel like I'm moving through deep water that's just about to go over my head. I see Charlie as soon as I get to the front of the wagon.

He stares at me, his face white. His hand trembles as it clutches his cane. "This true?" he asks, as I climb down from the wagon.

"Not like he said," I manage to whisper through my closed throat as I pull the rifle from the wagon's seat.

Charlie steps back and grabs for the gun.

"Don't," I snap, warning him.

He steps back and holds his hand up. "How else could it happen, Sarah? I know how babies happen." He stares at me for a moment before shaking his head and spitting at my feet. "You took me for the biggest damn fool."

I feel waves of disgust rolling off him.

The baby kicks. I know Charlie came after me, married me, saved me, but only I can save this child.

"I never did take you fer a fool. You knew. You knew before you ever married me that I was with child. You knew it wasn't yours, and you still married me, didn't you?"

He doesn't respond, just turns and walks away.

"Well, ain't that sweet. I guess you're mine after all," Jed says, laughter in his voice.

I lift the rifle to my shoulder, rest it on my splint, and wrap my fingers around the trigger. I point the barrel at him. "Jed Monroe, I will kill you if I ever catch a glimpse of your sorry hide again. You hear me?"

His eyes widen and the smile drips from his face, replaced by the sneer he normally wears around me. "Put that thing down before you hurt yerself."

"You know I can shoot," I say. "You best back up."

From the corner of my eye I see Charlie stop walking away from me. He's watching.

The fool takes a step toward me. I eye the place just above Jed's left shoulder but below the brim of his hat. I want him to feel, really *feel* the shot go right by that thick skull of his, get a taste of the fear he's made me feel. When he steps closer, I brace myself and pull the trigger. My bones grate on each other beneath my splint, and I grit my teeth in pain as he yelps and backs up, falling on his backside. Now it is my turn to smile. The sound of the shot reverberates through the canyon, and the bullet lodges with a loud thwack in a tree on the other side of the trail. Screams come from the nearby wagons.

"Sarah! What the hell you doin?" Charlie yells, but I ignore him.

"Damn't, Sarah! You tryin' to kill me?" Jed hollers as he scrambles to his feet.

"Not yet. If I was tryin' to kill you, you'd be dead right where you stand. Now git!"

"You'll hang if you shoot me. Then what'll happen to my son?" He stretches the word son, playing with it on his tongue, like a piece of tobacco he's suckin' on. Regardless, he backs up a few more steps. Good. I smile, giving him the same smile he's given me in the past, and I laugh. "If I shoot this again, the only thing hangin' will be your hat in the air where your head used to be. I won't hang, Jed. And you won't have me or *my* baby. He's Charlie's, anyway. I don't know what you're talkin' about, thinkin' he's yours. Take one step closer if you think I'm foolin' with this gun."

I lower the gun, rip the rag off my wrist so I can use my fingers to put another shot in the chamber, and hoist the gun up to my shoulder again. He watches, and wisely stays right where he's at. For once, my hands are steady. I'm not the same girl he attacked all those months and miles past. He'd best figure that out. I stare him down, not lowering my eyes for nothin'. I'd worried about bein' rude to him once before, and all it had gotten me was the worst ten minutes of my life and a child. Manners be damned.

I could kill him, without a doubt in my mind. Perhaps I'd hang, but my baby had a papa and it damn sure wasn't Jedediah Monroe. My baby'd be fine, and I realized I'd die to make sure my child would never lay eyes on the sorry cuss in front of me.

"Sarah? Put that gun down. Someone's gonna get hurt." I think it's Mr. Black, but I ain't takin' my eyes off Jed.

"No, sir. I ain't puttin' this gun down. This scoundrel means to do my family harm, and I mean to protect us. I've had about enough of you, Jedediah Monroe. Next shot won't miss. You ready to leave yet?" I cock the gun and look Jed in the eye. "Cuz you should be. And Mr. Black, don't you take one step closer neither. This don't concern you." I hear no more movement behind me.

Jed's true nature emerges, like a bear waking from the calm sleep of hibernation. His face darkens and he spits.

"You're just a whore, slicked up and pretendin' you're not."

I nod, not taking my eyes off of him. If he makes just one move, that's all it'd take. I'd take him out, and Mr. Black would probably shoot me, but Jed must be listening. He backs up another four paces.

"You can put that damn gun down. I ain't comin' over there, ya crazy woman."

"That's right. You ain't. You ain't staying here neither. Yer welcome here is all used up. Like I said, I see yer hide again, I'll shoot it dead."

He turns and walks down the track to his horse. I keep the gun up until he mounts and rides off, then I lower the gun slowly. My arms burn after holdin' it up for that long, then my hands, my arms, my whole body starts to shake. I would've killed him, I know, without a second thought. Feelings of horror and maybe even excitement sweep through me. I don't know where this murderous version of myself has come from. Then the baby kicks again, and I know.

"You all right?" Rachel stands behind me.

I glance around for Charlie, but he's gone, heading in the opposite direction from his cousin.

"I woulda killed him, Rachel, without even pausing. I'd a put a hole all the way through him." What kind of person does that make me? Putting my hatred above everything else? The shaking worsens as Rachel takes the rifle from my hands.

"We best get to work. We got to load the wagon and get these wheels off." She pauses to look around. "And it looks like we're on our own for a bit."

I look to where I last saw Charlie, and I wonder if I'll ever see him again.

Chapter 25

October 1847 - Portland, Oregon

ONLY A HANDFUL of buildings in the entire town of Portland might be suitable for Mr. Black and Charlie to start their businesses, but I don't want to head down the Willamette to Oregon City. What I've seen of Portland has convinced me that anywhere else might be better than here, but if that anywhere else has Jed in it, I don't want to be wherever that is either. He's not here, so it's better just to stay put.

I share a hovel with Rachel, her girls, Elizabeth, and her husband Mr. Black while we wait for Charlie to return with the stock, if he ever does. The ten foot by ten foot shack is attached to a larger home, and the owners seem happy to crowd as many of us overlanders as they can into the space while collecting rent. When we got here, it had been occupied for six weeks by a family who left it for Oregon City. My own family has not yet arrived, so I assume they took the Barlow road and are south in Oregon City, if they made it at all.

Rachel sits at the hearth, the rain dripping through the roof and onto the fire, extinguishing the meager flames. Water drips incessantly. In one day, we drew four buckets of water out of the hearth.

I close my eyes and think again about that afternoon on the Snake River. I imagine myself as the mouse the hawk kept hunting, until one day the hawk either couldn't find the little creature or found something easier to hunt. So it flew away. That's what Charlie has done. He's quit hunting me, chasing me. It's my turn to be the hawk and go after what I want. I've spent this entire journey, from the day I left our farm in Indiana, following orders: Papa's orders, Mama's commands, Jed's manipulations, even Pierce's auctioning me off.

"Mr. Black?"

The elderly gentleman sits in the corner, whittling a stick and whistling. "Yes, young lady?"

"Can I borrow one of yer horses? I'm goin' after Charlie."

He raises his bushy white eyebrows at me, then throws back his head and laughs, a hearty laugh. "You ain't goin' anywhere in yer state. Sit back down."

"Mr. Black, sir, I just walked two thousand miles through all sorts of trials. I think I can make it down the Willamette a few miles."

"Well, ye're walkin', then, cuz you ain't takin' the horse. She's still restin'. Girl, we just got here. Sit fer a bit, would you?"

"No sir, I ain't sittin' anymore. We've been here three weeks, and that's long enough for Charlie to get here."

"You sure he's even coming?"

I'm not, not sure at all. They all heard every word said between Jed and me, but now that I've decided to go, I want to leave right now. I've got to try.

"Sarah, you can't do this," Rachel says, her forehead scrunched in concern.

"Why not?"

"Ye're a woman, alone. It ain't right."

"She's right," Mr. Black adds.

I scowl at both of them. "Then would you go with me, Mr. Black? I gotta go after Charlie. I think you know why." I refuse to look down or give in like I would have before we left on this infernal journey. I don't want him with me, but I s'pose they're right about me being alone.

Mr. Black stands. "I can't let you do this."

"I'll git yer bedroll ready," Elizabeth says from the chair in the corner where she's been sitting watching the proceedings. She's a little like Mama. Mr. Black gets his way all the time—until he doesn't, and that's when Elizabeth has made the decision.

Rachel hands me her last pair of shoes.

I look down at my feet, red and swollen with the cold, rain, and baby. They were wet for the entire trip down the river. I'm not sure they'll ever look like my normal feet again.

"I can't take these Rachel. They're yer last pair."

"You can't go barefoot. Winter's comin' on. You'll lose toes if you don't wear them. If you find your husband, he can make me some new ones, can't he?"

"Thank you."

"Where you gonna look?" Elizabeth asks.

Her husband glares at me as he speaks. "I s'pose we'll just head south and see if anyone's seen him. It's been three weeks, as you say, long enough to get here with the animals."

"That sounds fine," I say then add, "thank you, sir."

"It won't take but a day to get to Oregon City, I s'pose. Let's leave at first light," he mutters, then he harrumphs and sits back down. His wife scurries around to get him ready.

I sigh but realize that is probably the best choice. I can make some biscuits tonight to take with us if I can beg some flour off someone and keep the fire going long enough to get some coals.

The next morning, miraculously, the sun shines across the dripping land. We load the pack mule with extra food, blankets, and a gun, then we saddle the horses and head south. The road is quiet this late in the season. Most of the immigrants are holed up, readying for the winter in shacks, wagons, and cabins. I will mark this year as one of the longest, most trying of my life, and I'm willing to bet most immigrants would do the same.

We ride silently for several hours and only see a few others on the trail. Each party we see, I ask after Charlie. We hear no word of him until the mid-afternoon when we catch a group of immigrants still in their wagons heading north to Portland.

"We're lookin' for a person missing from our party. You wouldn't happen to have seen him?" Mr. Blacks asks the grizzled man who drives the team.

His gaunt faced family stares at us. "Gotta name?"

"Charlie Dixon," says Mr. Black. "He's drivin' our oxen but don't know if he went over Lolo pass or the Barlow road outta the Dalles. He was thinkin' Lolo pass, but he mighta changed his mind. We just know we ain't seen him since the Dalles. He's got a cane, a bit of a limp. Light brown hair. Blue eyes."

"Walks funny you say?"

"Yes sir," I say, finally speaking up. "You wouldn't happen to know where we could find him?"

"Believe he's in Oregon City," the man finally says. "I mighta seen the feller ye're lookin' for in the store, talking bout settin' up shop."

228

My heart has almost stopped in my chest. If what this man says is true, then Charlie has no intention of coming back for me. Will he take me back if I keep going or is this a futile trip?

"Thank you, sir," says Mr. Black. "I'll let ya git on yer way."

He dismounts and leads both our horses to the side of the road. Finally, he breaks the silence. "Well, I guess I see this a couple a ways. One, we still gotta get the animals, but if we take 'em back to that shack we're livin' in we can't well feed 'em. I'm hopin' yer Charlie has them somewhere safe with feed, but I oughta check, as they're mine and Miss Rachel's. Two, you gotta decide if you want yer husband back, or else there ain't no reason fer you to keep ridin' this direction."

"Apparently he doesn't want me."

"Nope, I s'pose right now he don't. Let's go git the stock then. We's almost there."

"Mr. Black, I don't know anymore."

He turns to look at me. "Sarah, let me ask ya something. You love this boy?"

"Yes, I…do."

"You want him to forgive you?"

"Yes."

"Hasn't he already done that at least once? Chasin' you down halfway across this land of ours?"

I look down and fiddle with the reins in my hand. "Yes."

"And he still married you," he says, shaking his head. "Well, if you want him to forgive you one more time, you best find it in yer heart to forgive him. Are you gettin' this?"

"Yes, sir," is all I can manage to say. He's right. It's my turn to forgive. I'll even beg if need be. Really, I have no choice. He's my husband. And I love him. I always have since I first saw him.

IT'S EARLY AFTERNOON when we ride into Oregon City, which is nothing like Portland. It's actually a town with people and proper buildings. True civilization. I wished Rachel had come, but without the oxen she can't go anywhere. With that thought—that Charlie had stranded not only me but also Rachel—my temper flares as we approach the store.

"Sarah? Mr Black?" Charlie says from behind me. He stands next to the building, leaning on his cane.

"Well, hello there, Charlie. I'm after my oxen. Gotta move the wagons, get set in Portland, but you didn't make it. Did you have some trouble on the crossing?"

Charlie cuts his eyes at me before answering. "No sir, no trouble. I just hadn't made it up to you yet."

"So we noticed. How's the stock?"

"Good. The animals are round back if you wanna check on 'em." Charlie points to the corrals behind the store.

"I'll do that."

Before Mr. Black leaves, he helps me dismount then takes my horse with him. I'm alone with Charlie. A distance of ten feet separates us.

"I saw your family," he says.

"You did? Where are they?"

"They're south of here in the Willamette Valley. They were only a day behind us by the time you got on the raft. I came over the Barlow road with 'em. Your Pa's getting' a small cabin up. They're doin' all right." He pauses and eyes my growing stomach. "Jed's there too if you wanna go. He put in a land claim near yer Pa's. He'll do fine."

How dare Jed stake a claim near my family, but I can't worry about that now other than to know I won't be visiting them…ever. My concern in Charlie who's here with me now.

"What'd you tell my family? About us?"

"That we're married and ye're havin' a baby. Just like in yer letter."

"Am *I* havin' one or are *we* havin' one? Are you part of it? You are my husband."

He shrugs, but his eyes are dark with anger.

"Charlie, can we go somewhere? I wanna tell you the whole story, the entire awful story."

He doesn't move from the side of the building. "Ain't really got nowhere to go. I'm settin' up here. Got all my tools from my Pa, and I'm using a corner of this store until I can build my own place."

"There's a church over there." I point across the street. "Could we just sit in there?"

Charlie shrugs again but follows me as I head across the street to the church's pews. We can either go into a church or a bar, and I'd rather have this conversation in a church. We sit down in the quiet stillness, and I take a deep breath and begin to tell Charlie a story that I thought he already knew. I reach for his hand, but he pulls it back.

"Don't. Just tell me. Don't touch me."

I look down at my tummy, filling out with baby, and I begin to talk. Charlie sits tense and rigid as I talk. I start with Papa hiring Jed, Jed's inappropriate advances, his proposal and meeting with my father.

Finally, I tell him about Jed's attack in the hollow by the creek. "Against my will, against everything in me, Charlie, Jed ravaged me, on the banks of Alcove Spring. Remember the night I got sick? Mama had to give me spirits."

I see the surprise in his face. He remembers.

I don't tell him the details of my terror and physical pain, but I cannot stop the tears that drip down my face as I talk. "That's why I ran, Charlie. I couldn't marry that monster. I couldn't tell anyone what had happened, or I'da been a whore. You think anyone'd believe me? They all thought Jed loved me. I couldn't hurt my Mama like that, and I couldn't hurt you. My entire family would've been shamed, and you wouldn't ever look my way again." I swallow. "I thought you knew it was Jed when we married. I wouldn't have married you with that kind of lie between us. Jed's right. He fathered this child. I thought I told you that, that you understood that day on the Snake. Remember?"

I've told the story almost without breathing. I can hear the desperation in my voice. I want him to believe me, to believe in me.

"I remember you putting my hand on yer stomach." His voice catches, and he pauses before starting over. "I thought it was Joseph when you told me. When I thought back to hangin' that boy, I was glad he'd hung. I thought we'd done right, and that was before we even knew what he'd done to you. You never said Jed's name. When Jed said that at The Dalles, that it was his baby, I didn't believe it at first." He pauses, shakes his head. "During that hangin' I stood next to Jed, and it shoulda been him. It shoulda been Jed."

Charlie rises from the pew and begins pacing up and down the aisle, pausing, spinning his cane, tapping it on the ground. He stops pacing and turns to face me again. "Why didn't you say his name?"

"I thought you understood. Charlie, git over here and stop pacin'." My throat thickens. "I don't want you to leave me."

"Leave? *Me?*"

I shake my head and clench my fists in frustration. I deserve that, but how do I make him understand? "I didn't have a choice. If I hadn't left, I'd be married to Jed right now. He'd be standing here, not you."

"It probably should be him. That's his son ye're carryin'." For the first time, I can hear the pain in his voice. His cousin had beat him again. He'd had me first, but he hadn't ever had me willingly like Charlie had.

"When you thought this was Joseph's baby, what were you planning on doing with it? Why would you take Joseph's baby, a half breed child, as your own and not Jed's?"

"I wasn't planning on keepin' it. I thought we'd take it to a mission and let them have it."

"You were going to just take my baby and abandon it?"

"I didn't figure you'd want it either. Do you? Do you want that child ye're carryin'? Cuz I can't say that I want any part of it," he says, then he turns toward the door and leaves.

Mr. Black finds me curled up on a pew, my face wet with tears. He pulls me to a sitting position and puts his arm around me. "If it makes you feel any better, I saw him wipe away a few tears too."

It doesn't help. He's left me and I've become what I feared I'd be all those months ago: a whore. A woman with a baby and no husband.

"Git up, girl. We still got enough daylight left to get home to my Elizabeth."

I rise and blindly follow him out the door.

Portland, Oregon – February 1848

I groan, a violent bass harmony to the whipping of the wind through the trees outside. I holler again as another contraction seizes my body.

Elizabeth kneels between my knees. "Push for me. Push or this baby's gonna stay right there."

Rachel holds my hand. "I can see its head; we're almost there. Gimme one more push."

I grunt, heaving with every muscle in my legs and belly as I feel the head then a body slide from my womb.

"Oh, he's beautiful," Elizabeth croons. "He's got his daddy's eyes." I jerk my head to look at her, but she's gazing at the baby. "Look at him, Rachel. You see 'em? He's got Charlie's eyes."

I reach for my child. "Can I hold him yet?" The baby starts at the sound of my voice, looking for the source. Does he already know my voice? I lie back as Elizabeth lays the baby on my naked belly and begins to tie off the cord.

Blond, almost reddish fuzz covers the baby's pointy little head. He stares straight into my eyes, my soul. Despite all the anger and the hurt and the lies his coming had wrought, I see his little scrunched up face, the tiny perfect fingers, and realize this child is my light, and it isn't a light I could ever possibly hate, no matter who fathered him or how much fear and anguish it had caused.

"Elizabeth? Is this how you felt about your babies when they were born?"

Elizabeth frowns and tries to look severe, but she doesn't quite succeed. She sighs before speaking. "Yes, it's how all mommas feel at first. The hard part of lovin' comes later, but the fallin' in love, well, that's the easiest part there is, isn't it?"

Her words bring a smile to my face, and we both stare at the baby. "Let's get you both cleaned up." She pauses again before speaking. "He's a good man, Sarah. You remember that."

I glance up at her, "Charlie?"

She doesn't answer, and I wonder why she's bringing him up now. We haven't spoken of him since I returned, alone, from Oregon City three months ago.

I look down at my child and wipe Charlie from my mind. He is beautiful. Rachel and Elizabeth leave the cabin's curtained off space, and I watch his little mouth suckle, though he is not yet feeding.

The curtain moves again, and Charlie enters our makeshift birthing room in this small, wet shack. I thought I'd lost him forever, but now here he is, watching us. He closes the curtain and leans against the wall on the other side of the room. I'm not sure what to feel. Hope? Anger? Despair? I've felt them all, wondering, worrying about my fate, about how it all went wrong. But now, with Charlie here, I curiously feel nothing. It's as if I don't have the energy for it anymore, only for the small little bundle in my arms. And I'm too afraid to let myself hope anymore. I have to take my life one day at a time. If I've learned anything over the past year, it's that.

Charlie finally breaks the silence. "Mr. Black came for me two days ago, when it started."

"You've been here the whole time?" I had no idea, and I wonder that he didn't show himself earlier.

He nods in response, and now I see the exhaustion pulling on his young face. It's like what I feel in my body. I pull the baby closer, overwhelmed by a desire to protect this small human from the emotion emanating off Charlie. The baby begins to wiggle and fuss, and I ready myself to nurse him, not caring that we have an audience. He had his share of my bosom before he left. He turns aside, reddening while I push my nightshirt aside and guide the baby's little mouth to latch on and feed.

He suckles, making small baby noises. Elizabeth was right. The falling in love part is easy, too easy. Falling in love with Charlie was easy like this too, but since then, it seems not one thing went right. When I came home from Oregon City, I shoved that love into a tight little ball and locked it up with my memories of Granny. I haven't had the strength to unlock any of it and remember yet. Whenever I thought of Charlie these last months, the pain was physical, as if something was rending me in two. But the baby in my arms is protecting me now.

I feel my breasts tighten as he suckles. His little eyes seem to study me, and then I see what Rachel did, a bit of Charlie.

"He's got yer family's eyes, your eyes." I look up at my husband and take a breath. "You know, I've made some mistakes over the past months, and I'm sorry for that, Charlie."

"Nothing either of us can do can change the past few months, hell, the past year. We've both made some mistakes." He takes his hat off and spins it in his fingers.

"Right when this babe got here, Elizabeth told me something. She said it's the fallin' in love that's easy but the stayin' in love that's hard. I thought of you when she said that."

He still leans against the wall, but at least now he's looking at us, his embarrassment gone.

"I've missed you," I say, putting all the honesty I have in my heart into those words. I'm done lyin', and hiding, and trying to do the right thing for everyone else but me. That's what started this whole mess in the first place.

"Yeah?" He smiles a little, but it's a sad smile. "I've thought of you, but every time I think of you I think of Jed and … everything. I get so angry. I hate him. And then I don't want to think of you either."

My heart sinks. It's Jed again. Always Jed, keeping me from what I want, but not anymore. I look down again at the baby. He won't ever take my son, so now I at least have half of what I want. The other half is still standing across the room.

"Then why are you here?" I ask.

He doesn't answer just lifts his cane from the wall where it had been leaning and fidgets with it.

"I can't hate him no more," I say. "I look at this baby, and I can't hate him. Look what he gave me."

"You've forgiven him?" he asks, narrowing his eyes at me.

I think on that a moment and realize, in the last ten minutes, since I've held my son, that I have. "I guess so. I don't like him. I don't want him around my child, but I just don't want that black hate eating at my heart anymore. I can't love this child like I need to and have that hate in me. They don't all fit."

"I won't forgive him. Ever. I ever see him again, I'll kill the bastard."

"Maybe I just shoulda shot him in The Dalles?"

He smiles and comes toward the bed. "I wouldn't have minded."

"Charlie? I didn't think we'd see you again."

"I didn't think you would either until Mr. Black came. I've been so angry that that's all I could see. I'd think of you and then I'd think of Jed which would make me angrier. But when Mr. Black said the baby was coming, I got worried. I…well, I wanted to be here. Kind of surprised me how much I wanted to be here."

I carefully scoot my legs over and pat the cleared space on the bed for him to sit. He does, setting his cane on the floor.. After a moment he reaches over and strokes the baby's head.

"Did you miss me?" I finally get the courage to ask.

He nods.

"Say it. I need to hear it, Charlie. We can't ever have any lies, or secrets, or misunderstandings ever again." My voice cracks as I speak and tears fill my eyes. "Look at me, Charlie."

He lifts his eyes from the baby to mine. "I missed you, Sarah," he says, leaning over and kissing me.

I unlatch our child and off the baby to him. "Meet your son. His name's Lorenzo."

Chapter 26

Present Day

THE SMELL OF the place has become as familiar to me as the never ending rain in a Portland winter. They can't be separated, and yet I still can't define it. I can't put my finger on what exactly it smells like. It's cafeteria food, mashed potatoes and jello, the underlying tang of urine, the sour scent of sweat loaded with too much medication. The smell of human stagnation and fear. Sometimes, even after I come home from a long visit with Agnes, I can smell it on my hair, lingering like cigarette smoke.

Rain pours in an endless deluge as I pull into the parking lot. I open my car door and sprint to the main entrance. By the time I get there, water drips from my bangs, and I have to shake myself off like a dog. I wave at the receptionist in the lobby and head toward Agnes' room.

"Harper, wait!" she yells to my back.

I stop. "Yeah?"

"Agnes isn't down there anymore. We had to move her."

"You did? Why?"

"You didn't hear?"

"Hear what?

"She had an escape. Rosemary moved her into our higher security wing."

Escape? Is this a jail? "What do you mean 'escape'?"

"She decided to go for a walk on her own and got lost. They found her down the street at the Home Depot, sitting out front on their lawn furniture display in a porch swing. She had no idea where she was."

I want to cry for Agnes. She loved her porch swing. We spent hours there, rocking, as I told her my stories and then as I got older, we'd talk about school, my mom, boys and whatever else I thought of.

"She's on the second floor now, in the C wing. That way." She points in the opposite direction of Agnes' old room.

The new wing has security with coded locking doors, and her room is much more like a medical facility, with a large hospital-type bed in the middle. Agnes sits in a chair in the corner. She had never been a small woman, but the recliner almost smothers her, as if Jack had hurled the giant's chair down the beanstalk and it landed right here in C wing. The huge, pouffy headrest towers above her head. Agnes stares down at her lap, moving her lips in conversation with someone or with herself. It's hard to tell. She hasn't heard me enter, and I breathe in the smell of the place. It's stronger in her new room, as if the higher security and locked doors hold it in where it stagnates.

How had she possibly made it four blocks and across a busy street? It doesn't matter. No more Houdini moments for Agnes.

This room is spare, not filled with the crocheted afghans, photographs, and bric-a-brac like her old room. There's not a figurine to be found, and I wonder where it all went. A few books sit on the bookshelf, but they are not titles I recognize. Perhaps the facility provides them. I like to think that's the case. Either that or they belonged to the room's prior resident who died, which is a horrible thought. I take a step farther into the room, and Agnes looks up. Her hands flutter up, but they can't remember where to go, so they stay in front of her chest momentarily before dropping back down to her lap. She watches me warily as I step toward the bookshelf and read the titles.

"Home?" she asks. "Take me home?"

This sucks. Of course she wants to go home, but does she even know what that is? Rosemary won't have her. She's too much trouble, takes too much time. Who does she think cared for her the first eighteen years of her life? Apparently that's irrelevant. As long as she writes the check to the manor, she's off the hook. That philosophy is bullshit.

I turn from the books and face Agnes. "I know you do. I can't take you, though."

She seems to study my face for any memory. Confusion dances across her eyes, followed by fear. I can hear her breath speed up. Her hands begin to twist together as she gets more agitated.

"I have your quilt," I say, trying to calm her down.

I hold the bag up and she stares at it, uncomprehending. Rosemary has not contacted me about it since our meeting months ago. I've been waiting for a court summons but have heard nothing. The quilt simply sits in my closet, waiting to spur any vestiges of memory in Agnes' mind. Perhaps watching her mother wither away is making Rosemary's heart grow, kind of like the Grinch. Or maybe she figured out that she can't prove I stole the darn thing. Who knows? I'm done worrying about it. I'm not going to play her crazy games. I grew up playing crazy games with my mom, and I've learned—with help from Agnes—that all crazy-making people need are responses, and that's enough for them to keep the crazy going. So I don't respond, though it still surprises me when it works.

I sit across from Agnes and pull out the quilt. She makes no moves for it, and I wonder if she remembers it or the stories she has told me, her connection with it. She doesn't seem to. Instead, she closes her eyes and leans her head back. Her chair is reclined, and within moments she sleeps. Her chest barely rises and falls with the weakness of her breathing.

Is she still in there anywhere? Is this frail, thin body that doesn't recognize me when its eyes are open really Agnes? It looks like Agnes. Her heart and her brain are there, but whatever makes her Agnes is gone. I see a shell, a body, and that's all.

I look at the quilt in my arms.

It would be so easy to free her from this…and evil. Or would it be? Am I even thinking this? My hands begin to shake and I clench my fists into the quilt.

Her breath is shallow, barely moving her frail chest. Could I? Would I? I take a deep breath as I consider the thought, taking a step back from her bed. What kind of monster am I? Or am I a monster?

My Agnes would hate this life. She wouldn't want to spend her days lying in bed or this giant recliner, alone, afraid of everyone and everything, not knowing anyone, not remembering anything that makes her who she is. Not knowing where she was going when she went for a walk.

Agnes, the Agnes I love, would hate everything about this life. She would hate that Rosemary has accused me of theft.

It would be so horribly easy.

I take a step toward her chair. Her face twitches and the corner of her mouth rises in a half smile. I wonder if she's lucid in her dreams. Can I help her go? Would I? What does that make me, even having these thoughts?

I wouldn't have to watch this slow decline, and she wouldn't have to sink even deeper into nothingness and fear. Who says that keeping her alive and living like this alone and afraid is humane? I take another step and my hands shake. What am I thinking?

A knock comes at the door, and it swooshes opens. The nurse enters without asking. Agnes couldn't answer anyway, so I don't know why it matters. It just does. Tears fill my eyes as I grab the quilt to my chest and run out of this hideous place that has killed all the humanity not only in Agnes, but also, apparently, in me.

I throw myself in my car and call Claire.

"What's up?" she says.

"Are you home? I need to talk."

"Are you all right? What's going on?"

My breath catches. "I just need to see you."

"Do you want me to come to your house?"

"Yeah, meet me there." I pull onto the street.

Claire beats me to my house. She's sitting on the front porch, waiting for me when I pull into the driveway. "What's going on?" she asks, meeting me at my car.

I shake my head in response, grab the quilt and climb out. "Let's go inside." As soon as we get in the house, I collapse on the couch. "I think I'm a murderer."

"Oh my God! What did you do? Did you hit somebody with your car? Holy shit! What happened?"

"No, I mean I didn't kill anyone, but I thought about it. I was at the Manor, and Agnes, she didn't even know me, she was so scared and shaking, and little … she's so … little." My hands shake, and I clasp them in my lap. "Everything about her has shrunk and fallen into itself. Then she fell asleep, and I just thought about how easy it would be to just put the quilt or a pillow over her face and make it all go away." I can't even look at Claire as I say this. Shame pours through every cell of my body. I grab one of the pillows off the couch and bury my face in it. "I'm just like my parents. I obviously don't care about anything."

Claire sits down on the couch next to me and embraces me. "I don't think it's that at all. I think it's the opposite. I think you care too much."

"If I cared, that thought wouldn't have even crossed my mind," I say into the pillow.

"How could it not cross your mind? You didn't want to hurt her, you wanted her hurt to go away. Right?"

"Yes."

"Then I don't think that makes you a murderer. Criminals want to cause hurt. You wanted to make it go away." She sighs and hugs me harder. "And that's why I call you my best friend."

I take the pillow away from my face, and look at her. "Really? You don't think I'm horrible?" I sniff loudly. "I just want this all to go away, to go back to how it was when everyone was happy and healthy. Why can't it go back to that?"

"Because it can't. And really? When your mom was passed out and you stayed with Agnes was everyone happy and healthy?"

"No," I wail, knowing she's right. "But I hate this. Why do people have to change? Why couldn't my mom change and Agnes stay the same?"

"Why do you keep asking me all these questions that have no answers?"

She's right, but that's how I know she's a good friend. She listens.

"Okay, I'll ask an easy one," I say. "Can you go make me some cocoa please? Let's drink to Agnes."

Claire smiles and heads to the kitchen while I stare at the damn bag that holds the quilt. I've had it for months now and am no closer to a decision. What am I going to do with it? I wonder what Sarah would want me to do with it.

"Shari again called this morning. She held off on the article so it would coincide with some big quilt show downtown. She's got space for the article in the next week or two," Claire says as she returns with two mugs of cocoa. "She's ready for photographs."

"Okay," I say as it hits me. I know exactly what Sarah would do with it. "When? Can we do it soon? Like in the next day or two?"

She frowns. "Why the rush all of a sudden?"

"I just want to get it done." To get it done. To do it right and well. And to know that finishing won't trap me, it'll do the opposite. I'll be free. I take a sip of my cocoa and smile to myself, for the first time confident as to what I can do for Agnes, what I can give her as she gave to me for so many years.

"What are you grinning about?" Claire interrupts my reverie.

"Just thinking of Agnes. Why don't you call Shari?"

"Right now?"

"Yep, let's get it scheduled. The sooner the better."

Chapter 27

BEFORE SHE GAVE it to me, Agnes had stored the quilt at the manor in a giant gift box, complete with acid-free tissue paper. I want it to look exactly the same, something that might be recognizable to her. Not much is anymore. Not even me. And everything terrifies her.

I pull the box from the plastic wrap and put it together before laying the tissue paper in the bottom and up the sides. I lay the folded quilt in and secure the top of the box. It looks brand new—too new—so I set the box on the floor and smash it up a little bit with my foot. I step on one corner, mushing it down, and kick the entire package across the floor. It slides on the wood and crashes into my dresser. I smile, wishing the quilt appraiser could see me now. She would have a stroke. I kick the box again and watch the side dent in, but it needs one more good mashing. I step, right in the middle and watch each corner bend inward, creasing nicely. Much better.

I shove the entire thing into the gaudy gift bag. Agnes may or may not recognize the gift bag. I doubt it. She tends to only remember stuff from way back, not anything recent, and the gift bag is relatively recent, but the top of the box sticks out nicely from it. Hopefully one of the two will spark something within her, since I can't cart her cedar chest to her.

I don't make it to visit until 2:30 that afternoon. It's not the best time for a visit, but I couldn't come until after the quilt's photo shoot. Shari got beautiful pictures, and the story will run within the next two weeks. I've read some of her other pieces and she writes well. She'll do the quilt and Sarah's story justice.

I knock on Agnes' door but hear nothing. I punch in the code for her door and peek in when the lock clicks open. It's like a prison in this wing, but Agnes doesn't know it, and I'm thankful for that at least. She is sound asleep in her recliner, her head turned toward the side on the chair's cushions. I tiptoe across the room and perch on the couch, watching her sleep. Her mouth is slightly opened, and she snores softly. In sleep her face is slack; she has lost that fearful look that so often resides there. She looks like the old Agnes, the one who welcomed me into her home. That Agnes so rarely comes out anymore, I wonder if she is in there at all, if her brain has any of the connections left that made her my Agnes.

I wait for fifteen minutes, but I don't want to wait any longer. This may take some time, and I don't want to leave in a rush today as I always end up doing. The time before last, she cried when I left. I felt awful and had to get the nurse to sit with her. I don't want that to happen today. The visits have become more and more tiresome and difficult. Often I read or we sit together in silence. Sometimes she lets me hold her hand.

I reach across and rub her hand. "Agnes," I whisper. "Wake up."

She doesn't stir at all, so I try again, a little louder this time. She twitches a bit, so I continue repeating myself. Finally, she turns her head a bit and opens her eyes. She looks at me, but I'm not sure what she sees. I repeat her name one last time, and finally her eyes come into focus on my face. Her face maintains its relaxed state; the fear has not yet come into her eyes.

"I brought something for you." I set the gift on the couch next to me so she can see them.

Her eyes shift as she looks at them, but she does nothing to acknowledge their presence. I pull the box from the bag and set it on my left. She lifts her left hand slightly then lets it fall back into her lap. Her head is still leaning on the back of her chair. I lift up the box as she watches me, and I set it in her lap. Finally she gazes at the box. Her face does not register any emotion, and for that I am thankful. So far she is not afraid. Her fear is terrifying to both of us. I would rather have nothing at all than that.

"Would you like me to open the box? I brought you a gift. I think you'll like it." I smile at her. "I'm Harper."

She gives an imperceptible nod. I don't know if she's saying "yes" to open the box or "yes" that she knows who I am. I guess it's irrelevant at this point.

Her hands sit on her lap, trapped underneath the box. I thought she

243

would move them when I set it down but she hasn't, so I gently remove her right hand then her left from their entrapment. She makes no move to take the lid off, so I do it for her. She looks down at the tissue paper and then back at me. I peel back the tissue and reveal the gift below.

Finally, she responds. She moves her hands and lays them on the quilt, caressing the colors like she used to.

I begin to talk, to fill the silence. I start telling the story of Sarah, of the quilt. I reach for the box to take the quilt out, so she can see the whole thing as well as the gift in the bottom of the box, but her body begins to tighten up in fear. I sit back down and keep talking. She doesn't say a word, just pats the quilt like a friend.

I can't believe I didn't see this before. It is Agnes' quilt. Not Rosemary's. Not mine. It belongs to Agnes, and it's more than a blanket. It's her story. I always thought I could just make a new one, kind of like making a new cake out of a family recipe. Great Grandma's chocolate torte would not be saved and passed down through the generations, no matter how good it was. Her recipe? Yes. The cake? No. That's how I've seen this quilt. If I sold it, someday I could follow the pattern and make another one. It would be just as good.

But it wouldn't.

It wouldn't be the same at all.

Agnes needs to have this quilt, even if it only brings her a minute or two of comfort. I hope I can give her that. I feel like it should be buried with her, like Rebecca buried Katie, shrouded in a beloved quilt, wrapped up in love. And like Sarah, who attempted to use this quilt as her shroud when she ran.

"It's for you, Agnes. You can keep it. Would you like that?"

She nods again, but this time it is obvious, not an imperceptible shake of her head. I sit back in companionable silence for once, not feeling torn about the quilt. When I open my eyes, Agnes is watching me, nodding her head. For the first time in a long while, I feel like she's in there somewhere—not all of her, but some little part of her, and I still love that little part even though I don't know or understand much of who is left.

I give her a hug. She lets me. I take my gaudy gift bag and leave. On my way out the main door, I shove it into the garbage can by the front entrance. I won't need it any more.

244

I climb the stairs and open the door to my mom's old room. I had avoided it and college, and commitment to anything for fear I would become like her, unhappy and unable to find an escape in anything but alcohol. But as I survey it now, I realize this room has become my salvation.

The card table I'd set up at the end of the bed is covered with books, notes, and draft after draft of Sarah's story. It started as Sarah and Charlie's story, but it became Agnes' story and then mine. I took some literary license but the main events are all as Agnes told me. As I survey the pages, I realize I haven't even started a story, much less finished anything in over three years but this one...it's done, and I hope it's ready for publication. Even though that thought makes my heart speed up in fear, it's a good kind of fear. Agnes would be proud of me – I finished. This is the gift Agnes has given to me.

I sit at my makeshift card table desk and open up my laptop. The story is ready to go and who knows, maybe somebody will actually pay me for it, so I can afford to take more than one class a semester.

My finger shakes as it hovers over the "send" button on my email. I say a little prayer that some agent or publisher out there likes it and let it go.

Two days later, I stand in Agnes' door and stare in shock. She sits in her bed, covered with threads. Small pieces of fabric litter the floor. She has turned her agitation against the quilt, against the one thing that has held together for her. I step outside into the hallway and wipe away the tears that have filled my eyes. The quilt didn't help. It didn't bring her back or calm her like I had hoped. I take a deep breath and re-enter Agnes' room. She sees me, but as I approach her bed, she shies away from me, looking down, not holding my eyes.

Her fingers continue their incessant movement, their picking, their pulling. With her arthritic fingers, I can't imagine how she's done what she's done.

As she pulls on the thread she has worked free, a flower petal falls to her lap. It is a faded pink. She picks it up and throws it to the floor,

245

her hands never ceasing. I walk over, pick it up, and sit on the edge of the bed. I lay my hands across hers in an attempt to still them, but they continue their ceaseless picking. She does not look up at me, does not acknowledge my sitting near her, and I blink back another round of tears. I am gone to her and now, so is her quilt. I move my hands and let her continue. Somehow it calms her though she has destroyed an entire quarter of Sarah's quilt. I stand, pick up the larger pieces, one of which is a stiff piece of canvas cut in an oblong shape. I realize that is the batting that was in the tear. I pile the threads and pieces of cotton on top of it and set the whole mess on the bedside table as I survey the threads and small bits of fabric that cover the floor beneath her bed.

It is 10:00 on a bright Saturday morning in March, almost ten months to the day since Agnes moved into this place and began to tell me her story. I can see the printed copy of it that I typed up in the bottom of the large gift box that held the quilt. I wonder if she ever even saw it, though I doubt she could understand or decipher it any longer. It doesn't look like it, but it doesn't matter. Agnes knows the story; it is hers. The story is intact at least on paper, though it's no longer in her head.

I glance at Agnes' lap. Ten months ago, we had the quilt and no story. Now? A story and no quilt, but the loss I feel most deeply has nothing to do with either of those things. I'd give anything to have Agnes back. I thought the quilt might do it, bring her back for even a moment, but I was wrong.

As I begin to crawl about the floor around her bed, sweeping thread, cotton, and batting into small piles with my hands, the door swings open. I hear a gasp.

"Oh my God, Mother! What have you done?"

Rosemary enters the room. She stops when she sees me crouched behind the bed as if I'm hiding, and she turns her accusations to me.

"What have you done?"

"Just what you wanted me to do. I returned the quilt."

"To *her*?!?" she shrieks, pointing to Agnes as if the devil himself is lying in her bed. "You gave it to *her*? Oh my God."

"It's her quilt. She gave it to me, so I returned it to her." For the first time, I'm not afraid of Rosemary.

"You've ruined it." Her voice regains its icy composure. I'm not sure if she's talking to me or to her mother. It could be either, so I decide to clarify.

"Well, actually, I didn't. Agnes did. But I suppose it's hers to do with as she pleases. Not much else is anymore, so I think I can give her this."

Rosemary snorts in response. Lost in her own world, Agnes has not acknowledged either Rosemary or me.

I turn to look at Rosemary and hold up a larger piece of the quilt's top from Agnes' lap. "From what I can tell, she started at the original tear and worked from there."

"Collect them all," Rosemary says waving her hand.

"Really? Why?"

I scoop up my little pile of pieces from the floor in two hands and walk them over to her. She looks at them, looks at her mother, then turns and leaves the room. I drop the mess back onto the floor and sit back down on the edge of the bed. Agnes' old arthritic hands struggle to get hold of a thread until she gives up and pulls the two pieces of fabric apart. The cotton is old; the fibers have weakened over time and they give way easily. She smiles a little as she feels the fabric give way in her hands.

I pat her leg, pick up a piece of fabric, and begin to pull the threads right along with her.

Acknowledgements

In 2012, I woke up from a vivid dream, knowing that I had to write the story. My first thank you goes to my husband, Gary for not laughing when I told him I'd had a dream and was now going to write a novel, and for all of his unconditional love and support throughout the LONG writing and revision process.

I'd also like to express my sincere appreciate for the rest of my early supporters: my Dad, my sister, my Mom and my kids, all of whom encouraged me and kept me going through my journey to both write the story and figure out how to write it well.

My writing buddies, Gillian Archer and Paisley Hendricks, provided invaluable feedback. I'm grateful to my editor, Genevieve Graham, who helped me believe in myself, one of the greatest gifts.

About the Author

Amy Isaman spent most of her career teaching high school kids to write before finally picking up a pen (actually opening her laptop) and starting to write the stories that had been simmering inside for years. She's married to her high school sweetheart with whom she raised two amazing kids. After finally escaping the classroom, Amy now spends her days writing, designing websites with her web design business, and quilting.

You can find out more about her at www.amyisamanbooks.com.

Made in the USA
Middletown, DE
09 December 2018